MW00466920

LET THE BAND PLAY
DIXIE

By Lawrence Wells

LET THE BAND PLAY DIXIE
ROMMEL AND THE REBEL

LET THE BAND PLAY DIXIE

Lawrence Wells

To Mark Giannotto,
All best from Oxford!
Lawrence Wells
Aug. '23

DOUBLEDAY & COMPANY, INC.
GARDEN CITY, NEW YORK
1987

Library of Congress Cataloging-in-Publication Data
Wells, Lawrence.
   Let the band play Dixie.
   I. Title.
PS3573.E4924L4 1987   813'.54   86–32816
ISBN 0-385-23467-8

Copyright © 1987 by Lawrence Wells
ALL RIGHTS RESERVED
PRINTED IN THE UNITED STATES OF AMERICA
FIRST EDITION

To my parents,
Glenn and *Dorothy Wells*

Let the band play "Dixie." It is now Federal property.

Abraham Lincoln
Richmond, 1865

Every time you think you've discovered something new or innovative, go look it up in the library. You'll find that Mr. Stagg did it in or before the year 1900.

Bud Wilkinson
University of Oklahoma

In the East, college football is a cultural exercise. On the West Coast, it is a tourist attraction. In the Midwest, it is cannibalism. But in the South it is religion, and Saturday is the holy day.

Marino Casem
Alcorn State University

NORTH TO PLAY SOUTH
IN FOOTBALL GAME

The Philadelphia Athletic Club will sponsor the North-South College Football Game to be played December 21 at 1 P.M. at Franklin Field. The teams will comprise All-America and All-Southern players selected under the supervision of Walter Camp of New Haven, head of the All-America Football Committee.

Serving as honorary co-chairmen will be James Longstreet and Daniel Sickles. The coaches for the North team will include Amos Alonzo Stagg, Phil King, and George Woodruff; the South team will be coached by John Heisman and Glenn Warner.

Proceeds from the game will be donated to charity.

A spirited contest is expected, and the public is cordially invited to attend.

The Philadelphia Free Press
October 16, 1896

Part I

Chapter One

The powerful telescope lens disclosed, at a distance of a mile or more, intimate details of the impending battle. Union soldiers rammed charges into their muzzle-loaders and fitted percussion caps. As they formed line of battle in two ranks, men pulled caps tight, patted ammunition pouches, checked and rechecked weapons, bent to pluck a blade of grass.

The telescope's line of vision swung across a green field to observe a Confederate brigade. Red battle flags contrasted brightly with butternut gray uniforms. Troopers gentled their mounts. Infantrymen knelt, conserving energy. A colonel wearing a yellow sash spurred his mount forward. He drew his sword. Abruptly he pointed it at the Union line. Buglers ran forward to sound the charge. The gray line rolled across the field. From the Union side a cloud of smoke erupted. Men fell and lay still. Dense smoke crept hungrily over the battlefield. Only a few Confederates reached the Federal position. A second volley cut them down. The shooting ceased. Bodies were strewn over the ground like gray stones.

Slowly, miraculously, the dead and wounded began to hoist themselves up, exchange self-conscious grins, stand and slap the dust from their pants. The telescope's field of vision swerved to the trees surrounding the grassy meadow. Spectators applauded, men waved hats, women twirled parasols. Bicycles with oversized front wheels glided elegantly through the city park where the Civil War reenactment had been performed. On the far side of the park a naval shipyard could be seen, and beyond that the Schuylkill and Delaware met in a brassy riptide. A ferryboat's white wake sliced the shining water. The brown rooftops of Philadelphia seemed to wait expectantly for something else to happen.

As a breeze swept gunsmoke from the park, the telescope focused on a crepe-trimmed grandstand, from which a group of distinguished-looking elderly gentlemen had observed the mock battle. They wore military insignia and gold medals pinned to their lapels. The cynosure of all eyes was a large man with white hair. His bushy eyebrows were pinched in a frown over deep-set eyes. His beard was full except for shaved chin, which gave him a Mongol-like appearance. Like the other retired army officers present, he wore a conservative double-breasted coat with dark tie and silk hat. There all similarities ended, however. His unsmiling mask among the holiday faces was like an unexploded shell in an old battlefield.

"Ten to one he's a Confederate general," remarked the man watching through the telescope.

General James Longstreet, C.S.A., was on his guard. He realized that his host, Daniel Sickles, had just made some public remark, but Longstreet was hard of hearing. He assumed Sickles was talking about him. Too vain to let on that he was going deaf, Longstreet wished for T. J. Goree, his former aide-de-camp. Trying not to be obvious, he glanced at the man beside him on the grandstand.

"Excuse me. What did General Sickles say?" Longstreet casually asked.

"He speaks of Gettysburg, sir," the stranger replied, leaning away from Longstreet to get a better look at the famous face.

"Oh?" Longstreet stirred himself.

"The general was saying that the best possible course for the Confederates would have been a dawn attack on July second, the whole of Hill and Ewell's corps against Cemetery Ridge."

What business is it of Dan's to mess around with our battle plan? They whipped us. That ought to be enough.

Longstreet saw Sickles glancing in his direction, expecting a reply. Although many Union generals had been Longstreet's classmates at West Point, Sickles, who had lost a leg during the second day of fighting at Gettysburg, had been a Tammany politician in New York before the war. Longstreet remembered a rumor about Sickles' liaison with Queen Isabella. The Yankee King of Spain, they called him. Before the war he had killed Francis Scott Key's son for sleeping with his wife, Theresa.

A dandy and a ladies' man, Longstreet thought, but a pretty good soldier for a politician.

Longstreet stared over the meadow, where soldiers in blue and gray were mingling, talking, sharing food and drink. The scene had a surreal quality that confused Longstreet. He was seventy-five, and he would have liked to sit down. To him, reenactments resembled war the way kick-the-can resembled Pickett's charge. He avoided them whenever possible.

After the war he had shouldered the yoke of defeat with the same determination that he had fought the Union Army. He had joined the Republican Party and pursued a course of progress and reconstruction according to federal law. In New Orleans he had given his support to Butler, Stanton, and Stevens, consequently receiving appointments to a series of federal jobs: surveyor of customs at New Orleans, U.S. Marshal for Georgia, minister to Turkey. For these activities, combined with a flood of criticism from the poison pens of such critics as Fitzhugh Lee and Jubal Early, Longstreet had been branded a traitor and castigated in newspapers from Virginia to Texas.

Here in this Philadelphia park, with his former enemies awaiting his explanation of the failed strategy at Gettysburg, Longstreet felt less beleaguered than with certain of his former comrades-in-arms, such as Fitzhugh Lee, Pendleton, and Early. His twenty-year battle of vindication had swelled against the rock of censure until it had crested here, in 1896, with the publication of his book, *From Manassas to Appomattox*. Longstreet's explication of the true facts was a rising wave that would smash his opponents to ribbons.

"It's all in my book," he said. "Ewell's plan was indeed to attack early on July second, while my corps—First Corps—was to attack at the sound of Ewell's guns. Yet no definite hour had been set for beginning the attack. Ewell was to hit the left while First Corps hit the right, but no one knew exactly where the Confederate right would be the next morning. It had been at Seminary Ridge during the battle of the first day, but on July second it had shifted considerably to the south."

Sickles had led the Union salient at the Wheatfield and therefore knew how far the battle had shifted south. Longstreet did not feel any more explanation was necessary. He was concerned that his host was aware of Early's charge that he, Longstreet, had delayed First Corps's march into battle position.

The truth, if anyone cares to read my book, is that Lee's engineers did not properly prepare a covered march route. I was obliged to take personal control of the march. I doubled Hood's column and marched it into position. Now that it's over, the Old Man can do no wrong. But the truth exists. It's all in my book.

The costumed soldiers had separated and were forming up to make another charge. The telescope on a rooftop a mile to the north, near Market Street, followed them to their work. Then the man looking through the telescope stood back to give his eye a rest. He was small and swarthy. Blue beard shadow gave his face a brooding, Levantine quality. His dark eyes darted here and there like wrens flitting from one rooftop to another. He wore a thin black mustache poised as if in afterthought over full lips. His jet hair was brushed slickly back from narrow temples, giving his face a wolfish look. He wore a tailored navy pinstripe suit with a gray silk vest.

A hatch door in the roof opened and a head emerged. A gnomelike man with pallid complexion, drooping lips, frizzy hair, and eyebrows that grew together said, "New York is calling, boss. They found out. It had to happen."

"Call them back, Elston," said the man with the telescope. "Tell them I have ascended to Wall Street and sit on the right hand of John D. Rockefeller, and we are busy making up next week's list of gains and losses."

The gnome stared blankly at him.

"I'm making a joke."

"It's not funny," Elston said. "You better scram, boss. Mr. Canfield's gonna call out the boys."

"Thanks for the advice." The man turned back to his telescope.

Elston awaited orders, the hatch door resting on his head. "I'd scram if I was him," he grumbled to himself.

Arno (The Zipper) Ziprenian, twenty-eight, was the youngest son of an immigrant family which had left Armenia in the 1880s before the Turkish invasion began. "When the Kurds came down from the hills," Arno Senior often said, "the Ziprenians went to sea." In America The Zipper took to the Lower East Side of New York like a Black Sea sturgeon to the East River. Although a bright student, he left school at sixteen to go into business for himself. At eighteen he was discovered by Richard Canfield, the Faro King, running numbers and bootlegging on Canal Street. With a rapidly expanding operation, Canfield was always watching for new talent. He liked to hire promising young men and mold them to fit his organization. Ziprenian soon became Canfield's youngest lieutenant, distinguishing himself by his rapid rise within the Canfield empire. At twenty-five he had been placed in charge of faro operations in Philadelphia, Long Branch, and Atlantic City, where he set up deluxe pleasure palaces in record time.

Arno's prestige within the gambling organization was further enhanced by his having succeeded in spite of national origin. Everyone knew that Canfield's mob was Mick, not Spic. Success, however, only served to fuel Ziprenian's ambition. Lately he had begun to make investments of his own: a thousand here, a thousand there. Since each of the gambling halls under his purview averaged twenty-five thousand dollars in gross receipts per week, and since it was Ziprenian's job to deliver the money every Monday to the Faro Palace on Fourteenth Street in New York, appropriating funds had been a relatively simple matter. The Zipper was of two minds as to whether he should:

    1. Pay them back with interest.

    2. Pay them back.

Canfield was mild-mannered and conservative. He was a connoisseur of good food and fine wine. He took a stern view, however, of employees who borrowed from his organization. They had a habit of disappearing. In Ziprenian's dreams he was frequently visited by Canfield's head of enforcement, Archie (The Knife) O'Hara, who sometimes gave eulogies at the funerals of his victims. In the dreams O'Hara's eulogy for The Zipper pleased Arno's mother, Castoria, who was very religious.

"You really want I should phone New York, boss?" Elston loyally persisted. The hatch door was balanced on top of his head like an oversized square hat.

"I need," Arno said as he fixed his eye to the viewing end of his telescope, "to become indispensable. What does Canfield want that he hasn't got?"

Ziprenian could see the blue and gray regiments forming for another skirmish. The telescope was his favorite hobby. It gave him an overview and calmed his nerves.

"Don't ask me!" The hatch door grated on Elston's head. The thought did not occur to him, however, to hold it suspended above him.

"Canfield has got nearly as much money as Rockefeller," Arno mused. Cannons belched smoke in the distance. Mock armies clashed in a green meadow. "What has Rockefeller got that Canfield don't?"

"Don't ask me!" Elston grumbled.

The Zipper reviewed Canfield's history. At forty-one, Richard A. Canfield was generally acknowledged to be the foremost gambling-house keeper in the United States. In the late 1870s, when he was in his mid-twenties, Canfield had built his stake with winnings from snaphouses, deadfalls, brace games, wolf traps, and skinning houses from San Francisco to Saratoga. In his time he had played them all: poker, faro, brag, seven-up, chuckaluck, all-fours, bagatelle, rondo, keno, splendid hells, roulette, three-card monte, vingt-et-un, and rouge et noir. He had worked the wolf traps on Barclay Street in New York, where volunteer firemen mixed with political rowdies and shoulder-hitters from Tammany just around the corner, with ruffians from Five Points, with pickpockets and sneak thieves who quarreled over the suckers and countrymen coming out of Barnum's American Museum or Daniel Sweeney's House of Refreshment. He knew them all: cappers, ropers, thimbleriggers, pugilists, plug-uglies, pickpockets, watch stuffers, pocketbook droppers, *nymphes du pavé*, fancy men, sneak thieves, racetrack touts, confidence men, burglars, footpads, garroters, and safecrackers.

In 1888 Canfield became partners with a successful faro dealer, David Duff, and opened Madison Square Club in a four-story brownstone at 22 West Twenty-sixth Street. Their location in the heart of New York's retail and amusement district made them an overnight success. Some of New York's finest hotels were within a three-block radius of them: St. James, Albemarle, Brunswick, Fifth Avenue, and Hoffman House, as well as Delmonico's famous restaurant. Thus they were well situated to attract big-money suckers. Duff broke with Canfield after the latter locked him out one night for drunkeness and rowdy behavior in 1890. By that time Canfield virtually dominated the professional gambling scene in the state. He opened a summer clubhouse at Saratoga, which soon averaged a quarter of a million-dollar gross per month. He built a mansion at Saratoga with an Italian garden with imported sculpture and a French chef named Columbin whom he paid five thousand dollars for the summer season. The rest of the year Columbin was sent off to travel Europe in search of new dishes to surprise Canfield's rapidly refined palate.

Success had made a conservative out of Richard A. Canfield. He no longer gambled except on the stock market, nor would he permit his employees to gamble lest they lose and steal from him to pay their debts. As he lectured them, "It is impossible, impossible, impossible to win against the bank." And, "No man should play unless he can afford to lose." Canfield had no interest in politics other than prompt payment of protection money. He used honorable methods, no ropers or cappers, and never welshed on a bet. The squareness of his games was rarely questioned.

Ziprenian had been with Canfield for ten years, since the week the Madison Square Club had opened, and he had known a different Canfield in the beginning. That Canfield would match pennies for a thousand dollars a toss, would gamble on anything and on either side. He would hold bank at baccarat with no declared capital and would accept any stake his opponents wished to fix. He played poker with a dollar limit or a fifty-thousand-dollar limit or no limit. He played bridge up to one thousand dollars a point. Once, in Memphis, Canfield was said to have confronted a local sport with a thirty-five-thousand-dollar purse to wager and offered to flip a coin for it and save time. On a train between Chicago and Pittsburgh he bet a man on the speed of a raindrop sliding down a window and won twenty-two thousand dollars. Canfield would bet on how much a stock would go up in a given time: hours or even minutes. He would play poker for as long as three days without sleep, with winnings usually in the fifty to one hundred thousand-dollar range.

Ziprenian had once heard Canfield say to an opponent, "I'll bet one hundred thousand against your Rembrandt and let the issue be decided by a single turn at faro."

That Canfield, however, no longer existed. Being rich and famous had made Canfield careful. He was five feet, eight inches tall, weighed two hundred pounds, was clean-shaven with a small mustache and heavy jowls, had neat brown hair and gray eyes. He arose each day between six and seven A.M., breakfasted on eggs, rolls, and coffee, checked his mail, and went for a stroll to take the air. He selected his clothing with close attention to detail. He had once confided to Ziprenian, "My wardrobe contains twenty pairs of pants, nine overcoats, forty-four fancy vests, and a hundred morning, afternoon, and evening coats." Canfield always dressed for dinner. In New York he dined at Delmonico's, in Saratoga at his clubhouse. He ate heavily of rich foods, smoked immoderately, and drank large quantities of wine. It was not unusual for his evening menu to include frog legs, woodcock, quail, robins, trout, soft-shell crabs, and terrapins. Canfield slept in an old-fashioned nightshirt and was always in bed by midnight.

Although possessed of little formal education beyond grammar school, Canfield had read and studied art, Latin, and the classics. His favorite book was Gibbon's *Decline and Fall.* He became an art connoisseur of considerable distinction. He collected the works of James M. Whistler, who became Canfield's intimate friend and painted his portrait. He was a charter member of the exclusive Walpole Society of art lovers and men of letters. Christie's honored his opinion.

This was a man, Ziprenian thought, who had everything.

Could anything remain? Did Canfield yearn for a star? Ziprenian felt a trembling in his bones. He was on the verge of a startling discovery.

"*The Social Register!*" he cried over the rooftops. Elston ducked defensively. The hatch door bounced on his head. "That's it!" The Zipper peered gratefully through his telescope, as if it somehow had helped provide this new perspective, as if its god-like view held further revelation. He found that its angle had been altered. Now it was trained on another section of the park, where a different form of combat was taking place.

Spectators stood twenty deep around a field marked with white grid lines. Two teams opposed each other in neat formations. A ball was kicked into the air. The team receiving it swiftly resolved itself into a V-shape and shot forward. The opposing line converged on the V and both teams came together in a writhing mass that pushed slowly up the field like a many-headed creature. A runner carried the ball across the end line and touched it to the ground. A man in a white shirt raised his arm above his head. Spectators on one side of the field leaped for joy while those on the opposite side stood silent.

"What is this?" The Zipper demanded. Elston climbed out onto the roof and came forward in a loping stride, his head bent forward and bobbing like a camel's. He peered through the telescope, shutting his other eye and screwing his face up in a toothy grimace.

"I don't see nothing," he said.

"You see a *game* being played, don't you?"

"Oh, yeah—football. Anyway, what do I tell New York? That you're dead and in heaven with God?" Elston chuckled wetly at his joke, his cheeks sucking in and out.

"Wait a minute." Ziprenian reclaimed the telescope. "So *that's* football." He swung his instrument back to the reenactment, where the costumed troops staged hand-to-hand combat. Soldiers grappled or slashed at one another dramatically. Now Ziprenian trained the telescope on the football game, where one team kicked the ball to the other and the players clashed at midfield, bodies sprawling as though wounded. Arno panned

back and forth, observing a similarity between the soldiers and
the football players: attack and defend; chaos and order.

"Goodbye, boss," Elston said with a melancholy scowl. "I'll tell
my grandchildren about you if I ever get married and my wife is
fertile and we have children and they grow up and get married
and are fertile and they have—"

"I've got it!" The Zipper cried triumphantly. "Go back and
telephone New York. Tell them I want a meeting, as soon as it can
be arranged."

"You're giving yourself up?" Elston groaned. "You're not
gonna take it on the lam?"

"I will never take it on the lam, Elston," Ziprenian exclaimed,
his eyes darting. "I have ideas . . ."

"Once on Market Street," Elston lectured, "I had an idea I
would cut across traffic in the middle of the block and I nearly
got—"

"Just telephone New York like I say. Tell them I'll come any-
place they want, but soon!"

Elston loped to the open hatchway. His head sank below the
roof line. Ziprenian turned back to his telescope. The football
game had ended. Both teams mingled in the center of the field,
shaking hands with their opponents. Then the players separated
and each team went into a huddle, chanting fiercely. The spectators rushed onto the field to take part in the celebration.

A quarter of a mile away, on the other side of the park, Union
and Confederate regiments paraded before an appreciative audience. Bands played and flags fluttered in the breeze. A swirl of
red, white, and blue balloons was released into the sky. On the
grandstand, officials and distinguished guests gestured and talked
enthusiastically. The old soldier Ziprenian believed to be a Rebel
general stood slightly apart from the others, brooding and magnificent, impenetrable.

"Under the severest provocation I have remained silent, until
importunities have forced me to speak."

"Pardon?" said the man standing beside Longstreet. The general was not aware that he had been thinking out loud.

"What?" Longstreet became attentive. He heard a voice from the past.

"It does seem preposterous and absurd to me and must to any soldier of the army of Virginia, the idea of such an old granny *as Pendleton presuming to give a lecture on knowing* anything *about the battle of Gettysburg!"*

Good old Goree. Longstreet glanced around, almost expecting to see his aide, smiling under his white mustache. He spoke casually to the startled Philadelphian as though to Captain Goree.

"Bishop Pendleton sought to charge me with disobeying Lee's order to attack at sunrise on July second, 1863. He made such remarks from the belly of the whale: the Lee Chapel at Washington and Lee University. The funny thing is, how could the Bishop —nominally in charge of artillery at Gettysburg but actually involved primarily with ordnance behind the front lines—how could he obtain firsthand knowledge of what went on between Lee and myself?"

"I can only attribute Pendleton's statement about this order at Gettysburg to an absolute loss of memory said to be brought on by frequent attacks resembling paralysis."

"I recognize that voice! Colonel Venable." Longstreet looked over his shoulder seeking Lee's staff officer, whose letter refuting Pendleton's charge Longstreet had submitted to the New Orleans *Republican,* along with a quotation Longstreet remembered from a letter Lee had written to him in 1864:

"Had I taken your advice at Gettysburg instead of pursuing the course I did, how different all might have been."

"You don't say!" The civilian next to him was self-conscious and pleased.

"Lee's lieutenants demanded that I produce the full text of the letter from the Old Man," Longstreet confided, "but unfortunately it was nowhere to be found. I do remember clearly, however, the sentence in question."

"I see," the man said in polite confusion.

"It is altogether probable," Longstreet said ironically, "that the great military critics—Parson Pendleton, General Early, and Parson J. William Jones—are members of the Grand Army, but

even their combined authority as sage warriors does not in the
least shake my confidence in the ultimate triumph of truth."

"Good for you!" cried the man beside him.

Let the critics wail. Their voices are as dogs howling in the
wind.

Longstreet nodded in agreement with his thoughts. He was
determined to have the last word. His memoirs, *From Manassas*
to Appomattox, represented a triumph over old age, poor health,
paralysis of his right arm, financial difficulties, the burning of his
house, and the death of his wife. In July of 1896, six months after
they were published, he had attended—uninvited—a reunion of
the United Confederate Veterans in Richmond, Virginia. The
veterans had stood and cheered him with a thunderous ovation.
He had seen in their faces an abiding loyalty and affection. None
of those old soldiers had accused him of tacitly approving federal
plans that had carved the South into military districts. None of
those honorable veterans blamed him for supporting duly appointed federal officials. No, they had cheered him.

"No man who fought alongside Old Pete will ever raise his
voice against him!"

"General Longstreet's critics are unworthy to loose his shoe
latches."

"General Longstreet? Would you care to comment?"

Longstreet struggled back to the present. A newspaper reporter stood on the row below him, pencil poised earnestly over
his pad.

"It's all in my book," he muttered.

"I mean, in response to General Sickles's question," the reporter said. Longstreet turned his good ear toward the reporter,
who added, "The general was saying that he does not understand
why Pickett was allowed to attack Cemetery Ridge without a
strong supporting attack on both flanks, why Ewell's and Hill's
forces did not come up on either side of Pickett as might be
expected."

Incensed, Longstreet looked for Sickles. From where he stood,
Longstreet thought the former soldier-politician looked almost
arrogant. On impulse he grabbed the reporter's pad and pencil
and angrily sketched the attack as he had planned it.

UNION FORCES

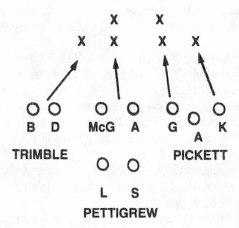

The Federal brigades on Cemetery Ridge were designated as X's. The troops under Trimble, Pettigrew, and Pickett were O's, identified by the surname initial of brigade commanders. Under Trimble: Brackenbrough and Davis; under Pettigrew: McGowan, Archer, Lane, and Scales; under Pickett: Garnett, Kemper, and Armistead.

"Our battle plan," Longstreet declared, holding up the sketch as though he expected Sickles to see it from twenty feet away, "called for Pickett to attack first, with Pettigrew and Trimble following in waves. Wilcox's brigade, of Hill's corps, was to cover Pickett's right. The objective was to penetrate the left center of the Union line and roll back the flanks. As general support, Johnson was to create a diversion by attacking the left; Ewell was to assault the extreme right and hold the Federal reserves in place; and Hill was to engage the center to create a diversion."

Longstreet recalled with stunning clarity the moment when he had knelt in a circle with Pickett, Trimble, and Pettigrew and drawn their attack positions in the dirt. He had not told them that he had begged Lee to reconsider.

A frontal assault across open ground against a well-entrenched enemy on high ground with twice our firepower?

The Old Man said, "General, the enemy is there and I am going to attack him."

Longstreet felt a hollowness in his chest. He looked at Sickles. Dozens of other dignitaries stared back at him with expectant smiles.

"You are correct, sir!" Longstreet called. "A strong supporting attack was needed on both flanks to give Pickett a chance to exploit any breakthrough."

Johnson attacked the left too soon and wore his men out by the time Pickett began his charge. Pettigrew's troops could not keep pace with Pickett and thus allowed a fatal gap to grow between them. Wilcox, covering Pickett's right, gave ground and permitted Union counterthrusts. When Pickett engaged the enemy positions on the ridge, the Union line, left and right of him, were free to concentrate their fire on Pickett and drive him back.

Longstreet thrust the pad and pencil into the reporter's hands and climbed down from the grandstand. He realized that his publisher would prefer that he smile, shake hands, and continue to promote sales of his book, but he had had enough. He ignored his hosts' murmur of surprise and headed for the park exit where his carriage waited with the others. Now, in the brilliant sunshine of this autumn afternoon, with the gentlemen and ladies of Philadelphia strolling arm in arm through the park, it did not suffice that *From Manassas to Appomattox* was selling like hotcakes.

Bring on the twentieth century, by God. Any change is bound to be an improvement.

Chapter Two

The window was patched, makeshift fashion, with panels of paper, wood, or cloth where glass panes had been. A single pane remained intact. Through it the woman watched the team filing out to the practice field behind the schoolhouse. Framed within the windowpane, muscular Negro youths of various heights and sizes carelessly tossed back and forth the football she had ordered from Montgomery Ward. The leather ball had become scuffed and torn, but the young men still handled it with respect.

It had not been easy for the woman to persuade their parents to allow their sons to stay after school to play a game. The book had helped. She had displayed, with a piety others reserved for the Bible, her copy of *A Scientific and Practical Treatise on American Football for Schools and Colleges,* by A. Alonzo Stagg and Henry L. Williams (Hartford, Connecticut, 1893). In the three years since its publication, she explained to the parents, this volume had become *the* handbook for football coaches and a major impetus for the expansion of the game as far west as Bardstown. The state university in nearby Lexington had organized a team. She had actually witnessed a game between Kentucky and Centre College.

The parents had argued that it was all well and good for white folks to chase a ball around a field, but black folks could ill afford to miss a day's work.

She had pointed out that not only was she a teacher at Post Oak

Normal School but the school nurse as well. Speaking in a medical capacity, she assured them that their sons had iron constitutions and were generally impervious to injury. "We must keep up with the times," she concluded.

It came as no surprise to the players' parents that the teacher and nurse was also to be the football coach. After all, it was her book, her time, and her football.

Mary Kathryn Kuykendall, thirty-seven—teacher, nurse, assistant principal, purchasing agent, and coach at Post Oak Normal —violently shoved her legs into the moleskin pants she had ordered from Montgomery Ward and pulled them up under her dress. Until the school found the money to buy uniforms for her team, she wanted them at least to know what a football uniform looked like. *Priorities,* she thought angrily as she yanked her dress over her head: whether to buy the uniforms for a team the Normal could rally around, or fix the broken windows? She shrugged into a nondescript white jersey with the cloth lettering POST OAK stitched on the front. She had an athlete's solid physique, thick but not fat, with sturdy arms and legs. All her life she had loved boys' games and had run with the best of them. Her body had retained a youth's muscle tone and natural strength, ready as ever to run a footrace or shinny up a tree. Her face was square with a prominent jaw, button nose, and gray eyes that turned flinty in anger or luminous in delight.

To complete the transformation, she slipped a chain with a brass whistle around her neck, picked up Stagg's *Scientific and Practical Treatise,* and went outside. The team had already started to fight. She hurried onto the playground to break it up. Blowing whistle bursts, she waded undaunted into the flying fists. The whistle shrieks were like screams of pain amid the groans and curses of the youths rolling on the hard-packed clay. She became one with the fighters, flailing and kicking indiscriminately at any available target—thigh or chest or head. The players sounded like wild beasts tearing one another apart.

"Brother, help!" she shouted at the team captain, who stood cynically apart. He rushed to her aid, and together they restored order. The players stood up with sheepish grins. To a man they wore denim overalls. All but two were barefoot. They did not mind the chill November air.

She scowled at them and blew a strand of gray hair away from her eyes. She impatiently brushed it back and left a red clay smudge on her forehead. The players milled about with a jollying hostility, awaiting her reproof.

"Football is a game with rules of order!" she bawled out. "Why must you fight? Why can you not play cleanly, like gentlemen, instead of clawing at each other like animals? B.C., you and Lincoln are the worst about fighting, and first cousins to boot. Shake hands!" Two huge linemen looked askance at each other and brushed palms with hands like hams. "Now, let's work on the halfback buck over left guard. Take your positions."

They moved reluctantly into opposing formations. It was more fun to make up their own plays, which were more daring than the diagrams of the great coach Stagg. Because the varsity always played offense and the scrubs defense—and because there were only nine scrubs to begin with—the defense grouped close together. They crouched low to the ground, ready to throw themselves in the path of the ballcarrier. Such positioning generally turned a line buck into an end run as the runner changed course to avoid being tackled, eliciting more kicks and scoldings from "Miz Kate."

They never tired of defying her, slyly and passively, enduring her ill temper in rebellious conspiracy while they experimented with the limits of her patience. In a recent game she had scheduled for them against Negro Normal of Lebanon, she had lost control of herself and embarrassed them by rushing up and down the sideline like a hen with a disturbed nest. Yet they knew to a man that if football ceased to exist, they would miss it desperately.

Brother, at quarterback, set his team and called signals. The ball was snapped and he feinted to Ulysses, the fullback, who plunged into the line to clear a hole for the halfback, Cassius. Kate held Stagg's book open to the diagram of the play and watched approvingly. So far the play was going as intended. Then the defense massed to plug the gap and Cassius swerved in mid-stride, swooping around the end with the speed and grace of a dove.

"No, no!" Kate screamed as they knew she would. She

crouched in their huddle and brandished the open book. "Does *this* look like an end run?"

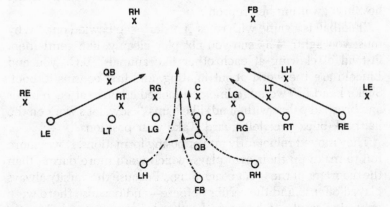

"It stands to reason, Miz Kate," Brother argued, "that if the hole is filled, the runner must take it wide."

"Thank you, Brother," she said stiffly. "This is practice, not a game. In practice, we do it like the book says. Do you all see what your assignments are? Good. Run it again. We are going to run it over and over until you get it right."

She watched them take their positions, knowing that somehow they would turn the buck into a reverse or a pass or even a punt. She watched Brother set the team. The son of a carpenter and a seamstress, the oldest of seven children, he was her favorite student. Short, compact, with broad shoulders and a small, well-shaped head, he directed the offense with composure and daring. A former valedictorian, he had applied to several universities for a scholarship to medical school. During the two years he had waited in vain for acceptance, he had halfheartedly studied divinity under Principal Rutledge (who was also pastor of Post Oak Church) and helped Kate tutor slow learners. Frustration and impatience had made Brother cynical. Although Kate admired his convictions, she tried to reason with him about the need for understanding.

Brother's heroes were John Brown, Geronimo, and Abraham Lincoln. He identified with their courage, ingenuity, commitment, and willpower. He dreamed of being an incendiary who exploded ideas into action. Waiting compressed his dreams and made them painful. Waiting was the most difficult thing he ever had done.

Football helped.

Kate watched her players turn the halfback buck into a reverse and made them do it over. Except for Brother, the rest of her raggedy team would become day laborers, farmers, perhaps tradesmen if someone cared enough to teach them plumbing or cabinetmaking. Except for Brother, they would merge with the black service industry which mortared and tacked together the white world of Bardstown. Looking now at the linemen—Henry Clay, Ulysses, B.C., Lincoln, Isaiah—with their heavy musculature, she sensed the rhythm of their lives, slow and measured. Hence she secretly exulted—although shrieking her disapproval —when they rebelled against the white man's formations and roared into some exotic triple-pass play; or when they complained about calisthenics yet gloried in the wind sprints, each day a new champion; or when a lazy, foot-dragging scrimmage exploded into the ferocity of combat and Kate would sally into the inevitable fight and empty the water bucket over their heads. It was manhood she was nurturing, valor she was sustaining.

Her motives were not entirely altruistic. At thirty-seven, she lived at home with her parents. She had allowed her family and friends to typecast her as plain but brainy, socially awkward but gifted, yet indispensable as a teacher and a fourth for bridge. She had found it far easier to become the person they perceived her to be than to break the mold and release her secret self. Her heroes were Joan of Arc, Geronimo, and Florence Nightingale, who, she perceived, had quietly gathered themselves for their leap into history. Kate rationalized that she, too, was biding her time. In the meantime, she smoked an occasional cigarette behind a locked door and read *Harper's*. She loved tales of faraway places. She cultivated a reputation in Bardstown as an eccentric recluse who sometimes galloped wildly around the courthouse in the moonlight. She kept a diary with occasional entries such as, "Nov. 3rd: first-period chemistry discovered elixir of youth." She read every page of the Louisville *Courier-Journal*—delivered by train one day late—and could rattle on at breakfast about streetcars in Chicago or tricycle races in Central Park or balloon ascensions in Atlantic City. She had nagged her father, a physician and mortician, until he had installed the first residential telephone in Bardstown. Then she could not think of anyone to call.

Football helped.

What she liked most about it was the contact. As a coach, she vicariously felt every crushing tackle and block, imagined herself scrabbling up to defeat the dread that nothing exciting was ever going to happen to her. On fall mornings, as she galloped hellbent to school on her beloved black mare, Diana, she often had football on her mind. Her students, parting beside the dirt road to let her pass, cheered as if she were winning a race, and tossed their caps into the air. She never acknowledged to herself that these students were cheering their *teacher*, Miz Kate, who praised, coerced, cajoled, and browbeat them into reading books, who forced them to respect what they might never again have the luxury to discover.

"Down!" She blew her whistle vigorously to stop the scrubs from piling on. "Stop that! Levester, you'll do ten extra laps for unsportsmanlike conduct."

As the players unpiled, one of them knelt on the ground, clutching at his groin. The rest of the players slyly waited for Kate to notice him. Her frown of concern was a signal that started them giggling. They cupped horny hands over their mouths and guffawed with gasps and belches.

"You mustn't laugh at a teammate who is injured!" she screeched. "It is unsporting not to help a downed comrade." Kate waded into them, pushing the big linemen out of her way. She knelt beside the injured player. "Where does it hurt, Sherman?"

"He ain't hurt!" one of the players roared. "He jest got the you-know-what stomped outen him."

Sherman gave her a baleful glance. She detected a telltale odor.

"Go clean your britches." She waved a hand toward the woods and turned her back so that she would not see the crouching lope with which the scrub made his way to the trees. The other players rolled on the hard ground, choked with laughter. Brother stifled a grin. Kate kicked the players to their feet.

"Why will you not *practice!"* she cried with each kick. *"Why* do
I have to *beg* you to do it *right? Why* don't you *have* any *pride?"*
One by one they rose, grinning sheepishly. Clay dust bur-
nished their cheeks. Kate glanced at Brother for support, but her
captain stared past her. He seemed to be waiting for some momentous event.

"All right. Let's try the tackle-back formation," she said. The
players especially liked this formation, in which the tackles,
Ulysses Jackson or Henry Clay (Tree) Jackson, shifted into the
backfield and took a handoff from the quarterback. It was comical to see a 250-pound forward metamorphose his bulk and
power into a back's quickness and elusiveness. Tree tiptoed expectantly into the backfield.

Kate wished she were able to get down with them in the dirt
and challenge them man to man, show them how to block and
tackle. Perhaps they would have respected her more then, she
thought. All she had was A. Alonzo Stagg's book. Yet she knew
that football could not be taught out of a book any more than
could ballet or bicycle riding. She knew that opponents did not
conform to neat X's and O's of diagrams. She took comfort in the
book, however. It not only gave her an ideal to strive for, but
represented in itself a marvelous array of new and interesting
facts: rules of the game, training, strategy, formations.

All her life she had loved facts. She respected knowledge, but
she adored the facts, such as: What is the capital of Wisconsin?
What is the estimated population of the world? What is the
world's highest waterfall? How many homicides occur annually
in the U.S.? What state is the largest potato producer?* And so
forth.

Facts. She loved without distinction chemical equations, mathematical hypotheses, geographical place names, quotable verse,
body organs and their functions, historical events and dates, bot-
any, biology, zoology, geology, history, philosophy, archaeology,
belles lettres, beaux arts, charts, statistics, and graphs. Facts were
the solid footing in the limbo of her life. Facts were the safe
terrain from which she sallied to face a shifting world.

So it was that Stagg's book provided a semblance of order for

* Madison; 1,450,000,000; Krimml Falls in the Upper Pinzgau; 10,212; New York,
52 million bushels. (Source: American Almanac, 1896)

this violent, dusty playground. Kate used the book because it was all she had. Ironically, also residing in Bardstown was one of the most celebrated football players in the South: Chase Riddle, quarterback. She had known him since he was a child. Theirs was a speaking acquaintance only, however, and she did not feel comfortable about asking him for advice. Also, she did not know his views on race. Bardstown whites generally tended to be tolerant of blacks as long as they kept to themselves, did their jobs, and stayed out of trouble. Four or five middle-class black families served as spokesmen and buffers between the races.

Although Kate was more a doer than a crusader, her heroine persona had led her to apply, fresh out of college with her teaching certificate in hand, to Post Oak Normal. The U.S. Supreme Court, with its recent *Plessy v. Ferguson* ruling, would have designated Post Oak as "separate but equal." Kate knew exactly how separate it was. Her parents and childhood friends strenuously objected to her "throwing herself away on those poor Nigrahs." In so doing, they merely confirmed to her that she was making the right decision.

Because of a chronic shortage of teachers, Kate was compelled to teach a variety of subjects: math, English, government, art, science, history—in fact, all subjects except religion, which was the special province of the Reverend Rutledge, the principal. With such a workload, she quickly learned to make tutors of her brightest students, positioning them in quiet corners, or outside in good weather, to quiz slow learners. She tried to make learning a game, to instill in her students a desire to excel. She made do with a terrible scarcity of materials. If there were five students to one tablet, the other four split logs for the school stove while they waited their turn.

She had become accustomed to repeating the curriculum every October, when school turned out for the harvest and many students forgot most of what they had learned during the first six weeks. She was prepared when bright girls became pregnant in the eighth grade or talented boys ran off to join a minstrel show. Yet every year or so a student like Brother would come along. In fourteen years of teaching she counted a dozen professional careers among her students: three nurses, four attorneys, an accountant, two engineers, a college administrator, and a physician.

Beside her satisfaction in helping her students, Kate's determination was fueled by the gossiping tongues of Bardstown who bemoaned her seemingly wasted talents at every wedding shower, sewing circle, or hearts tournament. Kate fed on their disapprobation like a jackrabbit on snapdragons. It was sustenance enough that Kate Kuykendall perceived herself to be at war with the white establishment of Bardstown, Kentucky. She would not have given up her teaching, her students, her football, if she had had to pay to work at Post Oak Normal.

The team was fighting. Kate blew her whistle and reached for the water bucket.

She pried apart the antagonists, two skinny scrubs and the varsity center named B.C., whose reddish hair and freckles hinted at a Scotch-Irish temper in his ancestry. B.C.'s grin revealed several missing teeth as he attempted to persuade her to reduce his sentence. "It a question," he reasoned, "of who hit whom first. Ax George."

One of Kate's pet grammar projects was the relative pronoun and its usage. B.C. was looking at her hopefully. Standing in the forlorn playground with twenty sweating, clay-streaked players awaiting her edict, she felt herself to be at the center of the universe. At thirty-seven, she knew that she would never bear a child, never touch the face of her own infant. Nor had she need to.

"Ten laps," she said.

Chapter Three

Richard Canfield, the Faro King, poured himself a glass of claret from a crystal decanter. He agreed with the French that wine was good for the digestion. He had ordered a light brunch of squab and omelets to be served after the meeting. Depending on how well Ziprenian defended himself regarding his misappropriation of funds, it could be the Armenian's last meal. Ziprenian had been a disappointment, but at least the odds remained in the house's favor, as always.

Canfield's smooth-shaven face was boyish and sly, ruddy from high living. He wore a cutaway morning coat with gray striped trousers and matching cravat with diamond stickpin. Diamond rings glittered on his fingers. In his lapel he wore a pink rosebud. He sipped his wine and watched his lieutenants with a mildly disinterested expression. Ziprenian was late.

Seated around the mahogany conference table were James (Bird) Mahoney, manager of Canfield's New York properties; Archie (The Knife) O'Hara, enforcement; and Freddy (Fingers) McGee, manager of properties in Hartford, Providence, and Boston. McGee and O'Hara passed the time by needling Mahoney about a john's roulette run at The Palace recently. He had won over a hundred thousand before his luck ran out and he lost all he had won and more. It was too bad the john shot himself afterward, they agreed, but at least he had the class to do it around the corner.

Ziprenian quietly entered the room. His face shone with an unnatural incandescence like oil on water. Canfield set his wineglass carefully on the polished sideboard. He nodded at a chair, and Ziprenian sat.

"Well," said the Faro King. "We're all here."

As usual, he did not sit, so that everybody had to look up at him. He also paced, or rather seemed to float, around the table so that his subordinates were forced to turn their heads continually to follow him.

"First generation off the boat." Canfield ironically addressed Ziprenian. "Traveling in steerage. Mahoney found you shining shoes in the Bowery, pitching pennies with schoolboys, matching quarters with sailors, running numbers for invalids . . . and wasn't there some particularly enterprising project?"

"Bootlegging for the nursing home on Canal Street," Ziprenian said.

"Oh, yes, very civic-minded," said Canfield. "Only in America, eh, Zipper?"

"Right, Mr. Canfield."

"Gave you a start right here on Fourteenth Street, didn't we?" Canfield steepled his fingers judiciously. "Dealing vingt-et-un at the nickel table. Eight years later, we put you in charge of operations in Philly, Jersey, and Delaware. Amazing what opportunities exist for a young man with wit and ambition. Supply and demand, eh?" He paused heavily. "I think you have something to share with us, Zipper?"

Ziprenian sat up straight with a small flourish. He spoke earnestly and without fear. "I have some advice for you, Mr. Canfield."

The lieutenants gaped. O'Hara felt for the razor in his coat pocket. Then they saw the corner of Canfield's mouth sag in the beginnings of a smile, and they released a loud, astonished laugh.

"Is it twenty-five thousand worth of advice?" Canfield said.

"Oh, I'll pay it back, don't worry." The Zipper's confidence was preternatural. "I'm talking respectability."

"I don't get enough respect?"

Canfield's gray eyes were leaden. In the stunned silence, a sparrow flew past the open window, its wingbeat like distant thunder.

"Why did the Athenaeum Club blackball you?" Ziprenian said calmly.

His colleagues leaned forward with elbows on the table, a gesture of neutrality. No one except The Zipper looked up at the Faro King. Canfield's face grew pale.

"One day," Canfield said with stiletto precision, "I must show you my Chippendales, my oriental vases, and my Whistler originals."

"Too much old money in the Athenaeum Club," Arno continued unabated. "No way to buy in."

"I'm a busy man, sonny, what's your point?"

At Canfield's deadly tone O'Hara crossed his arms, settling into his executioner's role.

"What does America love beyond all things?" Ziprenian asked.

"Something for nothing, a piece of ass, and a good night's sleep," Canfield replied without hesitation. The lieutenants chuckled in relief.

"Sports and patriotism," Ziprenian corrected him.

"Sports, you mean like the horses?"

"Sports like football."

"Is that like baseball?"

"No, it's different."

"Well, get to the point, sonny."

O'Hara glanced meaningfully at his watch.

"I'm gonna put you in the history books." The Zipper ventured a grin.

"Some sap is writing about me now. 'Father of Faro' he calls me."

"Who wants to be in a criminology textbook?" The Zipper said recklessly. "How does 'Great American Benefactor' sound? On the front page of every newspaper in the U.S.—Chicago, Baltimore, Boston, San Francisco, Philly. 'Founder of the greatest charity event in the nation's history!' " Ziprenian paused for effect. "The first annual North-South football game."

"What's this?" Canfield said.

"North and South. Union and Confederate. A hundred grand for charity courtesy of Richard A. Canfield . . ."

"You know," Canfield said with a flinty indulgence, "I appreciate a good bluff as well as the next one, even when it is temporarily costing me twenty-five thousand, but I only have so much patience." He gloomily sniffed the rosebud in his lapel.

Ziprenian broke a sweat, like a prize-fighter warming up. "All right, I'm proposing a charity football game, matching the best college players from the North against the best from the South. To be played in Philadelphia before Christmas. The Philly Athletic Club would serve as host organization and would officiate the contest. Walter Camp would be appointed to select the coaches and players who would participate—"

"Walter who?" Canfield said.

"Camp is to football what Canfield is to faro," The Zipper explained.

"So where do I come in?"

"You're the sponsor."

"You mean, the sap who puts up the money?"

"Loose change." The Zipper shrugged. "Maybe ten thousand. We get it back three times over from concession sales."

"And we handle the bets?" Canfield's interest was piqued at last. "Exclusive?"

"No bets," said Ziprenian.

"No bets!" they cried.

"It's gotta be clean," Ziprenian explained. "We are talking respectability. We are talking public recognition of your contribution to society, Mr. Canfield. We are polishing up your reputation. Consider this: does gambling get bad press every week? When a politician wants to make a name for himself, what does he do? He closes down some gambling joint. Isn't it time for a change? We need someone to make a grand gesture. Whose responsibility is it? Who is Number One in the American gaming establishment? I say the responsibility is yours, Mr. Canfield. I say ten thousand professional gamblers in this country are waiting for you to take the lead."

Canfield raised his eyebrows in appraisal. Drying sweat was cool on The Zipper's forehead.

"How much is this baseball game supposed to raise?" Canfield said.

"Football," Ziprenian gently corrected. "After making extensive inquiries, I estimate fifty thousand attendance at two dollars a head, plus fifty cents concessions per head. We should clear a hundred thousand."

"Fifty thousand johns would pay to see football?"

"I think, personally, there will be more than *sixty* thousand."

"Why will they come?"

"Why did they come to the War Between the States? When you mix athletics with love of country, you got something for everybody, like the Roman orgies."

"The Roman *games,*" Canfield corrected. "Patriotism and violence? I like it." He thought for a moment. "What charity benefits?"

"Children's diseases would be good." The Zipper examined his nails. "I've been thinking, a children's *hospital.*"

"You don't build a first-rate hospital with a hundred grand!" Mahoney scoffed, glancing at Canfield for approval. The Faro King was lost in thought.

"That's just the beginning," Ziprenian said expansively. "Look into the future. This North-South game becomes an annual event, like George Washington's birthday. A hundred thousand a year. The Richard A. Canfield Children's Hospital. In twenty years, one in every major city in America. Social standing for generations of gamblers yet unborn. This is a goal without historical precedent. I see laissez-faire laws for our profession. I see state-operated gaming establishments. I see the government appealing to the sporting instinct—no, the *soul*—of the American people to support lotteries which will earn millions for schools and hospitals and social welfare. The Athenaeum Club is begging you to accept its presidency. Ambassador Canfield at the Court of St. James! There's no end to it."

The mobsmen observed their chief's eyes widen dreamily.

"Say we don't handle none of the bets direct," Mahoney said shrewdly, "but take closed bids for the betting franchise. I'm thinking a quarter of a million . . ."

"Per annum!" McGee chimed in.

Canfield's fist smashed the table. "It's clean or it's nothing. Right, Zipper?"

"We oughta at least let bids on concessions," McGee complained. "Holstein Confections of Garden City will give us seventy-thirty—"

"No splits, no kickbacks." Canfield's whisper was like an ocean whirlpool. "We deal straight up or not at all. Right, Zipper?" Ziprenian grinned, showing perfect teeth. The Faro King gripped the back of his empty chair and stared at Arno with the full weight of his authority.

"All right, Zipper. I'll tell you what I think. I'm going for it, but it's your baby. You owe me twenty-five thousand, so *you* put up the ten thousand front money. *You* make sure everything stays clean. I say clean, I mean antiseptic, I mean germ-free. You make it a first-class operation. If it comes off as planned, if I get the good press you're talking about, if I'm satisfied in every detail, then you not only stay alive, you still got a job and you don't owe me the twenty-five grand. But if you screw it up—let's see." He cocked his head creatively. "Wasn't your father a tailor?"

Ziprenian's face was so pale that each blue-black follicle of beard shadow stood out distinctly. "Yes, but he's retired."

"You screw it up and I'm bringing him out of retirement. He'll personally sew you into the bag we drop in the East River. Got it?"

Ziprenian felt his colleagues staring. He sensed one-track minds humming with the challenge of how to skim a "clean" contest under the chief's nose. Cheating the law was business as usual. To pull one on R.C. and get away with it required uncommon boldness. If the chief caught on, they could hang it on Ziprenian. Their unblinking gaze reminded Arno of the attention that a wolf pack gives a freshly wounded member.

"Thank you, Mr. Canfield," he said.

Chapter Four

Cornelius Humboldt looked at the painting of Robert E. Lee hanging in his office and reflected on the nature of Providence. Was it of divine origin, which worked in mysterious ways? Was it an epic force for good, like God hurling Satan's fallen angels into a burning lake? Was it a cosmic irony which dispensed fate with savage nonchalance, a juxtaposition of human ambition with malevolent coincidence? Humboldt, professor of history, fencing master, and assistant football coach at the University of the South, looked out his office window at the fog that swelled thickly among the Sewanee oaks and the gray sandstone buildings. In his hand was a letter Coach Blair had given him that morning.

The letter, addressed to Coach J. E. Blair, University of the South, Sewanee, Tennessee, was from Coach John Heisman, Alabama Polytechnic Institute, Auburn, Alabama. Heisman was inviting Blair to serve as honorary coach, along with Heisman and Glenn Warner, of Georgia, in an all-star football match to be played in Philadelphia between the best players of the North and South. Blair, who was ill, had asked his assistant, Humboldt, to serve in his place.

Humboldt noted Heisman's enthusiasm:

> I view this contest as a means of engendering the spread
> of football throughout the South and other areas of the
> country. Also, it will be interesting to see how our play-
> ers from Georgia, Virginia, Ala. Poly., Sewanee, etc.,

match up with those from Harvard, Yale, Penn, Princeton, etc.

Yes, Humboldt thought, as a shark's jaws are interesting to a young porpoise.

Heisman went on to ask Blair's help in recruiting outstanding players in the Tennessee area, especially a fullback from Vanderbilt named Burke. Humboldt recalled having seen Burke play. The burly fullback was a nonpareil blocker, weighing 195 without an ounce of excess avoirdupois. The Gray squad, Heisman explained, would represent teams from the Southern, South Atlantic, and Southwest conferences.

Heisman mentioned some of the players he and Warner had recruited. From Alabama Polytechnic at Auburn, Heisman was bringing two linemen, Mike Harvey and Blondy Glenn. Glenn was captain of a 3–1 team that lost only to Georgia. Also Heisman had invited Eli Abbott, a hard-running halfback from the University of Alabama's Thin Red Line.

Glenn (Pop) Warner had selected from his undefeated and untied, 4–0 Georgia team his great captain, George Price. Captain Price tipped the scales at over 200 pounds, ran like a locomotive, and was a demon at tackle. Joining Price from Georgia was Cow Nalley, a fine halfback widely known for his ferocious play.

On their way to Philadelphia, Heisman and Warner planned to recruit other players: Carter, HB, and Martin, E, from Virginia; Joiner, C, and Wright, G, from North Carolina.

Humboldt silently appealed to Lee's portrait:

We're twenty years behind the North. We can't match them in terms of tradition and experience. The Blue coaching staff includes three of the best football minds in the country: A. Alonzo Stagg, of Chicago; Phil King, of Princeton; and George Woodruff, of Penn.

Humboldt sat morosely at his desk, which was covered by scholarly journals and periodicals stacked in overflowing piles. There were the *Southern Historical Society Papers, The Land We Love, Southern Magazine, Southern Review, Our Living and Our Dead, Southern Bivouac,* and *Confederate Veteran.* His eye fell on his favorite book, Edward Pollard's *The Lost Cause.* A felicitous phrase from Pollard came into the professor's mind: "In all standards of individual character, the South remains superior over the people of the North."

The face of Lee seemed to speak a name: *Chase Riddle.*

In 1895, when the University of the South played Centre College, Riddle, quarterback for Centre, had demolished the Tiger eleven almost singlehandedly. At six feet four and 200 pounds, Riddle ran like a deer, was a cunning signal caller, a fair dropkicker, and a sure tackler, especially good at reading offensive formations and alerting his teammates to a developing play. One play was indelibly stamped on Humboldt's memory.

In the second half, Sewanee was fighting to keep the score close. Centre had made a field goal and a touchdown against a single touchdown by Sewanee. Neither team had successfully kicked the point after, and the score was 9 to 4. Humboldt and Blair looked on from the sideline, encouraging their players. Sewanee had stopped Centre for no gain on two successive plays and expected Riddle to punt. He brought his team out of their huddle and set himself to receive the snap—tall and lithe and confident, his blond mop of hair streaked with sweat and mud, his hawk's beak of a nose aimed at his opponents.

Instead of punting, Riddle unexpectedly ran toward the Sewanee side of the field. Humboldt and Blair were dumbfounded. The Sewanee defenders closed on Riddle. He was trapped. In that instant, he spied a lone Centre player rising to his feet on the far side of the field, some 50 yards away.

To Humboldt's amazement, Riddle leaped high in the air and unleashed a sidearm throw over the heads of the tacklers. It was a humming spiral, thrown like a baseball in flat trajectory. The Centre wingman reacted automatically, plucking the ball out of the air and staring at it in astonishment. The other players stopped dead, tangled together like figures in an ancient frieze. Players, coaches, and spectators fell silent and looked to the referee in this historic moment of decision.

"Fair pass!" the ref shouted and waved his cap for play to continue. As if the official had in godlike fashion set mortal forces in motion, the wingman dashed for the goal with the Sewanee players in frantic pursuit. He touched the ball down. Centre went on to win, 18 to 4. Riddle's jump pass lay ticking like an

anarchist's bomb at the back of Humboldt's mind. He stared imploringly at the benign countenance of Robert E. Lee.

General, Riddle is a ringer.

I leave it to you, the portrait seemed to say.

Humboldt realized he was late for class. He gathered his lecture notes and left his office. As he made his way across the campus, charmed as always by the rush of black-gowned scholars to the various lecture halls, the hems of their robes swishing as they ran, he found solace in his favorite game of What if.

What if, he asked the mountain air, Lee had counterattacked the shattered Union Army when it lay astride the Rappahannock River at Fredericksburg in 1862? What if, he asked the towering oaks in their rusty plumage, Stonewall Jackson had not been shot down at Chancellorsville but had lived to march with Lee into Pennsylvania? What if, he asked the Gothic arches of St. Augustine Chapel, Forrest had been allowed his night attack to drive the disembarking Army of the Ohio back into the Tennessee River, thus destroying Grant's army at Shiloh?

Humboldt was in a properly melancholy mood as he climbed to the second floor of Forensic Hall and entered his classroom. A dozen students stood respectfully. He took his place behind his podium, forgetting, in his reverie, to give them permission to sit. He looked out the window. They fidgeted under their black gowns. It was not the first time such a standoff had occurred in Professor Humboldt's Civil War class.

"The issue, gentlemen," Humboldt said, still looking out the window, "is that of political morality."

No one said anything. The students stood like statues, waiting for him to notice them. Tolerant smiles creased their faces. They encouraged Humboldt in his eccentric digressions, his sentimentality and excess. Many students actually took notes of Humboldt's bombastic asides, such as, "Lincoln deserved to be shot. I would have shot him myself, given half a chance."

Danny Creech, of Cullman, Alabama, was late to class, as always. When he shut the door behind him and slouched to his row, Humboldt turned and saw the class on their feet. For an instant it appeared to him that they were standing to welcome Creech.

"Sit down, sit down!" he cried. "Creech, if you had been annointed by Christ himself to sit at the foot of God, you'd keep the Holy Ghost waiting."

Creech, a lanky, cadaverous person, folded his hands before him and assumed an expression of submission. Gowns rustled as the students took their seats.

"Well," Humboldt challenged, "did anyone read the book I assigned you? *A Constitutional View of the Late War Between the States,* by Alexander Stephens?"

Elliott, the star pupil of the class, tentatively raised his hand. Humboldt ignored him. Elliott always read everything.

"One in thirteen!" Humboldt cried. "I don't know why I bother. Be so good as to take out your tablets and write a paragraph in reply to the question, 'How can the South be said to be the rightful heir to the traditions of the Revolutionary forefathers?' You have five minutes."

Humboldt went to the window and stared into infinity. Elliott whipped out his tablet and began writing. The rest of the class glanced at one another with long faces. They went through the motions of turning to a blank page in their notebooks, arranging the notebooks symmetrically on their desks, testing the sharpness of their pencils. The only sound was the scratching of Elliott's pencil.

"Dr. Humboldt?" Creech mumbled. "Would you repeat the question?"

Humboldt stared imperiously at the Alabamian. The boy's father reputedly owned half of Cullman. Humboldt observed Creech's long johns underneath his gown. The lout had not taken the time, he thought, to put on his trousers.

"Never mind," he told the class. They relaxed with a sigh. "All right, Elliott, read us what you've written."

" 'The South faithfully observed the tenets of the American Revolution and the Constitution,' " Elliott read eagerly. " 'The North, on the other hand, violated the Constitution by attacks upon the expansion of states' rights, slavery, and other issues.' That's as far as I got, Dr. Humboldt." Elliott glanced up hopefully.

"All right, all right," Humboldt waved his hand in dismissal. He took up the argument.

"Now we see the postwar North devoted to a political Jacobinism and belief in rule by the masses over state interests, which violates the traditions of our Founding Fathers. The war, gentlemen, was a grand epic fought by a chivalrous South, a knightly Confederacy on plunging steeds, against a mongrel North. Our Christian knights made war against the political Jacobinism, irreligion, and greed." He paused dramatically. "In the end, the Confederacy was not defeated so much as overrun by Northern hordes. Our generals were superior to those of the North, but our armies were worn down eventually by the endless waves of blue that were sent against us, many of them European mercenaries. It all comes down to Gettysburg, the high-water mark of American history, the ultimate symbol of the South's nearness to obtaining the Grail. Why, gentlemen, why?"

Elliott was taking notes frantically. Creech had begun to doze. Humboldt was suffused with emotion as he continued.

"Lee took all the blame on himself, writing to President Davis, 'No blame can be attached to the army for a failure to accomplish what was projected by me, nor should it be censured . . . I alone am to blame, in perhaps expecting too much of its prowess and valor.' Yet Lee was the perfect embodiment of the purity, stability, and greatness of the South. How could he lose?" Humboldt allowed the eternal question to hang before them. "In a word, gentlemen, *Longstreet.*" Humboldt firmly grasped his lapels as though taking hold of history.

"After the war was over, the facts of what happened at Gettysburg began to surface and the truth became known. General William Pendleton was the first to charge Longstreet with disobeying an order from Lee to attack at sunrise on that fateful day of July 2, 1863. As a result of Longstreet's delay, the Union line had time to strengthen positions along their left, and so was able to hold when Longstreet finally mounted his attack. The lesser charges against Longstreet, brought by his fellow generals such as Pendleton, Jubal Early and others, include his unnecessary and deliberately circuitous march route to the Union left, which accounted for further delay, Longstreet's failure to support Pickett on July third, and a general attitude of disloyalty to Lee throughout the entire battle. As General John B. Gordon, Longstreet's fellow Georgian, wrote in his book, *Reminiscences of the Civil War,* 'General Lee died believing (the testimony on this point is overwhelming) that he lost Gettysburg at last by Longstreet's disobedience of orders.' Gordon went on to conclude, 'Lee was never really beaten. Lee could not be beaten.' Think about it, gentlemen. How, indeed, *could* he lose?"

Danny Creech had never, to anyone's knowledge, contributed to class discussion in his four years at the University of the South. Humboldt could not fathom why the boy suddenly spoke up. Was it some dark affinity with Longstreet? Was it a lack of proper respect for the Lost Cause? Was it simply that Humboldt had interrupted Creech's nap?

"What difference does it make?" Creech said. "We lost."

A thunderous silence filled the classroom. Humboldt stared austerely at Creech. Someday the lazy lout would own half of Cullman, Alabama. It was precisely at this moment that Cornelius Humboldt knew that he was going to Bardstown, Kentucky, to recruit Chase Riddle. He collected his lecture notes with crisp, decisive movements.

"For your next assignment," he said coldly, "read *Is Davis a Traitor, or Was Secession a Constitutional Right Previous to 1861*, by Bledsoe. It's on reserve at the library. Dismissed."

Humboldt headed for the administration office to request a temporary leave of absence. As he crossed the quadrangle, deserted now between classes, he felt a fierce elation. He hummed "The Bonnie Blue Flag" and unconsciously fell into step with the rhythm, marching to the bishop's office as if going to war.

Chapter Five

"So lovely, so nice," Cousin Minnie murmured.

Chase willed his body to go slack so she could do as she wished. It was her game, and she would cry if he did not let her play it. He conjured images of girls with sculptured breasts behind whalebone stays. The girls reached out to him as men hoisted him to their shoulders and carried him through a cheering throng.

"Let's do it *this* way, now," Cousin Minnie commanded.

With his free hand Chase held a football in his lap and imagined himself taking the heelback from the center, palming the ball neatly on first bounce. Then he feinted to the fullback going right, hid the ball on his hip, and rolled left all alone. The defense turned to chase him. It became a footrace down the sideline. His cleats flicked white dust from the yard markers as he outran his pursuers and crossed the goal line. The gun sounded. Spectators rushed toward him.

"Now do it *that* way," Cousin Minnie ordered.

She did not expect him to reply. They understood each other. He watched her stroke his arm, her withered cheeks close to his skin. He could feel her breath prickle the thick hair on his forearm. She was not his cousin or anyone else's that he knew of. But everyone at the nursing home called her Cousin Minnie. It had become part of his Sunday ritual to sit with her for a time, quiet and submissive, while she whisked the hair on his arm up and down, like a tiny field of wheat bending to the wind's will. Mrs.

Gaudchaux, the nursing home director, had encouraged him to let Cousin Minnie have her way with him, as the five minutes he spent with her every Sunday morning made her docile and easier to handle from Monday through Saturday. For Cousin Minnie, Mrs. Gaudchaux proclaimed it was a spiritual experience.

What if a capricious God had made Cousin Minnie His instrument? What if she raised her face with an awful truth in her eyes and spoke with the voice of an angel saying, "You are called"?

His grandfather, the Reverend Riddle, advised him to be patient. He listened to Big Dad, as he called his grandfather, because he liked to think Big Dad knew what he was doing.

"Getting the Call will be the most important thing that ever happened to you," Big Dad told him. "But don't worry yourself about anticipating how it will come to you. It varies from man to man."

Chase believed that being named All-Southern Quarterback in 1893 and 1894 was the most important thing that ever happened to him, but he did not argue with his grandfather.

"Some get the Call when an angel appears to them in a dream," Big Dad elaborated. "For others, it may be a moment of great physical strength, such as carrying a grand piano from a burning church building, which happened to my Uncle Henry. Some have heard a voice speak through a tree or a bird or a cow. Only a rare few are visited by a burning bush or pine."

"How did it appear to you?" Chase asked politely.

"God appeared to me as a crow."

"I thought crows were a form of the devil," Chase said.

"You are thinking of ravens," Big Dad corrected.

"What did the crow say?"

"It said 'Howdy,' natural-like, so as not to startle me, then went on to ask what I intended to do with my life. I realized right off that the Lord was talking to me and got down on my knees. The crow went on to instruct me to build my church, assemble my congregation, save souls, marry and beget children, shelter the homeless, succor the poor, and make the world a better place—which of course I did."

"That's all there was to it?" Chase had expected thunder and lightning, at least.

"What else you want, boy! When a crow talks, you'll develop a healthy fear. Don't ask too much of the Lord. Take what is your portion and be thankful."

"Let me get this straight," Chase said. "You actually heard a crow *talking* to you, and it was not imitation talk but real talk."

"That's right," Big Dad said, adding thoughtfully, "but it was not any ordinary sound the crow made. I know I heard him, in that I understood what he was telling me. But whether anybody else would have heard him—even if they'd been standing right next to me—that I cannot say. God moves in mysterious ways."

"So what you're saying is that you perceived the crow's meaning without necessarily hearing words spoken? Is that it?"

"All I can say is, that crow spoke to me. It spoke with the voice of an angel, which is not your ordinary human voice, is it?"

Chase ruminated for a moment. "Would you say that you *wanted* to hear that crow talk to you? I mean, before it said anything?"

Big Dad screwed his head around and squinted at Chase. "It was my crow and it spoke to me. It was my time to git the Lord's sign and I got it."

Something told Chase that the day's lesson was here ended.

"I don't know, Big Dad," Chase complained. "I may not be cut out for the ministry. I can't pay attention to every dog that barks. The only thing I was ever good at was playing football, and I have run out of colleges."

"There's more to life than playing football, boy. You got God's work to do."

"Maybe the church could organize a team?" Chase suggested. "A church league? I could be player-coach . . ."

" 'When I was a child, I spake as a child, I understood as a child, I thought as a child; but when I became a man, I put away childish things.' Corinthians one-thirteen, verse eleven," said Big Dad.

"That's another thing," Chase persisted. "I can't remember Scripture. I always mess up when I try to quote it."

"The Lord is on your side," Big Dad told him. "You got natural attraction. You got style. You in demand. Evening worship is up fifty percent since I turned it over to you. Collection is up twenty-five percent at the eleven o'clock. Forget football. You a preacher, thank the Lord!"

Cousin Minnie stroked faster and faster. She knew her time
was up. He gently detached himself from her. There was no need
to say anything. Her hand kept stroking the air where his arm
had been. She seemed to be making a priestly sign of absolution.
He waited to see if something significant was going to happen.
Her hand moved back and forth like a metronome. He told her
good-bye and went into the corridor.

Only a rare few are visited by a burning bush or pine.

Chase was dissatisfied with Big Dad's explanation. He brooded
on it as he left the nursing home and struck out on foot for the
church. He had ten minutes to get there. The singing started
precisely at 9:30 A.M. His job was to read the Doxology, lead the
congregation in their responses, and take up the collection. Big
Dad insisted that Chase take up the collection.

He followed a path up a wooded ridge. Tall beeches and oaks
formed a shimmering canopy of red and gold. He absently tossed
the ball in the air and caught it with one hand.

The crystal clear November air filled him with unfathomable
longings. To escape them he turned his thoughts back to the Call.
He had yet to find an ordained minister who was able to explain
it. The usual interpretation was that one simply *knew* when he
received it. This meant, Chase thought irritably, that he had to
take into account every birdsong, every cat's mew, every cloud
passing the moon, every breeze soughing in every branch. There
was no end to it, he thought, alert to a sudden movement of
falling leaves.

Tossing the football over a branch he tried to remember a time
when Big Dad had not directly or indirectly dominated his existence. It had begun in his boyhood when he sat Sundays without
end on hardwood pews, half-listening to Big Dad preach about
hellfire. He had stared at the rafters, half-expecting to see cher-
abim or seraphim flitting here and there. He saw only an occasional bird or wasp nest and once a sleeping bat, its grip tenacious
above a world slippery with sin.

Chase had gotten most of his height early—six feet at fifteen—
and it had seemed inevitable that the Reverend Riddle's tall,
handsome grandson would be invited to come forward and share
testimony with the congregation. Chase had discovered a talent
for mimicry. He could deliver a near-perfect imitation of Big

Dad's dramatic style. The congregation steadily increased in female attendance. The womenfolks were on the edge of their seats ready to shout "Hallelujah" the minute he approached the pulpit. Where was the challenge? When he called them his "flock" he meant it literally—just so many sheep waiting to be fed or foaled or cajoled or punished.

Big Dad, mindful of his retirement and desiring that Chase succeed him in his ministry, noticed signs that his grandson was being tempted by some of the sisters of the church. Nobody was to blame, especially the sisters. Big Dad prided himself on his tolerance but something had to be done. It was time the boy went to seminary and learned to interpret life's mysteries.

At seventeen Chase was packed off to Union Baptist College. During his freshman year a football team was formed. It was common knowledge that Brother Phillips, the headmaster, viewed football as an antidote for masturbation. Although nothing had been witnessed or confessed, Phillips had come to believe that solitary sinning had become epidemic at Union Baptist. The school board met in prayer vigil. They found inspiration. Since the student body numbered eleven students, all of them sound—too sound—of limb and body, and since eleven happened to be the number of players required to form a football team, Phillips declared football Union Baptist's salvation. He had seen the new game played in Louisville and considered it to be vigorous and manly. More to the point, each contest rendered the participants exhausted for up to twelve hours.

At six foot four and 200 pounds, Riddle quickly excelled at football. He had great stamina and a sinewy strength. He was a fast runner, extraordinarily agile for a big man. Although Union Baptist's football season consisted only of a six-week practice prior to a single Thanksgiving game (with sometimes a warm-up game against a high school team), Chase developed a knack for the game. The inflated leather ball, with its unusual spherical shape, seemed made for his grasp. He could throw it, kick it, hand it off, or hide it with a magician's sleight of hand. When he ran with the ball he somehow knew the exact instant to plant his foot, pivot, and drive past would-be tacklers. Time stood still when he scored a touchdown. He felt a fierce exultation, a militant joy that passed all understanding. He also flunked out of Union Baptist College.

Other universities invited him to attend their fall sessions, tuition-free. When the air was crisp and leaves were falling, professors did not seem to mind if he could not memorize Boethius or Longfellow. Crowds of cheerful people pursued him after a game. Men pressed money into his hands. Women gave him everything. For five years he played his way into the hearts of Kentuckians, Tennesseans, and Alabamians. Then Big Dad had sent for him. It was time, wrote Big Dad, to end his studies and begin his ministry.

A cow mooed in a field he was passing. Chase kept an eye on it. He had not, he realized, planned ahead. There had seemed no end to his happiness. The autumns had been full and exciting. Every spring he had returned home to help his father, Henry, plant corn and tobacco. Because of a stammer, Henry had not entered the ministry and so had made no objections when his son appeared able to satisfy Big Dad's expectations. Chase respected his father, but he often went to his maternal grandfather, Hudson Stroud, for advice.

Chase favored Hudson physically. They had the same hawk's nose, blue eyes, prominent jaw, and narrow head. Hudson possessed an aura of adventure, for he had ridden with John Hunt Morgan. Stroud had lost a leg at the Battle of Green River. But Hudson did not admire the minister whose son his daughter, Edwina, had married. The old cavalryman was not a churchgoer. He was violently opposed to Big Dad. Thus Stroud showed little sympathy when Chase complained about waiting for the Call.

"There's work on the river," Hudson would say. "Or you could go West. There's gold in Alaska. Or you could join the merchant marine. If preaching ain't what you want, go find something else to do and don't let old Riddle git your goat. Kick up your heels while you've got two heels to kick."

Chase appreciated his grandfather's concern, but Hudson had never seen him play football and did not understand his autumnal angst. The fall of 1896 was the second football season Chase had missed. He had begun to gain weight and recently had started to work out alone. He ran wind sprints and practiced his dropkick. He had gotten down to his playing weight of 200, he could sprint twenty 100-yard dashes in a row without becoming winded, and his running dropkick was again effective from 40 yards out. Yet getting his body tuned and ready for a nonexistent season only made things worse. He was a player without a team.

Chase stared at the football in his hands. Somehow it seemed to have betrayed him. He hurled it far into the trees and ran on.

Chase crested a ridge and saw Big Dad's church perched on the highest hill overlooking Bardstown, not far from "My Old Kentucky Home." The tiny white church rode the hills like a brave ship on a green and uncertain sea. The congregation had entered the sanctuary, leaving a young girl to fan flies away from the tables mounded with food and drink for dinner-on-the-grounds. He could hear a hymn faintly, "Nearer My God to Thee."

He entered the back door of the church, behind the choir loft, and slipped inside to take his place behind his grandfather. The moment he appeared, the congregation seemed to heat up. Women fanned themselves. Big Dad inclined his silver-maned head approvingly and handed Chase a hymnbook. Chase did not need the book to sing the closing refrain:

> There let the way appear, steps unto heav'n;
> All that thou sendest me, in mercy giv'n,
> Angels to beckon me Nearer, my God, to thee.

The congregation settled expectantly. The women's gaze clung to the broad-shouldered, golden-haired chaplain. The Reverend Riddle invited his grandson to testify. Chase knew then that the collection had not been taken. Big Dad liked to have Chase give testimony before the plate was passed. Chase approached the pulpit. A rustle went through the sanctuary.

"Brothers and sisters, I am here before you to give testimony to the saving grace of our Lord and Savior, Jesus Christ." His voice was quiet, yet it carried to the last row. He had not decided which testimony to give. "I am here to testify to the divine power of Almighty Jesus."

"Power!" the congregation responded.

"I am a sinner black with sin."

It was Chase's custom to testify about sins he had actually committed, rather than make them up. He never testified, for example, to drunkenness, even though it was a perennial favorite with the congregation, because he had never tasted alcohol. His testimonial repertoire included sloth, gambling, pride, and adultery. Sloth and gambling were strong suits, but he had used them recently during the August revival. Pride was his personal favorite, since it allowed him to mention his football career.

"So black with sin," he hesitated, "that I don't hardly know where to begin." At that moment his gaze locked electrifyingly with that of a redhead in the second row. The girl went into spasms.

"I'm *weak!*" he shouted.

"Praise the Lord!" the women cried.

"Brothers and sisters, I am weak in the flesh." Chase's gaze roamed the congregation, passing over the misty, fevered stares of the women, from octogenarians to eleven-year-olds just coming into puberty.

Behind Chase, seated in his straight-backed chair, Big Dad nodded benignly. Adultery provided common ground for fellowship. Most folks had committed adultery at least once.

"And a prey to Satan's temptations. When old Satan starts to tempt me, my heart flutters and I feel my knees go limp, and I cry, 'Help me, Jesus!' "

"Help me!" the women cried, their eyes darting at Chase.

"I've lusted after female flesh . . . sweet-scented flesh. I've wallowed in sin like a hog, help-me-Lord."

"HELP ME!" Fans whirred like motors.

"I've broken my vow to remain pure until marriage a hunnerd times," Chase continued blithely. "I've broken my mama's heart a hunnerd times. I started young in the madness of the flesh, lift-me-Jesus."

"LIFT ME."

"I was fourteen when I fell under the power of an older woman. She was nineteen. She led me astray, comfort-me-Jesus."

"COMFORT ME."

"It was the sin of adultery . . ."

"COMFORT ME."

"And we sinned together many times . . ."

"COMFORT ME."

"Sometimes as often as six times a night, come-unto-me-Jesus."

"SIX TIMES."

"Let thy power grow inside me . . ."

"POWER GROW."

"Let thy power become great within me . . ."

"POWER GREAT."

"Now and hereafter . . . now and forever . . ."

"NOW AND FOREVER."

"Amen."

"AMEN."

"Amen."

The women sagged against each other. Chase went to get the collection plates. He gave the Doxology. The women reached for their purses. As he passed the plate he tried not to look at them. As always, he felt only resignation coupled with an inexplicable sadness. On his way back down the aisle he saw Big Dad beaming proudly at him, and on the front row of the choir the lead soprano, Mrs. Cobb the widow woman, was singing the offertory in such open invitation that his hands shook and the coins rattled in his plate. The offertory hymn was "We Shall Overcome."

Chapter Six

The outhouse was dark and damp. A thin plane of light slicing through a crack in the door revealed a man's body curled around the base of the toilet. His legs were bent so that he seemed to cradle the curved wooden surface. His labored breathing paused as if he were listening to faraway sounds. He groped for the seat of the toilet, brushed his fingertips against it, and his breathing resumed.

A hand rattled the door to the stall. The man started violently and bumped his head against the toilet. His eyes opened, unseeing. Under a handlebar mustache his lips moved, barking small alarms. The door rattled again and the man weakly raised his head. His dry lips parted with a small popping noise and he cried, "Busy!" The door rattled viciously. The man's jowls trembled. He wrapped his arms about his head. A voice cursed outside and the door of another stall banged shut.

The man tried to snuggle back against the toilet but his eyes opened suddenly. Grasping the toilet, he pulled himself up and dry-heaved into it. After he caught his breath, he sank to the floor and sat propped against the toilet. He closed his eyes and began morning orientation. The events of the night before revealed themselves as if he were a one-man audience at a privately staged drama:

LOPEZ REMEMBERED

Scene: A crowded saloon; men stand shoulder to shoulder at a long bar. At the back of the room a poker game is in progress. Seated at the poker table are a hawk-faced dealer wearing arm garters and a diamond stickpin, a tall, lanky Indian with a gaunt, expressionless face, an overweight businessman who is drinking heavily, and a bald-headed cowboy with a handlebar mustache and a strongman's build. Behind the dealer sits a small man in a black suit and bowler hat. This kibitzer hovers behind the cowboy, who has amassed a large stack of chips.

BUSINESSMAN *(Gulping whiskey, speaking thickly)* Your bet, Lopez. Hurry up if you want any more of my money.

LOPEZ *(The cowboy, unhurried)* Raise you ten.

BUSINESSMAN *(Drunkenly thinking out loud)* You got two pair—three of a kind, anyhow. I'm gonna fold. Wait, let me see my cards, again. No, I'm gone.

(A telegram delivery boy enters the saloon, calling for "I. Lopez." Without taking his eyes from his cards, Lopez raises his hand. The delivery boy brings Lopez the telegram. Not in the least curious, Lopez drops the telegram on the table and gives the boy a cigar.)

DEALER *(Pushing chips into the middle of the table)* Raise you twenty.

INDIAN *(Folding his hand)* Shit.

(At the bar two arguing cowboys trade punches and begin fighting. Other bar patrons do not consider the fight eventful until a bottle smashes the mirror behind the counter. At the poker table the dealer irritably turns to watch. Lopez quietly reaches for a card in his boot. The fighters fall to the floor and roll toward the table. As Lopez exchanges a deuce for an ace a wiry hand grips his wrist. The Indian notices Lopez glancing under the table, where the little kibitzer is holding his wrist like a terrier.)

KIBITZER I got you, you rascal!

(Lopez leans down and hits the kibitzer with great force. The blow travels only a few inches but has the impact of a piledriver. The kibitzer is knocked unconscious. Lopez manages to add the ace to his hand before the dealer turns around. Lopez innocently meets the

dealer's stare, then realizes that all the players are look-ing at the backs of his cards. He has mistakenly replaced a red card with a green one.)

LOPEZ   Mal chance.

DEALER   *(Drawing a derringer)* Your balls.

(As the dealer cocks his pistol, Lopez kicks his chair out from under him. The gun goes off, missing Lopez and hitting an overweight hostess in the thigh. The In-dian laughs, and the dealer aims the pistol at him. The Indian dives under the table with Lopez. They begin to crawl from one table to another, enduring kicks from amused patrons. The dealer further entertains the crowd by shooting holes in the tables over Lopez's head. The kibitzer crawls after Lopez and sinks his teeth, ter-rier style, in Lopez's leg. The Indian helpfully dislodges the kibitzer by cutting off a piece of his ear. A bullet grazes Lopez's neck. They make a dash for a window, crash through it, and roll off a porch. Seeing Lopez has been knocked out, the Indian drags him by his heels down a garbage-strewn alley.)

LOPEZ   *(Coming to, his head bouncing on the ground)* This is mighty thoughtful, but I'd rather you drug me by the other end.

INDIAN   *(Stopping to change ends, remembers to give Lopez the telegram he left behind)* My name is Red Stick. I take you where safe.

LOPEZ   *(Absently stuffing the telegram in his pocket)* I need a drink.

INDIAN   We get.

LOPEZ   Why do they call you Red Stick?

INDIAN   Why they call you I?

LOPEZ   *Touchez.*

(Red Stick drags Lopez behind a building and knocks on the back door. A black woman peers out, sees them, and shuts the door in their faces. Red Stick knocks again. Nothing happens. He waits a moment, then knocks again.)

LOPEZ   It's cold.

RED STICK   Look miserable so she let us in.

LOPEZ I don't have to fake misery.

(The door opens a few inches and the woman looks out.)

WOMAN If you got money, go to the front do'. If you ain't got money, git lost.

RED STICK This your good customer. He hurt.

WOMAN Ain't none of *my* customer. I ain't no ho'.

RED STICK Excuse me.

LOPEZ She's the best damn cook in Texarkana!

WOMAN *(Giving him a closer look)* Who you is?

LOPEZ Aunt Sister, it's me, I. Lopez!

WOMAN Don't shine up to me. I ain't yo' aunt *nothin'*.

LOPEZ *(Groaning as if in pain)* I'm fading fast.

WOMAN All right. You can come in for a minute. But don't bleed on my floor. Take yo' hat off!

(Red Stick helps Lopez up the steps and into the kitchen. The woman tells a cook—a dubious little man —to pour the visitors some coffee. Lopez sits in a rocking chair by the stove.

LOPEZ *(To the cook)* Put some brandy in that coffee, would you?

WOMAN *(Taking charge, wiping blood off Lopez's neck)* You better find yo'self a good woman to keep you alive. Have some chilluns and keep out of trouble.

LOPEZ *(Sipping hot coffee)* I was kind of married but my mama broke it up.

WOMAN What for?

LOPEZ I grew up in Fordyce. My papa was Tex-Mex and my mama was from Mis'ippi. I had two sisters— Big Bertha and Little Agnes. What tortillas they could make! And how they could sing. I remember them dancing and swaying in time to the old songs. They was full grown at twelve. Early maturity ran in the family. We learned to do a lot of things early. Mama caught us in the barn one day and kicked me out. She didn't want no half-witted grandchildren. I respect her for that. She made a policy and stood by it.

WOMAN　Ain't no man sit in my kitchen and brag how he spoilt his sisters. You git!

(Before she pushes them out into the cold, Red Stick does some quick business with the cook. He slips a jar of corn liquor into his pocket. Outside, the two men sit on the steps in the dark. They can hear the woman complaining to the cook about brothers who ruin their sisters.)

LOPEZ　In my case it was the other way around. What's in that jar?

RED STICK　*(Passing the jar to Lopez)* Big medicine. Try some.

LOPEZ　*(Taking a big swallow)* Whewee! I hope it makes it through without burning too many holes.

RED STICK　*(Reflectively)* What happen next?

LOPEZ　We drink until we pass out.

RED STICK　After your mother kick you out I mean.

LOPEZ　*(Turning up his collar and hugging his jacket closer to his ribs)* I went to the sawmill and cut wood for four years. I got so proud of being able to feed myself and buy a new shirt every year that I started feeling competitive. Know what I mean? Won the Arkansas keg-lifting contest two years running. Weighed two-ten with a fifty-inch chest and twenty-inch biceps. Was only five foot three but being short didn't bother me after I discovered that tall women like short men. Discovered something else. Football. You keeping that jar all to yourself?

RED STICK　*(Passing the jar)* What is football?

LOPEZ　It's a game they play, up to the schoolhouse. Trick is to run with the ball and not git tackled.

RED STICK　Real people play that game on reservation. We call it War.

LOPEZ　So I ran the ball and crossed the white line. Man call hisself Coach come up and ask if I'd play on Saturday. I said, What for? He said, A dollar. So that's how I started playing football.

RED STICK　What happen next?

LOPEZ　Found out college paid more'n high school.

Played here and yonder. After a few years, began to experience some wear and tear. Coach didn't always let me run the ball, then, but I played any position Coach asked me to—center, guard, tackle, fullback. My mistake was, never stayed at a college long enough to make myself indispensable. Refs spotted me too quick and I had to move on. It was Texas one season, Missouri the next. Played in California one Thanksgiving. Colleges offered me free tuition but back then I couldn't read. They let me stoke furnaces.

RED STICK *(Drunk, attention wandering)* Sold my horse for whiskey. Wish I had ride back to reservation.

LOPEZ *(Just as drunk)* Lost mine in a crap game.

RED STICK Reach point in life when I no afford wake up outdoors with bad head.

LOPEZ I know what you mean. We are brothers in bad times, Red Stick. Bad times make us closer'n blood brothers.

RED STICK *(Whipping out a big knife)* Nothing closer than blood brother. Give me your arm.

LOPEZ We're close enough.

RED STICK *(Putting knife away)* Where we sleep tonight, Little Brother?

LOPEZ Good question.

(At the same time they notice a row of outhouses behind the building. The outhouses are built solidly. They are duplexes. Lopez looks at Red Stick.)

RED STICK *(Shaking his head)* Shithouse no good place sleep. Pissed on in dark. Red Stick no chief but no fool, either.

LOPEZ Whorehouse done closed for the night. It'll be daylight 'fore anybody needs to take one.

RED STICK Brother like you I not need. I need rich brother.

LOPEZ *(Holds onto Indian as they lurch toward the*

two-holers) Now that we're brothers, tell me. Why
do they call you Red Stick?

*   EXEUNT   *

As soon as Lopez remembered who and where he was, his
head began to ache. He tried to think of a single good prospect
but his imagination failed him. Then he remembered that the
Indian, Red Stick, had slept in an adjacent stall. He leaned over
and rapped the rough boards with his knuckles. There was no
answer. He knocked again.

"What you want?" Red Stick complained through the wall.

"Tell me some good news, Big Brother."

"Too early to tell," Red Stick said. "Head hurt."

"Mine too. Are we still brothers?"

"Go to sleep."

"Can't," Lopez said almost cheerfully. "The girls will be coming out for their crap before long."

There was a long silence. Then Red Stick said, "I too old wake
up cold and stiff with bad head. I thirty-six. How old you?"

Lopez drew a blank. He had lied to so many college coaches
about his age that he had forgotten. He began thinking out loud:
"I told Coach Babcock at Arkansas Western I was twenty-eight
when I was really thirty-two. Lost four years there. Told Coach
Rich at St. Louis Athletic Club I was twenty-six when I was thirty-
three. Add the seven years to the twenty-six and four to the
twenty-eight, and I oughta be thirty-two and a half on average.
But that was two years ago, and I may have been thirty-six in St.
Louis anyway . . ."

"What year you born?" Red Stick said. The question paralyzed
Lopez.

"Eighteen fifty-six," he said meekly.

"You forty!" Red Stick snorted with dry laughter. Lopez stared
bleakly at the wall. He drew himself together and listed his cred-
its.

"I have panned for gold. I can dance a buck-and-wing. I can tie
a Windsor. I know Eskimo wrestling holds. I have all but four of
my teeth. I play football."

"Knees bad?" said Red Stick, unrelenting.

"Yes."

"Arthritis?"

"Yes."

"Gout?"

"Yes."

"Flat feet?"

"I've got my boots on."

"Trouble shitting?"

"You mean, constipated? Hey, I don't think so!" Lopez was encouraged by this positive note. He pulled his pants down and sat on the toilet, his face screwed up in concentration. "Talk about something nice, will you?"

"Like what?"

"Something Indian. You know, learning to imitate the sound of an owl, killing your first antelope, living off the land, stuff like that."

There was a brief silence on the other side of the wall.

"Red Stick miss out on Indian stuff. Found whiskey at twelve. VD at thirteen. Fence stolen goods to soldiers at fort, not great but a living. But I have heard tell of these Indian stuffs you speak of. Ancient ones bullshit about it around campfire." A flatulent volley echoed through the stalls. "Congratulations," Red Stick added.

"Oh, shit," said Lopez, eyes darting around the corners of the stall for a scrap of paper, a corncob.

"Cobless in outhouse of life," Red Stick said intuitively. "Been there myself."

Searching his coat pocket, Lopez found a paper envelope. He smiled. This was a good omen. He bent forward and started to wipe himself, frowned in afterthought, and inspected the envelope.

"No news is good news," he muttered.

"What?" said Red Stick.

"Nothing. I found the telegram you saved for me last night."

"What does it say?"

"It's probably a creditor. It feels like the law."

"Read first, wipe later," said Red Stick.

Lopez carefully opened the envelope, unfolded the telegram, and read:

FROM: C HUMBOLDT   SEWANEE, TENN
TO: I LOPEZ   NOV 28, 1896
RECEIVED COACH BARLOWS LETTER RECOMMENDING
YOU STOP EXTEND INVITATION TO PLAY IN NORTH
SOUTH ALL STAR FOOTBALL GAME STOP STIPEND $25
PLUS EXPENSES STOP REPORT TO MAISON BLANCHE
CHATEAU PHILADELPHIA PENNA DEC 16 STOP

"What *is* this?" Lopez said.

"North-South football game," Red Stick repeated through the wall.

"But Coach Barlow died two years ago," Lopez said.

Then he remembered Humboldt's ad in the *Arkansas Democrat.* And he remembered having laboriously penned Humboldt a reply which he signed *Coach Barlow.* He could not remember Barlow's first name.

When did I do that? A month ago? A year ago?

After considerable effort Lopez recalled the ad:

STELLAR FOOTBALL PLAYERS

If you are of SUPERIOR ABILITY with outstanding varsity record SEND CREDENTIALS listing height, weight, statistics, college(s) represented, newspaper clippings if available, and letters of recommendation. If selected you will receive ALL-EXPENSE-PAID trip to Northern capital city to play in ALL-STAR FOOTBALL contest. Send vitae to C. Humboldt, Sewanee, Tenn.

The "college(s)" had caught Lopez's eye. Someone needed a *team* of ringers for a professional football game. At last it had happened. He had known all along it would, especially after baseball had gone professional. He had waited for this moment for ten years.

"Goddamn," he said.

"What?" Red Stick said.

For some time Lopez had become expert at ignoring the signs of aging: hair loss, dry skin, loose teeth, double chin. Ignoring outward evidence made it easier to disregard major deterioration. His knees were gone, his back was shot, his eyes were bad.

He had no speed beyond five yards unless being chased by a mob or a creditor.

Lopez is without equal at pulling guard, the deceased Barlow had written through the pen of ghostwriter Lopez. *In our game with Centenary he caused such mayhem and so demolished several of their varsity that Centenary defaulted the rest of their games for the season. Lopez has the strength, cunning, agility, and heart of a lion. His shortness of stature is an asset in line play, for he is able to penetrate under an opponent's stance and knock him off his feet. . . .*

Lopez's first and only effort at creative writing had succeeded beyond his expectations. He sat up straight and took a deep breath. There was money to be made in Philadelphia. He had never been east of Knoxville, but where there were sports, there were sportsmen. Who liked to gamble. Appearances, in a situation like this, could mean everything—and illusion was his primary resource. Invigorated by a sense of purpose, Lopez pulled up his pants and buckled his belt under a belly of heroic proportions. He opened the door and stepped out into the bracing November sunshine.

"What you do?" Red Stick exited his stall at the same time. Lopez was touching both hands to his chest, extending his arms shoulder-high on either side of his body, and breathing deeply.

"Calisthenics!"

"I mean, about game."

"I'm going to Philadelphia, of course," Lopez exulted. "First I'll get that Humboldt to wire me a train ticket. Then I'll have three days on the train to eat and sleep regular, cut down on my drinking, and get my color back. Hell, after three days' rest I may even *play* in this here all-star game!"

Red Stick despondently reentered the stall. Lopez followed him inside, seeking moral support.

"Can you believe this has happened!" he crowed. He glanced down as the Indian urinated. "They shoulda called you Elephant Man. Red Stick is an insult."

Red Stick irritably waved Lopez out of the stall and joined him a moment later. In awkward silence they stamped their feet against the cold and blew on their hands. A woman came out of the house clutching a bathrobe to her chin. As she hurried past them on her way to the outhouse she stared curiously. Lopez turned away.

"I make it a policy not to talk to whores in the daytime," he said as she entered one of the stalls.

"We not brothers," Red Stick said piteously. "Nothing in common no more."

"The hell you say," Lopez cried. "I never forgit a friend. Next time we see each other it's gonna be bonded whiskey and small-waisted women. Can you lend me four bits to send a telegram?"

Chapter Seven

The gravel road wound through the ridges and rolling valleys of bluegrass country. A sign painted on the buggy read, "Radcliffe's Livery—Complete Transportation—Elizabethtown." Cornelius Humboldt sat on the front seat next to the driver, a black man named Mac, who continually talked to his team.

"Come up, Maude, easy, Dolly. Dolly, she try to outstep Maude," Mac added in an aside to his passenger. "Dolly, she a two-year-old. Maude six. She'll learn, though. Dolly, I mean."

Humboldt was not interested in horses, but any kind of conversation was better than the driver's harmonica playing. Mac claimed that music made his team handle better. If so, Humboldt thought, it was because they were tone-deaf. The driver apparently knew only one song, "Camp Town Race Track." Cornelius saw Mac's hand edge toward the harmonica in his pocket.

"You say the Riddle church is just this side of Bardstown?" Humboldt kept the conversation going.

"That right," said Mac. "We be there in a few minutes." He glanced appraisingly at his passenger. "I spec won't nobody be there on a Thursday afternoon, though." Humboldt did not reply. "I hear tell some Eye-talian built hisself a wireless telephone," Mac said skeptically. "Did you?"

"They call it radio," Humboldt explained. "Marconi is the inventor's name." Mac digested this information. The buggy swayed and rattled.

After a moment Mac continued, "Well, did you hear somebody be working on a machine that fly like a bird?"

"I don't believe it will work." Humboldt said. "Radio, yes. Aeroplane, no."

Mac leaned back and stared down his shoulder at Humboldt. "Aeroplane make more sense than this footboil you been telling me about."

"Foot*ball*," Humboldt said. "Ball."

"Ain't that what I said? Do it hurt?"

"The players are used to it." Humboldt shrugged. "They wear nose guards and pads sewn to their uniforms."

"Ought not pad no boil. Make it fester."

"A foot*ball* is an inflated leather *ball* that can be kicked or passed." Humboldt wondered if he could stand to hear "Camp Town Race Track" again.

"I know 'bout passing stones. I never heard of passing no boils." In Mac's experience, the smarter the white man, the easier it was to rile him.

"Football is a game in which two teams try to advance a ball up and down a field. If one team crosses the other's goal line, they score a touchdown for four points. If they kick a field goal through the uprights they receive five points."

"Pitching horseshoes," Mac said judiciously. "Now that's a good game. And checkers. Checkers is good."

Play your harmonica, Humboldt thought. As if reading his passenger's mind, the driver slipped his hand into his pocket. The refrains of "Camp Town Race Track" soon echoed from the wooded ridges. Splashes of gold rippled like bright water through the trees.

They made a blond, handsome couple standing near the pulpit. Sister Cobb stood within a head of Chase's six foot four. He had heard her singing in the church, practicing her solo for next Sunday's service, "O Promise Me." They were alone in the sanctuary.

Sister Cobb gave Chase the same look she had given him last Sunday from the choir loft. She was three years older than Chase. He had first noticed her at a Chautauqua ice cream social. She had been so desirable that her nonstop conversation about a friend's new bonnet or how handsome somebody's little brother had gotten to be had seemed a strange language only he could understand. He had listened to her talk and heard a song of being alive. Her skin, her hair, her lips, her teeth, were perfection. Yet now, up close, as he reached for the widow woman he could see pouches under her eyes, fine wrinkles in her neck, blood vessels streaking the white of her eyes. He did not like the way she gasped for breath when he touched her, huffing and puffing through her nose when they kissed. He closed his eyes and tried to remember her as she had seemed, smooth-browed and serene and out of reach.

"Quick," said Sister Cobb.

After mutual exploration wherein he discovered, to his surprise, that she wore no undergarments, the widow began to unbutton him. He glanced around, expecting someone to tell them to stop. He had a feeling that someone was watching them. He looked over the widow's shoulders. There was no one else in the church. Chase continued to glance up at the rafters and behind the pulpit, while Sister Cobb hummed and moaned. She seemed on the verge of breaking into song. Chase remembered that one of the stained-glass windows had been broken and the pane replaced with clear glass. He twisted his head to look at the only place where a passerby might peek into the church. There was a face at the window.

So the Calvinists were right all along, he thought. *Clear glass, not the stained glass of idolatry, allowed the Truth to shine through.*

"Who is that busybody?" said the widow.

"Be still, Sister Cobb," Chase whispered. "God moves in mysterious ways." He addressed the man at the window with authority. *"Hello outside the sanctuary.* I am Reverend Riddle, Junior. We are conducting a private baptism. Please state your business." He could tell that they were in the man's line of sight only from the shoulders up. The Truth did not always shine through both ways.

"I am Professor Humboldt," said the man at the window. "From the University of the South. I have come about the game in Philadelphia."

Chase's heart leaped. "What game?" he cried.

"It was all in the telegram," the professor said.

"What telegram?"

"The telegram addressed to you at the Riddle Plantation, inviting you to participate in the North-South All-Star Football Game." Humboldt broke off and stared dubiously at Chase. "Sir, would you be the same Riddle who played quarterback for Centre College year before last?"

"I would be and am!" Chase exclaimed. Feeling the need to verify his identity, he cast about and saw the marble baptismal font half-filled with water. He scooped up a handful and doused Sister Cobb. "I baptize thee in the name of the Father, the Son, and the Holy Ghost!"

"Let go of me!" she said.

"Professor, please allow us to complete our ceremony." Chase willed calm into his voice. "If you will step around to the front door, I will be with you directly."

"God forgive me," Widow Cobb gasped into his lapel.

"God forgives those who forgive themselves," Chase automatically responded. "The Lord needs a Christian quarterback!" he added.

The widow gave him a disturbed look. Straightening their clothing they went their separate ways: she to the rear exit behind the choir loft, he to the front vestibule and the double doors. It was obvious to Chase that someone had intercepted the professor's telegram. However, he was willing to give his family the benefit of the doubt. The telegram probably had arrived during the harvest. He swept open the double doors and looked down on a dapper man wearing a bowler hat and three-piece suit. Nearby, a black man in a buggy watched skeptically while cutting a chew of tobacco.

"Chase Riddle!" the little man cried. "Six feet, four inches, two hundred pounds; speed—eleven seconds in the hundred-yard run; upper body strength—lifts two hundred pounds above head, age twenty-five; 1891—halfback, Union Baptist College; 1892—quarterback, Knoxville Athletic Congress, wing, Transylvania College; 1893—halfback, Birmingham-Southern; 1894—quarterback, Centre College. Career total points—469; sixty-six touchdowns, forty-one field goals."

Humboldt could have added: Left Transylvania after rumor of girl in trouble; attended Birmingham Southern only three weeks; at Centre, caught stealing examination questions from professor's desk, also rumor of affair with president's wife; currently assistant minister in grandfather's church, received ordination by mail order from Chicago.

"You have the advantage of me," Chase said, squeezing the professor's hand.

"Since you did not receive my telegram, let me explain." Humboldt flexed his fingers to get the circulation going. "There is to be a championship game in Philadelphia between teams from the North and the South. Amos Alonzo Stagg, of Chicago, and Phil King, of Princeton, will coach the North squad. Glenn Warner, of Georgia, and John Heisman, of Alabama Polytechnic, will coach the South. But do not be deceived. There is more to this than meets the eye. More than football is at stake here. Providence has placed within our grasp a golden opportunity to redeem the pride of a people fallen victim not so much to the prowess of their antagonists as to their own civilized and bucolic way of life, being more prepared to partake gracefully of the natural wonders of this world than to toil in squalid factories producing war materiel in vast number at the expense of the human soul, creating in its place an industrialized mongrel race devoid of honor, creed, or conscience. Now we meet man to man. This time, there will be a physical confrontation of skill, strength, and courage. This time, there will be eleven versus eleven. And this time—"

"I accept," Chase said.

"What?"

"I'll play," Chase said.

"Excellent!" Humboldt clasped his hands together. "Heisman and Warner will be delighted at such a"—he started to say, *pleasant surprise*—"splendid addition to the team."

"I see this as a Christian adventure," Chase added. "I want to dedicate this game to Jesus—"

"Excellent," Humboldt said dubiously.

"I'll just get my horse," Chase said.

Humboldt stood beside the buggy and waited. Mac worked his cud and patiently arranged it in his mouth. He leaned over the

edge of the seat and spat. Riddle came around the building leading a horse. Sister Cobb was nowhere in sight. He tied his reins to
the rear of the buggy and climbed into the rear seat. Humboldt
sat beside him. Mac made a clicking sound—no easy feat with a
mouthful of tobacco—and drove north into Bardstown.

"Wasn't Abraham Lincoln born around here?" Humboldt
broke the not uncomfortable silence.

"Down the road a piece," Riddle said.

"Nigh to Hodgenville," Mac added.

"Who's the opposition?" Chase asked.

"What?" said the professor.

"In the game."

"Oh. Well, All-Americas from the Big Four, I presume."

"Big four what?"

Humboldt stared at him. "Harvard, Yale, Princeton, and
Penn."

"Oh yeah." Chase stared reflectively at the road ahead.
"They've played football a long time up there."

"You have grasped the situation!" Humboldt exclaimed. "History would appear to repeat itself. The North seems to possess
overwhelming superiority. Their players are bigger and better
trained. Their coaches are cunning and greatly renowned for
their innovative formations. For example, the revolving tandem
devised by Phil King at Princeton is all the rage this season. By
contrast, the tackle-back formation, which is new to the South, is
considered all but obsolete in the Big Four."

"The Lord is on our side," Chase said.

"Yes, indeed," Humboldt said diplomatically. "But I was thinking also of pride. Let the Yankees scoff at us! Let them underestimate our spirit! Along with players such as yourself, reverend sir,
we will field a team with as much natural ability as that of the
Federals. We will return to Pennsylvania, this time, with scouts
aplenty—unlike Lee at Gettysburg with Stuart gone joy-riding—
and this time we will be ready for them. This time, there will be
rejoicing from Virginia to Texas!"

Mac had heard enough. Ordinarily he was able to tune out such
blather with a good chew and the sound of the horses. This talk of
footboils and tandems, Yankees and Lee, sounded awful. He felt

in his pocket for the reassuring weight of his harmonica. What they all needed was a nice song.

Chase listened to the driver softly begin to play "Camp Town Race Track." He felt better than he had in months. A broad grin threatened to take permanent possession of his face.

Humboldt noted the quarterback's pleased expression. It could mean only one thing, he thought: the time to negotiate had arrived. A religious ringer was still a ringer. He had prepared himself for this part of the recruiting process. He cleared his throat.

"Of course, there will be some compensation," he said.

"Beg pardon?"

"Financial compensation."

"Oh, yes."

He *would* play his cards close to his chest, Humboldt thought. "As a man of the cloth, a spiritual shepherd, you doubtless are above such mundane considerations," he said. "But you do not have to remind me that the clergy must eat, like the rest of us. What say you to fifty dollars and expenses, train fare, all meals, a week's comfortable lodging, guided tours of Philadelphia, and related banquets and entertainment?"

Mac shook the tobacco juice out of his harmonica. Fifty dollars and keep for kicking a ball around a field?

Chase was not surprised at the mention of money. Alumni had always pressed him to accept their gifts of money, clothes, watches, jewelry, even horses. He had sometimes wondered why otherwise intelligent, successful businessmen overlooked the obvious fact that he played football for the fun of it and had nothing better to do with his time.

"Fifty dollars," Chase mused.

"A fine sum for playing a game of football," Humboldt argued. "A month's wages for most of us."

Three months, thought Mac.

"I realize that besides the game you have the practice and the training," Humboldt continued, feeling his way carefully, "all of which carries risk of injury." He waited for Riddle to confirm these thoughts, but the quarterback remained silent. "Our budget for stipends, actually, is twenty-five per player. I offered you fifty because I recognize your superior skills."

"I appreciate that," said Chase.

"We do not have unlimited funds, you know," Humboldt complained. "The Philadelphia Athletic Club in association with Mr. Arno Ziprenian has been most generous in allowing us to make you an offer on their behalf, but well within reason. All right, then. Sixty dollars. What say you?"

"Hmmmmmm."

Humboldt was utterly confounded. He began to lose patience.

"Do you earn sixty a week farming, sir? For that matter, sixty a month? I must say, that amount is a quarter of my annual salary. Have our values become so distorted that a football player should earn more money playing in a single game than a university lecturer makes in two months!"

"It's distorted, all right," Chase agreed.

"Not a penny higher than sixty, sir!" Humboldt's color rose. "My budget for the entire Southern eleven is four hundred dollars for stipends and expenses. Some players are going to come out short as it is. I suppose you are thinking that tackles and guards do not score any points. Well, sir, a quarterback should respect his blockers. You should consider that your linemen may resent getting down in the dirt to block for a runner earning three times what they receive."

"I don't blame 'em one bit," said Chase.

Humboldt felt himself faltering. Haggling was unseemly for a Sewanee man. Then he remembered the Sewanee-Centre game two years before, when Chase Riddle ran a punt back for 99 yards, gliding through the Sewanee defense like a golden ghost.

"Seventy-five and that's my final offer," he declared. "I am cognizant that you work part-time on your father's farm, and your absence would leave him shorthanded. Doubtless you feel a filial duty to reimburse him for paying another worker in your place. Surely this sum will suffice for this additional expense! I must say you drive a hard bargain. I have done all that I can to meet you halfway. So, are we agreed?"

"Whatever you say, Professor," Chase said.

Mac's team lost cadence. He noted the change without conscious thought. Reining in the spirited Dolly, he whistled a warning for her to settle down to Maude's deliberate pace. He could see the red rooftops of Bardstown and smell the faint, overripe scent of sour mash cooking in the J. W. Dant distillery.

The Lord gave us horses and whiskey, he thought. This football business was yet another example of people with more money than sense and lacking the capacity to enjoy the natural satisfactions of this world.

Chapter Eight

Kate saw the men in the buggy. Even with the afternoon sun behind them, their faces silhouettes against the haze, she recognized Chase Riddle. In the slanting light his hair was like fire. Behind him dust rose from the wheels like spun gold.

"Tackle-back formation!" she yelled. Her players, rolling and kicking on the bare ground behind Post Oak School, did not hear her. She blew her whistle to stop them from fighting. "I said, tackles back! Brother, give the ball to Tree."

Then they saw the buggy coming. They got up and slapped the dust out of their overalls. For once, Brother did not change Kate's play but ran the one she had called.

When Chase heard the whistle, at first he thought he had imagined it. He instinctively thought, as a quarterback will, of taking the snap from center, hiding the ball on his hip, and rolling around the end. He looked to see who had whistled. His eyes sought the familiar sight of football players scrimmaging in a bare field behind a schoolhouse. He stood up in the buggy, causing Mac to rein in.

"That's Crazy Kate!" Riddle cried. "My God, she's got herself a nigger football team. Look, Professor, isn't that the tackle-back! See 'em shift?"

"Indeed!" Humboldt was intrigued. It had never occurred to him that blacks might be interested in football.

Mac spat and held his team steady. He could afford to let one offhand "nigger" pass but he was ready to cut the next one off at the tap.

From the road the men watched the team line up. The quarterback called signals in a high, clear voice. At his command they shifted, and two huge linemen drifted massively into the backfield and paused an instant before the center heeled the ball—an anachronism, Humboldt and Chase thought simultaneously—to the left tackle. He scooped up the ball carelessly with one hand and plunged ahead, smashing through the defense and dragging tacklers twenty yards before he collapsed under the weight of sheer numbers. Chase jumped out of the hack and cut across a fallow cornfield bordering the playground. Humboldt followed on his heels. They took long, gangling steps over old corn rows as if slightly drunk on the idea of Negro football.

Kate pretended not to see the tall blond man stepping over the rows with a farmer's sure gait and the diminutive, scholarly man in bowler hat and vested suit who hopped from one row to the next. She recognized Chase Riddle: an ex-ringer who took up collection at his grandfather's fundamentalist church. Her players turned and gawked at the newcomers.

"Run the tackle-back again," she hissed. "No, wait, do the end-around. Lincoln, you take the hand-off."

The players lined up again and Brother called signals. The big end dropped off the line and circled across the backfield to take a quick pass from Brother. The defense stampeded after him. The scrubs frantically wrestled Lincoln to the ground. Kate blew her whistle. The players peered out from among the twisted arms and legs, and watched the All-Southern quarterback offer Miz Kate his hand.

"Ain't no big thing," Weasel whispered scornfully on the bottom of the pile.

"What do you know about it?" Brother retorted. "Shut up. Maybe you'll learn something."

"Maybe the great Chase Riddle learn sump'm from *me!*" Weasel replied. The pile shook with laughter.

"Pardon the intrusion," Chase said.

"Pardon the intrusion," Weasel hissed and the pile heaved.

"May I present Professor Humboldt from the University of the South." As Cornelius greeted Kate, Riddle looked her over. She was square and sinewy. Her wiry gray hair seemed to stand on end. Chase was enchanted with her jersey, moleskin pants, and cleated shoes. He admired her level, confident gaze. He found her to be exactly what he expected and felt comfortable about her without wondering why.

"That was a real nice end-around," Chase told her.

"Thank you, Mr. Riddle." She spoke sternly, hiding her pleasure.

"One thing, though . . ." He hesitated, searching her gray eyes for permission to advise. She nodded abruptly. "The usual thing is for the right guard to pull and lead the end through the three-hole."

Three-hole, Kate thought happily.

"Right," she said, and awkwardly took Stagg's *Treatise on American Football* from her pocket. "I should pay more attention to the diagrams."

"You've read Stagg's book?" Humboldt said. He stared at the worn green book with clay dust on the cover. The germ of an idea was born in his subconscious.

"I reckon Coach Stagg couldn't put everything he knows in his book. How 'bout if I showed 'em?" Chase asked politely.

"By all means, Mr. Riddle. Please proceed." Kate called to her team: "All right, let's pay attention!"

Chase held out his hands for the ball. Brother reluctantly tossed it to him. Frayed and patched, it was the roughest football Chase had ever held. He saw that the players were alert to his every gesture. He spun the ball lightly in his hands. As a child he had organized kick-the-can games with the sons of black field hands on Big Dad's plantation. The Post Oak players approached him in a way that he recognized: shyly, with diffidence and curiosity—with one exception. Brother stared back at him, intelligent and defiant. Chase nodded in acknowledgment, one captain to another.

"If you'll bear with me," he told them, "I'd like to talk about positioning."

He began to coach them the way he had been taught. He showed the linemen how to stand in a slight crouch, hands braced on their thighs, partially facing toward the center; the wings, or ends, with arms extended, ready to fend off opponents.

He demonstrated how the center should snap the ball to the quarterback between his legs, using his hands rather than heeling it back in the old-fashioned way. The players followed his instructions with an urgent dignity, like novices attending to a priest. Next, Chase had them walk through an offensive play, clapping his hands to show them the rhythm. This device so intrigued Kate that she began to mince back and forth, looking over Riddle's shoulder. It would never have occurred to her to beat out the rhythm and walk through the play like a choreographer. She had never seen her team so absorbed, so determined to learn.

The players followed Chase's handclaps and shouts of "One, two, three, four . . ." as if dancing to a slow beat, moving in a perfect economy of motion.

"Men," he said, and the Post Oakians stood a little taller. "Assume starting positions. You know your lanes. Let's run it at half speed and then try it full speed."

Lanes, Kate repeated to herself in delight.

Brother called signals: "Ready, set, shift, hut-one, two, three, four . . ." Each player's lips moved silently in time with the count. Brother pivoted and stepped back, avoiding the pulling guard. His pirouette ended with the solid *chunk* of the ball thrust into Lincoln's midsection as the big man surged past him. The scrubs made a token effort to stop the play. Lincoln burst through them like an ox through a swarm of gnats. Riddle stuck thumb and index finger in the sides of his mouth and whistled. Brother laughed. Kate was beside herself.

"I must say," Humboldt exclaimed, "Riddle is a wizard!"

"What about my players?" Kate retorted.

"Yes, of course," he said quickly. "It's just that I am delighted to see Mr. Riddle perform his magic with the old pigskin."

"I thought his playing days were over," she said curiously.

"Not quite!" Humboldt exclaimed. "There is to be a football contest in Philadelphia between the best players from North and South. Mr. Riddle has consented to play quarterback for the South."

Kate suddenly felt airy, as if she had sprouted wings. "You are recruiting players for the Southern squad?"

"In Tennessee and Kentucky only," the professor said modestly, "although I *have* dipped into Texas via the U.S. Postal Service."

"What requirements must be met by the players you recruit?" She spoke casually without looking at Humboldt.

"They must be varsity scholar-athletes on the collegiate level," he quoted. "Whether they are current or former collegians is of no consequence. Our opponents doubtless will field a number of All-Americas . . ."

"Are you satisfied," she said, "that you have found the best players the South has to offer?"

Humboldt caught her meaning and was swept away on a wave of irony. "Of course these are high school players," he said, struggling toward solid ground. Kate was staring dubiously at him.

Chase had taken off his coat and tie and joined the scrubs. He was remembering what football had been like at Union Baptist when he had played simply because it felt good.

Seeing their new coach on their side, the scrubs swelled as if each had gained twenty pounds. Brother drew the varsity into a huddle and watched Chase position the defense. He shot a questioning glance at Kate.

"Make something up!" she called cheerfully.

"He's expecting tackle-back or some buck or other," Brother whispered to his teammates. He drew a diagram in the red dust. "I'm going to fake the hand-off to Lincoln. Cassius, you double back and take a reverse pass. I'm going to be right behind you. If you get in trouble, pass off. Got it? On two."

"Heads up!" Chase told the scrubs.

Brother met Riddle's challenging stare. He set his team. The scrubs dug in. The ball was snapped. As he feinted to Lincoln, Brother fixed on Riddle's golden hair as a beacon. Lincoln disappeared under a mass of angry scrubs.

Chase read the play and tried to hurtle the line. The center and guard, B.C. and Isaiah, turned him back. Hitting them was like running into concrete. Riddle staggered left to head off the reverse. He accidentally trampled two scrubs who were standing flatfooted. Chase threw himself at Cassius. He did not see the halfback flip a pass to Brother and buried by an avalanche of scrubs, he waited under the pile for Kate's whistle. He was amazed to hear the varsity cheering and looked out from under the squirming bodies to see Brother running down the sidelines with the ball tucked under his arm. He crossed the goal line, stopped, and elaborately touched the ball to the ground.

Several of the scrubs wept, but Chase praised them and made them smile. He shook hands with all the players.

"What do you call your team?" he asked Brother.

"The Post Oak Panthers," they told him self-consciously.

"Well, you are a mean bunch of cats," Chase said. The team broke out in brilliant grins and began punching each other joyfully.

"Reverend Riddle!" Humboldt called. "Shouldn't we be on our way?" He was privately worried about Chase spraining a muscle.

"Keep up the good work," Chase told the Panthers. "Maybe Miz Kate will let me help out sometime."

"Don't leave just yet!" Kate pleaded. "I want you to see this." She shrieked at her players, *"Line up for the hundred-yard dash!"* They obediently trotted to the opposite end of the playground.

Instinctively—Humboldt searched his pockets for his stopwatch.

Kate bellowed, *"Backs first! Ready? On your mark? GO!"*

The first wave of runners accelerated from a standing start, bare feet toeing inward as they pounded the clay. Small dust balls exploded behind them, marking their rapid progress. Cassius finished slightly ahead of the rest. Humboldt punched the stopwatch button. He brought the watch closer to his face.

"Nine-five?" he whispered.

"There's a bit of wind in their face," Kate said. "I think they can run it faster than that."

"My God," Humboldt said.

"I'm glad I don't have to catch them," Chase joked.

"No white man can." Kate smiled brightly.

Humboldt felt the wave of irony begin to build again.

"We have to go," he said. "Good-bye and thank you," he told Kate and turned away.

"I congratulate you, ma'am," Chase said. "You are making a great contribution here."

"It's all uphill. They don't call me Crazy Kate for nothing," she said testily. Chase was startled. He glanced down as if expecting to see his fly open.

"Whoever says *that* is the crazy one," he said diplomatically. "Good luck, Miz Kate."

Chase and the professor went to the buggy, where Mac was waiting patiently. "So that's football," he told them. "I'd just as soon chase fryers around the barn. Where to now?"

"Just up the road," Chase said.

As the hack started to move, Humboldt and Riddle watched the players running their sprints. They looked at each other and sighed.

Kate assembled her team. The Panthers towered over her, their breath frosty against the deepening shadows.

"Where them men going?" Lincoln asked.

"To the other side of the moon," she said. Without thinking she added, "And we're going with them."

The scrubs tittered nervously.

"Just the varsity," Kate amended.

The scrubs fell tragically silent. Brother digested this astounding news.

"Excuse me, Miz Kate," he said elaborately, "you mean, Post Oak is going up against Harvard and Yale?"

"Never mind that!" she snapped. "I'm talking about a trip to Philadelphia!"

"You really think they will take us?" Brother's face softened.

"Nothing is impossible." She had almost convinced herself. It could happen. "Did you hear what Chase Riddle said? He was glad he didn't have to catch you? Well, we're going to make him try."

"We don't know about dropkicks or trap blocks, the things he showed us today," Brother argued.

"There is time enough to teach you all you need to know. I'm asking you to trust me." Her intense stare fixed them with a happy dread.

"What are you going to do?" Brother spoke for them all.

"I don't know." She looked away at the surrounding woods and fields. "Whatever I have to. They're leaving tomorrow. I want you to go home and get your things ready—seniors only. Take your best clothes and don't forget your shoes. It will be cold in

Philadelphia, so find yourselves some warm coats and hats. Also some old clothes to practice in. Be ready before dawn. I'll come for you."

At this mention of preparations, the players suddenly began to hop from one foot to the other in a nervous shuffle. As Kate walked toward the schoolhouse, they bobbed and weaved behind her. She took the football and went to the back door. When she looked back, they were racing down the dirt road toward Bardstown, running faster than they had ever run before. They topped a rise. One of them paused, outlined against an amber sky. She recognized Brother's small, well-shaped head. Then he too disappeared over the hill and was gone.

She went into the building. The school consisted of two wings behind the church, separated by a long hallway. She entered a large room that housed grades one through eight and doubled as the choir's dressing room. It contained the violent stillness common to empty classrooms. Kate smelled chalk and paper and children. Arranged in crooked rows were desks of radically different sizes, like the children themselves, which Kate had helped glean from furniture auctions or neighboring white schools. The desks were scarred with penknife daydreams of generations of students, black and white. Stacked neatly under each desk were each child's books. A wood stove in the corner ticked as it cooled.

Kate measured fourteen years of her life within these walls: fourteen years of recitations and spelling bees and rhetorical contests and class plays. She strained to hear the hubbub of young voices as if they held the meaning of existence.

She went into the hallway separating the two classrooms. Standing in the dark hall, she began to hear voices swelling to a great roar, the cheering of thousands of spectators in a towering stadium. She saw herself leading her team onto the playing field. They were dressed in new jerseys and cleated shoes like the ones in the Montgomery Ward catalog.

"It's not for me!" she whispered fiercely down the hall. "It's for *them.*"

Taking a key from her pocket, she went down the hall to the principal's office, unlocked the door, and went inside. She opened a filing cabinet and flipped through the files until she came to an index headed: "Post Oak Seminary." The Reverend

Rutledge's lifelong dream was to establish a seminary. He had arranged to have application forms printed but had failed to raise the money to fund the seminary. Kate found a sheaf of blank application forms with the heading: "Post Oak Seminary, A Christian College Institution Sanctioned by the Methodist Zion Church."

She took pen and inkwell from a desk drawer, sat in the principal's chair, and practiced writing the florid signature of the Reverend E. Alphonso Rutledge.

The rest of the team had run ahead, but when they realized that Brother had stopped, they waited for him to catch up with them.

He stood in the road and looked back at Post Oak School. The T-shaped building seemed quite small in the descending night.

Brother was imagining himself sitting in his broom closet next to the coal-burning furnace that he stoked six times a day, for which—in addition to tutoring slow learners—he was paid two dollars a week. In his closet, which Kate had dubbed his office, he ate his lunch and read Aristotle or Tolstoy or Shakespeare. He filled his hours with work and did not dream lest the gods brush him aside like a fly. His only source of relief was the fierce combat of the playing field. Even so, Brother clung to the school. It was his only hope.

He saw the team wandering back up the hill toward him, their silhouettes moving awkwardly and hesitantly. It was just like them, he thought, to come to him rather than wait and make him come to them. Sometimes he wondered if the slavers had captured only the weak Africans, leaving the strong behind, free and unconquered. He had an immoderate respect for all wild creatures, pausing often as he walked to school to gaze at a deer or a hawk. He wondered who his African ancestors were. He imagined that they had been trapped because of bravery and daring, not fear or stupidity, and, like all wild and free things, had never ceased to struggle against their bonds.

"Where Miz Kate say we goin'?" Tree called softly, as if addressing a spirit of the night. The team fell into step with him, padding along reverently. He felt hemmed in. Impatience radiated from him, and they sensed its power.

"Philadelphia!" Cassius answered Tree's question.

"Philadelphia," voices echoed solemnly.

They waited for Brother to speak. He stalked along silently, changing cadence to throw them off stride. The scrubs shuffled to get back in rhythm. Tree slapped the nearest scrub as if to appease Jones.

"Philadelphia where the Bill of Rights was made," Lincoln said.

"First capital of the U.S.," Tree offered.

"Washington the capital!" cried an anonymous scrub.

"Not now, *then.*" Tree gave the scrub an instructive slap.

They waited for Brother to tell them if this momentous thing was possible. He walked in princely silence.

"Miz Kate say the best players from the North will play the best of the South,"· B.C. addressed the darkness. "Question is, how good is we?"

"Damn good," Lincoln growled.

Hearing the varsity speak openly about matters of such importance agitated the scrubs beyond endurance. They fell to scuffling and wrestling like eddies in a strong current.

"We beat Lebanon," Isaiah said, taking up the theme, "and they beat E-Town, and they beat Radcliff, and they beat *Owensboro.*"

"Owensboro is not Yale," Brother said.

They hushed and waited. He resented their expectancy, their hope.

"Who Yale?" Lincoln asked.

"See!" Brother burst out. "You can't *imagine* what you're up against." Philadelphia loomed in his imagination like a dark fortress bristling with battlements.

The clean lines of a gable rooftop were visible through the trees. They had reached the edge of town. In silence they passed the historic dwellings of Bardstown. The flat brick façades of Federal design, the ornate balance of Georgian architecture were uncompromising and exact.

"Miz Kate say we play as good as anybody," Tree began again. "She say . . ."

They had reached the lane which led to the Negro section of town. Suddenly Brother broke into a run. The others lit out after him. Bare feet slapped earth and merged with the sound of his own feet as he raced ahead of them, running from their fear, which was contagious, running from the waiting, running from the name his parents had given him:

Robert E. Lee Jones.

Chapter Nine

The dog crossed the field ahead of the man. Every few seconds it would stop among the rows of stubble and wait for him, twisting its long neck into a U shape and looking at him over its shoulder. It was a medium-sized black mutt, more terrier than anything else. It had a flat head with floppy pointed ears, a long snout, frizzy hair, and a tail which curled like a scorpion's over its back. Somewhere in its ancestry lurked a greyhound, because its muscular back legs were longer than its front legs, a condition that made it lean to the front with a speedy look. Sometimes when it ran to greet the man its back legs outran the front ones so that it skidded sideways and skittered out of control. The dog was content always to be near him.

The man crossed the field slowly, encumbered by crutches and a heavy pistol stuck in his waistband. He propelled himself forward with determination. His right leg had been amputated above the knee. The trouser leg was pinned neatly behind the stump. His clothes fit loosely, as though he had shrunk inside them. He was an old man, hatless, with thin white hair and a narrow face distinguished by clear blue eyes and a beak of a nose. His chin was peppered by a two-day beard. The way he cocked his arms over his crutches gave him a stubborn, waspish appearance.

When the dog saw the direction the man was taking, it entered the woods ahead of him, following an old deer trail. Eventually the man reached the trees and ascended the trail. Halfway up the long slope he stopped beside a tall hickory, threw down his crutches, and lowered himself with difficulty to the ground. The dog trotted back down the trail and sat near him, waiting to see what its master would do next and keeping an eye out for squirrels.

"The Indians could do it," the old man complained to the dog when he got his breath back. "Did it every day. Nothing to it. Just walked into the woods and found a place to die. They could put their minds to it and wish theirselves to death. You'd think if a squaw could do it, I could too." The pistol was uncomfortable in his waistband. He took it out and laid it on the ground beside him. It was a Navy Colt .44, dull and rust-streaked. The dog saw the gun and wagged its tail.

"No, Murphy, we're not hunting squirrels today," he said.

In silent rebuttal the dog stared intently at the treetops. The sun glinted through thin branches. A thrush called and from the cornfield a whippoorwill replied. Dust motes filtered through the trees.

"On the other hand," he continued, "the Indians usually did it in the wintertime when they could count on some help from the weather. It wouldn't hardly take much mental effort to die in zero-degree temperature. Just sit by the road and wait. Here we are with the warmest November in ten years. Goddamned elements are agin us. But we got an ace in the hole, Murphy!" He patted the pistol. The dog wagged its tail hopefully.

"It'll come a sharp frost tonight, though." He sniffed the air and the dog did the same. "Oughta be good'n stiff in the morning. Some kid hunting squirrels'll find us. Scare the bejesus outa him, us staring into the void. Resting in peace, thankee kindly." An ironical laugh bubbling up in his chest turned into a cough. "Hope no bobcat or wild dog goes to chewing on us. Well, it don't matter. Don't you worry, Murphy, I'm taking you with me. You're a one-man dog, and you'd lay down and die soon as they put me in the ground. So I'm goin' take you with me."

The man felt guilty because he was depending on the loss of his dog to give him the nerve to shoot himself. He held the pistol in his lap. He had hoped to do it quickly, but now he saw that he would have to take it by degrees. He leaned back against the tree and closed his eyes, getting used to the heft and feel of the gun.

Closing his eyes made the faces come back, the ones that came to him every night when he lay down to sleep. The pale faces called wordlessly to him across the divide, inviting him to come over. His wife, Marguerite, was there, and his brother, Edwin, and his cousin, Riley. He wondered if they would still have anything in common. Would Riley, for example, still be nineteen? Green River came back, then, in a rush. He had hoped to avoid it, but now he decided that thinking about it might help him do what he had to do. He lay back amid leaves and sunshine and birdcall and let it come.

He was twenty-one and a company sergeant with the 5th Kentucky under Colonel D. Howard Smith, part of General John Hunt Morgan's First Brigade. On the night of July 3, 1863, the Fifth rode through the night toward Columbia, Kentucky. At dawn, Colonel Dick Morgan's regiment, the 14th Kentucky, surprised the 2nd and 7th Ohio Cavalry and the 45th Ohio Mounted Infantry. After a hot running skirmish, the Federals beat a retreat to Jamestown.

"We held Columbia," the old man said to Murphy with his eyes closed, "and we thought war was fun." The dog lay down beside him and rested its head on its forepaws.

"We was making bivouac in Columbia," he continued, "when orders come down from Colonel Basil Duke, commander of the First Brigade, to ride picket north of town. We griped like hell to have to ride out whilst our comrades made theirselves comfortable. Men was camping in the yards, in barns, school, cemetery.

"The road was deserted and it was pitch-dark. We was armed with ever'thing from muskets, shotguns, and squirrel rifles to Springfield carbines captured from the bluebellies. Our mounts was making the usual, unavoidable noise, snorting, hardware jinglin'. I held the patrol up so we could listen. We heard axes in the woods ahead. Trees crashing. Couldn't see nothing, of course.

"We spurred forward at a walk. Our orders was to scout ahead to the Green River where the brigade was to cross next day. My scouts included my cousin, Riley Dunn. He was nineteen. I promised his mama I'd look after him. He wasn't scared of nothing.

"Sound of them dad-blamed Yankee axes was everywhere, getting louder every step we took. I give the order to dismount. Directly we spied a light off in the woods. We eased up to the edge of a small clearing. We seen a cookfire, a Yank lolling on a log with his tunic unbuttoned, and a *lady* in skirt and bonnet tending a skillet, frying bacon and boiling coffee. Smelled good. We hadn't et but hardtack for two days. A bluecoat and a lady.

"I positioned my men in the trees. Riley come over and said, 'Am I in on this?' I shoulda told him to stay put, but I let him come along. I went a-running to the fire waving my forty-four. Said, 'Yank, you are my prisoner, excuse me, ma'am.' The axes was still going in the woods beyond. I began to suspect something. The Yank raised his hands, but the lady stirred her bacon like she hated to waste good meat, irregardless who et it. Face hid under her bonnet. Showing off to Riley, I whip off my hat and give a smart bow, said 'Yo service, ma'am.'

"She pulled a sawed-off shotgun from under her dress and throwed down on us. Said, 'Long time no see, Hudson.' I recognized that crooked, gold-toothed grin. I had played cards on the riverboats from Cincinnati to Vicksburg across the table from that grin. It was Ernie Lieberwitz of Kalamazoo. He said, 'I believe you are *my* prisoner.' I cocked my forty-four and laid the business end to his head and said, 'It's you and me now, just like the old days.' I forgot about Riley, you see.

"Lieberwitz said, 'All right. Let the cards decide for us. Three-card monte.'"

"Riley speaks up, 'Nobody this side of Cincinnati kin touch Hudson Stroud at three-card.' I shoulda called my scouts in and settled it right then, but Riley had called the play and I said, 'Deal 'em.'

"Lieberwitz reached a deck of cards out of his bosom, smoothed his shawl on a flat log, dealt the queen of hearts and two aces, and started to shuffle them. He laid down the three cards, as smooth a lay-down as you'll ever see, but I was on top of it. I was sure the queen was outside right. Lieberwitz was grinning like a mother lode. I put the end of my gun barrel on the outside right. He flipped the card. It was the queen.

"I said, 'I win.'

"He said, 'You lose.'

" 'Bout that time thirty bluebellies come out of the trees. I yelled, 'Run, Riley.' And took off. Shots was fired. I looked back and Riley was down. Yankees got the drop on my scouts and we surrendered.

"I ran and Riley died," he told the dog and cocked the Navy .44. "Lieberwitz asked for my sword, polite-like.

"My wife, Marguerite, consecrated that sword with a kiss the day I went off to serve. It bore an inscription: 'Hudson Stroud, C.S.A., Go With Honor.' So there was Riley laying dead and Lieberwitz eating bacon off the point of my sword.

"I never knew where they buried Riley. They took us to their camp at Tebb's Bend on the Green River. Next day, Morgan attacked. I took a Minié ball through a gap in the stockade fence. Splintered the bone in my right leg. It got infected. I was delirious with fever. Shipped us to the prison at Sandusky, Ohio."

His story completed, he raised the pistol to shoot the dog. It looked at him alertly. A scrabbling noise came from above. The dog jumped up and began to bark.

It's found a squirrel, the old man thought in relief. He looked up and saw a squirrel flying through the branches like a soul in flight. He aimed at the middle of Murphy's side so he would not miss. At this range the dog would feel no pain but simply sail off into darkness. Hudson planned to follow close behind. He thought of his soul flying into space and felt suddenly light-spirited and free.

As he pulled the trigger, Murphy darted around the tree. The .44 kicked in Hudson's hand and numbed his wrist to the elbow. The report deafened him. The smell of cordite stung his nostrils. When he did not see the dog he supposed he had blown it to kingdom come, but through the roaring in his ears he heard it barking. He wondered if it was barking to him from across the Jordan. Then the dog spoke to him with a human voice.

"Where are you?" it said.

"Here I am," he cried hoarsely. "Wait just a minute." He brought the barrel to his head.

"Where are you, Sarge?" the voice said.

He hesitated. The voice belonged to his grandson. He lowered the pistol and immediately Chase was standing over him, smiling.

"What're you doing with that old forty-four?" Chase said

cheerfully. He extended his hand to help the old man stand up. "Ain't no Yankees left to shoot at . . ."

"Leave me be!" Hudson muttered, swatting at him with his free hand. "Murphy and me're doing just fine."

The dog continued to bark. Chase looked up and saw the squirrel. "Good Lord, you ain't *squirrel* hunting with that cannon!" He laughed. "If you *were* to accident'ly hit one, wouldn't nothing be left but tail. Listen, Sarge. I got some good news. I been called."

"Where to?" Hudson said irritably.

"My ministry, of course!" A lopsided grin threatened to unhinge Chase's jaw. "I'm playin' quarter for the South All-Stars. Ain't that sump'm!" He paused, sobering. "Do you know if a telegram came for me? The professor said he sent it but I never got it."

"Who's the perfesser?"

"He's waiting in the buggy. Let's go to the Big House and tell everybody the news. Don't forget your gun."

The Riddle house stood on a gentle rise facing west. Well-tended fields stretched away from it for a quarter of a mile. Fields dotted with corn stubble alternated with checkerboard plots of thick winter wheat ready for harvest. Surrounding the house and outbuildings was fenced pasture where grazing Herefords stood like black-and-white statues. The house itself was a plain, two-story white frame building with a wide roofed porch. A man sat in a rocking chair on the porch. He stood as the buggy entered the driveway.

"That's my dad, Henry," Chase told Humboldt.

The buggy rattled up the gravel drive. Mac stopped his team in front of the house and got down to unload the luggage. He was thinking how glad he would be to get shut of these white folks. The old man had not fooled him. He had not been hiding in the woods with his big pistol to shoot *squirrels.* First football, now suicide, Mac thought. Nothing about this group surprised him. If anyone had asked his opinion, he would have recommended that they rely on horses and whiskey to see them through. He climbed into his hack and called on Dolly and Maude to take him back to E-Town.

When Chase helped him out of the buggy, Hudson noticed that Humboldt turned his eyes away, as did most people, from his stump. He got his crutches under his arms and followed the others up to the porch. Henry Riddle stepped down to meet them. He was a tall, big-boned man in his late forties, dressed in khaki work clothes and mud-stained boots. With sandy brown hair and a deeply tanned face, he seemed part of the land he worked.

"Dad," Chase said, "this is Professor Humboldt, of Sewanee, Tennessee. He has invited me to play football up to Philadelphia, Pennsylvania. I been Called!"

"You have?" Henry Riddle said, shaking Humboldt's hand gingerly. He was looking at the Navy Colt .44 Chase held in his hand. "YYYou takin yo' gggrampa's firearm up there to ppprotect yo'self from them YYYankees?"

Hudson climbed the steps and thumped across the porch to sit apart from the others. He began to rock adamantly, as if to deny in advance any questions Henry might ask.

"Do you know if a telegram came for me?" Chase continued. "The professor sent me the invitation a while back."

Chase thought he remembered having seen Big Dad at the front door talking with a man, then turning away and stuffing an envelope in his pocket. Later, Big Dad had said it was a letter from a man who owed him money.

"*I* dddidn't see no tttelegram," Henry said, avoiding Chase's stare. Henry turned to Humboldt. "PhPhPhiladelphia?" he said.

"A stellar football contest," Humboldt said gravely, "pitting the best of the South against the best of the North."

Cornelius noticed a gleam in Hudson's eyes. He envied those fortunate enough to have fought in the glorious conflict. As he watched, Hudson became transformed: he sat up straight, sucked his stomach in, thrust his jaw forward as if facing Yankee cannon. His coat fit tighter about his chest and the dandruff seemed to have disappeared from his shoulders. His tobacco-stained lips grinned defiantly. Then Humboldt heard the wagon.

He turned to see a spit-and-polish trap coming up the drive behind a smart-stepping bay. At the reins was a big-shouldered man dressed in black. A mane of white hair flowed from under his hat.

"Here's Big Dad," Chase said. Hudson spat over the porch rail.

The Reverend Riddle stepped out of his trap and came to the porch. His stride was short and quick for a big man, as though to proclaim his humility. Chase introduced Humboldt to his other grandfather. Big Dad clasped the professor's hand with evangelical fervor. Then he turned to Hudson, lifting his hat politely.

"Afternoon, Sergeant," Big Dad said. He grasped Stroud's bony hand with the tips of his sausage-like fingers. "How are you?"

"Middling." Stroud sat ramrod-straight.

"Big Dad," Chase said eagerly. "I got the Call!"

His eyes grew moist and profound. He felt sorry for himself and wondered why. Big Dad stared closely at his grandson, seeking signs of metamorphosis.

"How did it come to you?" he asked skeptically. He noticed the pistol Chase carried.

"Here!" Chase pointed at Humboldt. "This man had the key that unlocked the door. I'm goin' to be a Christian quarterback!"

"What say?" Big Dad swayed as if blown off balance by a gust of wind. "Quarterback? No, no, that don't sound right, boy. It ain't right."

"Ain't there different Calls for different folks?" Chase grew plaintive, his face sharp and inquisitive.

"What do you think?" Big Dad complained to Henry.

"Chase oughta know." Henry's voice was steady now, with no trace of stammer. He reached into the pocket of his khaki shirt and got a can of Garrett's Red Leaf. Chase stared. His father never dipped snuff in front of Big Dad. Henry wedged a generous pinch between cheek and gum. Big Dad stared incredulously at the bulging lump.

"Pride goeth before a fall," Big Dad warned.

Inside the house, in the kitchen, Edwina Stroud Riddle stopped cutting biscuits and listened. She sensed that something was wrong. She took off her apron and went up the hall. When she saw the men on the porch, she stood behind the curtain and looked out. She was a tall, rangy woman with a lean face and the Stroud nose. One glance at the lump in Henry's cheek told her that a family crisis was in the making.

Humboldt, who was determined that his first recruiting venture be a success, turned to Big Dad diplomatically. "Sir, the South needs your grandson. The North will throw everything they have at us—All-Americas from the Big Four such as Heffelfinger, Newell, Barclay, and Rinehart—and the great Michigan quarterback, Ernest Liebowitz . . ."

"*OF KALAMAZOO?*"

Hudson's cry grated like an ancient rock being pried from its resting place. He gripped the arms of his rocker and kicked the chair around to face them.

"NNNo, no, it can't be *your* Liebowitz!" Henry sprayed a brown mist in his exasperation.

"Come to think of it," Humboldt replied, "I believe that Liebowitz *is* from Kalamazoo."

"PPPlease don't get him started," Henry said to Humboldt. "The Sergeant was a ppprisoner of war in Ohio. The man responsible for his cccapture was—"

"—from Michigan!" Chase exclaimed.

Hudson deliberately reached into his coat pocket. He took out a pint bottle of bourbon, unscrewed the cap, and drank. He pointed the bottle at Humboldt in a silent toast.

Big Dad, who agreed with Jonathan Edwards that the bulk of mankind is reserved for burning, glared at Hudson, dangling him, in his mind's eye, over the coals of hell.

"There may be a thththousand Liebowitzes in Michigan," Henry argued, his thoughtful expression marred by the lump in his cheek.

"But how many *Ernies?*" said Hudson.

His rocker began to jerk as if pulled by impatient warhorses.

"SSSergeant, even if thththis Liebowitz boy *is* bbblood kin to yyyour Liebowitz, what would it ppprove? It ain't ChChChase's grudge."

"The sins of the fathers . . ." Big Dad began, sonorous and grave.

"DDDon't ppput it on Chase," Henry pleaded.

"He's my blood," Hudson said.

"Football's just a game, Sergeant."

"Satisfaction ain't no game."

"Read Proverbs twenty, verse one," Big Dad commanded.

Stroud took a pull at his bottle. Whiskey had never tasted so good. Chase looked from one grandfather to the other.

"It pains me to say this, Sergeant." Big Dad's eyes blazed with good intentions. "But you are not a good influence in this house. In the past, charity has helped us tolerate your affinities for gambling and strong drink. Now you have gone too far. Chase is going to follow in *my* footsteps." He took two small steps forward. "He will build on the foundations I have laid. You would use your kin to accomplish your revenge? Well, now, I recognize whom I am dealing with, Sergeant. This I have had large experience with. Now I am on firm ground. For *this* is the work of Beelzebub."

Hudson considered Riddle over the rim of his bottle. He could not kill his daughter's father-in-law outright. Besides, Chase was holding the gun. He took a long swig of bourbon and licked his lips. Big Dad drew himself up, rich with responsibility.

"It pains me to remind you, Sergeant, that you are living on my property—"

"Whoa, here," Henry said. "Let's dddon't fly off the hhhandle." Big Dad turned on his son.

"Read Matthew seventeen, verse seventeen."

"I think I have a say in this," Henry said levelly. "We're proud to have the Sergeant stay with us, Liebowitz or no Liebowitz."

"I cannot condone his callous disregard for the future of my grandson." Big Dad's face was turning purple.

"He is my grandson too." Hudson's voice had a click in it, like a pistol quietly being cocked.

"Hey, it's *my* decision, ain't it?" Chase said. No one paid him any attention.

"I believe the Sergeant is overstaying his welcome," Big Dad told Henry pointedly.

"This is my house," Henry said. "He's part of it."

Big Dad swatted at the air as if warding off invisible demons. "Don't put the cart before the horse, Henry. Don't tempt fate. Read Romans sixteen, verse twenty."

"You know, Big Dad," Henry said thoughtfully, "I think what you object to most is the Sergeant's bottle."

"Read Corinthians six, verse ten!" Big Dad shouted.

Henry moved across the porch to his father-in-law. He reached out for the bottle and Hudson handed it to him. Henry raised the bottle to his lips, tilted it, and drank. His Adam's apple bobbed. Big Dad braced himself.

"Read Revelation two, verse twenty-seven," he said grimly. "The ancient enemy is here. Read Matthew ten, first verse. Satan has defiled your body, Henry. Read Deuteronomy thirty-two, verse thirty-nine."

Edwina had heard enough. She went to the drop-leaf table in the hall and got her silver bell. It was important to get their minds on food, even if she would have to kill herself to get it on the table in time. The house was clean.

The men were shocked by the violent ringing of a bell so close by. They all looked at the door. Behind the screen Edwina rang and rang. She leaned forward in a muscular attitude, as if braced against male appetites. Flour smudges on her cheeks and forehead gave her the appearance of an angry ghost.

"Oh, we have *comp*'ny!" she cried delightedly.

She emerged brightly from the house. Chase introduced her to Humboldt.

"Professah, you'll stay the night with us, of course," she said. "Chase, show the professah to the guest room upstairs. I'll set three more places lickety-split." She sailed fiercely away into the house.

The men were helpless in the face of Edwina's summons to table. Food was a mystery. They shuffled into the house, except for Henry and Hudson, who hung back to finish the bottle. Chase escorted Humboldt upstairs to his room. The professor noted the solid wooden furniture and handwoven rugs. A grandfather clock stood ticking in the hallway. Edwina's authority lingered in the ripe odor of pine oil. After a while, she called them in to dinner again. Everybody came except Henry and Hudson, who were nowhere to be seen. Edwina rang and rang for them. They had gone to the barn, where Henry kept a bottle. She marched into the dining room and told the men to sit.

"Let's go ahead while everything is hot," she said. "They'll be here in a minute. Daddy Riddle?"

Big Dad folded his hands before him and composed his thoughts. "Let us bow our heads," he said. "Our Heavenly Father, we offer thanks for this thy bounty . . ."

His words were drowned out by a clanking roar. The dishes

rattled on the sideboard. Edwina opened an eye and saw Henry drive his McCormick reaper past the window, harvester blades flashing hungrily in the air. Hudson sat on the fender waving a crutch. Edwina closed her eyes and the clanking gradually went away.

". . . ask that in thy infinite mercy You forgive us our manifold sins and wickedness. In His name we ask it. Amen!"

Edwina cast a critical eye over the table gleaming with china and platters of meat and vegetables. On the sideboard were extra biscuits and cornbread, spoonbread, and corn lightbread, and pitchers of ice water, iced tea, milk, and buttermilk.

"Professah," she said, "would you start the roast beef? Daddy Riddle, just start what's in front of you and we'll pass everything to the left. Henry and Papa'll be right along, after Henry shows off his new machine a little. I don't know what's gotten into him! You'll have to excuse us, Professah. I think everybody's still upset over Bryan's defeat. Is there room on your plate for the stewed tomatoes? Just when we were getting over the panic of ninety-three. Bryan's silver standard offered such hope. Are those biscuits still hot? Henry and Papa's plates'll be cold as ice."

The reaper circled the house and passed the window again. This time Hudson was jammed into the seat next to Henry, holding aloft a quart bottle of whiskey. Chase got up to see what was going on, but Big Dad raised a staying hand.

"Let us not give them the pleasure of getting a rise out of us," he said. "Let us eat our dinner as if nothing were happening. If it were not for your confounded football and this Philadelphia business . . ."

"What Philadelphia!" Edwina cried. Humboldt put down his fork.

Chase explained, with placating gestures, about the all-star game. Edwina tried to compose herself. Big Dad chewed stolidly as if eating sin. Humboldt came to Chase's aid with a lengthy description of Philadelphia: its historical monuments, parks, museums, and theaters; its modern trolley system and arc lights on street corners; amusements such as the new roller-skating rink, tricycle clubs, balloon ascensions, dime museums, and the Wild Bill Hickok Show. The McCormick reaper made another pass and drowned him out.

Edwina had barely listened. There was more than football at stake here. The family was in a state of collapse. She had always gone along with football, even though it seemed a needless risk. Looks were so important in the ministry. It was a miracle that Chase's nose had made it this far. But with Big Dad turning purple and Henry coming unglued, the sooner Chase left for Philadelphia the better. When the house was quiet she could catch up on her needlepoint and worry about Chase in peace.

"I can see you're set on it," she told Chase. "Well, the sooner you get it over with, the better. Daddy Riddle, you missed the okra first time around, didn't you? Isn't there room on your plate for it, now?"

"God's will be done," Big Dad intoned. He was relieved that his daughter-in-law had taken the responsibility on herself. "I *would* like a bit of okra."

"Save room for the pie," Edwina said. As soon as Henry calmed down, the crisis would be over, at least for the time being. Yet these things had a way of cropping up later, when a person least expected. "It's raspberry."

His mouth stuffed with biscuits and gravy, Chase grinned at Humboldt and held one arm close to his chest as if carrying a football, while with the other arm he pretended to stiff-arm an imaginary opponent.

After dessert, Edwina sent Chase to dig his wool overcoat and scarf out of the cedar chest. Humboldt went outside to smoke his pipe. He strolled around the house. The air was clean and cold. Stars winked in the eastern sky. He saw light gleaming through the barn door.

From inside the barn came the sweet smell of baled oats. The wavering flame of a lantern revealed stalls and rafters strung with harness and tackle. Tools were stacked neatly on nails. Feed bins were brimming with milo. In the center stood the yellow McCormick reaper. Henry sat at the controls, fiddling with the levers. Hudson was napping at his side.

"Big Dad paid cash for the new McCormick," Henry spoke deliberately and rather forlornly to himself. "It was the 1888 model, which bound with twine instead of wire, a big improvement over the 1876 model, according to the salesman in Lexington." Cradling a bottle of bourbon in his arms, Henry continued,

"I had a funny dream last night! Big Dad was at the controls, grinding through a field of winter wheat. I was running just ahead of the threshing reels. The machine caught hold of me and trundled me up its canvas belt to a chute, dropped me into a box with cut wheat, bound me into a neat bundle, and dropped me out the rear like a turd."

"A magnificent machine," Humboldt called.

Henry looked down at Cornelius. "Professor," he said quietly, "I want my boy to go play football in Philadelphia, if he wants to."

"Well said!" Humboldt cried. "Sir, you will be pleased to hear that your wife agrees with you."

"You don't say!" Henry said, surprised. "And what did Big—" He broke off and took a pull at his bottle.

Hudson opened his eyes but kept still. He wanted to hear his son-in-law stand up to old man Riddle.

"I been running this place for nigh on thirty years," Henry said. Whiskey smoothed away his stammer. "Big Dad ast me to take on the farm and leave him free to preach and run his revival meetings. Now, Big Dad can't help bossing us all around. He's got used to it, and we tend to go along with it. But just because we let him don't mean we roll over and play dead every time he barks." Henry took another reflective nip at his bottle. "This Philadelphia stuff has kind of shook things up out here, but maybe they needed shaking up. Professer, I'm glad you come and I'm glad you want my boy to play for you. I reckon you'll get your money's worth out of Chase, anyhow. One thing he can do, he can flat play football."

"If there's any whiskey left . . ." Humboldt said happily.

"Buy you a drink, Professer." Henry leaned down to hand the bottle to Cornelius. The Sewanee man solemnly raised it in a toast.

"Here's to the South!" he cried.

Hudson sat up alertly. "And to whupping Yankees," he added. "Don't leave *that* out."

Chapter Ten

The shadow of woman and horse flowed together over the clay gulleys. Kate's face, radiant in the moonlight, seemed suspended over the plunging neck of her mount like a small twin moon. The road was transformed into a silver band holding the dark earth together. There was nothing she could not do.

She turned without hesitation down the narrow lane to the Riddle plantation, although she had never been there before. Across open fields she saw two houses silhouetted against the night sky, one larger than the other. The large house appeared to be completely dark, while a light burned brightly in the smaller one. She slowed her mount to a walk, patting it on the neck. As she passed the small frame house set close to the lane, she peered curiously into the windows. An old man on crutches could be seen hobbling back and forth. He took something out of a closet, wrapped it in cloth, and packed it in an open valise lying on a bed.

Oh I wish I was in the land of cotton old times there are not forgotten look away . . .
Hudson hummed "Dixie" under his breath as he rolled a bottle of bonded sour-mash bourbon carefully, lovingly, inside a folded pair of long johns and stacked it alongside similar bundles in his valise. His black dog sat and watched him with sad eyes.

"Wish I could take you with me, Murphy," Hudson said cheerfully. "You ain't never been to Philadelphia. Well, neither have I."

He paused before wrapping another bottle, unscrewed the cap, and drank. The rich odor of whiskey mingled with the smell of leather and mothballs and oilcloth. Hudson rewrapped the bottle, packed it in the valise, and reached into an open trunk. One by one he took out his gambling clothes from his days on the river. It was like holding the past in his hands—the black broadcloth coat and pants, the white linen shirt with low neck and loose collar, black flowing tie, embroidered vest with pearl buttons and fancy hand-painted scene of the chase, high-heeled patent-leather shoes, a two-shot derringer—his "Betsy"—wrapped in oilcloth, and, finally, the gold Jeurgunsen watch on a long gold chain.

"Did I ever wear duds like these?" Hudson asked the dog.

Ordinarily at this time of night, all he and the dog had to do was go outside and relieve themselves, come inside the house, put his false teeth in a glass of water, turn out the light, arrange themselves horizontally on the bed, and listen to their hearts beating. But tomorrow was a new day!

"Murphy," he said as he carefully packed his poker outfit in the valise, "if you were asked to compare poker to another human endeavor, what would it be?"

The dog sat up and wagged its tail.

"War? Yes, you're exackly right! Why is that? Because in war or high-stakes poker *nothing else matters.* Both require attack and defense, bluff and counterbluff. A man has to put everything he is on the line. You rely on skill, memory, cunning, and boldness. You try to figure the personality, habits, strength, and weakness of your opponent. In battle you concentrate one hunnerd percent, same as you do when you've just bet your last dime. It's the element of risk, Murphy. Nothing else matters."

Hudson caught sight of the daguerreotypes in a twin frame standing on his dresser. On the left was his wife, Marguerite, serene and mystical in her wedding gown; on the right he stood, awkward and uncomfortable in his Confederate uniform. The photographer had made him pose in Napoleonic fashion, hand in vest.

Who was that young soldier? he thought. *What was in his eyes? Vainglory?*

"Murphy, it's done. Now we got a train to catch and some telegrams to send. Where?" He grinned at the dog. "One of 'em's to Kalamazoo, where else?"

Kate tightened the reins and patted the mare's neck to keep it quiet. She watched the old man hobble to the fireplace, take a poker and stir the coals. The fire blazed up suddenly. He stared deeply into the burning embers. She touched heels to the mare's flanks and walked it toward the big house farther up the lane.

The Riddle place seemed completely dark, but as she came closer she perceived a glow coming from the right side of the house. She walked the horse around the yard, its hoofbeats muffled by the frosty grass. No dogs barked. Through a downstairs window she saw a large man in nightcap and nightshirt kneeling beside his bed. His hands were folded and his expression was satisfied. His lips moved as if he were talking to himself. As he spoke he absently picked at lint on the bedclothes, straightened his nightcap, scratched himself on the rump.

Kate recognized the Reverend Riddle, who once had delivered a condescending lecture to a student assembly at Post Oak School. Riddle professed to be on intimate and friendly terms with his Maker. He prayed in the manner of a railroad engineer who leans on the stationmaster's desk and explains in a reasonable way why the schedule needs changing. Kate turned away and tied the mare to a maple tree beside the house.

Shadows danced against the ceiling of an upstairs bedroom. Kate rose in the saddle and caught hold of a low branch. Climbing up the tree she saw Chase, barefoot and wearing long johns, arranging an overstuffed chair and footstool in the center of his room. A football spun in the air and returned to his hand as though tied to it with an elastic cord. He laid the ball in front of the stool and crouched over it. He silently called signals. Then he snatched up the ball, feinted as if to an invisible fullback behind him, hid the ball against his thigh, and pranced around the armchair with an arm upraised to signal a touchdown.

Kate stifled a guffaw. In an adjacent bedroom she saw Professor

Humboldt lying against the pillows at the head of his bed, smoking a cheroot and smiling to himself. Did all Sewanee men think so well of themselves, she wondered?

She climbed out on a limb hanging over the roof, swung lightly to the roof, crept over the shingles and peered inside Chase's window. He was humming a tune as he played football with himself. The song was "Rock of Ages."

Chase was crouching over the footstool when he heard a tap on his window. His head swiveled around. Kate's face hovered in the night. He was so startled that when he went to the window to let her in he stayed bent in a crouch, like a hunchback.

"We've got to go!" Kate said as soon as he opened the window. Cold air rushed into the room. The schoolmarm's windblown hair stood out like wings.

"Go? Where?"

"To Philadelphia."

"Who? Us?"

"My players and myself."

"You mean, your nigger team?" He hurriedly added, "I mean, your team?"

Kate remained crouched in the window and waited for him to remember his manners.

"Would you like to come in?" he said.

"Thank you."

He held out his hand and helped her climb down into the room. "You shouldn't ought to be out, this time of night."

"Why not?"

Chase was taken aback. "You're a maiden lady!"

"So what? There are more important things in the world than my virginity. Aren't you going to ask me to sit down?"

He gestured helplessly at the overstuffed chair. She sat hunched forward with elbows resting on her knees, hands loosely draped between her legs. Her expression was so gauntly expectant that Chase wondered if Philadelphia was all she had on her mind. He glanced at the door to the hall. It was not locked. He sat on the footstool before her, careful not to let their knees touch.

"My players are raw talent." She spoke rapidly. "They are stronger and faster than any athletes I ever saw. All they need is an experienced coach to shape them into a real football team. You could see for yourself today how well they responded to a few minutes of your instruction. With you as their captain, they could be a great football team . . ."

"In three weeks? With no game experience?" Chase thought of offering to pray for her.

"My boys are strong as bulls and in perfect condition," she persisted. "They can run all day. All they lack is coaching."

"Don't look at me," he said. "I never coached a day in my life. Furthermore, nobody is going to teach a nigger—a Negro high school team to play as good as college men in three weeks. Not even Glenn Warner or John Heisman."

"Strictly speaking," she said, "my boys are no longer high school players. I enrolled them in our seminary program. They are college men now."

"What do you mean?"

"Professor Humboldt said that one of the eligibility requirements for the North-South game is that all players must be varsity men. So I fixed it." She smiled uncertainly.

Chase reminded himself that two minutes ago he had been on top of the world. A door had been opened to him. He was going to play football against All-Americas. Then trouble had climbed through his window. He sneaked a look at her wrists to see if they were hairy. He wanted to know what he was up against. Long sleeves covered her wrists.

"Miz Kate," he said, "I am only a participant in this all-star game. My one desire is to perform well on behalf of my family, the state of Kentucky, and Jesus Christ. I don't have the time to coach a Negro scrub team—"

"What did you say?"

Her eyes bored into him. He felt hair rising on the back of his neck.

"I said, 'I don't have the time—' "

"Scrubs! You said *scrubs.*" Her face was shining. "That's it! The Panthers will be the South's *reserves.*"

"Reserves?"

"Certainly. Don't all teams have substitute players?"

"Yes, but—"

"My players will make excellent reserves."

"On an all-star team," he reasoned, "aren't the reserves as

good as the starters?" He looked away and picked at the sleeve of his long johns. "And another thing," he continued. "I don't know if Negroes could get fired up about playing for the South. You know, with the bands playing 'Dixie' and Rebel flags waving everywhere. If I were colored, I don't think I'd get fired up. I mean, I can't see your boys—Brother, Tree, Lincoln, Ulysses—singing 'The Bonnie Blue Flag,' can you? And speaking of the fans . . ." He risked a glance at her. "Do you think *Rebel* fans would want to be represented by a team that was half black? Never mind that the black half was merely scrubs. It is also just possible that one of your boys might actually get to *play* due to injury or something. When he lines up in front of a son of Yankees that set his people free, and he looks into that Yankee's eyes, do you expect your player to wade into his *emancipator?* I can't see it."

Kate cast wildly about. "Some slaves accompanied their masters to the war and remained by their side for the duration!"

"What kind of argument is that?" he exclaimed. "I'm talking about free choice. Will your boys *want* to go to Philadelphia?"

"They will go if I tell them to."

Her face reminded him of a gnarled tree.

"So these Negroes are *your* Negroes?" He drew back. He thought she might strike him.

In the bedroom directly below Chase's room, Edwina Stroud opened her eyes and looked at the ceiling. She was not unduly alarmed. She often heard voices in the night. There was never enough time to get everything done. There were always loose ends that whispered to her in her sleep: a button not sewn, a pillowcase not ironed, dough not smooth, jelly not set. Even if the day's cleaning, baking, sewing, cooking, and washing were complete, her needlepoint never ended on the right row. She dreamed of doing needlepoint, surrounded by her friends in the Sewing Circle. The clicking of needles and voices lowered in gossip were life-saving; but ultimately all the voices became one —her own. She had a tendency to talk to herself, awake or asleep. Thus Edwina was not alarmed by the faint, muffled voices coming from the ceiling. She remained alert, however, and gradually realized that the voices were real.

Holding the coverlet to her chin, she looked to Henry for help. Heavy and unmoving, he snored beside her. She imagined she could see his whiskey breath, like black smoke from burning tar. Her father, Hudson, had kept a bottle in the toolshed when she was a child. Her mother had allowed no liquor under her roof. Whiskey, said her mother, was Satan in a jar. With Henry adrift in a state of sin, whatever was going on in Chase's room she would have to face alone. She listened intently. She realized that one of the voices was female and felt her strength rise.

Chase had decided to try another tack. He assumed a professional attitude, regarding Kate as a worshipper who sought divine guidance.

"I appreciate the fact," he said quietly, "that you believe in your team. I appreciate how you think they deserve a chance to compete, to show what they can do. Which brings us to you, Miz Kate. Is there some reason why you, personally, want to go to Philadelphia?"

Kate searched his pale blue eyes. She had known him since he was a boy.

"Have you ever thought what it is like to be female?" she said.

"Huh?"

"To start with, imagine dressing yourself in women's clothes. With your height and weight, you would wear about a size twenty-six dress with a forty-four-inch stay and size fourteen slippers."

He began to draw away from her. His face registered horror and suspicion.

"Feel those petticoats around your waist? Three layers or twenty yards of material weigh nearly five pounds. It is hot inside all that cotton. Hard to breathe or move your legs."

Chase fought against suggestion, but the image of himself swathed in petticoats and corset was too awful. His head tilted sideways, and he saw himself as a six-foot-four, 200-pound, twenty-three-year-old wallflower. Kate continued with grim satisfaction.

"Miss Riddle, you have way too much energy for a girl, and *they* are constantly on guard to keep you from slipping down to the crick to play with the boys. You like to fight and wrestle and run with the boys, don't you? Especially rough games like stickball and capture the flag. But *they* say you can't. Come inside the house like a good girl. You get too flushed playing so hard. It will ruin your complexion. If the sun burns your skin, you will have crow's-feet before you are eighteen. You skinned your elbows rolling in the grass with your cousins. If you are not careful, you will have to wear long sleeves for the rest of your days to cover the scars."

Chase stared at Kate's long sleeves.

"Uh-oh, here comes puberty. *Now* it gets serious. You are needed in the kitchen constantly. The way to a man's heart, *they* tell you, is through his stomach. Here's Grandma's recipe for dumplings. Put it in your hope chest with the pillowcases and feather duster. You have a definite talent for cookie cutting. When menfolks come tramping in from work or fishing or hunting or card playing, they like to smell stew in the pot and biscuits baking. Fetch them something cool to drink and give them a piece of your mind if there's whiskey on their breath. Pay close attention to your beau's mama's cooking and mind what brand of molasses he favors. Put your best foot forward."

Chase's nipples became sensitive. Puberty was upon him, and he did not know which way he would jump.

"You are so accomplished, dear. While your brothers and uncles and cousins waste their time fishing and playing baseball, you follow worthwhile pursuits, such as elocution, piano, and china painting. In the parlor you give a dramatic presentation of soliloquies and psalms and classical music. *They* keep requesting encores. Your 'Porphyria's Lover' would haunt Browning himself. What a repertoire you have. Your programs end on such a moving note with the Twenty-third Psalm. *They* all agree that the Bible contains the most beautiful poetry."

The Twenty-third Psalm struck too close to home. When Chase was thirteen it had been his specialty, constantly requested at evening worship services, ladies' sewing circle, and after Sunday dinner on the grounds. He fell into the past, thrust by memory inside a thirteen-year-old's body—arms too long, large joints aching, nipples red and uncertain, voice ranging two octaves. He heard his voice quavering somewhere between tenor and soprano:

> He maketh me to lie down in green pastures;
> He leadeth me beside the still waters.

He leaped up, resentful. Kate stood to confront him.

"Now do you see?" Her eyes were fierce.

Chase raised a hand half in benediction, half to ward off a blow. "It's not up to me! Ask Professor Humboldt. It's *his* decision."

He moved away abruptly, holding his arms stiffly away from his body like a bird poised for flight. He stumbled over the stool and fell to the floor.

Downstairs, the thump on the ceiling told Edwina to act. She heaved herself out of bed. Henry's snoring scarcely broke rhythm. She shrugged into her housecoat and scurried into the hall. On impulse she felt for the door of the linen closet under the stairwell and got out an armful of clean towels. Moving toward the stairs she bumped into someone in the dark. Big Dad loomed in his nightshirt like a ghost. His face seemed to glow with Christian responsibility.

"There is a female in the boy's room," he whispered.

"I know," she replied.

They began to climb the stairway together.

Chase rose, pressing his hand to his lower abdomen. Kate was concerned.

"I hooked my leg over the stool." His voice was unnaturally high-pitched. He lowered it to a husky baritone. "I think I pulled something."

"Groin pull?" She became clinically alert.

"It's not so bad," he said.

"Lie down on the bed."

"What?"

"I am a registered nurse," she said. "My medical training comes in handy on the playing field. Groin pulls can come back to haunt you if the muscle tissue is not properly massaged right away. Lie down and let me take care of it."

"Massaged?" he said hoarsely. "All I need is a good night's—"

She pushed him onto the bed. He sank into the feather mattress. She took off her jacket. Her severe expression reminded him of a cigar-store Indian.

"Are you really a nurse?"

"Unbutton your long-johns." She rolled up her sleeves decisively.

In the hall, Big Dad and Edwina put their ears to Chase's door.

Chase unbuttoned his fly and his penis flipped out, fully erect. He was as surprised as Kate was—perhaps more so, he reasoned in a strange moment of detachment, because she, at least, was a nurse. Where had it come from? He glanced anxiously at her rigid mouth, hard cheekbones, and button nose. Her solid breasts were not pointed or apple-shaped but wedges of pectoral muscle. He felt no more desire for her than he would for an opposing lineman. What had aroused him? Some vestigial memory of childhood games with his cousin Edna Mae, who had ministered to his feigned wounds with the provocative question: "Where does it hurt?" He concentrated to make it go away.

Kate did not flinch. She had studied anatomical sketches. A cursory glance, however, informed her that textbooks did not begin to illustrate shape, color, or size. The head was wider and flatter than the illustrations she remembered, the base thicker. She had never—or rarely—speculated on length. There was an arrogance about the male organ that no medical text could convey. In the nurses' manual, standard procedure for reducing an erection was a sharp blow to the head. Although her nursing instructors had not demonstrated, or indeed mentioned this maneuver, Kate felt capable of executing it as diagrammed.

Most nurses would have blushed or turned their backs, but Kate Kuykendall possessed a gift for level thinking. To begin with, it was *his* problem. He should be allowed to deal with it. She looked out the window with a sigh that could be interpreted either as forbearance or disapproval. It did not occur to her that she could be the object of lust. Sex had nothing to do with her, or vice versa. She had long ago resolved not to feel deprived due to lack of sexual experience. She had learned of masturbation from clinical texts but regarded it as petty and possibly habit-forming.

Chase directed all his willpower at the rebellious member. He felt his ears burning, as if there were more than enough blood to go around. It was ironic, he thought, that only moments before, while imagining himself swathed in petticoats, he believed he had lost sensation in his genitals.

"I'm sorry," he said.

"It is all right," she said, without looking at him. "Relax yourself."

In the hall, Big Dad and Edwina raised their eyebrows and kept their ears pressed to the door.

While Chase was grateful that Kate had turned her face to the window, he was also curious. He had often ruminated on woman's attitude toward sex. His mother, for example, was a mystery to him. When he was growing up she had been embarrassingly frank about bodily functions: quick to enema, to examine any moles, freckles, or warts, no matter where they were located. Once, during a walk through the woods, she had flabbergasted him by casually hiking up her dress and squatting beside the path to relieve herself. Yet his mother seemed interested in sex only if somebody else was doing it. In which case, she was quick to detect lustfulness or teenaged pregnancies or ordinary wickedness.

When it came to her own sex life, Chase sensed—with a son's intuition—that Edwina was niggardly. One night, however, as he tossed and turned in his bed upstairs, unable to sleep, he had heard her cry out. He held his breath and listened. Was she hurt? Where was his father? Then her rhythmic gasps, as regular and methodical as a mule plowing a field, told him where Henry was. He imagined his father's face, stern and expectant, looking straight ahead as though wearing blinders. He imagined his mother's face, eyes closed as though in prayer, gasps forced from her by the remorseless thrusting—a silent struggle in which Henry seemed to be trying to pump joy, a gasp at a time, out of his woman.

Chase was reminded of a joke that his mother's brother, Jake, had told him: "The good news is, the Lord created pussy. The bad news is, he put women in charge of it."

His erection had gone down. "You can turn around now," he said.

"What happened was quite elementary." She sought to distract him. "Stimulus received by the nervous system causes a flow of blood from the arteries which lead to the corpus cavernosum, which becomes engorged with blood, thus becoming firm. When the process is reversed, it returns to its original flaccid state. Now, let's see about that groin pull."

As soon as she tugged at his long johns the penis leaped up again. To Chase's embarrassment it weaved darkly, not unlike his Uncle Jake at a family reunion—inebriated, bald-headed, obscene—determined to tell his joke and make the women blush.

Kate decided she had no choice. Following standard procedure, she slapped the penis with her open palm—once, twice. It was hard as a piece of stove wood. Her hand stung but she resolutely struck again. The red eye of the urethra leered at her.

"It hasn't been this hard since seminary," Chase apologized.

"Shall we forgo the therapy?" she said crisply.

"I don't suppose you could work around it?"

"I am surprised at you," she said.

"Hit it again if you want to."

She thought she detected a bantering tone, which made her more determined than ever. "Think about something else. What is your favorite thing to do? I mean, like a hobby."

"Football, I reckon."

"Let's review the scoring system."

"What?"

"The *point* system." She folded her arms and did not look at him.

"A touchdown counts four points, a field goal five points, a safety two, and a goal after touchdown two."

"Offensive possession rule!" she barked.

"Three downs to advance ten yards and make a first. Runner is stopped when he calls 'Down' or when the referee whistles down." Perspiration wet his hairline.

"Dimensions of field!" she cried.

"One hundred ten yards in length, fifty-three yards wide."

"How long does a game last?"

"Seventy minutes, with two thirty-five-minute halves and a thirty-minute intermission."

"Substitution rule?"

"No substitution allowed except in case of injury to a player. If a player leaves the game for any reason, he mayn't return."

"How many players on a team?"

"Eleven—seven linemen and four backs."

"Define their function."

"The quarterback stands behind the center. He takes the ball and hands off to . . . it isn't working."

His penis remained erect, purple and proud.

"I don't understand," Kate said irritably. "What could be further from arousal than football?"

"I wish I knew."

They heard muffled voices singing a hymn in the hall.

> "Onward, Christian so-ol-diers,
> Marching as to war . . ."

The door burst open and Edwina swept inside, holding her towels like a shield. Big Dad hovered behind her.

> "With the cross of Je-sus,
> Going on, before."

"I brung you some towels!" Edwina shrieked.

Chase snatched his long johns up and fumbled with the fly buttons. Kate stopped him, laying her hand on his.

"We have not concluded treatment," she said.

The women locked eyes. Each intuitively perceived all she needed to know about the other. Kate saw in Edwina the closed ranks of Southern matriarchy, bristling with criticism, veiled insult, trifling cajolement, and competitive housekeeping.

Edwina looked at Kate and saw a pariah, a brazen hussy in long pants, a threat to womankind, a snake which came creeping in dead of night to perform unnatural acts.

"Madam," Edwina said, "what are you about?"

"I am examining Mr. Riddle," Kate replied firmly.

"She's a nurse!" Chase tried to sit up, but Kate pushed him down.

"I reckon this is a house call?" Edwina curled her lip in contempt.

"We were conferring about the trip to Philadelphia," Kate said, "when Mr. Riddle complained of abdominal pain."

"I seen what kind of pain he was in," Edwina said.

Big Dad hovered behind Edwina, grateful for the bulwark she made. He recognized Kate as Satan's harbinger, bearing a message from Big Dad's past. He remembered a night some thirty years ago—or was it forty?—when a husband had thrown open the door of an upstairs bedroom much like this one. Big Dad had rolled naked off the bed to kneel in prayer. In a climactic instant of inspiration, he had thanked the Lord for showing them the way to total humility by making them take their clothes off to become equal in His sight. His sister in worship gave testimony that for the first time she had seen God exposed. Thus in Chase's sweaty brow and wandering gaze did Big Dad see himself. He sank to his knees to ask forgiveness for them all. He began with the Lord's Prayer: "Our Father, Who art in Heaven . . ." Nobody paid any attention to him.

"Your son is suffering from a groin pull," Kate lectured. "It is a common athletic injury. Bands of fibrous tissue are stretched beyond functional limits and some are torn. Tearing of blood vessels may also occur, and pain often is severe. Swelling may occur . . ."

"We seen what swole," said Edwina.

"The Blood of the Lamb," Big Dad prayed, "shed for us in the hope of redemption for our manifold sins and wickedness . . ."

"I aim to git to the bottom of this," said Edwina. "Why didn't we hear you knock on the door?"

"I came through the window," Kate said.

Still lying on the bed, Chase turned his head back and forth to follow the women's conversation.

"I find that unusual," said Edwina.

"I did not wish to inconvenience anyone," Kate said.

"I bet," said Edwina.

Bearing the weight of Christian duty, Big Dad struggled to his feet. "Human frailty is in the blood," he said. "Shall we bow our heads together?"

"Yessir," Chase said, sitting up in bed.

"Wait a minute," Edwina said shrewdly. "What was that about Philadelphia?"

"Miz Kate has this Negro football team . . ." Chase explained.

"Nigra football?" Edwina said. *"And she wants you to take them to Philadelphia!"*

"They are the finest athletes in Kentucky," Kate cried.

"Oh God, our help from ages past," Big Dad began. His prayer was interrupted, however, by a polite knock. Professor Humboldt, resplendent in purple bedjacket, velvet slippers, and pince-nez, entered the room.

"Pardon my intrusion," he said, "but did I overhear someone mention Philadelphia?"

"She wants her colored team to be our scrubs!" Chase exclaimed. "They're seminary students. She forgot to tell you!" Both women now fixed their attention on the professor, who felt pinioned between them. The tide of cosmic irony which he had experienced earlier now rose up and swept him away.

"Capital idea!" he said.

Edwina was staggered by the professor's betrayal. At supper he had asked for second helpings of everything.

"Her boys can double as porters," Chase added, seized by invention. "There will be a lot of luggage."

"I will pay their expenses out of my own pocket," Kate said. "They are registered college students at Post Oak Seminary."

"The Rebel all-stars will have to have *somebody* to scrimmage against," Chase continued. "After all, none of us have played together. We'll need to work on our timing."

"You're right, of course," said Humboldt. "That will save our having to arrange a scrimmage with some local team."

Edwina looked helplessly from face to face. She groped behind her for Big Dad's shoulder. The Reverend Riddle felt equally deprived. He wished to focus on the sin that had brought them together in the first place.

"You say you will cover their expenses?" Humboldt asked, avoiding Edwina's gaunt stare.

"Out of my own pocket," Kate repeated as if taking a vow.

The professor shrugged his thin shoulders. "Coach Kuykendall," he said, "you have yourself a deal."

"*Ooohhhhhhh!*" Edwina roared her disapproval.

Kate gave a triumphant cry and shook Chase's hand so violently she almost dislocated his shoulder. She grabbed her coat and ran to the window, nimbly climbing out on the roof.

She stuck her head back into the room and called to the professor, "You won't be sorry!" Then she was gone.

They heard her whoop in the darkness. All of them crowded to the window to see her swing from a branch and drop into her saddle. She wheeled the mare and spurred it into a gallop. A silver cloud of dust pursued her down the lane.

The lights in Hudson's cabin were out when Kate passed it at full gallop. Inside, Stroud lay on his bed with his dog beside him. Murphy started up at the drumming of the horse's hooves but Stroud drowsily continued to recite the odds of being dealt a winning hand, which was better than counting sheep.

"A royal flush is 650,000 to 1, a straight is 72,000 to 1, four of a kind is 4,000 to 1, full house 700 to 1, flush 500 to 1, straight . . . 250 to 1 . . . three . . . of a kind 50 to 1 . . . two . . . pair . . . 20 to . . ."

And so he slept.

Chapter Eleven

The bereaved Allen family reported the facts in straightforward fashion. Harry Prescott drafted the obituary notice accordingly.

DIED

Allen—On Oct. 24, Mary Adelia Allen, daughter of Adelia and the late Herbert Allen. Funeral from her late residence, Pottstown, on Monday, Oct. 26, at two o'clock.

Harry began to doodle a bit.

DIED

Allen—On Oct. 24, Mary Adelia Allen, only daughter of Adelia and the late Herbert Allen, of dropsy. Funeral services will be held at her late residence, Pottstown, on Monday, Oct. 26, at two o'clock. Friends and relatives invited. Kindly omit flowers.

DIED

Allen—On Oct. 24, Mary Adelia Allen, beloved step-daughter of Adelia and the late Herbert Allen, after a bout of diphtheria. Funeral services at her late residence, Pottstown, Monday Oct. 26 at two o'clock, for family members only. Memorials welcome. Train leaves Pennsylvania Station at 10 A.M.

DIED

Allen—On Oct. 24, Mary Adelia Allen, estranged erstwhile daughter of Adelia and the late Herbert Allen, after a struggle against heart, lung, and mental illness. Private funeral arrangements from her late residence, Pottstown, Monday Oct. 26, at two o'clock. Invited are three members of the family. Flowers presumed. Train leaves

Tiring of doodling, he dropped the first one in his out-tray and swept the rest into the wastebasket. He had a dozen more notices to write before lunch. Fall was the busy season for obituary notices. Harry did not mind. He imagined that hundreds of readers scanned his death column as eagerly as they read front-page news. He tried to imbue his obits with a quiet drama.

Prescott liked facts not so much for themselves as for their potential. If, for example, a woman was reported drowned in the Schuylkill, he preferred to think of the circumstances as nefarious unless informed contrariwise. When it was discovered, as it invariably was, that she had been drunk and had fallen off a pier, he felt cheated. His selectivity regarding facts stemmed from their unlimited supply. As a stringer for the Philadelphia *Inquirer,* he was besieged by a swollen tide of murders, concerts, floods, divorces, fires, orphans, robbers, sale of public property, fistfights in public places, unknown men dead in the road, suffragists' meetings, prayer vigils, arrivals and departures of the rich—in all, the successes, failures, passions, crimes, disasters, valor, greed, charity, mayhem, and aspirations of Philadelphia and vicinity. He was a man paddling a canoe through a raging surf of facts. Doodling kept the canoe afloat.

He went back to work on the obits. He was looking forward to a siesta during lunch break. He had accustomed himself to sleep through the noise of the presses rolling overhead. His office consisted of a table and a chair in the basement of the *Inquirer* building. It was damp and cold with the single advantage of privacy. He stayed warm by wrapping himself in a buffalo robe. He had never seen a buffalo, but he trusted the Montgomery Ward catalog from whence he had ordered it. When he napped at his desk, his nose buried in the stiff, furry hide, he dreamed of mounting small herds of pubescent maids draped in soft pelts, grazing quietly as they waited their turn.

An open pipe rattled furiously against the wall. Prescott put his ear to the end. "Prescott," said a nasal voice. "I got an assignment for you. Get up here."

Prescott sat back and closed his eyes. Jimmy Larue could wait. Larue was city editor of the *Inquirer* and, as he often told Prescott, a graduate of the school of hard knocks. Harry was a Princeton man, a circumstance that nettled Larue, who had spent a lifetime climbing the *Inquirer* ladder. Thus the editor had made himself personally responsible for supervising the stringer's apprenticeship. He chose Prescott's assignments with fastidious delight.

As a would-be reporter, Prescott strove to find a voice that blended the literary with the prosaic, the romantic with the factual. His investigative report on the city's new sewer system had been entitled "The Feces of Change." Larue canned it. Prescott had never expected to work for a living. A wealthy aunt had left him an inheritance on which he expected to live comfortably if not lavishly all his days. His ambition had been to become a poet-philosopher with his own Walden Pond. Gathered at his feet would be women winsome and glad, enticing him to doff his satin cape and subdue them with gold chains; also classical scholars and gentlemen who knew when to talk and when to listen. And when he tired of his American school, Prescott would sail to France and establish a salon in Paris. Somehow, however, his aunt's money had run out—he had never fathomed his broker's explanations—and here he was.

After a few minutes Prescott's eyelids flopped open, blinked rapidly, and remained open. He put on his thick, rimless spectacles, threw off his robe, tugged his vest straight over his belly, and ascended the stairs with a heavy tread. At twenty-six he carried his portliness like a man thirty years his senior, but his blond cowlicks rising like twin horns from his forehead and his smooth, plump cheeks were decidedly boyish. His favorite authors were Dryden and Poe, his adopted style the heroic couplet. The obligations of earning a living had forced him to postpone his modern epic, to be written in the mode of Pope's *Rape of the Lock,* on the subject of strangulation during coitus. As a stringer, Prescott knew that such a *crime passionel* was not as esoteric as it might seem. He intended his opus to serve as a paradigm of the *fin-de-siècle*.

Jimmy Larue smiled grimly behind his cluttered desk. He was a thin, nervous man in his middle fifties, forever twisting his skinny neck inside his collar. He liked to make Prescott wait. He stared out the frosted window, running a pencil back and forth inside a curled thumb and index finger in a motion that reminded Prescott of rape.

"I got one for you, Harry," Larue said.

"Why me?"

"You haven't heard it yet!"

"No dark, odiferous places, I hope."

"Ha-ha, that's a good one." Larue's beady eyes gleamed. "This is an *outdoor* assignment, for a story with social implications and cultural significance. A football game . . ."

"Give it to Baker."

". . . between honorary teams from the North and the South . . ."

"Or Jones."

"It will be your brief, Harry, to cover every exciting moment, from the opening kickoff to the last bashing of heads."

"What is football?"

"A Princeton man should know. This is big news. A new American sport has attracted a nationwide following. And you're gonna tell the world about it, Harry."

"I detest sports."

"Then this assignment will be a real challenge. I can feel it, Harry, you're gonna build your own readership with this one. You're gonna become the voice of American football."

"I won't do it."

"You're fired."

"What is my deadline?"

"I need a preliminary draft by noon tomorrow, an announcement piece but with some flavor. Here's a statement the Athletic Club sent out. Work from that. Surprise me."

Harry read the public announcement:

The Philadelphia Athletic Club is pleased to announce its sponsorship of the first North-South All-Star Football Game to be played December 21 at one o'clock at Franklin Field. The game will be staged under the able supervision of Walter Camp, New Haven, eminent football authority and head of the All-America Football Selection Board.

"What is football?" Harry repeated.

"Philadelphia happens to have a lending library," Larue replied. "Research is no stranger to a Princeton man."

With his pencil Larue beat out a merry tattoo. Prescott scornfully drew himself up.

"Hibernation is over, Harry," Larue said. "Time to go out and earn your seventeen-fifty a week." As Prescott turned to go he added, "One more thing—I don't want to see the words *bucolic, ineffable, intoxicating, epicene,* or *bacchanal.* Do I make myself clear?"

At the Free Library on Chestnut Street, Prescott asked the librarian to recommend a book about football. She selected a compact volume entitled *A Scientific and Practical Treatise on American Football,* by A. Alonzo Stagg and Henry Williams. Harry suppressed a shudder, reminded himself of his undergraduate training, and went to the reading room. An hour later, having perused several chapters, he had acquired a general idea of the rules of the game, the means by which points were scored, and the point system itself. What he could not understand, however, was why people would gather to watch young men throw themselves in one another's paths. Flipping through the book he read passages at random:

When a man has a bruised and sensitive knee, a moistened sponge the size of a fist placed just under the kneecap will afford relief and protection . . .

Cleanliness is a hygienic necessity during the football season, and every team should, if possible, have hot and cold water shower baths connected with their dressing rooms . . .

> Long hot baths are weakening and should be avoided;
> though upon special occasions, when a cold has settled
> in the muscles, a Turkish bath may prove of great value.

The images of common baths and discrete droplets of perspiration on bruised skin appealed to Harry. He admired Stagg and Williams's aesthetic sensibility and continued to search the book for further sporting images:

> Squeeze the ball tightly when tackled or when going
> through the line . . .
> Never converse with an opponent during the game,
> but wait until the game is over for the exchange of
> civilities.
> Never play a "slugging game"; it interferes with good
> football playing.

Harry gave up on Stagg and Williams. As writers they could not hold his interest. He wandered into the periodicals room and, browsing through recent newspapers, found an account of a Harvard-Penn game. He read the first paragraph, seeking some point of view that he might adopt, cursing Larue all the while.

> When the football enthusiasts of Philadelphia arose
> from their beds this morning they found anything but a
> promising day to spend the greater part of it in the open
> air upon the unprotected stands of Franklin Field. Low-
> ering clouds covered the sky, and a fine drizzling rain
> was falling. The one compensation the weather vouch-
> safed was a rise in the temperature. Despite the nasti-
> ness of the day the air was soft and almost balmy.

The weather vouchsafed a compensation? he thought. *Where does Larue find such writers? In the linotype room? No, they have their standards. Wait. Soft and balmy. Southern breezes. North and South. Blue and Gray.*

To Harry, the War Between the States had little significance other than the fact that the Federals had contained the Confederates' wild abandon. Although Harry was all for abandon, he liked things orderly as a framework for his own personal rebellion. Philadelphia society, with its staid pace and moral countenance, made him dream of exposing himself, some hot June afternoon, on a bandstand in Fairmount Park. Yet the mind of the South—or rather, its lack of mental process—was fascinating to him. He admired Edgar Allan Poe's gothic South of dark dissolution pierced by bolts of spiritual lightning. What else did one need to know about the South? Yet now a vague thrill passed through Prescott as he contemplated a Southern football rabble, wild-eyed coaches, players, and spectators—a *force*—making its way north to Philadelphia.

He turned back to the newspaper account of the Harvard-Penn game:

> Early in the day crowds of men, boys and women made their appearance on the principal streets in the center of the city, bundled up to the eyes in their warmest wraps and bearing somewhere upon their persons the colors of their favorite college. While Philadelphia is naturally strongly Pennsylvania, there is a big Harvard contingent here, and the crimson of the Cambridge university was met with at every step. The cafés of the big hotels were filled all the morning with noisy partisans of either university. While the Harvard men were hopeful that their team would win, they were not willing to back the crimson at even money, and odds of 100 to 80 and, in some cases, of 2 to 1 were given. The Pennsylvanian who gave 2 to 1 was certainly an enthusiast, for the Quakers' play this year has been anything but encouraging, and Harvard today, for the first time this season, presented the full strength of its varsity eleven. Captain Wrightington, Dunlop, Wheeler, and Haughton were all to play for Harvard, and the presence of these men increased the strength of the Cambridge team over the eleven which played against Princeton earlier this year.

Harry imagined a gathering throng filling Franklin Field with blue and gray, growing steadily, not a festive, merry crowd, but a silent, ominous sea of gray surging in concentric circles around a beleaguered island of blue.

By noon all the cars leading toward Franklin Field were packed with people, and a constant stream of men and women who could find no foothold upon the trolleys was pouring westward. Enclosing Franklin Field was a great amphitheater of benches, rising tier upon tier high into the air. Through the numerous entrance gates into the field the crowd poured and sought their seats. Everyone had come prepared to sit upon damp boards, and all carried either shawls or rubber blankets to protect them from the cold and dampness. Anyone who has ever attended a great college football game knows by experience what an inspiring spectacle the towering stands filled with their mass of humanity, waving flags and howling, present. The Harvard people had a big section of the north stand reserved for them, and the followers of Cambridge turned out in sufficient numbers to fill all the space given them.

The west stand and the south stand were given over to Pennsylvania. Despite the drizzling rain, as 2 o'clock approached, the hour for the game to begin, a great multitude was present. The immense north and south stands were packed with people, and 20,000 is a fair estimate of the number present. The Glee Club of the University of Pennsylvania was stationed in the grounds before the Pennsylvania stand, and led their fellow-collegians in the singing of patriotic Pennsylvania songs. During this time the followers of Cambridge sat mute in their seats, only occasionally an individual cry for Harvard being heard. But finally the good feeling prevailing between the two universities was shown when the Harvard men arose and, raising the war cry of the crimson, followed it with a cheer for Pennsylvania. This courtesy was promptly responded to by 5,000 lusty Pennsylvania throats, which cheered for Harvard.

Harry heard a rumor of steel jangling, clashing against his inner ear, a clamor of bayonet and sword. The Stars and Stripes waved in the North stands, while the Stars and Bars waved in the South stands. From the North, a deep battle cry began, a bass tumult like tympani; from the South a cruel yelping, like dogs scenting a stag in the mountains of Appalachia.

A few minutes before 2 o'clock the Pennsylvania enthusiasts, armed with an immense magaphone, did a sort of wild war dance upon the ground, and then, raising the megaphone to his mouth, one of the number bellowed through it hysterically: "Here they come, boys; now three cheers for Penn'a." The sounding tin carried the speaker's voice throughout the stand, and as Captain Wharton jumped the fence into the field the followers of Pennsylvania arose to their feet, the stands broke out into a waving mass of red and blue, and in a mighty volume thousands of voices shouted in unison "Penn-syl-va-ni-a" three times three.

The Pennsylvanians tumbled onto the field and went through the acrobatic tumble act which characterizes the advent of all football games. Quite a wait followed, but at last the Cambridge men arose to their feet and began to shout as Captain Wrightington tumbled over the fence into the field. Then the men of Harvard made up for their previous silence. The long, slow cry of "H-a-r-v-a-r-d" echoed again and again across the field and was defiantly replied to by Pennsylvania.

Even now, from Tennessee and Georgia, from North Carolina and Mississippi, they rattle and sway northward on the railways of Dixie.

Harry Prescott lowered the newspaper. The muse was upon him.

A seething gray line moving inexorably toward silent figures in blue. They sweep into Pennsylvania by the thousands behind the ghosts of Stonewall Jackson and John Wilkes Booth, the rag-tag army of a slumbering defiance. The Southern giant awakes. He slouches toward Franklin Field to be reborn. Will Philadelphia become a new high-water mark of the Confederacy? The Quaker City prepares itself for siege.

Prescott jumped up and rushed out of the Free Library, anxious to get to his typewriter. He looked right and left for the Chestnut Street trolley. He heard its bell, the clanking of cables, and saw it approaching in the calm, orderly manner of the City of Brotherly Love.

Philadelphia, Harry thought, I am going to tear you a new sigmoid flexure.

Late the following morning Jimmy Larue returned to his desk from an errand to find a neatly typed sheet with the heading "Football Game" over the byline "H. P. Prescott III." Larue took his time, settling himself comfortably. Prescott was his private preserve, his secret source of diversion at the workplace. The grotesqueries that Harry's typewriter produced were never to be swallowed whole but rather to be savored—slowly, attentively— so that the appalling waste of Harry's expensive education could be fully appreciated. No one else shared Larue's hidden pleasure, because he had not allowed Prescott's pieces to be published under his byline. Harry was unaware of this circumstance, Larue knew, because Prescott considered it ill fortune enough to have to write for the *Inquirer* without having to *read* it too.

Larue picked up Harry's latest submission, his hands delicately trembling, and began to read.

> *Even now, from Tennessee and Georgia, from North Carolina and Mississippi, they rattle and sway north-ward . . .*

Chapter Twelve

At 2 A.M. Bardstown lay sleeping under a mantle of frost. The only sound was the rustling of leaves in the wind. Darkness reigned in the town except for a row of cabins across the railroad tracks. Here lamps were lit and shadows danced in the windows. On Second Street the Kuykendall home stood braced with its neighbors as if to repel invaders. A bedroom light came on.

"You're nervous as a watchdog," Mrs. Kuykendall complained to her husband. She sat up in bed and watched him don his robe over his nightshirt. He always did the proper thing. "What are you doing?" she said.

"I heard a noise. I am going to check on Kathryn." The doctor was a compact, squarely built man. Spectacles gave his face an owlish appearance.

"She resents being treated like a child," his wife lectured. "Let her alone. What time is it, anyway?"

"Be right back."

Kuykendall tiptoed down the hall and knocked on Kate's door. There was no answer. He tried the handle. As it turned his face softened, became indulgent and expectant. He opened the door an inch or two and was surprised to feel cold air puddle around his bare feet. He opened the door wider and looked into the room. The bed, illuminated by starlight through the open window, was unrumpled and unslept in. A night breeze moved suggestively through the curtains. Kuykendall took several adamant steps toward the bed, as if it were to blame for being empty, then went to the window and looked out. Kate was nowhere to be seen. He glanced around the room in confusion, then looked out the window again. He started to close the window against the night air, then hesitated, not wanting to lock her out in case she planned to return. It was not unusual for her to go for a night ride, but generally she used the back door. Then he saw the envelope on her dresser. He lit a lamp and opened the envelope. Kate's letter trembled in his hands.

> Dear Father & Mother,
> A wonderful thing has happened. I am taking my football team to Philadelphia with Chase Riddle (the chaplain) and Cornelius Humboldt (a Sewanee professor). I am sorry to be leaving like this, without warning. I only found out tonight that we would be allowed to go along. I borrowed the hearse. It will be returned first thing in the morning.
> I will be fine, so do not worry about me. This trip seemed such a grand opportunity that I could not let it pass us by. I will write as soon as we arrive in Phil.
> > Your loving daughter,
> > Kate
>
> P.S. I left Rev. Rutledge a note at school explaining the situation and taking full responsibility. I will make my players keep up their homework and will set study hours for them. This trip will be a magnificent learning experience for them. Also, I have some leave coming and have not taken sick leave once in fourteen years.

Kuykendall hurried to share this astounding news with his wife. He fidgeted impatiently while she read Kate's letter.

"Gone?" Mrs. Kuykendall lowered the letter to her lap. She was sitting in bed with the coverlet around her. "Well, it had to happen."

"We should never have sent her off to school in Louisville," Dr. Kuykendall complained. "That's where it all started."

"Is it dangerous for her to travel like this?"

"Not with those apes to protect her. Collectively they must weigh a ton."

"We must let her do what she wants. She's a grown woman."
Mrs. K was round and soft but none of the shopkeepers in Bardstown crossed her.

"Why did I let you talk me into letting her organize that silly team of hers!" Dr. K pulled at his hair until he took on an electrified look similar to his daughter.

"*Me?* I did no such thing. I was the last to hear about it, as usual. Anyhow, she didn't need your permission or mine either. It was a school project."

"I bet she's over there in colored town, right now."

"You're not going after her, are you?"

"I think I ought to, don't you?" He sat close to her on the bed. She stroked his back in the absentminded way she petted her cat.

"There is no point in making a scene. It's clear her mind is made up. She's as stubborn as the rest of the Kuykendalls."

As though to refute this charge, the doctor's shoulders sagged. "We used to have such wonderful sessions, Kathryn and I. She would stand at my elbow during autopsies asking question after question. She could sketch every human vein from memory, every ligament, by the time she was fourteen. Now here she is, abducted by darkies."

"I'd say it's the other way around."

"What will this do to her reputation!" he cried.

"The reputation she's got, night-riding with Negroes will only enhance it."

"*Where did we go wrong?*"

"*We* didn't do anything. Even when Kathryn came of age, *you* thought it was fine for her to climb trees and build forts with the boys."

"She led the pack," he said defensively. "At eleven she was as tall and strong as any boy her age . . ."

"*You* let her run wild. This willfulness should come as no surprise to you."

"Her spirit was too strong to be tamed," he argued.

"Are you hungry?" she said. "Would you like me to fix you a sandwich and a glass of milk? You'll be up all night worrying to death. It's not like she's a baby. She's thirty-seven."

"*She is?*"

* * *

Kate stopped the mule-drawn hearse in the narrow street between the cabins. No one was in sight. Then a familiar figure emerged from the shadows.

"Hello, Miz Kate."

"I have good news, Brother!" she called.

"Forty acres and a mule for every able-bodied . . ."

"No, they want us to go to Philadelphia with them!"

He came closer. "Who? That professor from Sewanee?"

"We're going to be All-Stars!" she said recklessly.

"Philadelphia." His face became open and wondering. "Really? They *want us?*"

"We must leave right away. I want us to be at Bardstown Junction to catch the L & N at daybreak. Our varsity eleven."

"There is going to be opposition."

"You mean Principal Rutledge? Don't worry, I am taking responsibility—for being absent from school, the train tickets, everything."

"Not him," he said. *"Them."* He gestured toward the cabins. Faces could be seen in windows and doorways.

"What do you mean?" Kate looked from Brother to the silent faces and back again. "What could they have against it?"

He shrugged. "Philadelphia is a long way away. What, seven hundred miles?"

"Seven hundred and forty-nine," she said without hesitation.

"You looked it up!" He grinned. "Anyhow, they think this is just another crazy white man's game, like football itself. Going away on the train may be safer than running niggers to hounds or matching bucks in a prizefight at the barbecue, but it's still dancing to the white man's fiddle."

"Oh, hush!" she said impatiently. "They trust *me,* don't they?"

He leaned against the hearse. The mules stirred in their traces. "I don't know if I can answer that to your satisfaction."

"I do my very best," she said defensively and glanced from cabin to cabin. Their squat shapes seemed to swell with doubt. "What do they say about me?"

"They don't know what to say." He smiled humorlessly. "They never heard of a lady like you, white or black. They don't know what to think of a woman who carries a football handbook and a clipboard full of diagrams and yells at their sons to 'haul tail.' I guess you could say that their general opinion of your connection with their sons is that it 'ain't natural.' "

"Is there anything you can do?" she said.

He shrugged. "I'm just one of the boys."

"I'll talk to them," she said.

He nodded and hurried to call people out like a town crier. "Come on out. Miz Kate wants to talk. Come out!"

Slowly people emerged from the houses. They were dressed for such an irregular occasion in skirts over nightgowns, coats over long johns, paper curlers and nightcaps. They could not seem to make up their minds whether to be amused or proud or uncompromising in the face of this dilemma that had popped up in the middle of the night. The children alone were free to enjoy themselves. Their shouts and laughter echoed up and down the street. Several dozen people gathered beside the hearse, hugging themselves to keep warm. Kate stood up in the driver's open seat. They gazed up at her, dignified and apprehensive. Young mothers jiggled infants to keep them quiet. Kate saw her players—Tree, Weasel, B.C., Ulysses and the rest—clustered together off to the side. Brother stood at her feet and held the reins for her.

"I have good news!" she said brightly. "The Post Oak football team has been invited to play in the all-star game in Philadelphia, which will pit the best players of the South against the best of the North . . ."

"Pit means buck-fights," Brother whispered. She dismissed him with an impatient wave of her hand.

". . . and our team is the best!"

The players, grouped together, gave a small cheer, which the children echoed.

"I know you are all as elated as I am that this honor has come to such fine young men. We will travel by train together, and I will take good care of your sons until we return. I'll have them back by Christmas, I promise. Now, we must hurry to get ready. Our train leaves in the morning."

A tall man wearing an undertaker's stovepipe hat and black broadcloth coat over striped pajamas stepped forward. "You say, in the morning? Excuse me, Miz Kathryn, but this ain't much advance notice." Voices murmured agreement. "Our boys got commitments. Tree is helping me put in a septic tank uptown. Cassius, over there, has got a brand-new baby."

Kate stared at the group until she found Cassius, grinning in spite of himself. He was only seventeen.

"Lincoln is helping his daddy build a new house," the undertaker continued. "These boys cain't just go galavantin' off someplace at two in the mawnin'. Now, everybody here respects what you have done for our chillun, helping get Post Oak School going—"

"It's only for ten days!" Kate interrupted. "Don't forget, our young men will be representing the Commonwealth of Kentucky. When they come home, all of Bardstown will turn out to welcome them!"

"Ain't *leavin'* as no heroes!" a woman shrilled.

"I'll get them back safe and sound," Kate said.

"Not worried about that."

"What, then?"

"It ain't right to come here, get us out of bed, and spirit our boys away. It ain't right." Again there were murmurs of agreement.

"We have a train to catch," Kate said lamely. She cast about and saw Brother looking up at her with a dubious expression.

"Excuse me," the undertaker said. "Will the other team up there have colored players too?"

"I can't answer that." Kate was afraid she was losing them. She held up her hands. "Wait, please listen to me. This game means a lot more than just football. The whole country is going to be reading about it in the papers. Don't you want our team to be there? It will be an experience that will last them the rest of their lives . . ."

Brother looked at the faces around the wagon. His parents were watching him to gauge his reaction. His father wore overalls with a coat slung over his shoulders. His mother clutched a shawl over her nightgown. Their hopeful faces reproached him —not, he thought, for going to Philadelphia but for daring to do something outside their experience. They were afraid and ambitious for him at the same time. It was like the name they had given him: a famous white name to help him get along in a white man's world. It was as if he had been branded a Tom in the womb. During the war Nelson County had been Unionist and his parents had been born freedmen, so it was with a strange magnanimity that they had named him Robert E. Lee Jones.

"Remember that it was Philadelphia," Kate tried another tack, "where the Declaration of Independence was written. 'We hold these truths to be self-evident, that all men are created equal, that they are endowed by their creator with certain unalienable—' "

"What Miz Kate is telling us!" Brother scrambled up beside her, shouting as he moved. Along with the rest, she stared at Brother. "She is telling us," he continued, "that she has found us a dream."

A hush fell. Even the smallest children stopped playing. The players stood braced together as if in a defensive formation.

"That dream may not come true," Brother said, "but look at it like this: if we actually *go* to Philadelphia, if we actually get to a place 749 miles from here, whether we play football or not, wouldn't that be *something!* But it's not true that we'd be going for Bardstown or for the Commonwealth of Kentucky or even for you—we'd be going for *ourselves.* Can you understand that? *Let us go!"*

Brother's voice shook. He stared down at faces that now looked unfamiliar to him, confused and without expression. He wondered whether they had heard a word he said. His parents were embarrassed. He was suddenly furious with their unending, patient suffering.

A cabin door slammed shut. People turned to stare at this welcome distraction. Lincoln padded barefoot toward the hearse, carrying his suitcase in one hand and his shoes in the other. He obviously meant to keep them clean and shiny as long as possible. His mother's voice broke the silence.

"You forgot your coat, Link! You could freeze to death up North."

As if this mother's lament were all they were waiting for, the community burst into action. Players ran to pack their bags, pursued, aided, and harassed by parents, grandparents, girlfriends, and envious brothers and sisters. Mothers held each other and wept. Children turned somersaults in the street.

Kate ran from house to house promising parents that she would take care of their sons and answering questions about Philadelphia. She flitted in and out of cabins amid an uproar of ironing, packing, moaning, weeping, praying.

Soon the team assembled at the hearse and climbed aboard with cardboard suitcases and carpetbags. The vehicle sagged under their combined weight. They stared out the long display windows on either side, stiff as corpses in their starched collars, their eyes wide with excitement. Kate climbed onto the driver's seat beside the undertaker, who had agreed to bring the hearse back to town. Cassius's wife added to the frenzy by throwing herself in front of the mules. She was dragged, kicking, away. Somebody's mother, crazed by the prospect of separation from her son, tried to hold onto a rear wheel. The hearse moved away slowly. The hatless, coatless throng shrieked farewell, mothers screamed advice, children clanged tin cans together like cymbals.

The players turned toward the rear window as the hurrahs faded behind them. The familiar sights and sounds of their community were replaced by darkness and the beat of the mules' hooves. They shifted in their seats and, shoulder to shoulder, looked solemnly at the gray road ahead.

Chapter Thirteen

His heroes were Napoleon and Billy the Kid. He was thirty-four and had played end on the Yale teams of eighty-four through eighty-six. There was no gray in his curly dark hair. He was compact and burly, with black eyes so sharp they held a man like teeth. He was coach and athletic director at the University of Chicago. His name was Amos Alonzo Stagg.

Stagg followed his host along the levee of a pond. The snow hardening on the ground was a week old. Their feet crunched through the brittle surface.

The second man was older, in his mid-seventies, tall, slender, with an elegant, gliding stride more suited to the carpeted decks of riverboat saloons than Michigan farmland. He wore a sheepskin coat and furry cap with earflaps. One of his sleeves was empty and tucked into a pocket. When he grimaced against the windchill, gold gleamed in his teeth. His name was Ernie Liebowitz, and he politely feigned interest in the football game Coach Stagg was telling him about. Stagg had come to invite Liebowitz's son, Ernest, Jr., to play in an all-star game in Philadelphia.

Liebowitz had never even seen his son play football. He was aware that Ernest played quarter on the college team at Ann Arbor, but Liebowitz did not know a quarter from a loin or brisket.

"Cold time of year to go fishing," Stagg remarked as they luffed along in the snow. Liebowitz saved his breath for walking. Ernest, twenty-two, was fishing off the levee through a hole in the ice. Stagg took off a glove and held out his hand.

"Mr. Liebowitz, I am Coach Stagg."

The young man dropped his fishing pole. He was tall, like his father, with wide, rangy shoulders and a grip like steel. He also had his father's crooked front teeth, minus the gold fillings. He grabbed the coach's hand.

"This is an honor," he said.

"Considering the damage Michigan inflicted on Chicago last year," said Stagg, "the honor is mine."

"Yes, but you beat us indoors this year!" Ernest said modestly.

"At the Coliseum on Sixty-third Street," Stagg explained to the elder Liebowitz. "It beats playing in the rain, don't you think? We were lucky to win. A close one, seven to six."

"It felt funny to play indoors," Ernest said. "I'm not making excuses, but the punts kept hanging up in the girders."

Liebowitz Senior, who did not know a punt from a girder, said, "Let's go to the house."

They retraced their footsteps in the snow. Coach and quarterback walked abreast, followed by the old gambler. Ernest said, "I read about that game in Philadelphia."

"I hope you will honor the Blue team by starting at quarterback," Stagg said.

"Ernest has been asked to clerk with a law firm in Ann Arbor," Ernie Senior interjected. "They may make him a junior partner: Smith, Jones, Brown, and Liebowitz," he added proudly.

"Congratulations," Stagg said patiently. "In the meantime, how about playing for us? It would only take a week of your time —ten days, tops."

"Who else have you got?" Ernest Junior said eagerly.

"How about the great All-America from Yale, William Heffelfinger!" Stagg said coyly.

"*The* Pudge Heffelfinger?"

"The same. Also, the 'little giant' of Harvard, Marshall (Ma) Newell."

"Newell coaches at Cornell now, doesn't he?"

"Correct," said Stagg. He had the quarterback walking in step with him. Their feet crunched the snow in perfect cadence. "From Wisconsin we have the Aussie kicker, Pat O'Dea."

"Hey, the Kangaroo Kicker from Melbourne. He's deadly from sixty yards out!"

"They call him the Toe of the Antipodes!" Stagg exclaimed. They laughed together. "We also have Cornell's first All-America, Clint Wyckoff, a magnetic back."

Walking behind them, Liebowitz brooded on such strange information. The only magnets in sporting events in his experience were used in craps or roulette, sparingly.

"At tackle," Stagg continued, "there is the Princeton immortal, Doc Hillebrand; at guard Charles (Babe) Rinehart; in the backfield, the Lafayette sprinter George (Rose) Barclay . . ."

"Didn't Lafayette beat Penn this year?" Ernest asked.

"Yes, and by the way, a savage game due to their money squabble. I do not mean to gossip, but Penn only allotted Lafayette a hundred-fifty out of a gate of ten thousand. A most unsatisfactory arrangement from the Lafayette standpoint. It is common knowledge, so I am not telling tales out of school. Business is business."

"So who's on the other team?" Ernest asked.

"I am not familiar with the Southern teams, but I know Heisman and Warner, who will coach the Gray squad. They will doubtless field a team of big, fast men who will give us a run for our money."

"Do they still use the flying wedge down South?"

"No, sir!" Stagg said firmly. He had long been an outspoken critic of the flying mass, because of the injuries it caused. "The Southern schools were represented at the Intercollegiate Conference this past February and voted with the rest of us to eliminate the wedge. For the game in Philadelphia, the wedge is out."

The wedge is out, Liebowitz Senior thought, *Whoopee!*

Stagg suddenly became preoccupied with a lump of snow in his path. Hands outstretched in perfect form, he kicked it as though it were a football held in place.

Liebowitz was glad when they reached the house and went inside where it was warm. His wife, Mary, invited the coach to have some cake and coffee. Stagg was used to being offered cake and coffee by an athlete's mother. He accepted.

"Oh, Ernie, this came for you." Mary gave her husband a telegram, then went to pour the coffee and slice the angel food cake, Ernest's favorite. Liebowitz knew his wife was irked that this Chicago coach wanted to take her boy off to play football and cut short his visit home, brief as it was. Before he had time to open the envelope Mary called them to the kitchen, the warmest room in the house. They sat at the table. She served steaming mugs of coffee. Oak chips crackled in the Franklin stove while sleet hissed against the window. Liebowitz read his telegram.

AS REGARDS NORTH SOUTH FOOTBALL GAME IN PHILA-
DELPHIA IF LIEBERWITZ TO QUARTERBACK BLUE TEAM
YOUR KIN I AM PLEASED TO INFORM YOU MY GRANDSON
QUARTERBACK GRAY TEAM STOP LIKE OLD TIMES STOP
IF YOU HAVE WHERE-WITHAL MEET ME STRATFORD HO-
TEL PHILADELPHIA DEC 17 UNFINISHED GAME OF
CARDS STOP BRING SWORD STOP HUDSON STROUD.

When Mary saw her husband's crooked grin she almost dropped the cake. "What is it?" she said.

"It's Stroud," Liebowitz said wonderingly. "He's still alive." He gave Mary the telegram to read. "Ernest," he said to his son, who stopped chewing, his mouth full of cake. "I think I'd better go to Philadelphia to see you play. It may be the last chance I get."

"Great, Papa!" Ernest sprayed crumbs across the table. "Coach, that *does* it. I'm gonna be your quarterback."

"I knew you would!" Stagg said and stuck out his hand to seal the bargain.

"You can't say no, can you, Ernie!" Mary accused her husband, waving the telegram in his face. "You can't refuse a scrap. But this one will be your last, mark my words."

"Excuse me, what scrap?" Stagg said politely.

"Show him the telegram," Liebowitz told his wife. "Looks like I got an extra stake in this game." He smiled at his son. When Ernest returned the grin, it was as if each was looking in a mirror. "The other team's quarterback is the grandson of an old poker player I used to know."

Stagg did not completely understand the telegram, but gambling was always a volatile mix with athletics. He ate his cake and considered the sticky question of how to take the quarterback and leave the father. Recruiting, he noted, squirreling away the observation, should never be left to assistant coaches.

"He still blames *you* for the loss of his leg. That's clear to *me.*" Mary kneaded dough with a vengeance.

Stagg looked up in surprise. This recruiting trip was becoming one of the most complicated in his experience.

Liebowitz reached for his coffee with his good hand. The other rested in a permanent sling. A Confederate bullet had shattered the bone in his upper arm. It had happened in Vicksburg, long after his encounter with Stroud in Kentucky. What a coincidence their meeting at Green River had been, he thought, like drawing inside to a royal flush. He had never wanted Stroud's sword. As he recalled, Stroud had forced him to accept it.

"Why don't you just mail him *back* his sword." Mary broke into his thoughts with witchlike intuition. "You don't *have* to go to Philadelphia. You *promised*, no more gambling. I'm sorry Mr. Stagg has to listen to this, but of course if it weren't for this *football* game, none of this would have happened."

"A million to one chance," Liebowitz mused, "that our boys would be the opposing quarterbacks. I'd say I've got no choice, considering."

"You've got no choice about your high *blood* pressure!" Mary said angrily. Flour flew under her fingers and dusted her to the elbows. "It's just not *worth* it. Why satisfy his grudge? He got in the way of a *bullet*, just like you did, and he has to learn to live with it just like *you* did."

"Well, he lost more'n a limb, along with the rest of the Rebs," Liebowitz said gravely. "And he can't leave it be. With those hot Reb feelings of his, he *would* wear his grudge all the time, like sleeping with his hat on."

"Well, go ahead and *go,*" Mary said. *"I* can't stop you."

Stagg stirred himself. "I'd be happy to arrange a place for you on the train, Mrs. Liebowitz, if you would like to accompany Ernest to Philadelphia and see him play."

Lon's intention was more than diplomatic. Having an athlete's mother in the stands made him play his best. It was sound football philosophy.

"On this short notice?" Mary spoke without turning around, but Stagg felt her wrath just the same. *"Somebody* has got to stay here and keep up the house and feed the stock, and that somebody is likely to be *me!*" She tried a different approach. "It's been forty years since you worked the river, Ernie. I won't have you going off and losing our savings."

"I won't lose," Liebowitz said.

He rubbed his fingertips together gingerly. It was true that he had not played cards professionally since before the war. Before retiring to his farm, he had earned a living as a surveyor and drainage contractor. Cards did not matter the way they once had, but it had pleased him to learn to shuffle and deal with one hand better than most men could with two.

God bless Hudson Stroud, he thought.

"He won't come alone, you know," Mary doggedly insisted. She had lost and she knew it.

Stagg looked from wife to husband and back again. To hear them talk, one might think that something more serious than football was going on. To Alonzo Stagg, nothing was more serious than football.

"Let's see," Liebowitz said happily, sipping his coffee. "He'll probably invite Harry Nelson to back his play at stud poker. Hudson always admired Little Harry. And he'd want Abraham Weinstein to handle straight poker. No, wait, Abe died last summer. Well, there's Colonel Isaac Pitts down in Cincinnati. For vingt-et-un he will probably turn to Knot Dickinson. Hudson also likes Babe Whittaker for vingt-et-un, but Dickinson lives in Baltimore."

"What's vantayun?" Stagg said, perplexed.

Liebowitz drew a deck of cards out of his shirt pocket. He dealt them each a hand, one card face down, the other face up.

"Aces count one," he explained, "or eleven. Face cards count ten. Goal is to hit twenty-one without going bust. Card?"

Stagg, a natural competitor, peeked at his hole card. Liebowitz did not look at his. He had a queen of hearts showing. Stagg showed a four of diamonds.

"Stroud and his bunch may have the advantage of us," Liebowitz remarked, thinking out loud, "seeing as how people seem to live longer down South. Don't know if their longevity derives from the warm climate or the quality of the liquor or the women's pampering."

Mary turned her back on her husband.

"I'll take a card," Stagg said. Liebowitz dealt him a six of clubs.

"Men last longer down there," Liebowitz continued. "Stroud's probably still going strong. But I've got a few friends and partners who can still cut the mustard. I'm good."

Stagg invited Ernest Junior to kibitz. The quarterback peeked at the coach's hole card and advised him to stand pat. Stagg flipped his bottom card over. It was a jack of spades.

"Do I win?" Lonny said.

"No, you lose."

Liebowitz turned up his ace in the hole.

Chapter Fourteen

The team stood bunched together on the tiny platform of the Bardstown Junction station. "What is it like on a train?" they asked Brother.

"Like riding a wagon, except faster," he said.

Actually, Brother had never ridden a train except the way they all had—having caught on to the bottom rung of a freight-car ladder until the slow-moving train began to pick up speed. Like his teammates, Brother gazed down the curving tracks where the L & N *President* would imminently appear.

As they waited, they nervously passed back and forth their patched, scarred football. It went from hand to hand. Everybody seemed to need to touch it.

Kate perched on a heavy trunk secured with leather straps. She felt overdressed in a velvet skirt and jacket, satin blouse and silk cravat. The players sneaked uneasy glances at her wide-brimmed hat with ribbons and a blue ostrich feather exploding from the crown.

Kate was unaware of their stares. She was having second thoughts about not having told her parents good-bye. She rationalized that they would have made a scene.

Packing her bags had been like taking inventory: what to keep and what to leave behind? Her prized possessions included riding boots of hand-tooled leather, bought with her first paycheck from Post Oak School; a pendant watch, a graduation present from her parents engraved *University of Louisville, 1881;* an Add-A-Pearl necklace with pearls from twenty-three Christmases; her grandmother's diamond ring which she had always known would someday be hers but which—with its tight circle of mortality—always made her sad.

Selecting these keepsakes was like trimming away the fat of her existence, the debris of birthdays and Valentine Days, a litter of earrings, colognes, chains, bracelets, buckles, bows and boxes, coats, dresses, nightgowns, hats, belts, gloves, stockings, shoes; and presents her students of fourteen years had given her: hand-embroidered scarves, quilted comforters, pencil holders made from tin cans, wood carvings of birds, dogs, horses, and lions, crayon sketches of Joan of Arc. Culling through her possessions and selecting for her journey only what was essential had made her feel lean and light as a bird, as free as she believed she could be.

Now she sat on the trunk containing her net worth—some eight hundred dollars in cash and coin and perhaps twelve hundred in jewelry—ready to travel. She knew she could get her team there and back. The rest was up to them. She felt their stares and flashed them a merry smile which they instinctively returned.

She told herself that she was doing it all for them, and knew that she was lying.

Eight miles south along the L & N line, steam and noise enveloped the Lebanon Junction station as the *President* came to a screeching halt. Joints locking between cars rang an iron chorus. Chase was the first passenger to board, carrying on his shoulder Hudson's footlocker without bothering to wonder what made it so heavy.

Humboldt was next to board, dapper in bowler and vest, full of expectations. Henry, with the fixed expression of a man fighting a king-sized hangover, helped Hudson board.

Stroud hummed an old Rebel marching tune as they took their seats. He was wearing a gray wool suit and his best mahogany peg. A starched handkerchief was folded neatly in his breast pocket. In his lapel was a brass pin that read *5th KY VOL.*

Before they left Bardstown, Henry had taken Hudson to the bank. He had been surprised to find that his father-in-law had over five thousand dollars in deposits. When Hudson asked to withdraw the entire sum, the banker had taken Henry aside and appealed to him. The banker suspected hardening of the arteries. It was not unprecedented, he said, for relatives to call a physician to administer morphine on the spot. Henry told him it was none of his business.

Their next stop was the Western Union office, where Hudson had sent a series of mysterious telegrams. It took over thirty minutes to dispatch them. He harassed the operator by watching him tap out each letter.

Hudson tried to explain to Henry what was going on. "For stud poker there's none better than Little Harry. He's in the banking business in Louisville now. For twenty-one it's a tossup between Babe Whittaker and Knot Dickinson. Knot's handier, in Baltimore. Abe Weinstein was my man for straight poker, but the heatstroke took him. Maybe Isaac Pitts can fill that slot for us. If these hosses are still kicking they can do some damage."

The conductor rang his bell. The *President* made a sudden lurch. Laughing at his father's hangover pallor, Chase waved goodbye to Henry, who stood on the platform. Then he stopped laughing. He pressed his face to the window and watched Henry receding in the distance until the station was no longer in sight.

As the clacking of the wheels increased, Humboldt began to pat his knee in time with it. Hudson propped his foot on his locker and reached into his pocket. He unscrewed the top of a flask and offered it to the professor.

"Let's drink," he said, "to passing the time."

Below Bardstown Junction, where the track curved out of sight, a white plume caught the team's attention. Kate and her players stood up. Above the trees a racing cloud marked the progress of the hidden locomotive. The *President's* whistle spoke to them and they responded with an excited murmur. Still, they were unprepared for the wave of fear and longing which burst over them when the train sprang around the bend, great wheels straining as if nothing could hold it back.

Part II

Chapter Fifteen

"We done left Nelson County?" Tree asked Brother.

"We're nearly to Louisville." Brother stared out the window at the passing hills. The farther from Bardstown they went, the quieter the Post Oak players became. Kate slumped in her seat, exhausted from the excitement of their departure. Hudson was the only one in their party who seemed to know what to do. He took a few reflective pulls at his flask and settled back for a nap. He awoke when the jerking of couplings told him they were entering Louisville.

As the train pulled into the Louisville station, Hudson saw a familiar figure waiting on the platform. Ross Fitzpatrick, Stroud's corporal and orderly in his 5th Kentucky squadron, leaned against a railing. Stroud recognized Fitzpatrick's determined frown.

There he is! Fitz, my man.

"Come 'ere, boy!" Hudson called to Brother, singling him out because he was the closest available black. Brother glanced up irritably, then let his face go blank. "See that gentleman standing there on the platform, the one in the brown suit? Go git his bags." Brother hesitated, glanced at Kate, who gave a subtle shrug of apology as if to say, "We have to humor him."

"I'll get it," Chase said quickly.

"No, that's all right," Brother said. "It's my job." Hudson was prepared to be irate. He watched Brother reluctantly leave the coach to fetch Fitzpatrick's luggage. "He didn't think he was just along fer the ride, did he?" Hudson called to Kate, who bristled but held her peace. The rest of the players looked out the window.

Fitzpatrick presented himself with a military salute that made Stroud feel thirty-five again. With his high cheekbones and narrow temples, Fitzpatrick resembled an Indian with blue Irish eyes. Hud saw that his former orderly, though pouchy of cheek, looked as undaunted and reliable as ever.

"Got your telegram, Sarge!" Fitzpatrick said. "Reportin' for duty."

Sarge, Hudson thought happily.

"Wife said, 'What about Christmas?' I said, 'Sarge needs me.'"

"Do indeed, Fitzy. Mighty proud you could make it." Hudson introduced his traveling companions. "Miss Kuykendall, meet Ross Fitzpatrick. And this here's my daughter Edwina's boy, Chase. These burly rascals"—he indicated the Post Oak players with a casual gesture—"are Miss Kuykendall's students at the Post Oak School near Bardstown. They like to play *football*. Ever hear of it?"

"I do believe I have," Fitzpatrick said, adding, "Sarge, I seen your friend Harry Nelson at the station. He'll be boardin' any minute. He told me a gentleman name of Pitts plans to meet up with you in Cincinnati."

"Colonel Isaac Pitts!" Stroud exclaimed. "It's coming together. Tell you what, let's see if we can find us an empty Pullman where we can do some serious card playin'." Hudson saw Brother enter the coach carrying Fitzpatrick's suitcases. "Don't put 'em down yet, boy. We're movin' next door."

Brother did not look at Kate or his teammates but held the bags and waited for instructions. His glance flicked across Chase's face. Chase crossed his arms in silent protest.

Harry Nelson soon found Stroud. Their reunion was cause for breaking out the bonded whiskey. Hudson was delighted to see Little Harry looking so well. Dapper and elegant, Nelson wore a tweed coat, affected a pencil-thin mustache, and carried a gold-knobbed cane. After celebrating for an hour or so, Hudson took a sudden nap. Fitzpatrick and Nelson, having just met, and with little to talk about, found it expedient to do likewise. Afterward they all went to the dining car and told war and poker stories over lunch.

As the train crossed the Ohio River Bridge, Kate noticed that her players grew tense. They stared at the shining water with eyes bulging.

"What's the matter with them?" she whispered to Brother.

"They can't swim," he said. "Neither can I."

In Cincinnati their party was obliged to change to the Pennsylvania Railroad line. They boarded the next train to Columbus, Pittsburgh, and Philadelphia. The gamblers welcomed Colonel Isaac Pitts to their Pullman car. Hudson appraised his old crony—once the vingt-et-un terror of the Mississippi—and was relieved to see Pitts as lean and straight as ever. Nelson confidentially asked Stroud about Pitts's title. Hudson replied that Pitts had been called Colonel as long as he had known him. The title apparently derived not from military service but from Ohio custom, as a mark of respect. Stroud had inferred that the title was honorary and had never inquired about it. As Pitts never volunteered any information, Hudson naturally assumed it was a closed topic.

"How's your wife?" he asked Pitts.

"She passed away."

"Sorry to hear it."

"That's all right. She's been gone these eleven years."

"I heard you live in a big, fancy house." Hudson steered away from death.

"Sold it. I stay at the retirement hotel now."

"How is it?" Nelson asked with sudden interest.

"Not bad," Pitts remarked. "If you like enemas." Everybody laughed except Hudson.

"How are your children?" Stroud inserted youth into the conversation.

"Fine, I guess. I don't hear from 'em except at Christmas. They send me a crate of oranges from Florida."

"That's nice."

"Well, you know, I can't digest 'em. Give 'em away."

"Let's play cards," Hudson said.

Little Harry dealt a hand of draw poker. At first Hudson enjoyed himself, but he could not help noticing hands fumble with cards, eyes and memory not as sharp as they used to be.

Nelson tried to deal from the bottom without their catching him at it—just for fun—and the cards slipped out of his hand. Harry grunted in embarrassment. Pitts and Fitzpatrick politely looked the other way. Hudson took a closer look at Nelson's hands. The knuckles were swollen.

"You got arthritis?" he said.

"Just a touch," Harry said.

"They say garlic rub is right effective for arthritis," Pitts said alertly.

"Tincture of opium's what I use," Nelson said, avoiding Hudson's disapproving stare.

Pitts attempted to stack the deck. When he dealt the cards Hudson said, "I was s'posed to have *what?*"

"Full house, jacks over fours," Pitts said hopefully.

"I got nothin'! I got trash. What happened?"

"I must've messed up," Pitts apologized. "Let me try it again."

"Let's just play straight poker, nothing fancy," Hudson said irritably. He refused to let it fall apart on him and concentrated fiercely on his cards.

"Actually, I didn't know if I'd be able to make the trip or not," Pitts said conversationally. "Catarrh had me down." Hudson glared at him.

"Cubeb berries are good for catarrh," Fitzpatrick said helpfully.

"Smoking jimsonweed's not bad," Nelson offered.

"Crush the cubeb berries up fine and smoke 'em in a pipe," Fitzpatrick added. "One pipeful will clean your sinuses out clear as a bell. You got to blow the smoke out your nose, though."

"It's your deal, Fitzy!" Hudson said. "Play cards."

During the next hand, Nelson tried a bluff that did not work. He had obviously forgotten how many cards the others had taken on the draw. Pitts drew attention away from Nelson's error by taking a swig from a bottle of patent medicine.

"Is that Triple Six?" Nelson was grateful for the diversion.

"Yes indeedy! Great little tonic. Take it six times a day."

"Ever try IQS?" Nelson displayed a similar-size bottle he kept in his inside breast pocket.

"Iron-quinine-strychnine!" Pitts exclaimed. "Know it well."

"The quinine's for a touch of malaria that won't quit," Nelson explained. Hudson could feel his blood pressure rising.

"You got to watch that strychnine," Fitzpatrick said sociably. "Too much of that'll put you in rigor mortis." He showed them some patent medicine he carried.

"Dr. Caldwell's Syrup of Pepsin?" Nelson read the label. "Troubled with constipation?"

"Off and on, like everybody else."

"I keep good old Epsom salts for that," Nelson confided. "With castor oil in reserve."

"The colon buster!" Pitts said. They had a good laugh, all except Hudson. Pitts added, "Wheaten bran in a glass of water's mighty good for constipation."

"What the hell!" Hudson exploded. "I'da thought you ladies carried Lydia Pinkham, too, 'cept you've all entered menopause." He threw his cards down on the portable table between the bench seats. "This bunch couldn't beat a moron playing Go Fish. Why the hell did I think I could count on you!"

The old men sat holding their cards in silence. Nelson cleared his throat. "Hudson, you're going to have a stroke if you don't watch out. Somebody get his heart medicine."

"Never mind my ticker. You cain't even hold on to yo' cards, Harry. Keep slipping outa yo' hand onto the table. Cain't remember what you discarded. Pitts cain't stack a measly full house for a four-hand deal. What's gonna happen in Philydelphia when the deal is for six, eight hands?"

They nodded tolerantly, which made Hudson even angrier. Fitzpatrick dug into Stroud's trunk for his heart pills. Hudson refused to accept the vial. "Don't patronize me! I'm the onliest one here knows what the hell he's doing."

Pitts's face grew solemn. "Maybe playing poker for that old sword of yours ain't the way to go about getting it back. If you want it so blamed bad, why not hire somebody to knock Liebowitz over the head and take it away from him?"

"You're missing the point," Hudson said indignantly. "Just getting the sword back ain't all I'm interested in."

"What else do you want?" Little Harry said.

"I reckon if you'da been in Sandusky Prison you wouldn't have to ask that question." Hudson threw the vial of heart pills into his trunk and reached for the bourbon.

In the adjoining day coach, Kate was eager to find something to distract her players from thinking about their stomachs. Once they had gotten used to riding on the train, they remembered how hungry they were.

How can their parents afford to feed them?

In twenty-four hours she had spent nearly fifty dollars, or one sixth of her cash, on meals alone, and she feared the food vendors who strolled through the cars hawking snacks: buns, tarts, apples, and cheese rolls. The players would cast pitiable looks at her while she stared sternly out the window and ignored the vendor until he left the coach. Her players were like huge nestlings who never got enough. Kate had an idea. She asked Chase to instruct her team in signal-calling technique.

"Pay attention!" she commanded them.

"Well, now," Chase said, standing at one end of the coach. The players leaned into the aisle and watched him. "There's hand signals, which you use when crowd noise is too loud to hear the quarterback. Such as"—Chase demonstrated—"pull up trousers on right side means Right-half-between-center-and-right-guard; or pull up trousers on left side means Left-half-between-center-and-left-guard."

To encourage her players' interest, Kate repeated Riddle's gestures. The Panthers looked back and forth between Chase and her as if they were crazy.

"Right hand on right thigh," Chase continued, "means Right-half-between-right-tackle-and-right-end. Likewise, *left* hand on *left* thigh means . . . what?" Chase pointed at Weasel for the correct answer. Weasel gave a five-second shrug.

"I doan know . . . yo' leg itches or sump'm," he said. All the players laughed, including Brother.

"It means Left-half-between-left-tackle-and-left-end!" Kate sang out determinedly. "Don't stop, Chase!"

"Right hand on right knee: Right-half-between-right-tackle-and-right-guard. Left hand on left knee? Brother?" Chase called.

"Left-half-between-left-tackle-and-left-guard," Jones said reluctantly. He could not help being irritated to see Chase replace him as Kate's first lieutenant.

"That's good!" Chase was quick to encourage participation. "Now, besides hand signals you have word signals, such as 'Brace up now' means Right-half-over-right-tackle. Or 'Now brace' means Fullback-over-right-guard. Or 'Hold them men' means Left-half-over-left-tackle. Stuff like that. Or numbers can be used. You number the holes away from the center: 4, 6, 8, 10 going right and 5, 7, 9, 11 going left. Then you number the players, with the center being 1, right side of line 2, 4, 6; left side is 3, 5, 7; the backs are 8, 9, 10, 11. So when the captain calls 9-5-8, the 9 means nothing, 5 is the ballcarrier, and 8 is the hole. So here we have left tackle (5) carrying between right tackle and right end (8 hole). Got it?"

With the exception of Brother, the Post Oakians fidgeted uncomfortably in their seats. Their faces grew long. They stared at Chase's chest or his shoes or over his head, anywhere but his face. He looked inquiringly at Kate, who nodded for him to continue.

"All right, here's a problem for you to solve. Using numbers as signals, how do you call Left-half-between-left-guard-and-left-tackle? How about you, big fella?" He pointed at Tree.

"I'd jest say, 'Give it to Weasel,' " Tree said. He paused while his teammates chuckled. "Weasel know how to pick his own hole, so I wouldn' take it on me to tell him which way to run," Tree concluded. The players murmured their appreciation.

"We *do* have signals," Brother told Chase defensively. "However rudimentary they may sound to you." Chase's face went blank as he grappled with "rudimentary." Brother continued, "I might say, 'Weasel around right end,' or 'Tree up the middle.' Then we have our own, secret signals, like 'ring around the rosies,' which means an end-around, or 'the rabbit play,' which is a double reverse. It's not fancy but it gets the job done."

"I see your point," Chase said diplomatically. "Still, there *are* the tried and true signals that everybody knows. Why don't we just practice a few more . . . just to kill time before lunch."

"There's no hurry!" Kate cried. "We've plenty of time."

That afternoon the train made a forty-five-minute stop at Zanesville, Ohio, to take on fuel and water. Chase suggested to

Kate that the team take advantage of the stopover by conducting a practice in a vacant lot. She thought it was a wonderful idea.

The Post Oak players self-consciously changed clothes, ducking out of sight of the windows. They folded their Sunday suits, put away their shoes, and donned overalls and homemade jerseys. Barefoot, they picked their way across the cinder roadbed, more concerned with the arrival of another train than with the cold, hard ground.

Chase assembled them in the lot. They waited to see what he would do. When he had played with them at Post Oak School, he had been their guest. Now it was different. They looked at Brother, who crossed his arms as if to say, "Riddle is on his own."

Kate hovered nearby. She could not help noticing that Chase stood with back arched and head thrust forward. He seemed to throb with energy. His head weaved back and forth. When he spoke his mouth was dark and red. She shook her head to drive out the unbidden thought.

"How about some cals to loosen up!" Chase enjoyed being out of doors. "Jones, help me lead them."

Irritated with himself for being pleased, Brother stood alongside Chase and faced the team. They stood solemnly in their homemade practice uniforms, waiting for instructions. Chase demonstrated a side-straddle hop. Brother caught on quickly and began to exercise in time with him. The team picked up the rhythm, clapping their hands. Some Zanesville boys came running to watch them. Brakemen paused while uncoupling railroad cars, interested in the spectacle.

"*One-two-one-two!* If you don't mind my asking," Brother spoke in an aside to Chase while jumping and clapping, "what are we letting ourselves in for? *One-two-one-two . . .*"

"You mean . . . Philadelphia?" Chase said. "*One-two-one-two! Just football, I reckon. I never been there . . . one-two . . .*"

"Well, if anybody ought to know, oughtn't you?"

"Why? *One-two-one-two . . .*"

"You've been around."

"What do you mean?" Chase stopped to assess Brother's face bobbing up and down beside him. The team also stopped. "All right, let's run in place!" Riddle addressed the team. "A hunnerd times. Keep 'em high. Count it out, Tree, Weasel! *One-two-three-four . . ."*

"What about us?" Brother ran in place beside Chase, jerking his knees high.

"Relax, enjoy the trip, don't worry."

"We're not actually going to get to play, are we?"

"Who knows?"

"Seriously, we're just along for the ride and to carry your bags? That's what your granddaddy says."

Chase looked at Jones and realized with a start that he did not see color, only intelligence, a man to be reckoned with. He stopped running in place and the team stopped again too. Grateful for any respite from Brother's dark eyes, Chase yelled at them, "Did I tell you to quit? Keep it up! *Twenty-eight, twenty-nine, thirty . . .* Weasel, pick up the count."

"What about us?" Brother said stubbornly.

"All right, you probably won't get to play. That shouldn't come as any big surprise to you."

"Why are we going through the motions, then?"

"Because it's a long time to sit on a train. Because it'll keep Miz Kate happy. She's gone to a lot of trouble for y'all."

They glanced toward the tracks, where Kate stood looking on anxiously.

"I know she has," Brother agreed, "and I appreciate it. It's just . . ."

"What?"

"Well, what would it take for us to play?"

Chase gave him a hard look. "You're serious, aren't you! You realize our squad will have some of the greats of the Southern Conference: Cow Nalley, Blondy Glenn . . ."

"Chase Riddle," Brother said. "No, why be modest?" He smiled disarmingly. Something Chase had said was worth smiling about: he had said *our* squad.

"One hunnerd!" Weasel cried and the players stopped running in place.

"Okay, let's run some plays," Chase told them. "We'll start with tackle-back, buck over right guard. Let's walk through it, first. Take your positions."

As he had taught them in the Post Oak playground, Chase first instructed them to shift formations at a walk, then at half speed, then full speed. One of the Ohio boys watching them ventured forward.

"You gonna play a game or what?" he yelled.

"Not here," Brother replied. "The game's in Philadelphia. Want to go?"

The team clapped and yelled excitedly. Chase saw Brother's wry look and grinned ruefully. The conductor rang his bell, and the engineer gave a short blast on his whistle.

"We got time for a few wind sprints before the train leaves!" Chase called. "Hurry and line up over there. Backs first."

As the players sprinted back and forth at his command, Chase heard a harsh cry of winter. He looked up in surprise. It was only a flock of gracklings, heading for roost against a darkening sky.

"What's the matter?" Brother alertly asked.

"Oh, nothing."

"It was just some blackbirds."

"I know. It's just habit. I been waiting to be called . . ."

"Called?"

"You know, to the ministry. I been watching for a sign."

"Sign? Like, from heaven?"

"That's right!" Chase sniffed, drew himself up. "And now I been called."

"To preach."

"Well, actually, for the time being, to play football."

"You mean, in Philadelphia?"

"That's right." Chase gave a go-signal and a wave of sprinters took off running.

"You received a sign?"

"Uh-huh."

"What was it?"

"I cain't explain it."

"What was it?"

"It wasn't so much what it was, itself, as how it happened." Chase nervously spun the football in his big hands.

"What was college like?" Brother changed the subject. Chase saw vulnerability in his eyes.

"You want to go, don't you?" he said.

"We can't all be laborers," Brother said angrily. "There aren't enough ditch-digging jobs to go around."

"I didn't mean anything! I think it's real good that you want to go to college. I hope you get there. Course, for some of us, college ain't all it's cracked up to be."

"Did you graduate?" Brother asked after a moment's pause.

"I was there to play ball. I didn't hardly go to class. Everybody ain't meant to graduate from college. But I think you'd be real good at it. You looking for a scholarship?"

"Yeah."

"We both waiting for a call. Where do you want to go?"

"I'm not in a position to be choosey: Fisk, Tuskegee, Morehouse, wherever they'll have me." He noticed that Chase was not familiar with the names of the colleges and added, "There's no football at those institutions that I know of."

When Chase again gave him a wary look, Brother smiled and Riddle's lean face flattened in a wide grin. The engineer blew his whistle, high and plaintive. The team gathered around, breathing deeply from their sprints.

"All right," Chase told Brother while the others listened, "you want to play football? I'll teach you quarterbacking if you'll teach me what Rudy something means."

"Rudimentary?" Brother said.

"That's him." Then Chase yelled, "Last one to the train has to walk to Philadelphia!"

The Panthers took off with a whoop, leaping the tracks in a pell-mell rush. Brother laid a staying hand on Chase's arm and pointed to the adjacent Pullman coach where Hudson and his cronies had established themselves. A Rebel battle flag was hanging in the window.

Couplings jerked and clanged as the train slowed to cross the Schuylkill River in Philadelphia. Hudson's friends were taking an after-lunch nap. Using his hat for a pillow, Little Harry lay curled up on the seat. Ross Fitzpatrick dozed with his mouth open. Isaac Pitts cat-napped sitting up, as if true to his military title even in sleep.

Maybe it's the alcohol, Hudson thought. *Maybe their wives ration them and they're not in drinking shape.*

As if his own body spoke in reply, Hudson's heart fluttered with an irregular beat. He took a deep breath and shrugged off the congested, stuffy feeling. From Wheeling to Pittsburgh, Altoona, and Harrisburg his friends had continued to joke about their ailments and share remedies for gout, rheumatism, and arthritis. They had been curious to see how Stroud's peg fitted his stump. Their card-playing ability had not noticeably improved, and Hudson had resorted to honeymoon bridge with Fitzpatrick. His companions occupied themselves with decorating the coach with Confederate memorabilia. At Harrisburg, Colonel Pitts had even persuaded the engineer to allow a Rebel battle flag to be flown on the locomotive. Their excitement had lasted exactly as long as a quart of bourbon before they went back to sleep. Hudson wondered if Liebowitz was also asleep on some train between Cleveland and Pittsburgh. How good was Liebowitz? he wondered. How much better would Liebowitz's backup players be than these gently snoring old soldiers?

Well, I'd rather go down with my own than win with strangers I don't care nothing about.

"Wake up, boys," Hudson said. "We're there."

In the next car Kate and her players sat motionless as the train eased into Philadelphia's Broad Street Station. Brother and his teammates watched dark steel pillars passing outside their windows. They took shallow breaths, unconsciously imitating the dying *chuff* of the engine boilers. A southbound freight hurtled past with a sudden, suicidal roar. Then the Broad Street terminal emerged into view, its vaulted ceiling brilliantly lit by arc lights. On the seat opposite Kate, Chase grinned. He was entering a new dimension, far from Big Dad, the Widow Cobb, or Cousin Minnie. Professor Humboldt, however, was not smiling.

"Look!" he said, pointing.

Hundreds of people crowded the center platform. Seeing the Rebel flag decorating the Kentuckians' car, the mob rushed forward. Men beat on the sides of the coach. Chase saw their passionate faces and was more puzzled than afraid. He glanced at his companions. Even the largest of the black players—Tree and Link—seemed to have shrunk two shirt sizes. Kate instinctively moved toward the door at the end of their coach, intending to lock it, but it burst open just as she reached for it. The conductor squeezed through the partly opened door and a wave of noise flooded the coach. He fumbled to lock the door. His hat was tilted as though in apology.

"You'll have to remain on board until things quiet down," he told them.

"What's going on?" Chase asked.

"I don't know." The conductor straightened his hat as if restoring order. "Please remain in your seats. There is no reason to be alarmed."

"He's crazy," Weasel whispered to Tree. "That looks like a lynch mob to me."

"Hush, Weasel," Tree said.

In the adjoining coach, Hudson was not unduly concerned. Any veteran knew a skirmish line when he saw one. His comrades looked to him for directions.

"It's nice to know somebody's expecting us," Stroud said.

Arno Ziprenian fought his way through the noisy throng. He had hoped for public response to the Southern team's arrival, but this was more than he had bargained for. In his pocket was a folded *Inquirer* containing Harry Prescott's article entitled "Rebels on the March." A heavyset woman poked her elbow into Ziprenian's stomach. Her nose was red. She had apparently been struck in the face and was clearing a space around her. The Zipper sank back to accommodate her. At the same time, a steam cloud wafted over the crowd, and people pressed forward expectantly, nearly lifting Ziprenian off his feet. He had never before seen Philadelphians so aroused. The riots of 1895 during the Amalgamated Railway Workers' strike seemed parliamentarian by comparison. Standing on tiptoe he saw men tearing at a window to raise it enough to pull out the Confederate battle flag. They got hold of it and ripped it out of the coach. A man was lifted to his fellows' shoulders. Ziprenian saw that he was chewing a piece of the Rebel flag, his cheeks stuffed full of cloth.

"Go home, Rebels!"

A chant began at the rear of the mob where people, being less pressed together, were at leisure to enjoy the spectacle and contribute inspiration.

"Go home, Rebels!"

At first only a few voices sang together. The crowd was slow to take up the chant. Philadelphians, Ziprenian noted, had little practice in mob action. Soon, however, the rhythm caught on and five hundred voices roared as one:

"GO HOME, REBELS!"

Stepping off a train that had arrived on another track, an elegantly attired young man observed the scene with scientific detachment. He was, in fact, a sociologist (Ph.D., Harvard 1895), newly affiliated with the University of Pennsylvania, where he had been hired to prepare a scholarly study of the Negro community of Philadelphia. His dissertation, *The Suppression of the African Slave Trade to the United States of America, 1638–1870,* would soon be published. He had studied abroad and affected the dress of a German student: high silk hat, gloves, and cane. He was slender, of medium height, with a Vandyke beard, a nut-brown complexion, and an air of assurance. His name was William Edward Burghardt (Will) Du Bois.

"GO HOME, REBELS!"

Du Bois was intrigued. During his brief tenure in Philadelphia he had come to know a corrupt and contented city incapable of such spontaneous emotion. He examined the crowd from a sociologist's perspective. Choosing a small section at random, he made some general observations: 16 percent female to 84 percent male; 50 percent working class, 48 percent middle class, 2 percent upper class; 90 percent white, 5 percent Semitic or Oriental, 5 percent black. Whether this small section of the mob was representative of the demography of the whole, Du Bois could only speculate. Curious as to what could provoke such a broad spectrum of society, he watched to see who would emerge from the train.

"GO HOME, REBELS!"

Inside the coach, the Kentuckians listened to the mob and looked at each other. Chase stood up.

"Excuse me, Miz Kate," he said, "but I'm going to see what the hell is going on."

Brother got up and followed Chase. He affected a swagger that belied his doubts. The other players, however, were happy to see their number-one man meet this challenge head-on.

"Look at Brother," Weasel told Tree. "Somebody in for trouble."

On the platform between the cars Chase ran into Hudson. Grandfather and grandson had never looked more alike, their lean faces chiseled into sharp angles. Hudson leaned on a crutch and carried a miniature Rebel flag in his other hand.

"GO HOME, REBELS!"

As though the mob had extended an invitation, the three men stepped forward at the same time. Brother, jostled accidentally by Chase, lost his balance and reached out to steady himself. He caught Hudson's little flag, and as he stumbled he seemed to wave it about. The crowd gasped and fell silent. A photographer's flashpan exploded. The smell of burning sulfur filled the air. A cloud of smoke boiled up. In worshipful confusion, the mob watched it rise. Into the silence a high-pitched voice inserted the word *"Tom!"* The exclamation rang through the terminal like a sexton's bell. Brother looked into the mass of hostile faces. Other voices picked up the cry.

"Tom, Tom, Tom, Tom . . ."

When Brother realized that he was holding a Rebel flag, his face burned in embarrassment. He thrust the flag back at Hudson and yelled at Chase, "What do we do now?"

"Get off the train, I reckon." Chase was sizing up the demonstrators. He was a head taller than most of them. He stepped down and the closest man silently gave way. Brother followed at Chase's heels. Hudson remained on the steps, unable to get down without assistance. He held up his flag and gave it a defiant little twitch. The crowd responded with renewed cries of disapproval while letting Chase and Brother through.

An avenue opened before them. Into their path stepped Arno Ziprenian. He firmed up the knot in his tie and pulled his coat straight. In sky-blue suit and beaver hat he gleamed with goodwill. Under his arm he carried an ebony walking stick with a silver knob. He showed perfect teeth in a winning smile. At the back of the crowd Will Du Bois stood on tiptoe to see.

"My name is Arno Ziprenian." The Zipper spoke loudly to be heard over the crowd. "It is my supreme honor to welcome you on behalf of the All-Star Game Committee."

"Excuse me, but is *this,*" Chase gestured at the people, "part of the welcoming committee?"

"Do not worry. It is part of our publicity campaign. I have not seen this city so excited about something in my life. Everything is fine, you'll see. And, sir, you are . . . ?"

"Chase Riddle, Bardstown."

Arno glanced at Brother, wondering if Southerners still traveled with body servants.

"This is Mister Jones," Chase said. "He's a football player, like me."

The Zipper paid attention. He had not seriously considered the football game or its players as anything other than devices for making money. No one had told him that Negroes played football. While Ziprenian was considering this new development, the crowd began to boo and hiss.

Weasel stuck his head out the door of the train and, followed timidly by Tree and Ulysses and the rest of the players, led his teammates onto the platform. A flashpan popped and smoked as they stepped off the train. Behind them were Kate and Professor Humboldt, then Hudson and his cronies, wearing Confederate insignia in their lapels and waving miniature Rebel flags.

Harrison Prescott urged his photographer to take as many pictures as possible. Prescott could scarcely believe his prophetic powers. In his mind's eye he could see tomorrow's headline: SONS OF SLAVES PLAY FOR SOUTH.

"Right this way, gentlemen!" Ziprenian cried. "Your transportation awaits. Come this way."

A squad of blue-coated policemen rushed to form a cordon between the mob and the flag-waving Confederates. Hudson glanced at his old companions. Now there was no talk of arthritis or psoriasis. With a riverboat saunter they made their way through the angry throng.

"What is going on?" Du Bois asked a stout Irishwoman.

"Oh, the paper says we be invaded by Johnny Reb!" she replied.

"Are they soldiers, then?"

"Footballers."

"What do they do?"

"Play football." The woman regarded him with Irish good humor.

"Is it like German football?" he asked. "Germans play *Fussball.*"

"Sure, I wouldn't know. I never seen 'em play that neither."

"And who are those Negro men?"

"Them?" she cried. "Why, they be the Black Rebels! Ain't that wonderful strange?"

The sociologist watched the crowd close in behind the players as they filed out of the station. Something "wonderful strange" was occurring and Du Bois was resolved to get to the bottom of it.

Outside Broad Street Station a trolley car waited on the tracks in the street. The Post Oak student athletes hesitantly boarded it, placing their feet carefully on the iron steps.

"What do you call this?" Cassius asked Brother.

"A streetcar, I think." Brother was still in shock over the "Tom" incident. The team watched, enchanted, as Italian laborers loaded their suitcases aboard the trolley.

As soon as the police disbanded, the mob made a last run at the team. Men drummed their fists on the sides of the trolley. They leaned their shoulders against the car and tried to rock it. The conductor threatened them with a piece of pipe. Kate and Humboldt boarded at the unattended rear door, while Stroud and his men hired a hansom cab to take them to their hotel. The conductor shouted at the engineer, and the trolley started off with a lurch. People ran alongside it for a block or so, cursing the players and telling them what they could do with their football.

As the trolley gathered speed and outdistanced its pursuers, Brother breathed a sigh of relief. Then to his horror, Ziprenian reached inside his coat, drew out a roll of red cloth, and unfurled a Rebel flag. He held it to the window, drawing the attention of pedestrians. People stopped and pointed, mothers sheltered their children, men shook their fists at the Confederate trolley car.

For their part, the Kentuckians simply stared at the sights of Philadelphia. High above City Hall the statue of William Penn looked out over his prosperous city. Workers cleaned the snow off the steps of Wanamaker's department store. The trolley passed Italian street markets, a Jewish bazaar with Hebrew signs, Chinatown. A freight wagon pulled by an eight-horse team crossed the tracks ahead of them. The drover thumbed his nose at the flag in the trolley window. A beer wagon raced alongside them. Children threw snowballs at the car. The conductor rang his bell again and again.

At first Brother was so confused and humiliated by the scene at Broad Street Station that he could hardly comprehend the city unfolding around him. Gradually he forgot the mob and its cries of "Tom."

His head continually turned this way and that to see posters of Gibson Girls, a billboard proclaiming Tony Pastor's Vaudeville Show, shop-window mannequins wearing the latest fashions. The trolley left the downtown district and entered neighborhoods of brownstone mansions. Then came wealthy Hunting Park, with three-story mansions and landscaped lawns under the snow. Farther north, smokestacks and factories crowded the horizon. They passed the John Stetson textile mills, the Kensington Iron and Steel Works, the Baldwin Locomotive Works, and a cramped workingman's suburb of boarding houses, taverns, and corner groceries. Gray houses leaned together in despair.

Ziprenian spoke to the conductor. The trolley car stopped in front of a four-story Victorian house with turrets and gables topped by a widow's walk with wrought-iron railing, all covered with a coat of blistering white paint—an aging dowager of a house overflowing her girdle. Behind a picket fence in the front yard, strapping young men tossed a football back and forth. They stared at the trolley and its occupants.

"Look!" Humboldt recognized two of the youths. "Cow Nalley of Georgia and Blondy Glenn of Alabama Poly."

"Gentlemen, we have secured accommodations for you at the Maison Blanche," Ziprenian announced. "You will be quite comfortable."

The Post Oak Panthers stared up at the widow's walk. None of them had been inside a building over two stories high.

"Lady up there," Weasel told Tree. "At the winder."

"More'n one lady," Tree observed. Other faces appeared ghostlike at the fourth-story windows.

Ziprenian noticed Kate and Humboldt appraising the peeling paint, the seedy neighborhood. "We secured these accommoda-

tions," he explained, "because of their proximity to training facilities." The Southerners followed his gesture past abandoned,
vandalized houses to a weed-choked vacant lot bordered by a
ravine full of rusted cans and other garbage.

"Training facilities?" Kate said.

"Open spaces," Ziprenian explained. "Where the team can
run and kick and keep fit. Shall we?"

As they got off the streetcar, two men hurried out of the hotel
to meet them. Humboldt recognized John Heisman, of Alabama
Polytechnic, and Glenn Warner, of Georgia. Heisman was lean
and spare, with a thick neck, a bullet-shaped head, short-cropped
brown hair, pointed ears, and a wide mouth. Warner was built
like an ox, with a blunt jaw, cauliflower ears, bushy eyebrows, and
a generous smile which disappeared when he noticed Ziprenian
loitering behind the streetcar.

"Are you Professor Humboldt?" Heisman asked. "Well, don't
unload your luggage yet."

Puzzled, Humboldt identified himself and introduced Kate as
Miss Kuykendall, with no further explanation regarding her or
her team.

"They promised us first-rate quarters," Warner growled. "Look
where they've put us—Mister Ziprenian?" Arno put his head
around the trolley, alert as a deer. "How do you expect us to field
a first-rate team operating out of third-rate facilities?"

The athletes in the yard listened attentively. Chase thought he
recognized one or two of them but hesitated to introduce himself
lest someone mention how many conferences he had played in.

"The man's an immigrant," Heisman muttered, as if this explained everything. "I don't know. The players don't seem to
mind this place." He shrugged as if conceding the unpredictabil-
ity of athletes.

Ziprenian slipped away and went around the house to the back
door of the Maison Blanche. He let himself in and, passing
through the kitchen, drew a curious stare from the cook, a large
black woman who was peeling potatoes.

"Put a few more in the pot," Ziprenian told her.

He went up a central hallway, where everything was red:

wallpaper, rug, lampshades, chairs. Gas lamps cast an intimate
glow. A faint, musky perfume hung in the air. On the first floor
were billiard, roulette, faro, and domino parlors. The second and
third floors housed suites for entertaining private parties. The
fourth floor was a brothel. Descending the central staircase arm
in arm were the proprietors, Mr. Dobson and Mrs. Adelaide
Brown. Ziprenian waited for them at the foot of the stairs.

Mrs. Brown dressed plainly, her black hair braided and pinned
severely. She was a head taller than her associate, Dobson, a tidy,
expressionless man with muttonchop whiskers. Ziprenian had
never seen him without his bowler hat.

"Who are the colored men outside?" Mrs. Brown began speaking before she reached floor level.

"Football players," The Zipper said. Mrs. Brown froze on the
next-to-last step, as did Dobson.

"They're not staying here?" she cried.

"Why, they're famous," Ziprenian said. "I'm surprised you
haven't heard of them already. They've only been in town a hour
and already they're famous, the notorious Black Rebels! Think of
the free publicity."

"Publicity I don't need," she snapped. "Ralph, say something,"
Without waiting for Dobson to speak she continued, "This is a
respectable sporting house. We don't allow the coloreds."

"Make an exception," Arno said.

"We'll lose business," she said.

"To the contrary, your customers will be honored."

"Ralph," she said.

"I'm with you," Dobson said.

"He's with me!" she said, as if it were settled.

"Let me put it this way," Ziprenian said wearily, "Mr. Canfield
is very interested in this football game. The players are supposed
to stay here. You are his employees . . ."

"I don't believe this is happening." Mrs. Brown went to the
window and peered out through the drapes. "Look at the size of
them. Where will they sleep? How does Mr. Canfield expect me
to feed them? I'll have to hire extra cooks."

"So hire them." Minor details bored Ziprenian. He was a man
of vision.

"It's not in my budget," she said.

"Mr. Canfield will make it up."

"The servants aren't going to like it. The cook and the maid and the houseboy. They don't like it, you know, waiting on their own kind."

Ziprenian began to move away, as if to emphasize that everything had been arranged. He waved his hand in a deprecating manner.

"You don't have to live here!" Mrs. Brown cried. "We all have to get along with each other, you know."

"You work it out. Mr. Canfield and I have every confidence in you."

"Where am I going to put them? They'll have to sleep on pallets. There aren't enough beds."

"Anything you say." Ziprenian had his hand on the doorknob.

"What about the white players?" Mrs. Brown fought a delaying action. "Maybe they won't sleep in the same room with the blacks?"

"They're on the same team, aren't they?" Arno called blithely and slipped out the door.

Heisman noticed the Post Oak players. "Who are they?"

"Our porters," Humboldt said quickly.

"Why is the conductor unloading their bags?" Heisman inquired.

"Why shouldn't he?" Kate replied. Heisman had not heard a woman speak so assertively since Rosalind in Shakespeare's *As You Like It*. Heisman was addicted to Shakespeare.

"Where are your other recruits?" Warner asked Humboldt.

"I. Lopez, the All-America center snapper from Texas, will arrive directly," Humboldt said.

"Lopez?" Warner said. "What All-America list was he on?"

"Offhand, I don't recall," Humboldt said distantly.

Warner offered to help Kate down from the trolley. She jumped down by herself. "Are you a football devotee?" Warner asked, intending to shed some light on her presence.

"I am a coach," Kate said.

"What say?"

"I am a coach."

"What sport?"

"Football."

Humboldt explained, "Miss Kuykendall is our nurse and trainer. She performs miracles with sprains . . ."

"The lady said she is a *coach,*" Heisman said.

"You may address me, sir, I am still present," Kate said.

"What team do you coach?" Heisman asked incredulously.

"That one." Kate nodded, indicating her players. The trolley pulled away with a creaking cable. Heisman and Warner observed the Negroes' patched clothes, pants too short, rawboned wrists sticking out of sleeves. Brother burned under the white men's appraisal.

"A Negro team?" Heisman said. He and Warner stared at the black players as if they were some rare species. "But the professor said they were porters!"

"They are seminary students," Kate said.

"What *is* this?" Warner said.

Humboldt hurried to explain. "I met Miss Kuykendall when I went to Bardstown to recruit Mister Riddle."

"And she recruited *you,*" Heisman interjected.

"They're here, John, we can't do anything about that, now," Warner said, shoving his hands in his pockets. "Let's go inside. I'm not used to the cold anymore."

"I haven't seen any black *college* teams," Heisman said suspiciously. "Maybe a high school team here and there." He did not wish anyone to think John Heisman was prejudiced. Didn't Auburn have a black mascot named Dabney?

"My players," Kate said, "are members of the Post Oak Methodist-Episcopal Seminary team in Bardstown, Kentucky. Their average height is six feet; average weight: 198 pounds. The backs run the hundred yards in under ten seconds. One of them runs it in nine point six."

"Nine-six!" Warner forgot the cold. "John, she said nine—"

"I timed them." Humboldt seized the advantage. "Miss Kuykendall is being too modest. All of the backs ran it in less than ten seconds, and that one"—he pointed at Cassius—"ran an honest nine-five. I therefore took the liberty of allowing them to join us here—as scrubs, or waterboys."

Heisman motioned to Warner to follow him off to one side.

"Waterboys that run a nine-five?" Heisman whispered, "What's going on?"

"I know one thing," Warner said. "That Riddle is a ringer. He's played for at least three schools that I know of. Fast, though. Great agility."

"What about the coloreds? I never heard of a colored ringer, did you?"

"How could there be? Negro colleges don't play football, do they?"

"I think Tuskegee Institute does," Heisman said thoughtfully, "just for fun, pickup teams on Sunday afternoons."

"Does this go back to Ziprenian?" Warner growled. "I wouldn't put it past him to meddle with our recruiting. That Jew is slick as a greased pig."

"I don't think he's Jewish, Glenn."

"What is he, then?"

"I think he's from one of those Bolshevik countries on the other side of Italy."

"Well, anyway, I wouldn't put it past him."

"I've never fielded a ringer." Heisman tucked his chin indignantly. "I'm not about to start now."

"Whew, it's cold," Warner complained. "Turns a man inside out." Heisman looked at him sharply.

"So, what's the verdict?"

"My toes are frozen." Warner hopped from one foot to the other. "Let's head 'em inside."

"Wait, what are you saying, dammit!"

"Cold as a witch's tit." Warner stamped his feet. "Listen, we haven't been here four hours or had the first practice. We don't even know all the players' names. Neither of us has ever coached a post-season game before, much less one this far from home. All I'm saying is, let's don't make snap judgments."

"I don't believe this," Heisman said.

"John, my friend." Warner hugged himself and shivered. "Do you mean to tell me you never had a fine, stout lad come out for the team in September, play havoc with the opposition, score a bushel of points, and then sort of disappear after Thanksgiving? And then come to find out the rascal had not attended class, failed to take final exams, nobody's sure what his real name was, and a rumor's going around that a well-heeled alumnus had something to do with it?"

"It's damned nippy." Heisman said briskly. "Let's go inside."

"Carter, Joiner!" Warner called to two players nearby. "Go help those boys with their bags. Let's go inside before we freeze to death."

Carter, a Jeffersonian scholar from Charlottesville, frowned, muttered angrily to Joiner of Chapel Hill that they oughtn't to have to carry a Negro's bags, but grudgingly did as his coach told him.

Seeing the white players approach them, Cassius edged close to Brother. "Who them?" he asked.

"Some All-Americas, probably," Brother said. He saw Chase laughing with the white players and wondered whose side Riddle was on.

"Best in America?" Cassius asked.

"That's what they say."

"We gotta play 'em?"

"We're on the same team."

"That's good."

Chapter Sixteen

Longstreet stood outside the Stratford Hotel on Broad Street. As he looked at Christmas shoppers rushing past, the thought occurred to him that he might have been mayor of Philadelphia—*hell, governor of Pennsylvania*—if Lee had listened to reason at Gettysburg. The image of himself in mayoral robes made the general smile.

On the other hand, I've been a lot of things I never expected to be: customs surveyor, railroad president, minister to Turkey, U.S. Marshal, hosteler.

He checked his watch—9:30 A.M., thirty minutes early for the meeting. Say what his critics would, they couldn't fault him on punctuality. He entered the hotel and looked around the lobby, searching for the mayor and aldermen. As no one came forward to greet him, he bought a newspaper at a newsstand and took a seat where he could see everything that was going on.

The general wore a dark suit with black tie and gray fedora. Peering over his newspaper he wondered if this was what it felt like to travel incognito. He was reminded of the Confederate spy, Harrison. *There* was a man with a comic aspect, like a mummer or a penny-theater actor. Longstreet idly wondered if Harrison's histrionics might have rubbed off on him. Today, behind his *Inquirer*, he felt clandestine, but more like a forward observer hidden in tall timber than a spy out of uniform. No West Point man would go into combat without his uniform.

Longstreet watched the lobby fill with people. He assumed that other general officers from Union and Confederate armies had also been invited. He hoped Jubal Early would not be among them. Longstreet flushed when he thought of Early's attack on him in the *Southern Historical Society Papers.*

As for General Early's ideas and information about Gettysburg, he has written just enough to show to military minds that he not only failed in his duties on the field of Gettysburg, but that he is not even capable of comprehending it after fourteen years of study . . .

Longstreet hoped he would not see Early. He did not know whether he could behave responsibly if they were to meet.

A group of men filtered out of the dining room. They looked fit and athletic and satisfied. They stood close to Longstreet, whose deafness in one ear made it difficult for him to hear what they were saying. They continually jostled one another in a muscular way, acting out their stories with abrupt movements and gestures.

"It was the Princeton-Yale game of eighty-nine," Lonny Stagg was saying. His eager listeners included the Father of American Football, Walter Camp, and the other coaches from South and North squads: Heisman, Warner, King, and Woodruff. Humboldt, knowing his place in such exalted company, stood behind Warner.

"In those days," Stagg continued, "the Yale quarter stood close behind the center to receive the foot-passed balls. Wurtemburg's signal for passing was to press two fingers on the hip of Hanson, the center. Princeton detected the signal, and House Janeway suggested to Long Tommy Thomas, who was six feet six, that he reach over and pinch Hanson's posterior. When the quarter, Wurtenburg, dropped back to confer with the halves, Long Tommy reached over and pinched Hanson, who automatically passed the ball back. Janeway broke through and fell on it for a Princeton first down. We were furious with Hanson and did not discover Princeton's infamous trick until the game was over."

The coaches laughed good-naturedly, yet they reminded Longstreet of opposing generals during an uneasy truce. Filled with well-being and a breakfast of scrapple and eggs, the coaches remained wary of one another. Their teams would soon meet in battle and they would face each other across the field, matching wits.

Heisman asked Phil King, "Can you teach Heffelfinger and company the Revolving Tandem in less than a week?"

"I doubt it," King joked. "Too complicated."

"How about those Negroes of yours?" Stagg asked Heisman, turning his head this way and that like a bear sniffing honey. Behind his newspaper Longstreet caught the word *Negroes* and leaned forward to hear better.

"You mean our scrubs?" Heisman said evasively. "They may shape up, and then again, they may not."

"How are they on signals?" Stagg said coyly.

"I don't know. What are you getting at?"

"I recall a story," Stagg said, "about a white man playing with a Negro pickup team against Tuskegee Institute. His captain called on him to carry the ball. He asked the captain, 'What about signals?' And the captain said, 'Dem niggers of mine couldn't learn no signals. I jes chatter some numbers to fool dem Tuskegees. De numbers don't mean nothin'. I'd say, 'Six billions, eighty-five millions, seven hundred and 'leven thousan', nine hundred an' ninety-nine, tek dat ball, Leroy, and go round dat lef' end!' " Stagg opened his mouth in a silent guffaw and the coaches laughed heartily, except for Heisman and Warner.

"There's no regular team at Tuskegee!" Heisman said.

"Pickup team, I think it was," Stagg said, subdued.

"I don't think Tuskegee Institute has a regular team, do you?" Heisman addressed Warner. "We were discussing that earlier, remember?"

"It was only a joke," Stagg said lamely. "Just a story I heard somewhere." The other Northerners, King and Woodruff and Camp, assumed conciliatory half-smiles.

"I'll have to check on that when I get back to Auburn," Heisman said, enjoying Stagg's discomfiture.

"Sure, I guess you . . ."

"Why shouldn't Negroes play football?"

"No reason in the world."

"I'm getting interested in Negro football."

"They're natural athletes," Stagg said hastily, "You have to give them that."

"All they lack is coaching."

"They have marvelous quickness!" Stagg was grinning a traditional type of grin.

"Very quick," Heisman said.

"How . . . uh . . . quick would you say?" Stagg added.

"Haven't timed ours yet." Heisman did not look at Humboldt.

Longstreet concentrated on his newspaper. A headline leaped out at him.

SONS OF SLAVES TO PLAY FOR SOUTH.

He remembered that scattered Negro Confederate units had fought in the war, but he had never endorsed such conscription or claimed that the slaves had fought willingly or even with full knowledge of what was happening.

What in the hell is going on?

Lonny Stagg noticed an athletic-looking young woman standing expectantly behind Heisman. He assumed she was someone's niece or daughter-in-law or wife, perhaps a member of a woman's club. These civic clubs were always after him to lecture on health and fitness. He wondered if Heisman was going to introduce her.

"Coach Stagg, Coach King, Coach Woodruff, Mr. Camp—may I introduce our . . . er . . . associate, Miss Kuykendall."

The lady's grip was as strong as a man's, her gaze frank and direct. Stagg had always liked women with strong hands. If he had not been a married man, he might have asked her to step into the tearoom for some strudel.

"In what capacity do you . . . uh . . . associate with Coach Heisman?" he asked.

Kate had joined the men late, not having been included in their breakfast plans. She had come to the hotel to stand on her rights. Heisman's evasive look stiffened her resolve.

"I am a coach."

"Tennis? Field hockey?"

"Football."

Warner looked for a potted plant to hide behind. Heisman stared at his shoes.

"She's part of your staff!" Stagg exulted.

Kate pointedly stared at Heisman until he mumbled his assent. Humboldt spoke up.

"Kate coaches our scrub team," he said. Heisman's head snapped up, with a frown of warning.

"Very interesting," Stagg observed. "Tell me about your team."

Kate flushed. She hardly knew where to begin. Her impulse was to tell everything: about organizing a team to restore school spirit at Post Oak; about ordering the ball, whistle, coach's uniform and cleats from Montgomery Ward; about crisp afternoons, the fighting, the shouts and laughter. Then she remembered that Post Oak had been transformed into a seminary.

"We run your mass momentum, tackle-back, and guard-back formations," she said.

"Oh, not mine!" Stagg proudly protested. "I don't claim to have invented them."

"They're in your book."

"You've read my book?" Stagg grew rosy with authorial pride.

"Matter of fact, I have it right here." Kate dug in a voluminous pocket and produced the treasured volume, *A Scientific and Practical Treatise on American Football for Schools and Colleges.* Stagg took the scuffed, clay-smeared book and held it up for the others to see. Over his newspaper Longstreet watched with interest.

"Would you do me the honor of inscribing it?" Kate added.

Stagg examined the dog-eared pages.

"I think you've gotten your money's worth," he said. "Your team obviously has a dedicated coach."

Kate dug in her pocket to find a pen. Stagg inscribed the book with a flourish:

> *To Miss Kuykendall,*
> *Good luck on the gridiron!*
> *A. A. Stagg*

While Stagg was writing, Heisman covertly asked Kate, "Do you mean you've read his book?"

"I've just about memorized it," Kate whispered.

"That's good to know," Heisman said. Stagg, having overheard this exchange, grinned uncertainly.

"Thank you very much," Kate said to Lonny. "It will be an honor to coach against you."

Confronted by this undaunted female who had memorized his book, Stagg experienced a premonition that was like wading into cold water. The cord in his sac drew his testicles close to the body cavity.

"Look at that!" Heisman pointed at the front door of the hotel, where General Sickles was making a grand entrance. Trailing clouds of reporters, civic leaders, and former military men, Dan Sickles swept into the lobby like a conquering hero. "Here comes the Civil War," Heisman added.

"Hey, where's the old Johnny Reb spirit?" Stagg joked.

"I was a Yale man, too!" Heisman was half indignant. "My people were for the Union."

"Well, let them wax and wave," Stagg said. "I'm for anything that sells football tickets, aren't you?"

"I'm not sure but there's a limit somewhere," Heisman replied.

When Sickles entered the hotel, Longstreet hid behind his paper. It had been pleasant to sit quietly, unobserved, and watch the people come and go. Sickles moved so dexterously on his crutches and with such autocratic bearing that one failed to notice immediately that his right leg was missing. With his pepper-and-salt walrus mustache and pince-nez, Sickles reminded Longstreet of a Prussian. Old Dan seemed to be enjoying himself. A Tammany Hall man, Longstreet thought, loved a parade. He watched the hero of Gettysburg greet businessmen and promoters who drifted out of the dining room under a bluish haze of cigar smoke. They bombarded Sickles with good cheer. The crisp voices of Pennsylvanians and New Yorkers made Longstreet feel strange and out of place. He wished he were walking the quiet trails of his Georgia woods.

As he peered at his old adversary over the top of his newspaper, Longstreet felt time collapse, so that he might have just ridden up to plead his case with Lee, who stood on Seminary Ridge studying the terrain through field glasses.

We could not call the enemy to a position better suited to our plans. All we have to do is file around his left and occupy good ground between him and his capital.

Sickles had seen him and was coming toward him. Longstreet had an impulse to hide behind his paper, but since it was impossible to avoid Sickles, who was bearing down on him like a freight train, he got to his feet, tugged his vest straight, and prepared to give as good as he took.

"Jim!" Sickles sang. "You've come."

"Hello, Dan."

Reporters clustered around them alertly. They reminded Longstreet of terriers that had treed a squirrel.

"It looks as if they've made us honorary chairmen of this event," Sickles said. "I want you to know, General, that I cannot think of another man I'd rather serve with on such a commission."

"That's most kind."

"Are you a football 'rooter,' as they say?"

"What?"

"A rooter—a follower of the sport!"

"I've read about football," Longstreet replied, "in the Atlanta *Constitution*. The university over at Athens has a team, I believe."

"Never seen it played?"

Longstreet heard pencils scratching on pads. "I don't get down to Athens very often."

"Well, then, it's gracious of you to go along with all this . . . folderol." Sickles gestured comically toward the lobby rapidly filling with men.

"I don't think it's folderol."

Sickles became alert. "Oh, really?" The reporters all looked up from their pads.

"What we have here is an interesting tactical situation." Longstreet meant to amuse, but with his fierce eyes and Mongol-like whiskers he looked anything but amusing.

"I had the impression," said Sickles, "that you placed less emphasis on tactics than on terrain. I believe I read somewhere that you said, 'The only way to fight a battle is to occupy good ground and hold it.' "

"I must have said that before Manassas and Seven Pines and Mechanicsville." *No, no, this is a social occasion.*

Combativeness ached in Longstreet like an old shrapnel wound on a rainy day, and he made a conscious effort to suppress it.

"I reckon if anybody had seen me at Blackburn's Ford, July 18, 1861," Longstreet added self-effacingly, "they wouldn't accuse me of being a tactician. We floundered around in Bull Run creek like sitting ducks."

Sickles appraised Longstreet as sharply as he once had done through field glasses at Gettysburg's Little Round Top.

"Well, sir," he said, "we must agree that there is no high or low ground on a football field, just good, clean sport between athletes of the highest caliber. I think you'll also agree," Sickles paused to let the reporters catch up with him, "that this contest is in the nation's best interests."

"How is that?" Longstreet said.

"Well, for one thing," Sickles said expansively, "it shows that North and South have entered a new age of understanding. Whatever hard feelings still exist, scattered hither and yon below the Mason-Dixon Line, will dry up once America gets itself a small war somewhere. In the meantime, we've got this all-star game to show that we're all together again!"

"Let's don't tell the football players about the 'new understanding,'" Longstreet said. "They've still got a game to play."

Sickles's eyes were keen and watchful behind a bright smile. "Well, sir, will you accompany me to meet our hosts?" He extended an arm, bent at the elbow.

Does he think I've forgotten the Peach Orchard at Gettysburg? That salient of his broke up McLaws's attack or we might have taken the Federal left.

"I'll join you directly," he said.

Sickles adjusted his crutches under his arms and inclined his head. Then, smiling, he moved away to greet admirers. Reporters trailed in his wake. Watching Sickles, cheerful and confident, surrounded by well-wishers, Longstreet suddenly knew what had brought him back to Pennsylvania.

Across the lobby, Cornelius Humboldt stood at Heisman's elbow, absorbing football talk with a poet's memory. What songs he would sing when he returned to Sewanee Mountain. He basked in the camaraderie of the scholar-athlete ideal. Warmed by such sentiments, the professor glanced around and happened to see a familiar figure on a sofa. As the gentleman turned a page of his newspaper, Humboldt caught a glimpse of a narrow forehead with craggy eyebrows and deep-set eyes.

James Longstreet.

Humboldt was transfixed by conflicting emotions. Here was Lee's nemesis, antagonist supreme of the Lost Cause, and yet— Humboldt struggled against an unbidden impulse. What was it he felt? *Not celebrity worship!* Humboldt reached for righteous anger, on behalf of Robert E. Lee, and came up empty-handed. Now that he viewed Longstreet in the flesh, the professor was awed by the living presence of history.

Who am I to accuse James Longstreet of anything?

What was Longstreet doing here? What could it mean? Had Longstreet come to Philadelphia to pick up the fallen banner? Humboldt saw the white-haired general glance up, and he edged out of sight behind Heisman. The academic who worshipped Bobby Lee trembled lest he dash forward and beg Longstreet for his autograph.

Hudson Stroud got off the hotel elevator and made his way across the lobby. He was headed for the barroom to meet Liebowitz when he, too, saw James Longstreet. He changed course and made for the corner sofa. The general looked up from his newspaper. Hudson drew himself up and saluted. Longstreet noted the commemorative pin in Stroud's lapel, the peg leg, and the stiff-necked admiration. It reminded him of his reunion in Richmond the previous summer, with the Army of Virginia. He stood and tipped his hat.

"Hudson Stroud, Fifth Kentucky, Sergeant of Mounted Rifles," Hudson sang out.

"Fifth Kentucky," Longstreet mused. "Under John Hunt Morgan?"

"Yes, sir."

"Let's see, his men called him the *Beau Sabreur?*"

"That's right, sir, like your Virginians called you Old Pete!"

Longstreet laughed out loud. The old soldier's presumption was refreshing. Then he respectfully asked Stroud where he lost his leg.

"Green River, in Kentucky."

"I've heard of that fight," the general said. They fell silent, remembering. It was not unpleasant. "What brings you to Philadelphia?"

"Football and poker," Hudson replied. "We got us up a game 'twixt North and South. You a gambling man, General?"

"I've played some cards in my time, mainly before the war."

"Well, sir, I'm on my way to set a game up, over to the saloon there. Would the General allow a sergeant the honor of buyin' him a drink?"

"Thank you, Mr. Stroud, another time perhaps. But your poker game intrigues me. If you'd leave me a message at the hotel desk telling me when and where, I'd like to sit in for a hand or two if I may."

"That can be arranged, sir!" Hudson piped. "And so can a drink of the best Kentucky sour-mash whiskey."

"That sounds most delightful, Mr. Stroud. Thank you very much."

"My pleasure, General, sir. Now, if you will excuse me."

Longstreet watched Stroud thump with crutch and peg leg past businessmen, politicians, promoters, and reporters without paying them the least attention.

Football. Poker. Kentucky bourbon. Not a bad combination.

Hudson paused at the door of the dimly lit barroom and saw an old man sipping from a glass. His heart thumped. He needed assurance that the man at the bar was no ghost. Then he saw Liebowitz's Adam's apple bob as he swallowed. So strong was the grip of the past that as Stroud entered the barroom, he was surprised that his step lacked the spring of a thirty-year-old.

Liebowitz heard the peg thump on the wooden floor leading down to the lower level of the barroom. Without turning around, he raised his glass in salute. Hudson saw a gold tooth shine in the mirror.

"Glad you could make it, Lieberwitz!" Hudson's voice almost shook. He brusquely signaled the bartender to bring two more of what Liebowitz was drinking. Stroud leaned his crutches against the bar and eased his weight onto a stool.

"What has two heads, three arms, and three legs?" Liebowitz turned his glass this way and that, contemplating the light trapped in the rye whiskey.

If Lieberwitz is senile, all bets are off.

"Two heads, three arms, three legs," Ernie repeated.

"I give up—what?"

"Us."

Liebowitz turned, and Stroud saw the arm in its sling, the gloved hand curling on itself like a dry leaf. Hudson's stump itched.

"We could form a sideshow act and go on the road," Liebowitz said.

"How did it happen?" Stroud said.

The bartender brought their drinks. Liebowitz hesitated until the man had served them and moved away.

"Not long after Green River. Minié ball broke my arm. Surgeons said nerve damage."

"Too bad."

"Yes, well.—There's a lot a man can do with one hand."

They drank in silence.

"About this football game," Liebowitz said. "Some coincidence about our quarterbacks, eh?"

"Shoot, Ernie, I thought you come seven hundred miles just to see *me.*"

"Here's to our boys." Liebowitz raised his glass again. "How good is your grandson?"

"Chase? He's the best."

"In the South."

"The best, period."

"We're here to find out, aren't we?"

"Did you bring the sword?" Hudson squinted suspiciously at him.

"Oh, that."

"Where is it?"

"Hotel vault."

"Suspicious scoundrel."

"Your telegram said cards."

"We come to play."

"*I* came to play."

"Who's backing you?"

"Old friends." Liebowitz swallowed the dregs of his rye.

"Does tomorrow suit you?"

"Name the place."

"I checked at the hotel desk," Hudson said. "We can reserve a private suite up on the fourth floor."

"That's thoughtful of you. I appreciate it."

"Think nothing of it. I 'preciate you coming seven hundred miles to allow me to whup your ass. —Does it hurt?"

"What?"

"You know, the, uh . . ."

"Hand? Only when it rains. How about your . . ."

"Stump? Itches a lot, mostly in the summertime. I don't reckon you deal much monte one-handed."

"No, but I can deal 'most anything else."

"Too bad. I was hoping I might try you at monte." Hudson's eyes glittered in the gaslight.

"War's over, Stroud."

"May be, for you."

"You crazy Rebel. I think you miss it."

"What?"

"The war."

"That's right, like I miss passing kidney stones."

"I mean it. Why do you Southerners have such a hard time facing facts?"

"It ain't the facing that bothers me. It's having some hard-tailed son of a bitch like you sticking his nose in my bizness."

"So? Do you miss it? Was I right?"

Stroud frowned at Ernest's reflection in the mirror behind the bar. "Sometimes," he said. "When I'm alone. I can smell powder burning. Keen as anything."

"We lost a lot of good men."

"Well, *I* didn't say I missed it. *You* said I missed it."

They hunched over their glasses, speaking to each other's mirror image.

Hudson said, "Being old is more intolerable than war. I felt better when I was getting shot at than I do now."

"Nobody plans on getting old."

"It's a real surprise to be eighty-three. How old are you?"

"Seventy-eight."

"Aw, you're older'n that!"

"My wife says I don't look seventy-eight."

"You look a hunnerd to me."

"You're one to talk."

They drank.

"What do you do up there?" Hudson said.

"Where?"

"Kalamazoo."

"When?"

"Anytime, all the time."

"Well, I got my woman, you know."

"Yeah."

"She kinda keeps me moving around."

"Yeah." Hudson shifted on his stool. "Let's get down to it."

"Shoot."

"How's this sound? No weapons, frisk search before the game —both sides—half-hour limit for recess unless due to medical emergency. All right? Now, draw or stud?"

"Suit yourself."

"I favor stud, then."

Liebowitz sipped his drink. "Stud is more chance than skill."

"Stud is more guts'n anything else."

"Fine. Stud it is. On the other hand, we may need some variety."

"All right. Draw poker, nothing wild. Now, how many players?"

"I have three. I'm inclined to say three per side. To keep the betting lively and have a fresh man in reserve at all times."

"All right, three per side. Now, betting limit?"

"How about five dollars?"

"I didn't come eight hundred miles to play penny ante! Let's open it up. You ain't about to wager the sword agin my first raise."

Liebowitz eyed him askance. "Feeling lucky? Well, maybe stud will give you a shot at it."

"Did I bad-mouth you? Let it be draw, then. Makes no ne'mind to me. I don't care, long as the game is square."

"No limit." Liebowitz got out a small pad and a pencil and began to write a list.

"What're you doin'?"

"Putting the ground rules on paper. That way nobody can bellyache later."

"You gettin' kinda persnickety in your old age," Hudson sniffed. "Did your wife learn you to be so careful?"

"If she did, more power to her." Liebowitz looked up sharply from his tablet. "I brought my life's savings. My wife thinks I've gone crazy."

Stroud sipped his drink contemplatively. "Make me a copy of that list, will you?" He listened to the scratching of Ernest's pencil. "I reckon we may *be* a little crazy. Too late to worry 'bout that."

"I never knew a gambler that wasn't crazy. Here's your copy."

"That brings up a question," Hudson said, tucking the paper in a coat pocket. "If you start off crazy, do you get crazier as you go along, so folks have to make allowances for you?" He grinned. "If the world adjusts to crazy folks, it's only a matter of time 'fore we take over."

"I'll drink to that."

They drained their glasses. Hudson called for refills.

"All right," Liebowitz said, "but two's my limit."

"Whiskey don't affect me like it used to," Hudson observed, "now that I got me a hollow leg."

They watched the bartender pour fresh drinks.

Hudson became solemn. "At Sandusky Prison, being crazy was the only way to stay alive. After a while it seemed normal to gripe about the extra burial detail we was pullin'. And rat meat was the best thing we ever et. We got to be right at home in hell."

"And you blame me for everything!"

The old men glared at each other. The soft light shone equally on their balding heads and bony faces. Hudson was the first to give way.

"I reckon it's natural to hunt somebody to blame."

"Who do I blame for this?" Liebowitz held up his shrunken arm. "The Weird Sisters? You count yourself lucky to have somebody to blame, Stroud, and you're *damned* lucky I showed up for this game of cards."

"*Me* lucky!" Hudson snorted. "Hell, Ernie, you wouldn'a missed this for the world. —Hey, look who's here."

Little Harry Nelson, accompanied by Knot Dickinson, who had just arrived from Baltimore, Pitts, and Fitzpatrick joined them at the bar. Liebowitz remembered them from his Mississippi River days. After he greeted the Southerners, he asked them what had two heads, three arms, and three legs. He let Stroud have the punch line.

In the lobby, which was now packed with Philadelphians of all stripes, Harrison Prescott sniffed the air for a story and made for the expensive cigars. He did not care that no one paid him any attention. He was content to move unseen among them, like light in water.

Prescott's confidence was due partly to his improved circumstances at the *Inquirer*. Ever since national wire services had begun to pick up his reports about the all-star game, Harry's stock had risen. He now had his own, centrally heated cubicle in the Metropolitan Department. A secretary was available to him. He had been given exclusive coverage of the all-star game under his own byline, setting a precedent at the *Inquirer*. The city editor, Jimmy Larue, addressed him in tones of respect. Nobody laughed at Harry Prescott.

Near the ballroom entrance stood an elephant of a man who towered over other Pennsylvanians of wealth and distinction. Prescott recognized Boies Penrose, all six foot four and 295 pounds of him, among aldermen and civic leaders constituting a roll call of Main Line Philadelphia: Cadwalader, Biddle, Ingersoll, Wanamaker, Pepper, Wistar, and Wister.

Penrose was like a magnet to Harry, who liked to imagine that they had a lot in common. Born to wealth in a prominent Philadelphia family, the Harvard-educated Boies had turned away from a life of ease to enter the political arena. In his early twenties he underwent an apprenticeship in Philadelphia ward politics, rapidly gaining a reputation as a backroom dealer and manipulator of the first order. Part of his attraction as a politician was due to the fact that, having inherited a fortune, Penrose was vastly uninterested in stealing from the public till. What intrigued Boies about politics was manipulating voters. Penrose made a point of buying stock in local newspapers and entertaining reporters at every opportunity. He sided with the city political machine and was rumored not to be above bribery, fixing juries, or paying political debts with patronage. He had run for mayor of Philadelphia in 1894 but withdrew from the race when his opponents published a photograph of Penrose leaving a known house of prostitution. (Prescott had rushed off to visit the brothel as soon as the picture appeared, but the place was so busy he was turned away at the door.) Now, at age thirty, Penrose was running for the United States Senate.

Harry threaded his way through the crush of cigar wavers until he was standing just behind Penrose. The roll of fat on Boies's neck represented living proof of his gargantuan appetites. Prescott yearned to emulate such cravings. At breakfast, Penrose had been known to consume a dozen eggs, an inch-thick slab of bacon, six rolls, and a quart of coffee. At a victory party for Matthew Quay, Penrose's political mentor, upon his election to the U.S. Senate in 1887, Boies was said to have drunk six quarts of Pennsylvania Highspire whiskey and devoured two turkeys, a chicken, and most of a ham. On another celebratory occasion Penrose ordered reedbirds at a Philadelphia restaurant. The waiter brought a chafing dish containing twenty-six birds to the head of the table to be inspected before serving. Penrose ordered the dish set before him and, while the rest of his party gaped, stolidly ate all twenty-six reedbirds and all the wild rice, then drank the gravy from the bowl—this after having drunk nine cocktails and five highballs.

Penrose was known to frequent low dives, where he drank Highspire whiskey and cheap gin until he passed out. Harry had heard rumors that Penrose's coarseness extended to prodigious fornications as well. He not only approved of Penrose's desire to wallow in the mud, he wished he could wallow with him. Prescott wished he had the nerve to ask Boies what he thought of capes, whips, and chains.

"Excuse me, Mr. Penrose." Harry gazed respectfully up at the beady-eyed, fleshy face. "I am Harrison Prescott of the *Inquirer.* Would you care to make a statement?"

"About what?" Penrose stared disdainfully at the owlish reporter.

"About, well, *football!*" Harry gestured at the commotion in the lobby. "Did you play the game at Harvard?"

Penrose's grimace lent truth to the rumor that he hated to be touched, even refusing to allow people to whisper in his ear.

"I dislike physical contact with other bodies," Penrose replied in a low voice, "especially dirty, perspiring ones."

Harry imagined Penrose unbuttoned at ceremonial banquets, uncouth with food stains on his vest, his boots tied—on one occasion, it had been said—with corset strings borrowed from a prostitute. He could not help wondering how Penrose avoided body contact during coitus and thought thrillingly of harnesses, straps, and pulleys suspending a woman over a bed.

"Er, could you explain, then," Prescott continued, "your interest in this football game between North and South?"

"Of course!" Penrose snapped. "It is for the good of the city."

Boies's eyes gleamed as he recognized Richard Canfield lingering near the scions of Philadelphia's first families. "Excuse me," he told Harry and moved off to reconnoiter the Faro King.

Penrose had met Canfield in Saratoga, where Boies had bucked the tiger at Canfield's gambling casino. Canfield had invited Penrose to visit his private suite and view his Chippendales, oriental jade and porcelain, and original Whistlers. As an aristocrat who aspired to low company, Penrose was amused by Canfield's converse desire to join the gentry.

When the all-star game was proposed to the Philadelphia board of aldermen and they learned of Canfield's sponsorship, they had been adamantly opposed to the game. Penrose had astonished them by backing Canfield. He had found an ideal means of revenging himself on a proper Philadelphia establishment which had scotched his candidacy for mayor.

In fact, Boies perceived the aldermen's Canfield dilemma as peculiarly Philadelphian: it was Franklin versus Penn; Franklin's crackerjack, Yankee, money-making spirit versus Penn's gentle, symmetrical, myrtle-and-brick Philadelphia. Penrose despised William Penn. In his secret heart he had always wanted to rape a Quaker.

"How do you do, Mr. Canfield."

"Oh, Mr. Penrose!" Canfield grabbed at Boies's hand, happy to have been noticed. To make a good impression on the Philadelphians, he had dressed conservatively in black cutaway, gray vest, and dark tie. The businessmen around him appeared flamboyant by comparison. Many of them were turned out in colorful school ties or blazers with mums in the lapels. "Or may I presume to hope, *Senator* Penrose," Canfield added unctuously.

"Anyone may presume to hope, sir." Penrose's jowls grew pink with satisfaction. "Let me say that your financial backing of this charitable endeavor is much appreciated. Highly commendable."

"Not at all, my pleasure!" Canfield glanced about with a shade of apprehension.

"Have you met our aldermen?"

"Not socially," Canfield said.

"Ah. Professionally speaking, you have entertained some of them at Saratoga?"

"Or possibly Boston or New York." Canfield could not resist listing his properties, just as Penrose could not resist sticking a pin in the King's balloon.

"Is it true that you once bet twenty thousand dollars on how fast a raindrop would roll down a window?"

"You must be confusing me with someone else. That kind of wager sounds like Bet-A-Million Gates to me. I am a businessman. I go with the odds."

"Sir, if you are a businessman, I am a Baptist missionary. You are too modest. At any rate, allow me to introduce you to my associates." Penrose invited the civic leaders to join them. "Gentlemen, I believe you know Richard A. Canfield of New York and Saratoga? Canfield, this is Mr. Pepper, Mr. Ingersoll, Mr. Cadwalader, Mr. Wanamaker, Mr. Wistar, Mr. Biddle, Mr. Wister."

Penrose had anticipated having to pressure the board of aldermen to accept Canfield. To his surprise they stood in line to meet the Faro King. Canfield was beside himself with pleasure, almost fawning. Boies could not believe his eyes. Main Line Philadelphia had let him down, once again, and he was manifestly disappointed.

Canfield listened pleasantly to their conversations about stocks and bonds, the price of sugar or timber or dairy products. He mingled cheek by jowl with the Philadelphia elite and felt that here at last were his true peers, men who could appreciate what he had accomplished: the art objects bought in Europe, the Chippendale set purchased at auction at Christie's, his rewarding personal association with James Whistler. (Had any of these Main

Liners sat for a portrait by Whistler? The artist had promised to paint Canfield someday.) Here were men of sensibility who could appreciate him for what he was, a connoisseur, a patron of the arts, a member of the Walpole Society.

Hovering nearby behind a potted plant, Canfield's associates, Bird Mahoney and Fingers McGee, observed their chief ingratiating himself with the bluebloods. They were horrified at Canfield's obsequiousness. The King had become a gentleman-in-waiting. They averted their eyes so neither would be forced to acknowledge the depths to which he had fallen. Their fear was left unspoken: As Canfield went, so went his mob.

Penrose led the promoters, aldermen, civic leaders, sports figures, and guests of honor into the ballroom. There was a buoyancy, a feeling of conspiracy among the board of aldermen that Boies had never seen before. He felt somehow violated as they took their places. Longstreet and Sickles, honorary chairmen, were seated at the head table. Kate sat very straight in her chair between Heisman and Warner. She was the only woman in the room, yet the aldermen seemed to ignore her completely. The Faro King sat discreetly at the rear, mild as any Quaker.

Penrose suppressed an ironic smile. He recalled City Hall's adamant opposition to the all-star game when the concept first was presented to them. When he discovered that Canfield was behind the idea, Boies had invented a trickle-down theory by which the tourist dollars at the ball game would be multiplied throughout Philadelphia. He created a mathematical formula to illustrate how the gate at Franklin Field would increase tenfold. His projected figure of five hundred thousand dollars' potential profit had gotten the board's attention. Soon they would be competing among themselves to refine Boies's theory.

When everyone was seated, the mayor looked at an alderman, who looked at Penrose, who nodded. The mayor then called the meeting to order. After recognizing various dignitaries such as Sickles, Longstreet, and Walter Camp, and introducing the coaching staffs of each team, the mayor turned the meeting over to Mr. Cadwalader, who in a melodic, pragmatic manner presented the city's game plan, including a schedule of events, publicity and promotional arrangements, estimates of costs, and the establishment of a limited, one-time parlay gambling permit to be operated on behalf of the city. Cadwalader pointed to a chart graphing the upward curve of anticipated revenues. Everyone was delighted.

Richard Canfield was pleasantly agog at the way his dream had taken hold. Gradually, however, he realized what Cadwalader was saying. Despite the dulcet tones, Canfield recognized exploitation of his charitable cause. He became agitated, though he took care not to display his emotions. If he spoke out, the Philadelphians might withdraw their support. What could he do? How could he rescue his dream from the mire of profit?

Cadwalader concluded, "And so, city share of said revenues will accrue to the recently established fund for city management. Any questions?"

"See what they're doin', Chief?" a voice whispered hoarsely in his ear. Canfield glanced with distaste at Mahoney.

"Certainly, they are attempting to raise as much money for charity as they can," Canfield replied, arguing as much with himself as with Mahoney.

"Sure they are," Mahoney said. "How d'ya think these fellas got their millions? Takin' suckers, only they do it legal. Me, I'm enjoyin' watchin' masters at work. This is like goin' to business college."

Canfield gave his aide a horrified glance. He refused to allow doubts to defeat expectations. Surely a compromise could be reached. Surely the city fathers would listen to reason. They ran the banks and factories in which Canfield invested his millions. They operated by a strict code. They were the real world.

"They know what they're doing," he told Mahoney.

"I believe it!" the Bird agreed.

The mayor thanked everyone for coming and urged them to attend a rally in Fairmount Park, to follow immediately. The meeting was adjourned.

To Harry Prescott, the gathering at Fairmount Park resembled a Civil War reunion. Among the holiday throng—ladies wearing the latest fashions, gentlemen in Newmarket coats, roller-skating clubs on parade—Confederate and Union veterans stood grouped around the bandstand like ghost companies drawn up for review. They wore old army caps or blue or gray coats. There were hundreds of them, many leaning on crutches or canes like a great flock of herons. When Harry approached them, however, he saw the fight in their eyes.

A Fire Glows in the Furnace of America.

His next article pulsating in his brâin, Prescott approached a veteran whose Confederate Army cap was tilted over a face like saddle leather. The old soldier might have been embalmed, buried, and exhumed for the occasion. Aware of his influence in luring these veterans out of retirement, Harry regarded the patriarch with the respect—and curiosity—with which a fiction writer views his characters.

"Excuse me, sir," he said, "I am with the *Inquirer*. Are you a football fan? Come to cheer the Southern team?"

The old man looked at him, uncomprehending.

"I see from your cap that you're for the South. Are you, sir, a veteran of the war?"

"He cain't hear you," said the man's companion, also well advanced in years, who wore a Confederate coat with faded gold braid.

"Is he deaf?"

"I'd say so."

"But a football fan?" Prescott noted that the object of their conversation did not so much as glance at him.

"Not that I know of."

"May I ask, what is he here for?"

"He hates Yankees."

Prescott experienced a thrill. This venerable misanthrope represented Mortality itself, summoned by Harry's typewriter. Looking into the old Rebel's stonelike face, he felt like a sculptor who chisels a figure out of marble and waits for it to speak.

"We come up from Bal'imore," the tall one continued conversationally. "We fought in the same regiment, and now we stay at the Old Soldiers' Home . . ."

"Where's the fight?"

The old warrior's voice rasped like a nail being pried from a plank. Prescott was delighted.

"You mean, the game?" he said.

"He cain't hear you. He means the fight. You can bet your

bottom dollar we didn't come all the way to Phillydelphia just to see some *game.*"

At that moment, a brass band which had been entertaining the audience with Strauss waltzes struck up a staccato rendition of "Dixie." Old Rebels tossed their hats and waved their canes. Harry's mossback looked at his companion for an explanation.

"Dixie!" he shouted into the old man's ear. "The band's playin' 'Dixie.'"

The stone face cracked in a grimace of joy. The veteran clapped his cap over his heart. Harry heard booing. Ex-troopers wearing Union caps and coats shook bony fists at the Southerners. Trapped between elderly armies, Prescott held up his reporter's pad to signal his neutrality. Graybeards cursed one another. Harry was solidly whacked in the shoulder by a Confederate cane. He lurched away and collided with a Union flagstaff, which knocked him to his knees. The brass band now played "The Battle Hymn of the Republic."

"Rally, Vermonters!" voices cried. The air bristled with crutches, walking sticks, and a sword or two. Harry crawled to safety as the canes clattered overhead. Looking up, he saw a pistol tucked in a man's waistband.

Like Frankenstein, I am attacked by my own creation.

Seated on the reviewing stand with her players, Kate heard the commotion, saw heads turn.

"It's only a minor disturbance—don't worry," she told her students.

As if to contradict her, a policeman blew his whistle. Kate was determined not to let anything spoil the occasion. "Isn't this exciting—the flags and banners, the brass band? I could not imagine a grander time."

"Fights and police notwithstanding," Brother replied.

"You hush," she said.

The black players sat on the back row of the wooden bleachers behind their white teammates. Abbott, the Alabama halfback, passed up to Kate a pink envelope addressed simply, "Miss Kuykendall." Puzzled, she tore it open and read a hand-printed invitation:

The Schuylkill Rowing Not Drifting Club
requests the honor of
your presence
Meeting topic: Woman's Role in Education
(social hour and refreshments to follow)
Wednesday, December 17, 7 P.M.
1127 Linden Ave.
Regrets Only

Kate looked up to identify the person who had delivered the note. In her self-conscious state, however, many spectators seemed to be staring at her. She wondered if the Schuylkill Rowing Not Drifting Club was anything like the Bardstown Service League which she had assiduously avoided all these years. At any rate it was an invitation, she decided, that she could not refuse.

Brother watched Kate put the pink envelope in her pocket. He was momentarily envious. He knew that, for Miss Kate, it was enough to be there. It made no difference to her that they sat on the back row behind the white players. Directly in front of him, Cow Nalley's head was as square and uncompromising as a cypress stump. The only consolation to a back-row existence was that he was not continually exposed to the crowd's inspection. At least no "Tom" chants had erupted today. He almost welcomed the fracas between the old veterans.

Brother noticed the Northern All-Americas moving confidently into their section of the grandstand—clean-shaven, broad-shouldered, at ease with the crowd's adulation. He was glad not to be compared with them. As he watched them file into place, everything he had heard or read about the legendary Harvard, Yale, and Princeton came together. He could not suppress a sense of awe.

Chase Riddle caught Brother's eye and winked at him. Some of the Gray squad—Nalley, Abbott, Joiner, Price—stared with reverence at Heffelfinger of Yale, Poe of Princeton, Rinehart of Lafayette. Chase coolly tipped his hat to them.

The Northern All-Stars were too busy to acknowledge Riddle's salute. Gentlemen and ladies pressed up to them with a dovelike cooing. The Blue team were handsomely turned out in blazers and waistcoats. Some of them sported well-brushed mustaches.

Behind the grandstand, Arno Ziprenian, who had paid the band director twenty dollars to play "Dixie," awaited the mayor's opening address. With him were two actors dressed in authentic Confederate and Federal army uniforms complete with rifles and fixed bayonets. Through the bleachers the Zipper caught sight of Canfield attended by Mahoney and McGee. The King seemed to be in good humor, but Ziprenian remembered how Canfield had smiled the day he inquired if Arno Senior could sew a shroud. Like a ferret in a cage, The Zipper looked through the bleachers and waited for the festivities to begin.

The band played a fanfare and the mayor approached the dais. Speaking through a megaphone he welcomed distinguished guests and fellow politicians, and went on to say what a fine occasion it was, what an honor to host an event such as the North-South All-Star Football Game. On cue, Ziprenian's costumed actors marched out and took a position in front of the dais. A flapping and cawing arose from the old veterans. The mayor turned to ask an aide where the uniformed men had come from. Accordingly the aide asked an assistant who asked another assistant. The mayor resumed his remarks, recognizing the honorary chairmen. As Longstreet and Sickles waved, the actors turned and crossed bayonets.

The Philadelphians gave an astonished cheer, while the old soldiers quickly formed skirmish lines. The mayor called for order, police moved in. Walter Camp approached the dais with a determined smile.

"Guide on, Vermont!"

"Assemble on me! Tennessee Volunteers!"

Canes and crutches were brandished as veterans of Pennsylvania, New York, and Vermont squared off against Virginians and Carolinians. Eddies of motion swirled through the audience. A policeman fell. Blue-coated officers rushed to protect him.

"It is my privilege," Camp shouted through the megaphone, "to participate in what I hope will become an annual contest . . ."

Players, coaches, and spectators alike craned their necks to see what was going on. Ladies raised their eyebrows as if to express the sentiment that William Penn would not have approved of such ill temper.

"Hurrah for the Bonnie Blue Flag!"
"Hip-hip for the Rhode Island Artillery!"

". . . pitting the finest athletes of North and South in an unexcelled football match. It is hoped that this contest will engender the expansion of football throughout the land, especially in the Southern states . . ."

Seated next to Sickles, Longstreet was embarrassed by the fighting. The wooden *clack* of cane against crutch had an otherworldly sound, like a medieval joust. Yet he hated to see the mounted police spur their horses into the melee. The Confederates seemed to be winning.

"At this time," Camp yelled into the megaphone, "I'd like to introduce the coaches! For the North, from the University of Chicago, Amos Alonzo Stagg . . ."

Camp could hardly be heard amid the birdlike din. The Civil War vets had actually formed into ragged platoons, which wheeled in cadence until they grappled hand to hand with their enemies. As the mounted police rode yelling into their ranks, a pistol shot rang out. Ladies dropped their parasols and ran; roller skaters raced ahead of the panicked throng to keep from being trampled.

On the grandstand Kate took a stand in front of her charges, ironically protecting the most able-bodied persons in Fairmount Park. The mayor reappeared on the dais and ordered the band director to play the national anthem. He stood at attention, hand over heart, although the only spectators remaining were the elderly fighters, many of whom clearly needed medical attention.

In the next issue of the *Inquirer,* Prescott's headlines read:

CIVIL WAR IN FAIRMOUNT PARK
CITY UNDER SIEGE

Chapter Seventeen

Brother unrolled a ball of twine to mark the sideline, while B.C. poured a steady stream of lime on top of the string. The lime bucket looked like a toy in the lineman's huge hands, which were white with powder. Their teammates from Post Oak labored alongside them, clearing trash from the empty lot near the Maison Blanche. Some of them chopped weeds with scythes while others dragged heavy boards to smooth the surface. They wore a wild assortment of overalls and patched hand-me-down clothing for "practice uniforms." In the thirty-degree weather Kate had made them wear their Sunday shoes.

"If I bust my shoes playing ball," B.C. complained, "my mama'll kill me."

"Want to catch pneumonia?" Brother said. Yet he had been careful not to let any lime fall on his shoes.

"Ought not to be the onliest ones to lay down this lime," B.C. grumbled.

"Watch out, you're getting it crooked."

Brother was glad to have something to do at last. He enjoyed being out of doors with the great city all around him. He imagined exotic and commonplace happenings going on in Philadelphia homes: the snap of newspapers being opened over morning coffee; teakettles whistling; trolley bells ringing in the street; the clip-clop of the milkman's horse. He wrapped himself in these fantasies and made them his own.

Surrounding the vacant lot, the row houses with their mournful façades and steep roofs were to Brother as mysterious as Buddhist temples. For him the sky was not so much bleak as fecund with the promise of snow. It did not matter that he and his companions labored over the field like slaves picking cotton, or that the white players, including Chase, had been exempted from this chore. He felt a sublime sense of expectation. Something exciting was going to happen.

Kate had protested when Heisman assigned her players the task of clearing the vacant lot. "You got them here," Heisman had told her within the players' hearing. "At least let them be useful. It's bad enough that we have to prepare our practice field. Let's don't make it worse by complaining."

The white All-Stars stood in front of the Maison Blanche tossing a football back and forth, touching their toes, limbering up. Chase was the only one of them who glanced in embarrassment at the scrubs laboring in the empty lot. The white players wore brand-new gray jerseys over moleskin pants. Their shoes had cleats.

"Why don't them white boys he'p out?" B.C. complained, looking up from his lime bucket.

"You can't expect a Virginia gentleman to get down in the dirt —except for sport—can you?" Brother said good-naturedly.

They saw Kate coming toward them. She wore her Montgomery Ward football shoes, moleskin pants, and jersey under a hunting jacket. A red wool cap was pulled down over her ears. Her coach's whistle hung on a chain around her neck. She walked with the gangly strides of a teenager. They saw her lips move and knew that she was muttering to herself.

"Heisman and Warner are right: we should be housed in a proper hotel, not one with a gambling casino on the third floors. What's on the fourth floor? Nobody's saying. Ziprenian's responsible. I don't trust that man. It's nothing against immigrants, but they have their own standards. At least my boys are getting enough to eat. The Maison Blanche has had to hire two extra cooks, which is a kind of revenge, I suppose."

In mid-stride she turned and looked back at Heisman and Warner. It had been enough at first simply to get out of Kentucky. Now that her players were here, under a Philadelphia sky, anything was possible. For the first time she seriously sized up the white players. They did not seem any larger or more muscular than her Post Oak team. Tree and Ulysses were in fact bigger than any of them. It was the whites' experience and knowledge of the game that made them formidable. Kate reached the practice field ahead of Heisman and the others.

"Listen up!" she called. Her team gathered around her. Something looked different about them. She realized it was the shoes. "Let's try to learn all we can. Pay attention to what Coach Heisman and Coach Warner say. Concentrate and do your best. Watch the other players to see what they do."

They were staring at her with the intensity of nestlings.

"Is any of them from Yale?" B.C. said nervously.

"Yale's in Connecticut," Brother sighed. He remembered the night when they had stood on the Bardstown pike and wondered about Philadelphia. "We play against somebody from Yale on Saturday, if we get to play."

"That's good," B.C. sighed. "I ain't up to Yale today."

"What is this 'City Under Siege' business?" Heisman was saying to Warner as they led their players onto the field. In his hand Heisman waved a rolled-up copy of the morning edition of the *Inquirer*.

"Selling papers," Warner said equably. "Actually, that article didn't stretch the truth much. If the police hadn't moved in when they did, somebody could have gotten hurt."

Blondy Glenn, the All-Southern tackle from Alabama Poly, trotted past them, and Warner genteelly swatted Heisman's captain on the rump. Since boarding their train in Atlanta, each coach had petted the other's captains. Heisman had brought Glenn and Mike Harvey, his quick, small tackle, while Warner's Georgia representatives were halfback Cow Nalley and George Price, tackle.

"Coach, will we scrimmage today?" Glenn called.

"No." Heisman saw Glenn glancing at the Negroes policing the vacant lot with their rakes and scythes. It was a credit to Humboldt and Kuykendall's persistence, he thought, that the varsity athletes had begun to perceive the blacks as scrubs. As far as

Heisman was concerned, now that they had prepared the practice field the Negroes' participation was complete, except for setting up tackling dummies, and water bucket duty.

Scrubs, indeed!

Heisman glanced irritably at Humboldt, who walked briskly along behind them, smoking his morning cheroot. How much more damage, he wondered, could the Sewanee man do?

"If you will take the backs," Heisman said politely to Warner, "I will take the forwards."

"Fine," Warner said. "Glenn can lead calisthenics."

Ordinarily the captain led warm-up exercises, and Warner's selecting Glenn would alert the players as to the coaches' choice for captain.

"I was thinking Nalley might lead cals," Heisman protested.

"Why not Glenn and Nalley together?" Warner said.

"Capital."

The coaches approached the vacant lot forthrightly. Kate watched the white players begin their warm-ups, bending and stretching, running short sprints, their breath like steamy extensions of their egos. The Panthers stood on the sideline of the field they had made and watched the white players exercise.

"Get out there and do what they do!" Kate shooed the Panthers onto the field.

Chase saw the blacks hesitating and waved them on. He surprised the white players by tossing the football to Tree, who, equally surprised, tucked it under his arm. He assumed Riddle wanted him to hold it until it was needed. It was so new and smooth that he hated to get it dirty. He could not remember when the Post Oak ball had been new.

"Here you go, Tree, throw it back!" Chase called. He grinned to see the big lineman awkwardly toss the ball to him, as if this were the first time he had ever touched a football. Chase began to play catch with the other the Panthers. His relaxed attitude was contagious.

Glenn and Nalley formed the team for calisthenics. The Panthers lined up on the second row. They tentatively began touching toes and bending from side to side. *"One, two, three, four!"* Nalley cried. Standing near her players, Kate began to demonstrate the exercises.

"Not now, Miz Kate!" Brother pleaded. She retreated reluctantly to the sideline.

After the warm-ups Heisman yelled, "Forwards over here, backs with Coach Warner!" He noticed the Negroes tagging along and suggested that they wait on the sideline. Kate roamed up and down, fuming.

Warner worked with the backs, running bucks and sweeps to let them get used to each other's movements. Heisman worked the forwards in cross-blocking, pulling to lead interference, and shifting into guard-back and tackle-back formations. The big men shifted position smoothly, without waste motion.

"They move pretty good," Lincoln whispered.

"We could do that, with a li'l practice," Tree said.

They watched Burke drop-kick the ball sixty yards. "We cain't do *that*," Weasel said.

"Who needs to kick," Cassius sniffed, "when you can *run?*"

After fifteen minutes of drills, Heisman called the forwards and backs together. They began to work out in full formation. For a time the only sounds were of feet drumming on the hard ground, harsh breathing, and Heisman shouting, "Shift together—together!" Or Warner: "You've got to lead him a bit more with your pass, Riddle. He's five yards outside you when you turn. Try it again."

Kate saw Heisman looking at her and hopefully ran up to him.

"Where's the water bucket?" he said.

"Is that all?" She stood flat-footed in her disappointment, her cheeks ruddy with cold, her eyes piercingly blue.

"We need water." Heisman's expression was noncommittal.

"Isn't there anything else we can do?"

"I'll let you know." Heisman's long-suffering expression made Kate suddenly furious.

"Maybe I should go back to the house," she said coolly, "and bake up some tea cakes."

"That would be nice." Heisman turned back to his work.

"I have a better idea. How about a scrimmage?"

Her challenge was so personal that for a second Heisman thought she meant the two of them, woman against man. "Oh, your scrubs versus the varsity? Oh, no," he added in some relief. "Just bring the bucket."

"Afraid my players will show yours up?" Kate stood braced, fists against her hips.

"Madam, get hold of yourself!"

Heisman was turning away when a hack pulled up in the street. A passenger leaped out, staggering before he caught his balance. He was a short, barrel-chested man, wearing a black cape and a Western-style ten-gallon hat. He started to walk onto the practice field, but the cabbie called him back and made him pay his fare. Then the stranger proceeded onto the field, walking a not-so-straight line. With a sweeping, dramatic gesture he whipped off his cape and flung it aside.

"Which one-a you is Coach Humboldt?" he cried.

The professor spun around. His cheroot turned sour in his mouth.

"My God," he said.

"I. Lopez," said the stranger.

Phrases echoed cruelly in Cornelius's memory: *All-SWC, heart of a lion, without equal at pulling guard.* Looking down at the five-foot, three-inch Lopez, Humboldt feared for his reason. He smelled liquor.

"Lopez?" he said faintly. "From Texas A&I?"

"The same!" Lopez boomed. Heisman and Warner regarded Lopez askance, as if they could not bear to look directly at him.

"May I have a word with you, Coach Humboldt?" Heisman said. "Is this your idea of a joke? That man is older than I am." Humboldt hugged his chest as though to protect himself. "Get him out of here!" Heisman hissed. "The players are laughing at us."

Humboldt took Lopez aside, saying, "Coach Heisman says, since you are tardy for practice, please wait over there until we take a break. Then Coach Heisman will consider your situation."

"My si-chation?" Lopez glanced toward the sideline. "You're puttin' me in the nigger section? *What is this?*" He raised his voice to a bellow. "I done come ten thousand miles mostly at my own expense and now you say, 'Wait with the niggers!' "

"I never said—"

"Don't I git a tryout?"

Humboldt glanced slavishly at Heisman.

"Blondy!" Heisman called to his big tackle. "I need you for a tackling drill. Okay, Professor. If Texas wants an audition, he can have one. Right *here*."

"Lopez," Humboldt said, "Coach Heisman wants you."

Lopez did not move. In an empty cattle car between Baltimore and Philadelphia he had put away his last fifth of tequila. Drunk as he was, however, he had enough sense not to rush into anything. He saw Blondy Glenn waiting for him. The man had a head like a bighorn ram.

Did I say anything to make anybody mad at me?

Lopez had meant to save the tequila for a celebration after he joined the team; but after he lost his money in a Birmingham crap game and had to hop freights the rest of the way, he needed something to take the edge off reality. As there appeared to be no way out of his predicament, Lopez strutted toward Blondy, hoping that the tequila would dull the pain. He stood before Blondy, looked up, and said, "If this was a game I'd butt you in the nuts and chew on yo' leg. I probably wouldn't make the team if I was to do that now, though!" Satisfied with Glenn's dubious expression, Lopez crouched in his best defensive posture, about waist-high to Glenn, and hoped for luck.

"Don't you want to take off your hat first?" Heisman asked.

Lopez started to take off his ten-gallon hat, then inspiration seized him. "That reminds me," he said with massive dignity. "I didn't git no chance to warm up. Just got off'n the train, y'know."

"Sure, take all the time you need, cowboy." Heisman waved him off the field. "Okay, everybody, let's get back to work!"

Practice resumed. Lopez wandered over to the sideline and squatted down. He was having a sinking spell. He looked around for a tree or bush where he could throw up in private and noticed faces staring at him—dark faces. Curiosity overcame nausea.

"What're you doin' here?" he asked.

"Nothing much," Lincoln said.

"I kin see that. I mean, you handle the equipment or sump'm?"

"We players," Tree said. He could not bring himself to utter the word "scrubs," which in Bardstown was synonymous with "nothing." Lopez looked him over.

"Are you sittin' or standin'?"

"I hunkered," Tree answered precisely.

"Jesus, I thought we were the same size. What's yo' name?"

"They call me Tree."

"I believe it. So, when do you fellas git to play?"

"Not anytime soon, the way it's goin'."

"That's some kinda horseshit, ain't it? Bring us thousands of miles to freeze our asses off in some—what is this, a vacant lot? Where's the stadium?"

"I don't rightly know."

Lopez focused on the silent faces around him. He was at home among underdogs. He struggled to his feet and whipped his cape back over his shoulder, exposing his rawhide vest and jeans soiled with cow dung. He hitched up his belt and marched out onto the field. Downwind, the players caught his scent and started laughing. Heisman tried not to look at him.

"Coach, when you goin' to put the scrubs in?" Lopez demanded. "I'm talkin' 'bout them niggers over there."

Heisman glared not at Lopez but at Humboldt, who wished he were invisible.

"What about the scrubs?" Lopez persisted. Politics cleared his head.

"Don't talk to me, talk to *Humboldt.* He's your man," Heisman said.

"Excuse me, Coach, but bringin' a man ten thousand miles and then tellin' him you don't need him is grounds for civil suit in Arkansas. I respectfully ask you to reconsider. I druther settle this without recoursin' to legal remedy."

"You are messing up my practice," Heisman spoke out of the side of his mouth. His players from Alabama Poly, Glenn and Harvey, recognized this facial tic as a sign of oncoming fury.

"Sir, I respectfully request—"

"Go sit yourself down and leave us be."

"Sir . . ."

"GO! SIT!" Heisman thundered.

"Sure thing, Coach." Lopez headed for the sideline with contrite steps which changed into a swagger as he reached the scrub team, of which he had appointed himself captain. He gave them a cocky wave.

"It won't be long," he said. "Stay ready."

Tree loomed over Lopez. "You ought not to call us that," he said.

Lopez's head was just about level with Tree's stomach. He looked up. "What?"

"You know what."

"Oh, yeah. You can call me greaser if you want to."

"I ain't goin' call you greaser, and you ain't goin' call me nigger."

"Good deal, big fella."

A carriage stopped on the street near the vacant lot. Richard Canfield got out, accompanied by Ziprenian, Mahoney, and McGee. Although Canfield was not curious about the football team, Bird and Fingers, who were building an investment in the all-star game, had persuaded him to put in an appearance at practice. Ziprenian, who also had come along to protect his investment— his life—scurried ahead to set up a folding chair for the King. Resplendent in beaver coat and mink collar, Canfield approached the field like a feudal lord. In fact, in a strange way Canfield viewed the football players as serfs, their hulking size, brute struggles, hoarse cries somehow all part of the Richard A. Canfield empire.

"Do I own this property?" he asked. The ground felt as if it might belong to him.

"Yes, boss," Mahoney said.

From such a bemused perspective Canfield's eye fell on Kate Kuykendall. She still wore her red cap with her hair tucked into it, but she had taken off her hunting jacket. Nervous as a cat, she stalked up and down the sideline. Lopez's demand that the scrubs be allowed to play had made her more determined that they get their chance.

"Is that a *woman?*" Canfield stared with intense interest. Heads bent to attend him, faces turned to follow his glance.

"Yes, boss," Mahoney said, after a moment's hesitation.

"What is her name?"

A whispered conference took place. "Kathryn something," Ziprenian offered.

"Something? Get her name!"

Canfield watched Ziprenian move gingerly across the field, avoiding the yard lines as if he had no business there. His gaze continued past Ziprenian to Kate. Her aggressive manner, square shoulders, and thick neck charmed him. He appreciated size in a woman.

Ziprenian sat on his heels in the manner of the Negroes. Tiny snowflakes swirled in the air. He addressed the young man next to him.

"Could you tell me that woman's name?" he said.

"Miz Kate," Weasel said.

"Mrs. Kate what?"

"She ain't married."

"What is her last name?"

Weasel thought for a moment. "You know, I don't know."

"What about them?" The Zipper gestured at the other players. Weasel's question went to the end of the row and back again. Brother told B.C., "Kuykendall." When it reached Weasel it was "Kitengale."

"Or sump'm like that," Weasel said. "Down home she mostly go by Miz Kate."

"Sump'm like that?" Ziprenian echoed. He had cultivated a speaking acquaintance with Negroes in New York and Philadelphia—houseboys, cooks, street sweepers, hansom cab drivers, bartenders, launderers. Arno wondered if Southern blacks were a different breed. Could it be possible that men trained under a coach, even a female one, for any length of time did not know her *name?*

"Do you go to school?" Arno asked. Weasel did not appreciate the skeptical expression.

"Natchally," he replied. "Post Oak."

"Post Oak *Seminary,* fool!" Cassius whispered.

"Until I graduated to the seminary, that is," Weasel said.

Ziprenian was confused. First they did not know their coach's name; then they were unsure about where they went to school. At least they were consistent, he thought, as he returned to his boss to report the name, Miss Kate Kitengale, or something like that.

A trolley stopped in the street, its bell muffled in the distance. Will Du Bois got off. He came toward the field, picking his way carefully through the icy stubble to keep from getting mud on his shoes. At Fisk and later at Harvard, Du Bois had taken little notice of athletics. He would not be interested in sports now, except for the sociological phenomenon of the Black Rebels. He saw them huddled together on the far side of the field and wondered if he was wasting his time, if the scene at the Broad Street Station had been so much sound and fury. He could see at a glance that the Negro players were being denied the opportunity to play with the whites. He looked across the field to pick out the flag-waver of the "Tom" incident. He recognized Brother.

Close behind the departing trolley, another carriage arrived. Du Bois turned and saw a large, white-bearded man getting out of it. Something about this man's authoritative bearing stirred Will's memory. He recalled a photograph in the *Inquirer.* It was James Longstreet.

Du Bois had never spent much time thinking about Confederate generals, whom he regarded as devils or worse. Now that he stood almost shoulder to shoulder with one of the most famous of them, he was disappointed. Longstreet looked tired. Du Bois expected Lee's lieutenant to resemble Milton's Satan, complete with scales and horns, hoary wings furled after a flight through Chaos. Sneaking a glance at Longstreet, he felt deprived.

For his part Longstreet was uncomfortably aware of the slight, well-dressed man scrutinizing him. He glanced at Du Bois and read intelligence and sensitivity. The general was prepared to give educated Negroes their due, but they made him nervous. He concentrated on the football practice and was struck immediately by the similarity between football and combat. Linemen pushed forward or held their ground like infantry, while the backs slashed through or flanked the line like cavalry. Punts and dropkicks reminded him of artillery. The ball sailed end over end like canister. When it landed he half-expected it to explode. In his soldier's mind a thought was born.

"Our team seems to be doing well," Du Bois remarked loudly. Longstreet cut his eyes at him.

Our team? the general thought. "Yes indeed," he said.

"What are our chances?"

"Of winning? Not bad, I reckon."

"Better than first predicted?"

"Absolutely!" Longstreet warmed to the role of underdog. Du Bois took this for a sign of amiability.

"I am W.E.B. Du Bois," he said and made a little bow.

"I am James Longstreet."

"Pleased to meet you. Congratulations on your book."

Longstreet brightened. "Thank you. Thank you very much."

"I hope sales are going well."

"Very well indeed. The first edition has almost sold out."

"Is your publisher going into a second printing?"

"I hope so. However, these decisions are quite out of an author's hands."

Du Bois solemnly nodded. "I can imagine how you must feel. My first book is at press now."

"Really?" Longstreet realized that some further response was required, one author to another. "What is the title?"

"The Suppression of the African Slave Trade to the United States of America, 1638 to 1870."

"I see." Longstreet wondered uncomfortably if he himself were a footnote in Du Bois's book.

Aware that spectators were watching them, the players ran smartly, kicking up their heels. Heisman was pleased. He smiled when Blondy Glenn begged him for a scrimmage. Chase asked him the same thing.

"How about letting the scrubs work out a little bit with us, Coach?" Riddle said. "I trained 'em during water stops on the trip up here. They're awful quick."

Heisman glanced at the blacks. To him they seemed satisfied to be doing nothing. "We don't have time to indulge in curiosity, Mr. Riddle. Things are going fairly well. I won't have my workout messed up again."

"They won't mess up," Chase said.

"Come on, Coach," Blondy said. "It might be interesting."

Heisman had always made a point of humoring his captains. He relented. "I'll let the Negroes play five minutes on defense. Maybe we can get our timing down if we have an alignment to run at." He saw Kate looking at him. "Coach Kate, kindly assemble your team."

Kate masked her delight behind a businesslike expression. She pushed her players onto the field. Lopez followed the scrubs nearly to the line of scrimmage, then dropped back beside Kate. When she clapped her hands and shouted encouragement, so did he. Heisman watched the Negroes amble self-consciously into

position. He silently asked the gods of football to forgive him for
what he was about to do. He huddled with the white players and
said, "Full speed, halfback sweep left." Then he stepped back to
watch.

On the far sideline, Mahoney said to Ziprenian, "I'll back the
whites against your blacks and give you ten to one for a fiver."

"*My* blacks?" the Zipper said, annoyed. He glanced at Canfield. The King was watching Kate Kitengale-or-sump'm.
Ziprenian decided that, orders to the contrary notwithstanding,
private side bets might be allowed.

"You're on," he told Mahoney.

Chase followed the white linemen up to the ball. He watched
the Panthers move tentatively into position. It occurred to Chase
that they might be afraid to hit a white man. They certainly had
not been timid about tackling him, however, behind the Post
Oak schoolhouse. As he called signals, Chase's eyes sought Brother's determined face.

Joiner of Carolina snapped the ball. Chase pitched it to Abbott
running left. Although the Panthers instantly recognized where
the sweep was headed, they were slow to react. From his left
linebacker position, Brother had to pursue the ballcarrier all the
way across the field. The big linemen—Link, Ulysses, Tree, and
B.C.—stood and grappled with their opponents. Abbott gained
ten yards before Brother, Cassius, and Weasel caught him by the
shoulders and rode him to the ground.

"I'll take my five now," Mahoney told the Zipper.

"It's not over yet," Arno said.

Heisman nodded to Warner as if to say, "There you are." The
white players huddled jubilantly and looked at their coach for
the next play. Chase glanced back and saw Brother talking to his
teammates.

"You know what they're saying?" Brother hissed. "Don't look
at the ground, look at me! They're saying we're a bunch of scared
niggers. Let's show 'em, dammit!"

As the Post Oak players took their positions, Brother happened
to notice the slender, well-dressed black man standing on the
sideline. The man was small, almost frail, but his eyes burned
with an intensity that Brother could sense from across the field.

Using precision blocking and deft passes, the whites pushed

the blacks down the field. Chase played automatically, his heart with the scrubs.

"Hey, this is fun!" Alabama's Abbott said to Georgia's Nalley.

"Did you hear that?" Weasel whispered to Tree. "Let's tear his head off."

"Coach wouldn't like that," Tree whispered back.

On the next play, the Panthers swarmed over the ballcarrier and held the All-Stars to no gain. In the ensuing pileup, pushing and shoving began. Kate yanked at their bodies, startling the white players and embarrassing the blacks.

"Get off me!" Joiner told Ulysses and elbowed him in the stomach.

"Don't take that off'n him," Weasel told Ulysses.

The All-Stars tried another buck, but the scrubs stopped them for no gain.

"You can't hold thataway!" Joiner accused B.C., and added in a low muttering, "Damn fool."

"Well, *he* was doin' it, too." B.C. complained to his teammates.

"Don't take that shine off'n him," Weasel advised B.C. Joiner paused to listen. B.C. saw that the big Carolinian seemed to be challenging him.

"Rule work both ways," B.C. said. "You don't believe me, you can ax Coach."

"I don't need to *ax* Coach, you ignorant nigger," Joiner muttered. An inscrutable calm settled over the scrub team.

"What did he say?" Lopez bellowed.

Chase thanked the Lord for Joiner.

"Coach Heisman," Kate sang, "I believe your center owes my center an apology."

"I just said *Nigrah*, that's all," Joiner complained.

"Just calling a spade a burrhead," Brother grunted.

"Hush, Brother!" Kate said.

"I said *Nigrah*," Joiner stubbornly repeated, looking at his teammates for corroboration. They stood with their arms hanging woodenly at their sides.

"He said 'Nigrah' meaning 'Negro,'" Heisman explained to Kate. "If he said *nigger* he would owe your man an apology and me twenty laps."

"Only twenty?" Brother said.

"Hush," Kate said.

On the sideline Du Bois and Longstreet stood like statues, straining to hear what was going on. Canfield was looking at Kate's buttocks.

"Joiner meant 'Negro,' " Heisman said, "only he did not pronounce it correctly. This is a common mispronunciation in the South."

"That's right, Coach," said Joiner. "I mispronounced *Nigrah.*"

"You mean, *Nee*-gro," Heisman corrected. He turned to Humboldt. "Professor, can you explain this from the philological point of view?"

Humboldt took hold of his lapel. "Southern dialect, as you doubtless have observed, is famous for its leveling of vowels and inflections. I think it may actually have been black people themselves who reduced 'Negro,' with its nasal fricative, extended vowels, and bilabial consonants, to 'Nigra.' The derogative slang term 'nigger,' however, probably was first used by Arab slave traders operating in the Niger River Basin of Africa . . ."

Brother and the Post Oak players stared at Humboldt in disbelief.

"Thank you, Professor," Heisman said dryly, thinking the least Humboldt could do was to help defuse the situation. "So it's actually nobody's fault we Southerners don't speak correctly. Everybody satisfied? Joiner, shake hands with—uh, what's your name, son?"

"B.C."

"With B.C. and let's get on with the practice."

Joiner grudgingly stuck out his hand and B.C. just as reluctantly shook it. Longstreet and Du Bois observed this ceremony with the predatory interest of a bald eagle and a kingfisher roosting side by side. The teams separated into respective huddles. Lopez crawled among the scrubs.

"I cain't believe you-all goin' to let that college boy git away with callin' you *niggers,*" he said.

On the next play, the scrub team surged forward as one, knocking the All-Star linemen on their backs and burying the ballcarrier. Chase got up and sidled over to Heisman.

"The scrubs got their blood up, Coach. Why not let them run the ball a few times?"

"I'm not interested in what the scrubs can do," Heisman said. "It's the varsity that needs work."

"They'll surprise you," Chase persisted.

"Why not?" Warner interrupted.

Heisman had not noticed Warner moving up beside them. Crossing his arms impatiently, he nodded, turned away, and kicked at the ground. Chase trotted off and assembled the scrubs around him. Kate and Lopez hovered nearby.

"All right," Chase said. "You whupped the college boys on defense. Show 'em what you can do on offense."

Lopez said, "Excuse me, but I would like to show our linemen a little trick or two." He put his false teeth in his hat, handed it to Kate and demonstrated to Tree, B.C., Ulysses, and the other forwards how to hit low and drive the head and elbows up through the opponent's chest, then grind him into the ground. He intended to show them also how to gouge an eye or break a nose but the discs began to give way in his back.

"Remember that li'l ole triple-pass play you cooked up that day behind your schoolhouse?" Chase grinned at Brother.

"Listen up!" Brother told them. "This is the rabbit play, repeat, rabbit play." He drew lines in the dirt with his finger. "Right side of line, block left. Riddle passes to Cassius running right, who passes to me on reverse, and I pass to Weasel on double reverse, with left side of line pulling late. Got it?"

"Lord, if it be Thy will," Chase prayed.

"Amen," Weasel said.

They came up to the ball, where the All-Stars were dug in. Du Bois understood only that the black team had a chance to turn the tables. He bent over with his hands on his knees.

Strike them strike them strike them.

Longstreet watched the teams face off. His soldier's instincts told him to expect a flank attack.

Chase called signals. The play broke fast. A step behind the blacks, the white players swerved left, then right, then left. Weasel rolled around right end untouched for a touchdown.

"He gone," B.C. told Joiner.

Kate leaped in the air and cheered. Du Bois rammed his hands in his pockets with fierce satisfaction. Longstreet watched the

black halfback ceremoniously touch the ball down and understood that he had scored.

We did not fight the war to preserve slavery. Did we?

"It was a fluke," Heisman told Warner. "Don't you think it was
a fluke?"

"Try it again," Warner said.

Chase looked into the clouds. Was that a sign, Lord? he silently
asked.

"What did you say the odds were?" Ziprenian asked Mahoney.

"Ten to one, North over South," the Bird answered solemnly.
"But if these niggers can do it to the white boys like that, what
can the Blue team do?"

"The South's varsity won't be white," the Zipper said
shrewdly. "You owe me fifty."

"Not until practice is over," Mahoney stalled.

In the huddle, Brother drew another play in the dirt. "Same
play, but this time I fake to Weasel on reverse and take it around
left end. Left side of line pulls right, just as before, and Weasel,
you hunch over and act like you're hugging the ball to your chest.
Got it?"

"How 'bout the 'Abe Shuffle'?" Cassius suggested.

"No arguments," Brother retorted. "Run the play I said."

B.C. snapped the ball to Chase. The Blue defense bellowed like
bulls to see the scrubs attempting the identical play again. They
barely responded to Cassius's feint or Brother's but galloped to
meet Weasel. Brother hid the ball against his thigh and was almost across the Blue goal line before they realized what had
happened.

Watching these athletes running up and down a frozen vacant
lot in North Philadelphia, Longstreet was inexplicably drawn to
the past, to Gettysburg.

*Sir, I want to move around the right, Hood said. Let me move
right and put a battery on Round Hill. If we attack straight
ahead through those boulders I stand to lose half my division. If I
can get a battery up there on Round Hill . . .*

*We must attack as ordered, Longstreet said. I asked General
Lee the same thing. He would not approve a flanking movement
around the right. We have our orders, Sam. We must do our duty.
God bless us all.*

"You're going to get your flanking movement, Sam," Longstreet said.

"Pardon?" Du Bois said.

Heisman motioned Warner to gather near. He cleared his throat. "Ever see team speed like that?"

"I did not imagine," Warner replied, "that it existed."

"What in the hell have we got?"

"I'm willing to find out if you are."

"Coach, I don't think that play was legal," Joiner complained.

"Don't worry," Warner said diplomatically. "You're doing just fine."

"Will we get to work some more on offense?"

"You're doing fine on defense. Let's contribute to the team any way we can."

Joiner, All-Southern at Chapel Hill three years in a row, had not heard "contribute to the team" since he was a high school freshman in Winston-Salem. He sullenly rejoined his white teammates.

"All right!" Heisman called crisply. "We're going to scrimmage under game regulations. First team will kick off to the scrubs. Warner and I will act as referee and field judge. Take your positions, gentlemen."

As scrub captain, Chase assembled his team. He saw a wolflike confidence in their eyes. "Forwards form a wedge on the left, and ballcarrier run behind it," he told them. He walked them into their respective positions. At home their strategy had been to bunch together to receive a kick and fight for the privilege of returning it.

Cow Nalley kicked deep. Heisman and Warner witnessed the most amazing runback they had ever seen. Weaving with elflike quickness, crisscrossing, dodging, and, when seemingly trapped, tossing the ball back to a trailing runner, the scrubs advanced the ball ninety yards upfield while maneuvering some three hundred yards between sidelines until Cassius danced into the end zone and looked back at the tacklers sprawled in his wake.

Humboldt, glancing about for someone with whom to share his excitement, saw Longstreet leaning forward, brooding, hands folded behind his back. The professor recalled a line from Fitzhugh Lee's biography:

> Over the splendid scene of human courage and human
> sacrifice at Gettysburg there arises in the South an appa-
> rition, like Banquo's ghost at Macbeth's banquet, which
> says the battle was lost to the Confederates because
> someone blundered.

"Yes, there are ghosts," Humboldt whispered to himself. The
Sewanee man wished for the courage to go up and confront the
old war-horse.

Will Du Bois watched the black team score four unanswered
touchdowns. By the time the scrimmage ended, he had come to
realize just what he was witnessing. It was more than an almost
all-black team (with Riddle at quarterback the only exception)
beating an all-white team.

It is the beginning of a revolution, right here on this vacant lot.

Heisman dismissed the team. The white players slouched off
the field, bruised and baffled. Joiner told Price, "I'm goin' home if
Coach puts a Nigrah in mah place." The Panthers lingered behind in possession of the field they had laid out and won.

Lopez said to Kate, "Now these boys know what whuppin'
white boys is *like.*"

Kate glowed like a bride. Heisman fell into step beside her and
asked her about Stagg's book.

"The early chapters contain basic information about rules,
training, playing the various positions; the later chapters are very
revealing of Stagg's technique, especially the chapter entitled
'Field Tactics.'" Kate grinned expectantly at Heisman.

"Let's have lunch and you can tell me all about it," Heisman
said.

Richard Canfield hurried across the field to intercept Kate, his
assistants fluttering behind him like kites. The King wanted to
see her close up. He admired her square jawline, thick shoulders,
and muscular thighs. "Permit me . . ." he began, but Kate
brushed past him. Being snubbed by a woman was a new experience for Canfield. The connoisseur shivered inside his beaver
coat but not from the cold. The sweaty athletes filing past him,
their cleats clattering like hooves on the hard ground, were like
satyrs. This small, seedy abandoned lot was an Elysian field. One

tiny, postage stamp of Canfield holdings, it seemed ideal for an athletic infatuation, hard and rugged.

Harrison Prescott hurried onto the field. He had arrived in time for the final touchdown, which he observed with genuine interest. To see brutes bash each other was of little moment, but the possibility that the South's team might be all-Negro set him on fire. Nalley and Harvey, captains-designate, spotted the reporter and waited for him. Harry walked past them. He selected the biggest Negro and approached him ingratiatingly. Tree regarded the reporter with blank suspicion.

"I'm with the *Inquirer*. Could I impose on you for an interview?"

"What interview?" Tree said.

"It's for the paper," Harry explained. "Your name, please?"

"Henry Clay Jackson. They call me Tree."

Looking up at the brown face dwarfed by massive shoulders, Prescott imagined banana or breadfruit trees springing up overnight, full-grown, in a rain forest.

"What's your name?" he asked another of the treelike men.

"Lincoln Jackson."

"And yours?"

"Levester Jackson. They calls me Weasel."

"W-E-A-S-E-L," Harry spelled as he wrote.

"I spell it W-E-A-S-L-E," Weasel said.

"W-E-A-S-L-E." Harry abruptly turned to Tree. "Will the South rise again?"

"I don't rightly know."

"What do you think about Plessy versus Ferguson?"

"Say what?"

"The 'Separate But Equal' ruling."

"I ain't thought much about it." Tree looked to Brother for help.

"Are you by any chance the son of slaves?"

Tree looked at his friends for assistance. "I just came to play . . ." he began.

"(. . . to the best of my ability)," Weasel offered.

"(. . . using my God-given talents)," Cassius whispered.

"(. . . if I give my all)," B.C. put in.

"(. . . the rest will take care of itself)," Lincoln concluded.

"Write it like they said," Tree said.

Brother, fascinated by his teammates' first newspaper interview, felt a tap on his shoulder.

"Excuse me," Will Du Bois said, "I am somewhat confused."

"About what, sir?"

"About Confederate generals and Black Rebels."

"What generals? Where?" Brother was at a loss. At the same time he felt drawn to this compact, well-dressed man with his air of assurance.

"Over there." Du Bois pointed toward the street. "See that man getting into that hack? That's James Longstreet."

Brother shrugged, then hiding a grin said, "All Confederate generals look alike to me."

I was right, Du Bois thought.

Will reached into his vest pocket and gave Jones his card. Brother handled it as if it were a talisman. It read:

W. E. Burghardt Du Bois, Ph.D.
Sociology Department
University of Pennsylvania
Philadelphia, Penna.

"I would like to invite you to have tea with me tomorrow afternoon. You have the afternoons free, do you not?"

"I think so. Nobody has told us what our schedule is."

"And you are?"

"Oh, uh, Jones."

"Mr. Jones, it is a pleasure."

Du Bois's small hand had a surprisingly firm grip. Shaking it, Brother had the strange sensation of being led into another dimension.

"By the way," Will said, "I saw you arrive yesterday at Broad Street Station." He hesitated.

"You saw the flag-waving incident," Brother said immediately, "and heard the crowd yelling 'Tom.' "

"Yes?"

"I slipped, getting off the train," Brother explained. "I grabbed that flag by mistake. It was all a mistake."

Du Bois threw back his head and laughed, a short, barking laugh. "I thought to myself something *strange* must be going on down South. Nothing so dramatic ever happened when I was in Nashville."

"Are you from Tennessee!"

"Oh, no. I grew up in Massachusetts. But I attended Fisk College." Du Bois pointed to the card Brother was holding. "I have written my home address on the back of it. Do you think you can find me?"

"I'll try." Brother studied the small, neat handwriting: *College Settlement, second-floor apartment above cafeteria, Seventh and Lombard streets.*

"Take the Broad Street trolley, get off at Lombard, and walk east toward the river," Du Bois said. "Shall we say two o'clock, then, tomorrow afternoon?"

"Yes, I think so."

"Good! I will look forward to it." Du Bois's sharp eyes were mesmerizing. "You have a rare opportunity to do something important," he added mysteriously, "for our people."

Brother watched the dapper stranger pick his way across the vacant lot now churned into mud. It took him a few seconds to realize whom Du Bois had meant by "our people."

Several miles away, on the west bank of the Schuylkill River at Franklin Field, Amos Alonzo Stagg watched his Blue squad practice. He looked like a monk under the hood of his flannel jersey with "U. of Chicago" printed on it. King and Woodruff were conducting carefully orchestrated drills. Here on the University of Pennsylvania campus, at historic Franklin Field where Stagg had once played end for Yale, Heffelfinger and his All-America teammates ran their formations with the precision of a threshing machine. The shouts of the coaches, the drumming of feet, the harsh breathing of the athletes were like music to Stagg.

"I wish the game were tomorrow!" King exclaimed.

"Don't be in such a hurry," Lonny told his assistant from Princeton. He glanced up at clouds heavy with snow and thought about the South All-Stars practicing under the same sky.

What are Heisman and Warner cooking up?

"I once read," he told King, "about a black strongman of Vicksburg who could lift a five-hundred-pound bale of cotton over his head."

"Yes, Coach?" King said.

"I'm wondering about Heisman's Negroes," Stagg mused. "How well do they play? We know they're fast. What defense do we use? Do we concentrate on containment? How fast are they?"

"Nine-six, we heard," King said glumly.

"Yes, but are they faster when being chased?" Stagg continued.

"Maybe Heisman won't play them," Woodruff said, joining them. The assistant coach from Pennsylvania kept an eye on his forwards who were hitting the tackling dummy.

"Don't count on it," Stagg said.

"I heard General Longstreet appeared at their practice," King said wryly. "Maybe we ought to ask General Sickles to pay our squad a visit."

"Longstreet!" Stagg was concerned. "What was he doing there?"

"Probably trying to promote his book," Woodruff suggested.

"What book?"

"From something *to Appomattox*—I forget."

"I want a copy," Stagg said. "Where's a bookstore?"

"There's Leary's . . ." Woodruff said.

"Good. Go buy me a copy." Stagg dug some money out of his jersey pocket.

"Now?" Woodruff said.

"Now?" Stagg echoed. "Yes, now, if you want to win this ball game."

"What does Longstreet's book have to do with football, Coach?" King asked tentatively. Stagg fixed him with a black-eyed stare from under his monk's cowl.

"What's a military commander's first maxim?" he demanded.

"I don't know, Coach," King said.

"Know your enemy."

Woodruff and King exchanged an uneasy glance.

"Better get to Leary's before it closes," Woodruff mumbled

and lumbered off. King returned to tutoring his backfield in the revolving tandem.

Stagg wandered into the end zone. He leaned on the goalpost, looked at the sky, and sniffed the air. He could have sworn he smelled jasmine.

Chapter Eighteen

Hudson's companions watched respectfully as Fitzy helped strap on his mahogany peg. They had gathered in his hotel room while he dressed for the game. Dickinson held out his white shirt for him.

" 'Preciate it, Knot." Hudson slipped his thin arms into the sleeves. " 'Specially seeing as how I couldn't beat you at vingt-et-un in a month of Sundays. I oughta be holding yo' shirt."

"Reno ain't bad his own self," Dickinson said modestly, referring to O'Shea, the blackjack specialist among the Northerners.

"Reno's seventy-eight," Little Harry said. "Maybe he can't cut it anymore." Little Harry, at sixty-seven the youngest member of their group, never let anyone forget his junior status.

"I wouldn't count on it," Hudson warned. Fitzpatrick was buffing a single patent-leather high-top. "If Reno crosses his legs, look out. He carries cards in a holler heel."

"I'll watch for that," said Fitzpatrick, who had been placed in charge of security. They fell silent, watching Hudson's ex-corporal lace up his shoe.

"Anybody heard from Holliday lately?" Isaac said. They groaned and smiled at the old joke. Every gambler claimed to be a friend of Doc Holliday.

"Ain't he out in Colorado somewheres?" Dickinson kept the joke going.

"Down with the bad lungs," Hudson said. "Retired."

"I heard smoking opium was good for tuberculosis," Nelson said scientifically. "It relaxes the lungs." Hudson frowned at him. Before the subject was silenced altogether, Harry added, "And inhaling brandy fumes from a charred oak keg has been known to cure the TB."

"Let's don't forget to check the seals." Hudson steered them away from home remedies. "Feel the edges for smoothness and check the backs for indentations or markings."

"Right, Sarge." Fitzpatrick rubbed Hudson's cuff links with his handkerchief. Pitts helped Stroud slip into his vest embroidered with scenes of the chase.

"By the way," Pitts said, "happy birthday." The others chimed in, surprising Hudson.

"I plumb forgot," he said.

" 'Zackly how old *are* you?" Little Harry said.

"It don't matter," Hudson replied. 'Least I ain't got arthritis."

"Mine's under control." Nelson added defensively. "I take alfalfa tablets for it."

"My coat!" Hudson cut him short.

The old gamblers looked on appreciatively as Hudson stuck his arms into the black broadcloth coat. They murmured their approval as he displayed his watch, trademark of the river gambler. He looped the gold chain three times around his neck and inserted the watch in his vest pocket.

"Does it work?" Colonel Pitts teased.

"It's a Jeurgunsen, ain't it?" Hudson grinned. "Time ain't no account, nohow. All I need is 'bout a week." He put on his slouch hat, tilted it at a rakish angle, and turned to face his associates.

"You forgot your teeth," Little Harry said.

They were soaking in a water glass next to the washbasin. Fitzpatrick dried them off with his handkerchief. Hudson turned aside to pop them into his mouth. While Stroud's back was to the others, Fitzy slipped into Hudson's pocket four vials containing his heart, liver, cirrhosis, and blood-pressure pills. The riverboaters self-consciously patted their own pockets. Fitzpatrick handed Stroud a flask of sour-mash whiskey.

"For energy," Hudson needlessly explained. All of them carried flasks. "Where's my button?"

Fitzpatrick rummaged in Stroud's traveling kit and produced

the "5th KY" pin, which he attached to Hudson's lapel. Stroud examined his reflection in the mirror. Behind him he saw the faces of his partners: expectant, clear of eye, living in the present.

Whatever happens, at least we come this far.

"Let's whup Yankee butt," he said. Swinging his crutches, he led them into the hall.

They took the elevator to the fourth floor, where a private room had been reserved. They had taken an open-ended rental. No one knew how long the game would last. Hudson knocked. Liebowitz opened the door. He grinned at the sight of Stroud wearing riverboat clothes. Ernie wore a conservative dark suit and his "lucky" red-flannel shirt, open at the neck.

"You look smart, Hudson. Come in." Liebowitz made introductions to mark the occasion, although everybody knew everybody. "Reno O'Shea, Diamond Ed Baker, Dutch Trott, Bones McCain —Knot, Harry, the Colonel, Fitzpatrick."

The gamblers shook hands. Smiling, the Southerners glanced at the ceiling for peepholes, casually felt under the table rim for hidden cards.

"Go ahead, check it out," Liebowitz said. "You don't hafta be shifty about it! It's clean. But I want you to be satisfied."

"If you're satisfied, we're satisfied," Stroud said.

"No, no, let everybody be happy. Go ahead, be my guest."

Hudson nodded to his men, who left off their small talk and immediately made a thorough search for hidden devices. They turned chairs upside down. They crawled under the octagonal table. They frisked their opponents and checked the contents of their pockets. In turn, they allowed themselves to be searched. At last the old men squared off around the table. Without another word, they took their places. Reno asked Dickinson if he would care to check the seals on the decks. Knot slit the paper seals with his penknife, expertly examined the cards, then nodded. Hudson and Ernie cut for deal. Hudson showed a queen, Ernie a ten.

"Draw poker," Hudson said, "nothin' wild, pair opens, no limit, ante one hunnerd. Cards, gentlemen."

Nelson and McCain served as co-bankers and distributed the chips. They played in silence for the first few hands, checking more often than betting, exploring, feeling each other out. Neither Hudson nor Ernie looked at each other over their cards, though each man's concentration was fixed on the other.

Hudson felt his energy begin to fade and reached in his coat pocket. All eyes were on his hand as it disappeared from view. He took out his silver flask, unscrewed the cap, drank, replaced the cap, and returned the flask to his pocket. The whiskey burned pleasantly in his stomach.

"What's the biggest raise you ever heared of?" he said.

"You always were one to talk," Liebowitz complained. It was obvious that Hudson was trying to break his concentration. At the same time Ernie could not help remembering poker raises. McCain had just dealt. Everyone was considering the cards and Hudson's question at the same time.

"Dealer checks," McCain said.

Liebowitz was sitting next to McCain, under the gun. He studied his hand: four low hearts and an ace of diamonds. Possible flush, he thought, and remembered a story.

"Gun checks," he said. "Biggest raise I ever heard of . . ."

Everybody put his cards down. Flasks came out of pockets. Cigars were lit.

". . . was at the Palace Hotel in San Francisco, in the old Cinch Room. Jackpot game between Senator Sharon of Nevada— the Comstock Lode man—and William Ralston, president of the Bank of California. They built up a pot of a hundred and fifty thousand dollars. The way I heard it, Sharon raised Ralston fifty thousand. Ralston came back with a raise of a hundred and fifty thousand. Sharon folded. Ralston could not resist showing his cards. He was holding a pair of tens. For years Sharon would not tell anyone what he had in his hand that day. Then Ralston's bank failed in seventy-five, and he drowned himself the next day. At Ralston's funeral Sharon revealed that he had folded a pair of jacks."

The players murmured their satisfaction. Poker stories had a redemptive quality, like going into a church on a rainy afternoon.

"Colonel, your bet," Hudson said.

"Check," Isaac said.

"Check," Reno said.

Hudson looked at his pair of jacks. *Damned if I'm folding mine,* he thought, and flipped two $100 chips into the pot.

"John Dougherty actually made the biggest raise in the world," he said, raising Liebowitz's story. "At Bowen's saloon, Santa Fe, no-limit straight poker, for the poker champeenship of the West, 1889. Dougherty's opponent was Ike Jackson, cattleman out of Colorado City, Texas. Among their spectators was New Mexico governor L. Bradford Prince. The pot held one hundred thousand dollars. Jackson wanted to raise Dougherty one hundred thousand but found hisself out of cash, so he wrote a deed to his ranch and ten thousand cattle. Dougherty called for pen and paper, scribbled on it for a minute, drew his revolver and handed the paper to Governor Prince.

"Dougherty said, 'Now sign this, Guv, or I will kill you. I like you and would prob'ly fight for you, but I got my reputation as a poker player to think about.'

"Governor signed the paper. Dougherty tossed it in the pot. He looked old Ike in the eye and said, 'I'll raise you the Territory of New Mexico. There's the deed.'

"Ike threw in his hand and said, 'All right, take the pot, but you're damned lucky—' "

" '—that the governor of Texas isn't here!' " Liebowitz chimed in. Everybody laughed. Stroud sulkily regarded his cards. If there was one thing he hated, it was somebody cutting in on his punch line. Lucky for Liebowitz, he thought, that I left my Betsy in the room.

On reflection, Hudson was glad Ernie had revealed his true, obnoxious self. For a minute he had forgotten why he was there.

"Where's the sword, Lieberwitz?" he said.

"The hotel safe."

"It won't be there long.—Dutchman?"

"I'm staying." Trott tossed two chips into the pot. Betting resumed. Nelson and Baker folded, but the others stayed. McCain dealt the cards.

Liebowitz took one card. He slipped it into his hand without looking at it, then fanned the cards by degrees until the new one was revealed. It was a queen of hearts. Liebowitz tapped the flush together, laid the cards on the table perpendicular to himself, and waited.

Hudson had drawn a four of clubs, six of diamonds, and king of diamonds, which did nothing to improve his two jacks. He checked the bet, lowering his eyes modestly as if daring them to come on. The Dutchman bet one hundred. Baker and McCain folded. Liebowitz raised Trott two hundred.

Hudson studied Liebowitz's face. What was happening behind those black eyes? Were the gray cells as sharp as ever or had slow blood cut back on the brain activity? Ernie had taken one card, which could mean that he was trying to fill two pair to a full house or a flush or a straight. His raise said he had filled it; but even if he hadn't filled it, his two pair would beat Hudson's jacks. On the other hand, if Ernie hadn't filled a flush or a straight, Hudson's pair might take the pot. But what if Ernie had been dealt three aces, say, and had asked for one card to confuse the players? Hudson had noted a slight hesitation on Ernie's part before he raised the bet. Was it too obvious? Did Liebowitz want him to think he was working up his nerve to bluff? No, Hudson thought, Liebowitz would anticipate such a reaction, from Hudson, which meant he *had* improved his hand by the draw, in which case it was not worth $200 to find out how improved it was.

Hudson placed his cards face down on the table and rapped his knuckles twice. Trott also folded. Liebowitz raked in the pot.

Hudson thought he saw a flicker of disappointment on his rival's face. If so, that meant Liebowitz had been laying for him.

Ernie's gray matter is still in operating condition.

Kate Kuykendall looked in the mirror and felt sorry for herself. It was bad enough to get gussied up for a fancy banquet, but quite another to be asked to serve as a team sponsor. She was a coach, not a corsage wearer. She had come to Philadelphia to knock the blocks off the men of Yale, Harvard, and Princeton, not to charm them.

"We need you," Heisman had said. "We don't have any other Southern belles up here. Help us, please."

There was nothing to do but slap rouge on her cheeks and smear on lipstick. The last time she had put on makeup she was twelve, playing dress-up in her mother's closet.

You gave up then, and you'd better give up now.

She tried to think about her players, knowing how nervous they must be feeling and wishing she had a new suit of clothes for each of them. But the sight of herself in the mirror was so unnatural that she could think of nothing but her own predicament.

She yanked and tugged at her new dress, which had arrived without warning from an exclusive dress shop, with a mysterious card:

> "You are the brightest star
> in the Southern Cross.
> Shine on, angelic beacon."
> Secret Admirer

The dress had a hoop skirt. The last time Kate had seen a hoop skirt was in 1870. When she moved around the room, she felt like a bell—not a belle—inside the dress, which swayed back and forth.

"If I find out who sent me this," she told the mirror, "I'm going to flatten his nose." Her painted face stared back at her like a caricature of a Southern simp.

"Yea-es, but you-all ditn' think to bri-ung any evenin' clo-uthes up heah, so what-all else are we supposed to we-ah, honey?"

Snow sifted against the window, a downy invitation. She longed to rip off the dress, rush outside in her bloomers, and run in the cold, clean air. Instead, she grabbed a washcloth and scrubbed her face until the cosmetics were gone. Her features glared pinkly back at her: plain, blunt, unlovely, but no longer those of a stranger. She wriggled out of the petticoat with its three hoops and exchanged a plain one for it. At last, satisfied that she would not embarrass her players, she went to join them in the Maison Blanche parlor.

Brother, Tree, Weasel, and the others were milling around in the front hall, looking as awkward as Kate felt. Having spent more time than usual on their own grooming, they did not seem surprised to see her dressed in an evening gown. They had slicked and pomaded their hair until they gleamed like seals. The team had split into two competitive groups. Carter, Joiner, Martin, and Wright had threatened to quit if they were not assured of full playing time. With black on one side and white on the other, Chase and Kate tried to make small talk until Heisman came to tell them their transportation had arrived.

"Is everybody ready?" he said with a cursory glance at Kate. "Let's have a good time tonight. Don't forget that you are gentlemen and scholars."

Gentlemen! Kate thought. *I should have worn cleats with my evening dress.*

Lopez led the South All-Stars into the Grand Ballroom of the Stratford Hotel. The Bardstown scrubs stood with their hands shoved into their pockets, waiting for someone to tell them what to do. Brother saw the North All-Stars watching them patronizingly. Lopez intercepted a waiter with a tray of champagne glasses and began passing champagne to his teammates. The Panthers held the slender-stemmed glasses with exquisite care, waiting for Brother to take the first sip.

Brother would not look at them. They were afraid of everything: strange food, tall buildings, stray dogs, bedbugs, getting lost, having wet dreams on the hotel sheets, catching gonorrhea in the Maison Blanche outhouse. Everywhere he went they clung to him. They marveled when he picked up a newspaper in the hotel lobby and began to read. "What's goin' on?" they asked. "Read it for yourself!" he told them. Yet they refused, as if they could see the world only through his eyes. He knew they were curious about the champagne, wanted to tickle their noses in it, but would not drink unless he did; knew without a doubt that the moment he lifted his glass, nine other glasses would rise as though connected to his by an invisible wire.

Ziprenian brought Kate a bouquet of lilies and ushered her to the head table, where the North team sponsor was already seated. Arno introduced her to Colette O'Hara of Chestnut Hill, a Dresden doll with shining blond hair and blue eyes. Her practiced smile made Kate feel like a turtle without its shell. In a moment of uncertainty she wondered whether she had acted rashly in washing off her makeup. She sat, smoothed the ruffles on her dress, and glanced around the ballroom at the otherwise all-male gathering. Her players stood like statues with champagne glasses frozen to their fingers. She willed them—across the room —to relax and have a good time.

Miss O'Hara seemed perfectly at ease with all this male attention. It occurred to Kate that her secret admirer might be present. At that very moment he might be looking at her. She looked down at her lap in crimson modesty.

Richard A. Canfield was, in fact, at that very moment feasting his eyes on Kate's size 16½ neck jutting out of her white lace collar. Seated inconspicuously at a corner table, he was enjoying the banquet he had paid for.

Longstreet declined a waiter's offer of champagne. Sickles accepted. The former Union general raised his glass in a toast to his old friend.

"I'll quote to you," said Sickles, "from 'The Lady of Lyons': It is astonishing how I like a man after I've fought with him!"

"Thank you, Dan," said Longstreet. "If I had me a good whiskey punch I'd surely return that toast in full measure."

Seated side by side at the honorees' table, the generals amiably looked over the company. Longstreet was curious about the opposing coaching staff.

"Tell me about your man Stagg," he said.

The question amused Sickles. "I'm afraid I am not conversant with the sports scene. Ask me about politics, ask me about railroads—hell, ask me about Spain!—but football, that's out of my province."

"Not *now,* it's not," Longstreet countered cheerfully.

Sickles had been speaking loudly, to compensate for Longstreet's hearing loss. Kate, seated on the other side of the rostrum at the same table, could not help overhearing. She leaned forward so Longstreet could see her.

"May I be of assistance, General Longstreet? My name is Kuykendall. I am here with the Southern team."

"Of course you are." Longstreet struggled to his feet, bowed. "It is an honor, missy. I've seen you at the football practice and, before that, at the promotion meeting yesterday."

"You were asking about the Northern coaches," Kate continued. "They're seated over there with our staff, Heisman and Warner. That young man is Phil King, of Princeton, and beside him is George Woodruff, of Penn. They look young enough to be players instead of coaches, don't they! And across the table is Alonzo Stagg."

"He's the commanding—I mean, the head coach?" Longstreet said. "Did I see him autographing a book to you?"

"Yes. His *Treatise on American Football*. It has become the standard text for coaches."

"Are you familiar with it?"

"I have it by heart, General."

"Oh, yes, you're a coach too, aren't you. Well, young lady, that's most commendable. And you've brought your team from—is it Bardstown? Lovely place. Wasn't Abraham Lincoln born near there?"

"Yes, sir, near Hodgenville."

"I spent the night there once; stayed at the McLean House, sampled Jim Beam's bourbon. My business associates had to drag me away or I might have stayed there for good. Listen here, missy, do you reckon you and I might get together tomorrow and go over Mr. Stagg's book?"

Kate glowed. "General Longstreet, I would consider it an honor."

Sickles, overhearing, interrupted sardonically, "Taking up coaching, are you, Jim?"

"Seeing as how I am chairman of the Southern contingent," Longstreet said, "it behooves me to learn something about the rudiments of the game. It wouldn't hurt you to do the same, Dan. When we attend the contest, what will we talk about, otherwise?"

"We'll think of something," Sickles said.

Stagg had seen Longstreet and Kate looking at him. He turned to Heisman. "John, have you met General Longstreet?"

"Have I *met* him?" Heisman said with a straight face. "He's my number-one assistant!"

Stagg did not let on that he had suspected as much. Now more than ever he wanted to meet Longstreet, whose book he had begun to study during the free period right after practice. "How about introducing me?"

"Sure thing. Come on."

They approached the generals. Heisman introduced Stagg and Longstreet, then introduced himself to Sickles. Longstreet and Stagg sized each other up. Stagg's bright black eyes and energetic manner reminded Longstreet of John Bell Hood.

"I'm enjoying your book, sir," Stagg said deferentially. "I'm only up to chapter four, but I find your account of the battles fascinating and most informative."

"Are you interested in military tactics?" Longstreet asked. As an author he was pleased to hear a reader's praise. Yet he had the feeling he was being stalked.

"Very much so," Stagg replied, "though I am certainly an amateur looking on from the sidelines. Tell me, General, is your predilection for offense or defense?"

"Are you speaking of war or football?"

"Both." Stagg's eyes were full of mischief.

"Oh, so you're both reading each other's books, eh?" Sickles put in. "What's this? A mutual admiration society?"

Stagg gave Longstreet a quick look of surmise. "Are you a student of football strategy, sir?"

"I'm very much the novice," Longstreet said, "but I'm getting more and more interested in it."

"Do you find that football tactics bear some resemblance to military tactics?" Stagg continued tenaciously. Longstreet gave himself a little shake, as if trying to loosen Stagg's grip.

"I reckon they might," he said indifferently.

Heisman and Sickles exchanged a surprised glance. It both amused and perplexed them to witness coach and general feeling each other out in such a manner.

"I'm looking forward to reading your chapter about Williamsburg," Stagg persisted, "and the one about Second Manassas. Wasn't that the battle where you gained your reputation for picking the exact moment for a counterattack?"

"Heavens!" Sickles cried in mock alarm. "I am getting an inferiority complex. Can't we talk about something else? And I'm out of champagne, to boot!"

Heisman and Stagg both signaled for a waiter. Walter Camp drifted over to their table, and the talk became more casual. Yet Longstreet was not unaware of Stagg's continued watchfulness. Behind an impassive exterior, Longstreet had to admit to himself that he was having a marvelous time.

At the entrance to the banquet hall, Hudson Stroud's poker group entered at the same time as Liebowitz and his men. They found the champagne and toasted one another as if they were meeting for the first time.

"I'll be glad to get this over with," Hudson told Ernie, "and go back to doing what we come for."

"Cards, you mean," Liebowitz said.

"That's right," Hudson said.

Liebowitz reached for something under his coat. Stroud was surprised to see Ernie present the captured sword.

"What're you doin'!"

"Take it back," Ernie said.

"What the hell has got into you?"

"I'm giving it back. Let poker be poker and bygones be bygones."

"I'm ashamed of you, Lieberwitz, tryin' to weasel out thataway."

"What weasel? I'm doing you a favor."

"I thought you and me had an unnerstandin'. Let the best man . . ."

"Take it, Stroud." Liebowitz thrust the sword at him. Hudson recoiled.

"Goddammit," Hudson cried, "it's a question of *honor*. Can't you see that?"

"You don't say!" Liebowitz grinned crookedly. "How about pistols at dawn, rapiers at dusk? An even fight: three arms versus three legs."

"You sumbitch, I reckon I ought to thank you for puttin' things into place. I was beginnin' to forget you're a goddamned Yankee."

"And I had forgotten your muleheadedness."

"Say anything you like, just hold on to that sword. It's mine, and I plan to take it back my way. I'm gonna drag you kickin' and screamin', broke and beggin' for mercy, into the street. Then, who knows? I just might offer you my sword as a memento of yo' ignominy and shame!"

Heffelfinger led his teammates, Ernest Liebowitz, Jr., and Edgar Allan Poe, across the room to meet the Southern players. He was especially curious about the blacks. Heffelfinger was acquainted with many Negroes, but Negro footballers were another species. They certainly had the bulk for it, he told his friends.

"Did you ever see musculature like that?" said Poe, nephew of the famous writer. "Are those their *scrubs?*"

"They're too big to be scrubs," Liebowitz Junior agreed.

"William Heffelfinger," Pudge introduced himself to Chase Riddle.

"Hi, Pudge," Chase said. "Meet I. Lopez. Lopez, Heffelfinger."

"Pleased." Heffelfinger leaned down to shake Lopez's hand. "My associates, Liebowitz and Poe."

Chase and Ernest took each other's measure. "Your name means a lot in our family," Chase said.

"A lot of what?" Ernest said.

They laughed and shook hands.

When Brother saw Heffelfinger turn his way he nervously gulped his champagne. Nine other glasses were simultaneously quaffed. All the Bardstown players were aware of Heffelfinger's approach. Eyes glistening from the champagne, they whispered to one another:

Who he what position he play how much you think he weigh I say two-fifty he mean-lookin' glad he ain't my man Tree he yo' 'sponsibility Go git him Tree.

To Heffelfinger, the Negroes' chatter was somehow mystical, like wild turkeys feeding somewhere over a ridge. He asked his companions if Southern Negroes spoke a kind of dialect not immediately understood by white men. They did not know.

"Mr. Heffelfinger, Mr. Jones," said Chase. "Mr. Jackson, Mr. Jackson, Mr. Jackson, Mr. Jackson, Mr. Jackson, Mr. Jackson, and Mr. Jackson."

Unaccustomed to looking up, Heffelfinger stood back from Henry Clay Jackson. "What position do you play, sir?"

"Who, me? Uh, tackle."

"So do I!"

"Also guard, end, ever'where Coach want me," Tree added.

"Most *versatile!*" Heffelfinger exclaimed. "Where did you get your size?"

"My mama's side of the fam'ly."

"Ask him what he eats," Poe whispered.

"Do you eat any special foods down South?"

Tree thought for a moment. "Cain't say as I do."

"He must have a staple," Liebowitz suggested.

"Is there any particular food, Mr. Jackson, that you are fond of?"

"I eats most anything."

Weasel nudged Tree and whispered, "Corn bread."

"Corn bread," Tree said.

Heffelfinger, Liebowitz, and Poe exchanged quizzical glances. They were familiar with corn cakes, cornmeal mush, and corn pudding, none of which noticeably affected their athletic performance. What was corn bread?

"Ask for the recipe." Poe mumbled against the back of his hand.

"How does one prepare corn bread?" Heffelfinger masked his seriousness with an easy manner. Liebowitz and Poe were fiercely attentive.

"Easy," Tree said. "Just mix cornmeal and water . . ."

"Shortnin'," Weasel said.

"Salt," Cassius said.

Holding their champagne glasses like shields, the rest of the Panthers tried to improve on Tree's recipe:

"And a egg—don't leave that out."

"Put in bakin' powder or it won't rise."

"If you talkin' pan-fried, leave off the bakin' powder."

"My mama use lard."

"It make a powerful difference which kinda cornmeal you use."

"*Stick to stone-ground.*"

"And you?" In his bewilderment Heffelfinger turned to Brother, who had not spoken.

"Corn bread is truth: truth, corn bread," Brother said.

Someone tapped a knife against a water glass. Everyone turned toward the speaker's podium. The hubbub of voices ceased.

"Welcome, one and all, to this festive occasion!" said Walter Camp. "Yesterday the general public had an opportunity to meet you. Tonight we hope you will get acquainted with one another.

So, gentlemen and ladies, be seated. Dinner will be served presently. You will find your places marked."

There was a smattering of applause. Then the guests began to look for their place cards.

"His hand," Poe told Heffelfinger, referring to Tree, "was as big as a lapdog."

"A *dead* lapdog," Liebowitz interjected. "There was no life in his grip."

"I couldn't get my fingers around his hand," Pudge admitted.

"Jackson is not sure how strong he is," Poe observed, borrowing his uncle's preternatural understanding. "He's afraid he might crush your hand."

In the milling confusion Lopez grabbed a bottle of champagne off a waiter's tray. His natural inclination was to turn it up and drink the bubbly like soda pop, but he refrained, gulping it a mere glass at a time and belching politely behind his hand. He found his seat, with the rest of the Gray squad, and organized the waiters to keep a constant supply of champagne coming. The Bardstown men soon lost all shyness in toasting each other.

To yo' health thank you to yo' health and happiness to yo' mama and daddy to Cassius's baby no to Cassius's babies to Miz Kate yes to Miz Kate!

"To Pancho Villa," Lopez joined in.

An army of waiters began serving soup. Brother examined the menu printed on the inside of his folded place card:

NORTH SOUTH ALL STAR BANQUET
18 Dec. 1896

She-crab Soup Virginia
Suckling Pig Pennsylvania
Creamed Duck Carolina
Venison Vanderbilt
Wild Rice Princeton
Almond Beans Harvard
Candied Yams Yale
Bombe Alabama
Coffee Sewanee

"What's that?" Tree said.

"The recipe for supper," Weasel explained.

"This menu makes a nice souvenir," Brother said. Sipping his champagne he added, "Tree, you ought to autograph one for Heffelfinger."

Walter Camp called on Alonzo Stagg to say Grace. Stagg rose with hands folded reverently. Chase motioned to the tipsy scrubs to bow their heads.

"Lord, give us this day our daily bread," Stagg intoned, "to the nourishment of our bodies, and we will strive to give one hundred and ten percent—in life as well as on the playing field. Keep our players free of injury. And if it be Thy will, Lord, help Heffelfinger learn to shift into the tackle-back formation. Amen."

There was a startled silence, then light laughter. Stagg, accustomed to asking the Creator frankly for what he wanted, squared off before his soup bowl and initiated a discussion with Walter Camp on the demise of the flying wedge.

As the soup bowls were being cleared away and entrees served, Camp rose to announce the banquet speakers. Kate was taken by surprise when Camp said, "Our lovely sponsors from both North and South of the Mason-Dixon Line will provide some dinner entertainment for us. First I would like to present Miss O'Hara of Chestnut Hill, who will sing"—Camp referred to his notes—"a medley, *a cappella,* of popular favorites. Miss O'Hara!"

Kate watched stiffly as the Dresden doll went to work, hands clasped over her bosom, singing like a bird. No one had informed Kate that she was on the program. She searched her repertoire for an appropriate recitation. Her nervousness faded, however, when she realized that the menfolk had paused only momentarily while Colette began to sing, then resumed feeding. She saw Lopez whispering—lewdly, she thought—to some of his teammates. Eli Abbott, of Alabama's Thin Red Line, choked on a spoonful of she-crab soup. The Bardstown players, after six glasses of champagne, teetered on the edge of hysteria. At the next table the Northern players indignantly left off eating and gave Miss O'Hara their undivided attention. When she finished her song they stood and applauded loudly. Lopez gave a razorback version of a Bronx cheer.

"Your boys are in high spirits, tonight," Stagg said to Heisman.
"Well, we're here to have a good time."

Heisman gave him a wary glance.

"Have a good practice today?" Stagg added.

"Not bad," Heisman said. "Excuse me." He leaned over and
whispered to Warner, "The scrubs are a bit out of control. Tell
Humboldt to do something about it."

Warner said to Humboldt, "Do something about Lopez and
them."

The Sewanee professor put down his fork and spent the next
few minutes waving his napkin, trying to catch Lopez's eye.

O'Hara took her seat, glancing smugly at Kate. Camp rose to
introduce her: "I give you the Gray sponsor, Mary Kathryn Kuykendall, of Bardstown, Kentucky."

By damn—I'm going to make them cry.

"*My Lost Youth,* Henry Wadsworth Longfellow," she announced. Some hissing arose from the Blues, but Heffelfinger
squelched it. Above the clanking of tableware, Kate began to
recite:

> Often I think of the beautiful town
>   That is seated by the sea;
> Often in thought go up and down
> The pleasant streets of that dear old town,
>   And my youth comes back to me.
>   And a verse of a Lapland song
>   Is haunting my memory still:
>   "A boy's will is the wind's will,
> And the thoughts of youth are long, long thoughts."

Eyes glistening, Canfield applauded prematurely. He de-
plored the disruptive noise coming from the Northern players'
table. He wished someone would serve them Mickey Finns.

> I remember the black wharves and the slips,
>   And the sea-tides tossing free;
> And Spanish sailors with bearded lips,
> And the beauty and mystery of the ships,
>   And the magic of the sea.
>   And the voice of that wayward song

Is singing and saying still:
"A boy's will is the wind's will,
And the thoughts of youth are long, long thoughts."

Everyone at the head table—with the exception of Longstreet, Sickles, and Colette—mouthed the final couplet in unison, lost in reverie, venison and creamed duck suddenly forgotten. Stagg and Heisman had their arms around each other's shoulders. Canfield unashamedly wiped the tears from his eyes.

Strange to me are the forms I meet
    When I visit the dear old town;
But the native air is pure and sweet,
And the trees that o'ershadow each well-known street,
    As they balance up and down,
        Are singing the beautiful song,
        Are sighing and whispering still:
        "A boy's will is the wind's will,
And the thoughts of youth are long, long thoughts."

Many voices now joined Kate in reciting the lines. Walter Camp fought to keep his emotions under control. Lonny Stagg dabbed at his eye with his napkin.

And Deering's Woods are fresh and fair,
    And with joy that is almost pain
My heart goes back to wander there,
And among the dreams of the days that were
    I find my lost youth again.
        And the strange and beautiful song,
        The groves are repeating it still:
        "A boy's will is the wind's will,
And the thoughts of youth are long, long thoughts."

Everyone chanted the final lines in a winey chorus. Men wept like babes. Kate made an awkward curtsy, severely pleased. Canfield was on his feet clapping wildly, leading a standing ovation. The applause died down, replaced by an expectant murmur.

"To Robert E. Lee."

Lopez was on his feet, swaying, his glass raised, grinning evilly beneath his black mustache, bald head gleaming under the brilliant chandelier. Humboldt looked immediately at Longstreet, who pretended he had not heard. Sickles, however, stood affably, glass in hand, setting a fine example, murmuring, "Yes, General Lee." Longstreet now had no alternative but to get up and put a good face on it.

Get up, you old war-horse! Humboldt exulted.

"To Bobby Lee!" Hudson Stroud chorused from the farthest table, standing and clutching his chair for balance.

Stagg and Heisman exchanged an uneasy glance, as if to ask where this was leading.

"To Robert E. Lee *Jones!*" Weasel cried and set the scrubs howling. Brother was furious.

Heffelfinger was fascinated with the Negro table, as he referred to it. "What do you call a family of gorillas?" he asked Poe. "Not a *herd,* is it?"

"To Ulysses S. Grant!" Colette O'Hara sang in a brave soprano. She glared at Kate in open challenge.

"Ulysses S. Grant!" Many voices, including the senior Liebowitz's, cried in unison. As Brother drank to Grant, so did the rest of the Panthers. Joiner and Carter glared at them as if they were traitors. Longstreet and Sickles linked arms in a display of unity.

"To John Hunt Morgan, the *Beau Sabreur!*" The wavery falsetto belonged to Hudson Stroud, whose companions applauded.

"Sit down, you old fool!" Liebowitz shouted.

"To Sickles and Gettysburg!" cried the young Edgar Allan Poe. A cheer went up for Sickles, who could not resist taking a bow. Longstreet pretended to disengage himself from Sickles's grasp.

"To Longstreet and Chickamauga!" screamed Cow Nalley of Georgia.

"Do you think this is in good taste?" Camp asked Stagg.

Camp approached the podium.

"Gentlemen, ladies!" he called optimistically. "It is our fervent desire that our All-Star footballers will not only enjoy spirited competition on the field of play but that they will form friendships here to last many years. Let us raise our glasses in the holiday spirit and say, in the words of the poet, 'God rest ye, merry gentlemen . . .'"

Camp was interrupted by a small splat. What appeared to be

an orange eye patch appeared instantaneously over his left eye.
Longstreet, who was nearest to the speaker, identified the foreign substance as candied yam. Camp continued, as if yam-drop-
pings were an everyday occurrence in the Stratford banquet hall.

". . . let nothing you dismay," he sang. A yellow viscid glob
whacked Camp (Longstreet guessed egg custard, from the wisp
of meringue) and silenced him.

"I'd say it was a thousand to one," Lopez bragged to his companions, "that I could hit him two times in a row."

Creamed duck smacked Lopez's face. He scowled slickly and
looked for his assailant. So efficiently and quietly had the exchange of missiles taken place that many honorees still sat with
glass in hand awaiting the toast. Longstreet almost told Sickles
what he was thinking.

*Here we have three quick hits in a row. What would Brigadier
Alexander, my chief of artillery at Gettysburg, say about it?
There is no substitute for an athlete's hand-to-eye coordination.*

Lopez stood, clutched the table for balance, and headed for
the dessert trays which held a variety of cream pies and cakes.
Lopez chose a berry pie, hefting it for balance and weight. He
stretched himself to his full height of five foot three and walked
to Heffelfinger's table.

" 'Tis the season to be jolly . . ." Camp said desperately, but
no one was listening.

The room hummed with anticipation. Stagg and Heisman
waved their napkins like white flags of surrender. Heffelfinger
rose, all six foot four of him, to meet Lopez. As Longstreet observed these mismatched antagonists, he became aware of a
stealthy, multitudinous arming: dozens of hands reaching for
pastries, pies, yams, wads of rice, duck legs, ham hocks.

Lopez steadied the dewberry pie on his fingertips and regarded Heffelfinger, the Yale man. He thought of all the rich
college boys he had known, flashy dressers with their fathers'
silver jingling in their pockets. He spoke carefully to Heffelfinger
so as to convey the spiritual weight of his berry pie.

"This is for my mama and 'em!"

As Lopez mashed the pie in Heffelfinger's face he had the
instinctive feeling that Pudge welcomed it.

The ballroom erupted. People ducked for cover. Lopez, given

his proximity to the enemy table, was drenched to the skin with soup, sauce, gravy, tea, coffee, and wine. Meringue clung to his scalp like a thick, wavy head of white hair. Tables and chairs were overturned. Heisman vaulted the head table and dashed between the throwers. Caught in a crossfire of fruit cobbler, he hit the floor hard.

Longstreet sat untouched. He could not help smiling when Sickles took a hit in the face. Sickles calmly wiped whipped cream off with his napkin. Neither general wished to take cover before the other did. Longstreet saw Hudson Stroud brandishing his crutch, exhorting the Southern players to *charge*, and remembered Stroud's invitation to play poker. Longstreet continued to sweep the room with his extraordinary powers of observation. The Blue team seemed to be winning, in that they had more ammunition. They had commandeered the punchbowl and gained a supply of ice cubes. The clear nuggets whizzed like bullets. Howls of pain rose from the South table.

Throughout the fight the Negro squad, Longstreet noted approvingly, remained in their places, taking random hits without moving a muscle. Longstreet again thought of the black regiments that had performed faithfully and well, on both sides, during the war.

That's the way to hold a defensive position. Don't yield an inch.

"What's got into you, Longstreet?" Sickles said. "You Rebels have ruined our banquet."

Kate, too, saw her Bardstown players sitting like statues. She wished she could hike up her dress and lead them in a glorious assault. Brother was so still and alert, he might have been attending an art lecture. His teammates tried to emulate his self-control, but now and then one of them moved by reflex to avoid a flying éclair or bombe. Kate intuitively understood that their main concern was food stains. She saw Weasel examining Tree's coat.

"That peach cobbler, now, it come out awright," Weasel was saying, "but that 'ere raspberry, that's bad."

"You reckon would it come out if I soaked it?" Tree asked.

"My mama soak stain in lye."

"Lye eat up a nice white shirt!"

At that moment a blackberry cobbler exploded in Tree's chest. He and Weasel wiped the splashes from their eyes and inspected the damage.

"Forget soakin' it, Tree. It don't matter now."

"How can I show Mama this? She won't let me in the house! You know, that make me mad."

"Don't get mad. This a nice party."

"It ain't no mo'."

Brother filled his glass with champagne and settled back to watch the fight. Weasel told him about Tree's problem.

"Don't worry, we'll find you another shirt," Brother soothed.

"Why they do that to me?" Tree said.

"I don't know. White folks have got so much they don't know what to do with it."

"Order, gentlemen, order!" Walter Camp shouted. He turned to the sponsors. "Would you sing our national anthem?"

Kate, itching to get her hands on a pie, ignored him, but Colette crawled out from under the table and began to sing, "Ohhhh, say can you see?" She took a pie full in the mouth and retreated under the table.

Canfield, seeing that Kate had come under fire, made his way toward her, intending to shield her with his coat. The Faro King got within ten feet of the head table before he slipped down in the syrupy mess.

Lopez burst out of the kitchen door pushing a full pie cart. He stiff-armed a steward and rammed the cart against the enemy table, but before he could start throwing, the Blues (literally blue with berry stains) leaped howling over the table and ravaged Lopez with his own pies.

Longstreet could hear Lopez's screams, muffled within a mound of crust and filling. The general chuckled and turned to Sickles just in time to see a lemon chiffon whop Dan. Longstreet grinned and offered Sickles his napkin.

Canfield, hit by the barrage that missed Lopez, got up and made his way, slipping down once more, to the head table. His coat was now a mess, but he took it off and tried to put it around Kate's shoulders. In fending off this unwanted attention, Kate failed to duck for a pie barrage. She and Canfield were hit at the same time. Her hair flattened against her head, Kate glared at

Canfield and looked around for something to hit him with. She found half a German chocolate cake and raised it in both hands. Canfield offered no resistance as she buried his face in cake to the ears. He had never felt closer to another human being.

For a few moments, except for Longstreet and Sickles and the Post Oak Panthers, everyone went berserk. Heisman got Stagg, Humboldt got Heffelfinger, Camp got Canfield, Liebowitz Junior got Chase, Stagg got Warner, Hudson got Liebowitz Senior, and Harry Prescott of the *Inquirer* got a picture of it all just before Lopez got him.

Suddenly it was over. Camp's "merry gentlemen" stood and looked at one another. The banquet hall was in ruins. The master steward could be heard weeping. The hotel manager ran in, too late, and slid in the muck.

Walter Camp rummaged around for a glass and a spoon. His face was purple. Crumbs clung frostily to his eyebrows. Camp tapped on the glass. Stagg came to attention, hands folded respectfully. A pie shell framed the back of his head so that he resembled a medieval saint.

"These festivities," said Camp, "are concluded."

Longstreet nodded to himself. It had been a good fight. He checked his clothing. He had not been hit, but then he rarely had been. Sickles, on the other hand, was a brown-and-yellow mess.

"Just a skirmish," Longstreet told an incredulous Sickles. "Each side wanted to feel the other out. It's lightning before the storm."

Sickles's disbelief changed to solicitous concern. "Jim, are you all right?" he said.

Displaying his celebrated sportsmanship, Heffelfinger went to apologize to the South team but slipped down on the floor. Tree surprised his teammates by going to Pudge's assistance. He lifted Heffelfinger gently, as one picks up a child, and set him on his feet.

"How did you do that?" Pudge said, amazed.

"It ain't nothin'," Tree allowed. "It awright 'bout my shirt. Here's sump'm."

He pressed a card into Heffelfinger's hand and went back to his table. It was a place-card/menu, inscribed as follows:

TO HIKKAFIGER
GOOD LOCK.
H.C. JACKSON
(TREE)

Chapter Nineteen

The knocking on Ziprenian's office door was so bold that he assumed either the police or Archie The Knife was paying him a visit. Elston needed no instructions but began clearing away incriminating materials: betting sheets, accounts from gambling houses, reports from loan shark, protection, and prostitution operations. Into drawers and cabinets went the papers, quickly and efficiently. Satisfied, Ziprenian nodded. Elston opened the door.

A short, wide man filled the doorframe. He wore a ten-gallon hat. His Western boots clunked loudly on the floor as he entered. He tipped his hat but did not take it off. Arno regarded him narrowly. Lopez sprawled in a chair without waiting to be invited.

"Howdy," he said.

"How did you find me?" Arno said.

"I asked one of the girls out to the Maison Blanche. Got anything to drink?"

"Girls?"

"Yeah, the working girls on the fourth floor." Lopez saw Ziprenian's cagey expression and waved away denials before the promoter made them. "Whorehouses and me, we go way back. I never trained for football in a whorehouse, but I ain't complainin'. After a hard day's practice on the gridiron, a professional woman can help take the kinks out. I don't know why the two haven't been combined before. It could revolutionize physical therapy. Anyways, I'm here to make you a deal."

"Not interested."

"It involves compromise," Lopez continued smoothly. "You git sump'm, we git sump'm."

"Who's we?"

"The South All-Stars."

"What's the deal?" Ziprenian could not help being curious. He half-admired Lopez's style, crude though it was.

"You need publicity. We need compensation."

"We have all the publicity we want. A stipend has been set aside for the players. Do not forget that you have the honor to represent—"

"Honor my ass." Lopez took out his false teeth and showed them to Arno. "I had the honor of having my teeth knocked out playin' for various conference champeenships. That's all the honor I need."

"You want money," The Zipper said flatly.

"Well, now, it ain't like it's out of yo' pocket, is it?" Lopez said. "I mean, the city fathers of Philydelphia is in this thing to *make money*, ain't they?—Say, can a man git a drink around here?—A strike could double the paying customers and set us all up."

"Strike? What strike?"

"A players' strike." Lopez crossed his legs and shifted his weight to show how comfortable he was.

"A players' strike?"

"It's sump'm new." Lopez picked at a scab on his knuckles. He had gotten it while showing Tree defensive technique. Tree had skin like sandpaper.

"I heard of *workers* striking," The Zipper argued, "but ballplayers?"

"Players are workers too."

"Playing is work?"

"You don't think it's work, *you* run wind sprints after a three-hour scrimmage."

"But the players, they do it for fun."

"There may be a few strange players who think pain is fun, but this Texican ain't among 'em. The fun is when you examine yo' body after a game and find no permanent injury. The fun is knowin' you will recover from bein' stomped on, given plenty of bed rest. Fun? Is rammin' yo' head through a brick wall fun? They don't call it a gridiron fer nothin'.''

"All right, so it is work and not all play. Still, the public has its view . . ."

"John Q. Public is waitin' to be influenced in the right direction. I'm the fella's gonna educate him."

They eyed each other. Somewhere in their disparate ancestries a common bond existed: if they missed a deal, it would not be because they refused to listen.

"Just for the sake of curiosity," The Zipper said, "whatta you want in the form of compensation?"

"Five hunnerd."

"Dollars?"

"Yep."

"Per team?"

"Per man."

"Ha, ha, don't make me laugh. Look, Elston, he's making me laugh!"

Elston bared yellow teeth.

"Table scraps compared to the increased gross I goin' to git you," Lopez said calmly.

"At twenty players per team," Ziprenian calculated, "that's twenty thousand dollars' worth of table scraps!"

"I'm speakin strictly fer the South team, of course, but I 'magine if we git five hunnerd the North'll want it, too. So, yeah, you can figure twenty grand. The strike'll quadruple yo' gross, so it *is* strictly table scraps, by God."

"You want to put on a strike for publicity purposes."

"You got it by the horns."

"What if the local businessmen and politicians who are in charge of arrangements do not go along with your strike? What if they shut the game down?"

"They reasonable, ain't they?" Lopez opened his arms in a gesture of accord. "They unnerstand give and take. That's what it's all about. Look, what do you project as the total gate? A hunnerd thousand bucks, with thirty-five thousand payin' spectators? A strike could double attendance! Git folks riled up and indignant 'bout these uppity niggers jackin' up the ticket price to pay for their demands and fans'll be roarin' to see 'em git the tail-whuppin' they deserve. I'm talkin' a minimum of fifty thousand fans at five bucks per head and concessions of another two hunnerd grand. Near half a million gross, hoss."

"What if the city fathers agree to go along," The Zipper asked shrewdly, "and when you get to the bargaining table, you ask for more than five hundred?"

Lopez, who had thrown out the figure of $500 in hopes of getting $250 or even $150, felt momentum shifting. "I'm givin' you my word," he said sincerely.

"Elston, what am I hearing!" Ziprenian cried. His assistant conjured up expressions of amazement, consternation, hope, and sympathy.

"You want me to sign a paper?" Lopez offered.

"Yes, please incriminate us both for labor racketeering."

"Then you'll hafta take my word." Lopez dug in his pocket. "You don't mind if I chew, do you?"

"What authority do you have to negotiate for your team? Are the coaches behind you?"

"Don't need the coaches' approval." Lopez worked a wad into his cheek. "I am the authorized player representative."

Accustomed as Ziprenian was to dealing with all types, Lopez was one of the strangest specimens he had ever seen. Yet he recognized, in this sawed-off cowboy, the musky magic of the American dream.

"The newspapers're goin' to love this strike," Lopez said, looking for a spittoon. "It's twenty thousand bucks' worth of free publicity. What's the current line on the game?"

"Elston?" Ziprenian said.

"Six to one, boss!" Elston replied alertly.

"Down forty percent from the opening line of ten to one," Lopez reflected. He tried to spit into a waste basket, spraying brown mist across the floor. "Word got out 'bout the scrimmage my niggers won, eh?"

"There has been speculation," The Zipper admitted. "It's natural. People enjoy it."

"Yeah, well, the niggers're natural athaletes and all that, but they ain't Yale or Harvard. I doan care how big and fast these pickaninnies are, they ain't experienced like Heffelfinger and his bunch. Those Yankee boys know all the tricks. But, now, consider how a strike will affect your house odds. I mean, when my players come struttin' up to the negotiatin' table, the odds got to come down, artificial-like. Nobody'd figure they'd do sump'm as wild as go on strike if they wasn't some kind of super-hosses. Only a man damn sure of hisself makes bodacious demands. When we strike, watch that line drop to near even. The house cain't lose."

Lopez saw a light in the Armenian's eye. The Zipper made a final show of resistance, to keep Lopez respectful.

"My employer, Mr. Canfield, has issued strict orders that no one in his organization is to participate in any betting propositions. Our purpose is charity."

"Canfield can skim off his charity. I'm all for charity. I wouldn' be tryin' to raise up our underprivileged colored players and put a few dollars in their pockets if I wasn't."

"That is the first thing I noticed about you, Lopez," Ziprenian remarked. "Your charitable spirit."

Kate dubiously approached the row house, which looked exactly like all the other well-kept red brick houses along Linden Avenue. Its circumspect exterior revealed nothing of who, or what, awaited her. Glancing again at the hand-printed invitation, Kate checked the house number: 1127.

What kind of club, she wondered for the dozenth time, was the "Schuylkill Rowing Not Drifting"? It was whimsical and sophisticated beyond Kate's experience. In Bardstown ladies' clubs had names like Our Christian Circle, Nelson County Literary Society, Industry Club, Gethsemane Service Association, Stephen Foster Restoration Society.

Kate remembered a photograph of her mother's music club: sixteen ladies in two rows, tough and sharp as sparrows, wearing hats with feathers, plain skirts, suits, and shoes, only a bit of rouge here and there which revealed a rebel among these wives of merchants, distillers, bankers, railroad men, insurance agents. Even within their group they sought no identity beyond that of marriage; no Mary, Carol, Alice, or Betsy, but *Mrs.* Peter Arnold, *Mrs.* Andrew Belcher, *Mrs.* Albert Reynolds, *Mrs.* Henry Peacock. Their resolute faces bore testimony to sewing machine, oven, and piano; to starched curtains, shiny floors, and polished brass; to children and grandchildren; to talents whetted like knives; to their Kentucky homes. When the 1896 Biennial Convention of Women's Rights had met in Louisville earlier that year, not only had these ladies not attended—considering they were only three hours from Louisville by train—they did not even know the event had occurred. In the photo, these mothers of Bardstown sat shoulder to shoulder—friends and enemies, allies by necessity, whose motto might have been: Us Versus the World.

"Rowing Not Drifting" dared an outsider like Kate to rock the boat or to ask, Rowing, yes, but where to? Maybe the point was to row, row, row (not gently) *upstream* and perhaps to ram any craft drifting irresponsibly *down* the Schuylkill. Kate remembered the low rapids she had seen near Boat House Row in Fairmount Park. A barrier of roped buoys stretched across the river to protect small craft from the low falls. Were the Rowers-Not-Drifters simply fighting the current to avoid going over?

Kate knocked on the door. It opened. A pleasant, moon-shaped face smiled at her.

"Miss Kuykendall! How good of you. I'm Elizabeth Robins. Won't you come in!"

Her hostess ushered her inside. They went into a parlor, where some dozen ladies made a pigeon-like murmur as they rose to receive her. Kate smelled sherry. She was surprised that they greeted her with such respect. *What have I done?* she wondered. She was intrigued by their appearance: instead of the dour, well-to-do, staid dowagers she had expected, here were clean-faced, energetic young women who dressed casually but well and who possessed a knack of seeming down-to-earth and polished at once. There was a raw sense of anticipation about them. Kate felt that she had found her own kind at last, even if her shoes *were* caked with Kentucky clay.

At the end of the informal receiving line was a young woman subtly apart from the others. She had introspective hazel eyes, a bemused air, and was smoking a small black cigar. Kate had never seen a woman smoke in public. She was thrilled.

"I am Agnes Repplier," the smoker said. She did not immediately extend her hand, having a cigar in it. Kate got the impression that Agnes was waiting for her name to register. "I write," Repplier added helpfully.

"Kate Kuykendall. I coach."

They smiled and shook hands. Elizabeth Robins went to the center of the room and gave a sharp command: "Unstack oars, face upstream!" The club members took their seats. Robins motioned for Kate to sit next to her.

"The meeting will come to order," Robins continued. "Today we are privileged to have in our midst one who is doing more than most in carrying woman's banner into the world of affairs. It is no exaggeration to say that she is a true pioneer in her field, inasmuch as she is the first female football coach in America. She has come to Philadelphia as one of the South team's coaches for the college all-star game. On behalf of Schuylkill Rowing Not Drifting, I extend warm greetings to Kathryn Kuykendall."

Kate felt her face grow warm. The members applauded. Robins added, "Perhaps our guest would entertain questions from the floor?"

"I'd be glad to."

"What is it like," one of them asked, "coaching an all-Negro team?"

"Wonderful and awful," Kate said spontaneously. The Rowers-Not-Drifters murmured their approval.

"Is there resistance in your community to what you do?" asked another member.

Kate shrugged. "They think I'm crazy, to tell the truth."

To her surprise there was a burst of applause, the women sitting forward now and clapping ardently with hands raised in tribute.

"Do your players have reservations about a female coach?" someone asked.

"I think sometimes they wish I could run faster or tackle harder, so I could show them instead of tell them," she said, "but they don't complain. After all, it's my football."

"What about the women in your community?" Elizabeth Robins asked. "What is their attitude about women's rights?"

Kate thought about the photograph of the Bardstown Music Club—the familiar, homely, resolute faces—and was suddenly on the defensive.

"Before the war," Kate said, "I guess you'd say that Southern women were a pioneer race. In addition to household chores, they helped plow, plant, and harvest. They maintained kitchen gardens. There was birthing and rearing, sewing and cooking and cleaning for three generations under the same roof. You'd think that here was a superior breed of female who brooked no comeuppance from the menfolk. However, the war came along. The North not only inflicted military defeat on the South, but killed off a preponderance of husbands and fathers.

"So what you had were thousands of mothers, from Virginia to Louisiana, hovering over their sons, hanging on little Buster's every word, and creating an egocentric race who roamed the earth with absolute assurance that females would cater to their every whim. Equally dismaying was the fact that, as the mothers reared these son-protectors, daughters and sisters were watching and absorbing the process, so that the cycle would be repeated over and over again.

"This situation is one that Southern women rarely, if ever, discuss; but if they did, I imagine they would call it the Yankee's revenge: Southern men exist today as a living deterrent to political rebellion."

The Rowers-Not-Drifters exploded with appreciative laughter. They had become quite infatuated with Kate. Because she had responded naturally, her words struck home.

"Thank you so much for sharing your thoughts with us," Elizabeth Robins said. "We are thrilled to have a Southern sister here with us. I think all of us will agree that Miss Kuykendall—may we call you Kathryn?—is the very person to represent our organization in the demonstration . . ."

"What demonstration?" Kate said.

"The civil rights demonstration, dear."

"Whose civil rights?"

"Why, *your* players'." Robins smiled patronizingly.

"This is the first I've heard of it," Kate said. The SRND members murmured in surprise.

"That's odd," Robins went on. "I suppose that the word simply has not had time to get back to—"

Kate frowned. "Would someone please explain what is going on?"

"The idea came, I think, from a social worker in the Seventh Ward," Robins said.

"He's connected with the University of Pennsylvania," someone confided.

"A colored man," Robins continued, "very well-spoken. A Harvard graduate. Du Bois, his name is. Susan Wharton, who runs the College Settlement on Lombard, recommends him. When Mr. Du Bois approached the Union League and other civic clubs, everyone naturally was in favor of supporting Negro rights."

"Let me get this straight," Kate said. "A sociology worker from the University of Pennsylvania has proposed a political demonstration on behalf of Negro rights in Philadelphia using as a rallying point my black football players from Bardstown, Kentucky?"

"That's correct."

"Excuse me, but nobody asked me."

The Rowers-Not-Drifters regarded Kate with suspicion. She thought how she must appear to them: wind-chapped, iron-haired, wide-shouldered, calloused and muscled. They were abstract, she was concrete. They played with rebellion, she lived it. They needed her like a wood fire needed kindling.

"I'm sure everyone is eager to get to know our guest," Robin diplomatically resumed, "but first to business! Perhaps, Kathryn, you would allow our publicity person, Ann, to take a photo for the papers?" She gestured to a corner of the room set aside for that purpose. Glad to avoid further scrutiny, Kate did as she was asked. A sharp-faced woman with perfect makeup led her to a chair. A camera waited on its tripod. Ann produced a football, presenting it with a flourish.

"Do you mind using a prop?" she said.

Feeling foolish, Kate took the ball. Then she saw Agnes Repplier wink at her. The photographer ducked to look through her Kodak. In the meantime, Kate heard Elizabeth Robins call on the secretary to read the minutes of the last meeting. Kate listened, feeling like an eavesdropper. The secretary read with authority:

"November thirty: Motion made by Cynthia Pearsall to subscribe *in toto* to Miss Emmeline Hart's Home School for Etiquette; seconded by Shirley Bingham. Report on Hart: classes given in privacy of home, etiquette rules defined, how to develop personality and self-confidence, make most of oneself, succeed in business, etc. How to make introductions, acknowledgments, formal and informal entertaining, social correspondence, letter forms, art of being a guest, travel etiquette, office and business manners, telephone courtesy, poise without pose. Discussion followed. Consensus: Hart's Home School on firmer ground than other such courses intended to develop charm, etc. Vote: Nineteen in favor, one opposed, one abstaining. Motion carried. Bingham to collect fees: Fifteen dollars per member, course to be given at Pearsall's home, February third to fifth, six to eight P.M. Business concluded. Refreshments followed."

"Smile," Ann told Kate and took the picture. "Let's try it again," she said firmly.

"Don't you think," Kate spoke through her teeth, "that a football looks a bit out of place when I'm wearing a dress?"

"Oh, the *ball* is all right. It's your features."

"What features?"

"I'm not really a photographer," Ann began explaining. "All I do is follow Eastman's motto: Press the button and we do the rest! But I have done a lot of portraits for the newspapers, and I see a bit of a problem here."

Kate imagined how she must look through a camera's eye, stiff and heavy, holding a football, her face uncompromising. She did not want to know what Ann was thinking but she had to ask. "What is it?"

"Well, your mouth is somewhat small for your other features."

"Oh, is that all?" Kate relaxed, then was on guard. "Meaning that my nose is too big?"

"I can give you a tip," Ann confided, coming forward and lowering her voice. "Practice stretching your mouth. Like this." The publicity chairman of SRND spread her lips by tightening unknown muscles. It was like seeing a deep-sea creature smile on the ocean floor. In spite of herself Kate could not resist trying to follow these instructions. She worked her cheeks, spreading her lips first in one direction, then the other.

"No, not like that, dear! Don't bare your teeth while stretching."

Kate caught sight of Agnes Repplier watching her and gave up. She pressed her lips firmly together. "Just get it over with," she said. Ann sighed and returned to her camera. At least, Kate thought, the other SRND members were busy considering motions for a new club motto.

"No footsteps backward!" someone said.

"Man grows as higher grow his aims," another said.

"Knowledge is the treasure of which study is the key."

"Self-culture is the basis of all culture."

"Women give and forgive; men get and forget."

The Rowers-Not-Drifters had a hearty laugh, then became serious again.

"More light."

"Strive to understand great minds and learn to think."

" 'Tis life, more life, and fuller that we want!"

This final slogan caught the fancy of the group, and after a brief discussion it was adopted. Now they adjourned the meeting and went for the refreshments.

"That ought to do it, then," Ann told Kate. "Thank you for your cooperation. It's so nice to have you here." She gave Kate a deprecatory smile, as if to say, "I've done the best I can," and moved off.

"Don't mind Ann." Agnes Repplier cheerfully appeared at Kate's side. "Since we elected her publicity chairman there has been no stopping her. We worry too much about looks. It gives Ann power. It's easy for me to talk, since my mouth is already too wide for stretching!"

Kate grinned in relief. She glanced around to see if the others were within earshot. "Maybe you can explain something. I'm a little out of touch with what is going on in the women's movement. What do charm and etiquette have to do with political activism?"

Repplier, too, looked to see if anyone was watching. "Most of us come to these meetings," she explained, "for the fellowship. That's why I come, anyway. I'm not sure if they believe this any more than I do, but the idea is, charm is to be utilized as an asset for attaining success in business or civic service. Etiquette is used for the sake of personal progress. The purpose is to go beyond husband-hunting and achieve success in both worlds, the world of affairs and the world of the home."

"I see," Kate said.

"You're thinking maybe we don't practice what we preach?"

"Oh, not at all."

Repplier waved her cigar, dismissing Kate's protest. "Give us credit for trying. We can't all be like you."

"What do you mean?"

"Lead an adventurous life."

"Who, me?"

"You are a rugged individualist, more than the rest of us can ever be."

"Oh," Kate said, not unpleased.

Agnes hesitated. "You don't hold it against us, do you?"

"What?"

The author's eyes sparkled. "Winning the war and begetting the egocentric Southern male."

Kate grinned. "Well, not today, anyhow!"

"What can we Yankees do to make it up to you?"

Kate thought for a second. "Losing to my team this Saturday would be nice."

The farther down Lombard Street Brother went, the worse the neighborhoods became. He steered clear of derelicts standing around a fire built in a garbage can and continued past Eighth Street. The address Du Bois had written on the back of his card was "Seventh and Lombard streets, second-floor apt. above College Settlement cafeteria." Brother had a hunch that Du Bois had not chosen to live in this neighborhood by accident. These slums were too incongruous an environment for a university man. Brother remembered the thoughtful eyes, sensitive mouth, Vandyke beard, the affectation of a cane. He already felt he knew Du Bois. The sociologist conformed to an image of manhood that Brother had long nurtured in his subconscious—complete with a Harvard Yard accent—and he would have sought Du Bois in hell or Seventh and Lombard.

Jones found the cafeteria. Du Bois's card was pasted in the doorway of a narrow, airless stairwell. As he climbed the steep steps he heard a woman scream, children crying, and somewhere a steady pounding sound. He thought of the criminal types he had seen lurking in every alleyway and hoped he was hearing someone scrubbing clothes on a washboard and not a fist methodically pounding a face. He shivered as he knocked at the top of the stairs.

"Here you are!" Du Bois exclaimed, throwing open the door. "Come in."

Brother timidly entered the one-room apartment. He automatically compared it to his family's house in Bardstown. Though his home was much larger, eight people lived in it; thus Du Bois's apartment seemed neat and spacious. There was a stove, a small table and two chairs, a wardrobe, an overstuffed chair, and a sofa wide enough for three. Brother wondered where they slept. In the middle of the spotlessly clean room stood a petite woman with shining eyes and a bright smile.

"This is my wife, Nina," Du Bois said, "and this is—I'm sorry."

"Brother—I mean, R. Jones," Brother stammered. Du Bois noticed his guest's embarrassment and gestured for Brother to be seated.

"You're wondering where the bed is?" he said, smiling at Brother's amazement. "Everybody does, so I thought we might get that item out of the way. You're sitting on it. The sofa folds out into a bed. It's the latest invention for modern apartment dwellers." His eyes sparkled with amusement. Brother stared at the mysterious sofa under him.

"Would you care for some tea?" Nina asked. Her voice had a musical quality that pleased Brother. It seemed strange to be drinking iced tea in the wintertime, but he nodded politely. Nina went to light the kerosene stove and fill a teakettle. Brother noted that the Du Boises had water on tap. He imagined himself occupying an apartment such as this one, someday. He glanced at Du Bois, who sat on the edge of the overstuffed chair leaning confidently forward, elbows resting on his knees.

"How is the football training coming along?" Du Bois said.

"Fine." Through the thin walls Brother heard an infant crying.

"Fine," Du Bois repeated with a hint of irony. "A most unusual circumstance, wouldn't you say: Negroes representing the South?"

"We're just the scrubs," Brother said quickly. "We don't really represent anybody."

"I see." Du Bois's gaze was intense. Brother hoped the profes-

sor was not going to bring up the flag-waving fiasco again. He did
not want to have to repeat his explanation.

"Did you play football in school?" Brother changed the subject.

"With my size?" Will grinned wryly. "I'd have been the tackling dummy. I made up games, like racing through mazes formed
by alleyways, intricate marathons. Things like that. Sports are
supposed to be fun, aren't they?" He paused. "What do you do,
besides play football?"

"I've, uh, been graduated from high school but I am employed
there as, uh, tutor." DuBois's candid glance convinced him there
was no way to glamorize what he did. "I'm basically the school
handyman. I stoke the furnaces every morning before school
begins."

"That was my first regular job, too," Du Bois said, surprising
Brother. "Stoking an old, base-burning stove—but quite a modern appliance back then—in a Massachusetts millinery shop."

Brother saw Nina smiling at her husband. "What was it like,"
he eagerly asked, "to grow up in Massachusetts?"

Du Bois settled back sociably on the sofa and reminisced.

"Great Barrington was really just a village. It was a boy's para-
dise for swimming and climbing and skating. We roamed and
played. I never noticed much discrimination in village activities,
except maybe toward the Irish. —You are surprised by that? Well,
let me add that in our community of perhaps five thousand there
were not more than fifty colored people. In high school I suppose
we were protected from discrimination by the fact that there
were no school dances or fraternities. If I noticed any racial
antipathy I treated it with disdain, but this came easy to me
because I was the leader of my class. —You too?" Will had seen
Brother nod to himself.

"It's not much of an accomplishment where I go to school,
though," Jones said.

"Oh, you mustn't be too hard on your classmates," Du Bois said
intuitively. "In a mostly white school, I confess I felt such shame
at the shortcomings of my fellow black students. I wanted us all to
excel and be accepted. I was the only black student in my class,
and I expected the younger colored students to live up to my
standards. I was fairly awful in my expectations."

Du Bois paused. Brother did not know what to say. Nina gracefully served the tea. Brother was surprised to find that it was hot tea. Thankful that he had not made a remark about serving iced tea in December, he watched her fill two cups from a steaming porcelain teapot.

"It's a Bavarian tea service," Du Bois noted, as if anticipating Brother's inquiry, "a gift to me when I was a student at the University of Berlin."

"Milk or lemon?" Nina asked. Brother hesitated, then took the plunge.

"Both," he said.

Without a word Nina poured a dollop of milk into his cup, then gently squeezed lemon on top of it. Brother watched the cream curdle. He was afraid to look at his hosts.

"Will?" Nina said. Their eyes met for the briefest instant.

"I'll have both," Du Bois said.

Brother watched the cream curdle in Will's cup and stifled a sigh of relief. They sat with teacup and saucer balanced on their laps. Nina set the tray on the table and pretended to find something else to do in the tiny kitchen.

"How did you do it!" Brother said suddenly, the words torn from him by a terrible sense of inadequacy.

"What?"

"Make it."

Setting his cup and saucer on the table, Du Bois shook his head reassuringly. "I had a lot of help. There are ways. It takes a little time, but the means can be found. We all give each other a helping hand. Scholarships are available."

Brother was sitting hunched forward. He turned his eyes to Du Bois without raising his head. He did not dare ask.

"Tell me," Will said briskly, "who do you read—Negro writers, I mean."

"Frederick Douglass, Wendell Phillips . . ." Brother began, relieved to be able to show what he knew, but the names jammed up in his mind. He was terrified that he would fail to please, and just when Du Bois seemed on the brink of helping him.

"I gave my senior oration on Phillips," Du Bois recalled nostalgically. "He influenced me greatly in high school, gave me direction. But when I was at Fisk, Bismarck was my man. I admired his strength, the way he created a nation out of a mass of divergent peoples. I admit I was something of an imperialist in those days."

The student in Jones made him eager to hear more. He forgot his anxiety. "Who else besides Phillips and Bismarck?" he said.

"Well, at Harvard it was William James. He was my teacher and friend. He entertained me in his home. He was my guide to clear thinking. It was James who turned me from philosophy to sociology. He told me it would be hard to earn a living with philosophy. He neglected to add that sociology is not exactly a cakewalk."

"Who else?" Brother said doggedly.

"Let us talk of the present," Will said. "Let us talk about you and your teammates."

"All right," Brother said in some confusion.

"I think you have an opportunity to stand out above the crowd, to make a statement and to bring honor to your people."

"To Bardstown?"

"To your people, *our* people!" Du Bois said impatiently. "You have been thrust into the public eye of this city. You are in a position to command sympathy and generate public opinion."

"Miz Kate brought us to Philadelphia," Brother said defensively.

"What does that have to do with it? Who is she?"

"Our teacher."

"Oh yes, I remember. The female coach. So, are you obligated to her, then? Does she have some kind of hold on you?"

Brother had never thought to question Kate's motives. He accepted her for what she appeared to be. An image came to mind, of Kate stoking the fire at Post Oak while listening to Weasel recite the multiplication tables. She was frowning, her lips pursed, as she attacked the potbellied stove. It was hard to see which made her frown the most: the dying fire or Weasel's faulty memory.

"She cares about us," Brother said.

Du Bois, who had been regarding him intensely, relaxed and said, "That is high praise. I think of my principal, Frank Hosmer. It was he who opened the college doors for me. That's what I'm talking about: commitment. I have been in touch with the Union League of Philadelphia, through the able person of Miss Wharton, who runs our College Settlement. The consensus is that they will support you."

"At the game?"

"No, with your protest!"

"What protest?"

"I am asking you," Du Bois said heavily, "to help lead a protest against exploitation of the Negro people."

"How?"

Du Bois sat militarily erect. "I got the idea from seeing you waving the Confederate flag at the train station." Seeing Brother's momentary embarrassment, he hurried on. "The focus of your protest would be the Board of Aldermen's sanctioning the display of Confederate symbols, which are offensive to our people. But your statement of protest would be expanded to draw attention to the plight of the Negroes of Philadelphia. We would demand that the board establish a commission or panel to prepare a study of the problem, which would subsequently be published in the *Inquirer.* The panel would include black members. It is a demand which can easily be met; therefore I believe that it has a chance of succeeding. I admit that it is not exactly a frontal assault on the color barrier, but it would definitely represent a step forward. The first thing we have to do is to make people aware of injustice and to keep it before their eyes so they cannot forget it."

Brother was not sure what was required of him. He was afraid to say anything lest he make another mistake, as with the tea. Du Bois, however, waited for him to reply.

"What if they do not agree to your panel?" Brother said at last.

"You strike."

"Strike? You mean, like a union? Us?"

"No, *us.*" Will's face was fierce. His Vandyke looked finely honed and dangerous. Brother, who was physically larger and stronger, felt fragile next to him.

"We came here to play football," he said in confusion. "We're out of our territory. It's not that I don't want to help. It's just that I never thought of myself—much less my friends—as a crusader."

Du Bois thought for a moment. "I once heard Negro spirituals sung at a church in Great Barrington," he said. "I was moved to tears. I wanted a chance to open up my spiritual isolation—and I went South to do it."

Brother was amazed. "South!"

"Do not underestimate the South's advantages. When I attended Fisk, I went South in the New England missionary tradition." Du Bois smiled disarmingly. "I went to furnish leadership for a black electorate. I went with great expectations. I was seventeen. For two summers, while I was at Fisk, I taught at a country school in east Tennessee, near Alexandria. Only once since the Civil War had there been a Negro public school there. The schoolhouse was a windowless log cabin, with rough benches and no blackboard. We walked long distances to get there, my students and I. For those summer sessions I was paid twenty-eight dollars a month. I was a student, too, of the race problem at its most fundamental level. I learned volumes about it, from my students and also from my employer. I learned to sing the old songs of sorrow. Once, when I called on the white superintendent on business, he invited me to stay for dinner. I did not accept, because I knew that he did not dream that I would not only have expected to eat at the same time as he, but at the same table. After those summers, I became somewhat bellicose in my attitude toward breaking the color bar. Later, Harvard taught me more sophisticated forms of segregation. Then Berlin taught me about European colonialism and exploitation of the African masses on a grand scale. You have to live this, as I did, to perceive it down deep, to feel it, but here in Philadelphia you have a chance to leapfrog, to act instead of observe. I suppose what I am trying to say is, I want you to take *me* with you."

All Brother could do was sit and balance his teacup and saucer on his knees, adrift in a sea of ideas.

"I'll tell you what," Du Bois said, getting to his feet. "Why don't I take you on a battlefield tour."

"A what?" Brother exclaimed.

"Walk around the neighborhood." Du Bois shrugged into his overcoat. He turned to Nina. "We'll be back presently. I'll stop by the bakery for some tea cakes, and we'll try another cup of tea when we get home."

Still in a state of polite confusion, Brother put on his coat, awkwardly took his leave of Mrs. Du Bois, and followed his host out into the cold. Du Bois took Brother's arm and guided him west on Lombard Street. "Our ward is an interesting mix of white and black, rich and poor. Here, between Seventh and Eighth streets, we have criminals, gamblers, and prostitutes living next door to decent, if not very energetic, poor people. This is Ratcliffe Street. Stay close."

Brother followed Du Bois down a dark alley. He saw faces hidden in dark corners and doorways.

"Come through here." Du Bois went between buildings so close together Brother had to walk sideways. He noticed that his slender guide was better built for such dark passage. An ammoniac stench of urine made Brother's eyes water. Behind the tenements was a space just large enough for a ramshackle outhouse.

"Forty people use this one outhouse," Du Bois said.

Brother breathed shallowly. The worst outhouse in Bardstown was a model of hygiene compared with this.

"The patricians of Philadelphia," Du Bois said sarcastically, "are fond of observing that Philadelphians scorn exterior show: their homes are plain outside but impressive inside. In this part of the Seventh Ward, what you see is what you get."

Du Bois opened the back door of a building and led Brother up a rickety flight of stairs. What sounded like a celebration drew them to a second-floor landing. Through an open doorway Brother saw a small boy eating bread that was green with mold.

"In this Christmas season," Du Bois continued ironically, "the discriminating shopper buys his cakes at Dexter's, his beef at Margerum's, his oysters at Jones's, and his ice cream at Sautter's."

From the end of a dark hallway came shrieks, curses, and children's cheering. Du Bois went to investigate, with Brother on his heels. Through an open doorway they could see a woman threatening a man with a knife. She was a heavy woman with wild hair, and she repeatedly stabbed the air as though killing ghosts. The man, bleeding from a cut on his arm, brandished a stick of wood but kept a table between them. It was the only piece of furniture in the room still standing. The children—two boys, two girls, one of whom held a squalling infant—were screaming like magpies. While Brother had seen his share of domestic quarrels, this standoff between strangers with unknown grievances had an air of unreality. The knife stabbing the air, however, was very real. Brother was surprised when Du Bois did not hesitate but walked up behind the woman and told her to give him the knife. The children stopped their squealing and listened. The room became quiet, the only sound the woman's hoarse breathing.

"Give it to me, I said," Du Bois repeated. The woman was half a head taller than he was. She glanced at him but kept an eye on her husband.

"If he touch me again I cut his heart out," she said.

Brother was startled to feel a small hand slip into his own, little fingers curl around his thumb and hold on tight. He looked down and saw the younger of the two girls, as tall as his waist, looking up at him, all eyes.

"Give me the knife," Du Bois said.

The woman hesitated, thinking it over, and just then the man moved. She stabbed the air again, keeping him at bay. The husband looked mean and surly but also relieved that someone had come to break up the fight.

"She start it," he told Du Bois.

"Like hell," the wife said.

"Give me the knife," Du Bois said. "Think of your children."

The woman began weeping, but remained vigilant of her husband. "He'll start up again soon as you leave."

Will addressed the husband. "I want you to promise you won't hurt her afterward. If you do, she is to send for me and I will have you arrested."

"She start it," the husband said doggedly.

"I don't care. This is no way to treat your family."

The wife suddenly threw the knife on the table and staggered backward with her hands covering her face. She wept through her fingers, then said quite clearly and audibly, "It gonna be Christmas next week."

The husband dropped his piece of wood on the floor. It made a hollow thump. Brother felt the little fingers tighten on his thumb, holding on for dear life.

"There ain't no food in the house," the woman sobbed.

"Come to the settlement," Du Bois said. "Bring your children, and we will feed them."

The woman collapsed on the floor as if felled by a blow. She rolled over on her side, weeping uncontrollably. Her older daughter knelt beside her, holding the infant. The husband stared at her with no sign of emotion.

"Why don't you go for a walk," Du Bois told the man. "Go anywhere. Just let it be for a while."

As though relieved to have someone else decide for him, the husband shuffled out of the room and down the hallway. He did not look back. For their part the children ignored him. Their eyes were riveted on Du Bois. Brother could feel the weight of their need and wondered how Du Bois stood the pressure.

"Come to the settlement," Will repeated to the sobbing mother.

"How'm I gonna make it?" she cried.

"You'll make it."

"I ain't gonna make it."

"You have to make it," Du Bois said. He shook his head at Brother, as if to say he had done all he could, and went quietly into the hall. The small fingers relinquished their claim. Brother could not bear to look at the child and left quickly.

As they went downstairs Du Bois said, "This is not part of my job here, but one cannot ignore suffering when it is all around him. There's not much we can do, without support from City Hall." Ahead of Brother, Du Bois was silhouetted against the open front door. Brother looked at his slim neck and narrow shoulders and marveled at his courage.

He saw a small shadow following them up a debris-strewn corridor, and was afraid to look back. He shivered as they exited onto the sidewalk, but not from the cold. Du Bois again headed west on Lombard. Glancing at Jones, he saw that the Kentuckian was shaken.

"I want you to understand what I am doing here," he told Brother. "I believe that the answer to the Negro problem begins with systematic investigation which can lead to understanding. My job is to present the facts, so that the world will stop misjudging the Negro and lumping all into a single category: lazy, shiftless, stupid, and venal. The cure for this gross error in perspective is knowledge based on scientific investigation. The University of Pennsylvania hired me to prove the prevailing notion that Philadelphia is going to the dogs because of the increasing crime rate

among Negroes living primarily in the Seventh Ward. I welcome
the opportunity, because it gives me a forum from which to
dispute their theory. When my study is published it will show
that Philadelphia Negroes function on distinct, individual levels
—that there exists a successful, progressive Negro middle class—
that Negro criminals prey mainly on fellow Negroes and not
whites—that Negro crime is a result of poverty and ignorance—
that the Negro problem is a result of historical development and
not an innate characteristic—that our people are a striving, palpitating group and not an inert, sick body of criminals."

Brother fell into step with Du Bois. He admired Du Bois's
ideas, especially the one about the white man's tendency to view
Negroes as a group rather than as individuals, but his attention
was suddenly distracted. He felt rather than saw the girl from the
tenement following them. When he did look back, she seemed
even smaller out in the open, her hair uncombed and clothes like
rags. She followed him like an echo of despair. He saw her eyes
shining from a distance of a hundred feet.

"I see you've made a conquest," Will said cheerfully, glancing
back at the girl.

"What'll I do?"

"Don't worry. She'll be all right. Children will follow us all over
the ward. They have nothing better to do. She'll go home."

Du Bois resumed his lecture on the Seventh Ward neighborhood. He pointed out the middle-class residences side by side
with tenement slums. Brother kept glancing back to see if the
girl was still following them. She was.

"Some of the best Negro families of the ward live on this
block," he said. "Oh, see there? Coming out of that brownstone?
Mr. Carver and his daughter. Carver owns a laundry service and
a grocery store. He is well-to-do, at least by my standards. Com
pared to me, Carver is a very wealthy man."

"You? A university professor?"

"No, not a professor. Not even an instructor. The university ha
bestowed on me the title of *assistant* instructor. What else coul
they do with the first Negro on their staff! Still, for my purposes, i
suffices. It's only a one-year appointment. Here come the Carv
ers. I'll introduce you. —Hello, Mr. Carver, Miss Carver! How ar
you? Allow me to present Mr. Jones, who is one of the footbal

players the city is honoring. Perhaps you have read about it in the papers?"

Brother was stunned. Miss Carver was the most beautiful girl he had ever seen. She had flawless almond skin with a faint flush of rouge on her cheekbones. Her face was framed by a fur-lined hood. Her smile was elegant, assured; her eyes were curious and unafraid. Brother realized that Mr. Carver had had to repeat a question, though with amusement, as if accustomed to young men temporarily losing their senses over his daughter.

"What college are you representing?"

"College?" Brother was distracted by Miss Carver's appraising glance. His clothes felt shabbier and more ill-fitting than they actually were. "Uh . . . Post Oak Seminary."

"Post Oak?" Carver was brisk. "Haven't heard of that one."

"It's in Kentucky," Brother said lamely. "It's new." He sensed Du Bois's questioning look as well.

"I see. Well, good luck to you, young man. Come along, dear." Carver took his girl's arm and guided her away, apparently accustomed also, Brother thought, to separating the wheat from the chaff. He marveled at Miss Carver's fluid grace. Then he sensed the slum child standing behind him. He looked back and she was there, small and unprotected. When he turned to catch a glimpse of Miss Carver before she and her father turned the corner, he felt suddenly that he was suspended between his future and his past. Du Bois was looking at him with an intuitive understanding.

"So you've never seen a black princess before?" Will said. "Now you know how the other half lives." He glanced at the child, who waited patiently for them to move on. "The problem is, people like Carver are reluctant to share their influence with less fortunate members of their race. Having gotten into the boat, they don't want to rock it. What we need is a rallying point."

"And I'm it?" Brother was on the defensive.

"Don't be afraid of who you are."

In spite of a trapped feeling, Brother smiled ironically. "My name is Robert E. Lee Jones."

Now it was Du Bois's turn to be surprised, but only for a moment. He heard the despair in Brother's voice.

"Drop the *Lee*," he said with conviction.

"What?"

"Drop it. Why not?"

"In Bardstown, people die with the name they were born with."

"You're not in Bardstown. Listen, when I gave a commencement speech at Harvard graduation in 1890, do you know what my topic was? Jefferson Davis. That's right. The New York *Nation* said that I handled my subject with good taste, moderation, and 'almost contemptuous fairness.' So I feel qualified to advise you: it would be in good taste, fair and moderate, to drop the Lee. You are now Robert E. Jones!"

Brother stared at him in wonder.

"Now that we've solved that problem," Du Bois continued amiably, "how about helping me with mine?"

"I'd like to . . ."

"But?"

"But I'm not alone. My teammates will have to vote on it. I could set up a team meeting after practice. Say, five-thirty this afternoon? At our boardinghouse?"

"Is that what they call it?"

Brother grinned. "It's a gambling place, isn't it."

"Among other things."

"Would you come and speak to the team?"

"Most assuredly," Will said.

"I can't make any guarantees."

"I don't ask for any." Du Bois suddenly linked arms with him, as though to seal the bargain, and together they continued up Lombard. When they reached the corner, Brother remembered to look back. The little girl was gone.

Chapter Twenty

Hudson Stroud called for a counsel of war.

The Southerners met in his room before returning to resume the game. "Notice anything unusual about your opponents?" Hudson asked.

"Liebowitz has a tendency to bet before the draw," Colonel Pitts said. "He may be overeager."

"He'll settle down," Stroud predicted.

"Reno is getting stubborn in his old age. He wants to stay regardless of the cards he's got," Nelson observed.

"McCain's hot streak is due to cool off," Fitzpatrick offered. "He must have won three pots yesterday."

"Four," Pitts corrected.

"Dutchman's arthritis is getting so bad he can't handle the cards!" Knot Dickinson cackled. "Dutch hit too many folks in too many barrooms. His knuckles are calcified."

"You're one to talk," Hudson said. "But back to particulars: I recall a hand last night where Diamond Ed pushed his luck with a pair of nines against Knot's queen-high flush. Ed had no business staying in that hand. And what about that two-discard of his? Remember that? He held an ace as a kicker and tried to bluff Knot into thinking he had three of a kind and was drawing for a fourth. I think ol' Ed's not thinking straight."

"Speaking of which," Little Harry said waggishly, "anybody

bring any patent medicine?" Dickinson and Pitts reached for their coat pockets. Hudson scowled. "Just kiddin'!" Nelson said.

"Don't get off on ailments," Hudson said irritably. "We got work to do. And in case I forget myself and start actin' like it's just another game of poker, somebody give me a swift kick."

There was a knock at the door. Fitzpatrick went to answer it. James Longstreet stood in the hall. Delighted, Hudson went to greet him. The general tipped his hat.

"Reporting for poker," he said.

"Come in, General. This is an honor," Hudson said.

Every man stood at attention as Hudson introduced them to Longstreet. Pitts swelled with pride when Longstreet acknowledged his "title" with a little military salute. Then the general turned to Stroud.

"I believe you mentioned something about a drink of sour-mash whiskey?" Longstreet said.

Four flasks were immediately produced from coat pockets. Glasses were found.

"Gentlemen, your health," said Longstreet.

"Health!" they chorused and drank.

"What's your game, sir?" Hudson asked.

"In my old army days—the Union army, that is—it was brag and chuckaluck," Longstreet replied.

"Our game is straight poker."

"That's fine with me. I'd like to play, if you'll allow me to join in."

"That would be our pleasure."

"What's the limit?"

"No limit. We've got twenty thousand to wager, and we hope to take at least that many Yankee dollars back South with us."

"Uh-oh," Longstreet said. "I may be out of my depth."

"They say poker is a lot like war," Hudson observed. "If that's true—and I think it 'tis—I can't think of a man I'd rather have on my side. We'll be proud to back yo' play, sir."

"Hear, hear!" echoed the others.

"Well." Longstreet pulled at his mustache. "Yankee dollars, you say? I hope this game is more friendly than that donnybrook of a banquet, eh?"

"Just a civilized game of poker, General," Hudson lied.

Longstreet noticed Fitzpatrick and Nelson exchanging guilty looks. "Didn't I see you," he alertly asked Hudson, "at Fairmount Park when that ruckus started up?"

"I reckon I was there," Hudson said innocently.

"Can't say I approve of that sort of display," Longstreet said. "War's over. Best forgotten. Bury our sectional differences. For the good of the country."

"Yes-sir," Hudson said and made a show of looking at his watch. "It's time we played cards, General. Are you ready?"

Longstreet knocked back the dregs of his bourbon. "Lead on, Sergeant."

When they reached the fourth-floor suite, the Northerners were so impressed that such a personage as General Longstreet had joined them that they dispensed with the ritual of frisking their opponents. Before Hudson could introduce his important guest, however, he saw that something was wrong. His sword was lying on the table.

"What's this?" Longstreet said, amused but wary.

"Liebowitz, what do you think you're doing!" Hudson said.

"What do you mean?" Liebowitz countered. "Winning it back is your idea, not mine."

"Well, you don't mean to put it up, first hand we play," Hudson said lamely. "Put it away till we're ready for it."

Longstreet drew Stroud aside. "This is obviously a private game," he said. "Perhaps I should retire."

"Oh, no, General," Hudson said. "Everything's fine and dandy. Don't worry 'bout that old sword. We want you to play." He motioned to Liebowitz to come forward and help make amends, then introduced Longstreet to the other players. At last they sat down. Pitts insisted on giving up his place for the general. Liebowitz took the sword off the table. To put them at ease, Longstreet leaned forward to tell a story.

"Ever play with Indians?" he said.

"Can't say as I did," Liebowitz replied sociably.

"It's funny—they like their poker," Longstreet said. "But you have to put yourself out considerably to play with them. They want you to smoke their peace pipe, give them whiskey, make friendly sign talk, watch them dance, and generally pass the time until they decide to spread the blanket and deal the cards. I knew a lieutenant who played with some Sioux once. An old buck started to cheat. He laid his hat upside down on the blanket. It had a mirror in the crown, so that on his deal he could see every card. The lieutenant asked him to put the hat away. When the game continued, a young buck commenced walking around the players babbling Indian talk. The lieutenant realized he was giving away his hand to the chief. Pretty soon the chief got a good hand and began betting strong. The lieutenant decided to meet fire with fire and slipped four eights and a jack up his sleeve. He then let the wandering buck see the weak hand he was dealt. The buck jabbered away to the chief. After the draw the lieutenant managed to exchange his hand for the cards up his sleeve and made a large wager. The chief, thinking he was bluffing, sent his squaw to bring a bag of silver from his lodge. He then called the lieutenant. They showed down. The chief just sat there, staring at the four eights. Then he grabbed his tomahawk. The buck who had been doing the talking started to run. The lieutenant raked the money into his hat, jumped on his horse, and cleared out. When he looked back, the buck was still going through the woods with the chief right behind him."

After everyone had finished chuckling over the story, Liebowitz said, "Pardon me, General, but that lieutenant . . . he wouldn't happen to have been you, would he?"

"Like I said," Longstreet replied, pulling on his mustache, "he was a friend of mine."

"Whose bet is it?" Hudson said, jealous of Longstreet's attentions to Liebowitz.

When play resumed the Southerners began to win steadily. The game continued for an hour or more, until they broke for lunch. They sent out for a tray of cheese and cold cuts. Stroud took Longstreet aside to talk strategy. He had noticed that Liebowitz, who had not been getting good cards, had begun to bull his luck, raising when he held weak hands. Hudson had observed that Liebowitz went against the odds by staying in a game with a possible straight. He had seen the look of relief on Ernie's face when he filled his middle card on the draw.

"Liebowitz is feeling lucky," Stroud whispered to Longstreet over cold cuts. "Let's push him a bit. He's bound to overplay his hand."

After lunch, on the first deal Hudson's hand contained two jacks, a five, a six, and a queen. Liebowitz cautiously fanned his cards and saw a nine, another nine, a king, a nine, and a nine. Reno O'Shea opened with a hundred-dollar bet. Liebowitz raised two hundred, hoping not to frighten the Southerners out. He slumped in his chair, pretending that it was a matter of indifference to him whether they stayed or not. Dickinson folded, but Stroud, Nelson, and Longstreet saw the three-hundred-dollar bet. O'Shea and Trott were in, while McCain folded. O'Shea said, "Cards, gentlemen?"

To stand pat, Liebowitz knew, would signal that he held a full house—or a flush or a straight—and the betting might end. So he threw his king of hearts down and shook his head, as if to say, "Here we go again." Barely looking at the card dealt to him— another king—he inserted it into the middle of his nines as though filling an inside straight.

Hudson asked for three cards. He looked at his draw and ignored a pain in his chest like heartburn. He had drawn a jack and two deuces.

Lord don't let me die before I finish this hand.

Liebowitz opened with a two-hundred-dollar bet. Hudson raised him five hundred, and the others dropped out. Longstreet watched the betting escalate until the pot held over twenty thousand dollars. Ernie raised Hudson five thousand after Stroud had called with every chip the Southerners had. Stroud had a whispered conference with Little Harry. He showed Harry the cards he was holding.

"I *got* the sumbitch if you can just round up some money."

"Ask for a recess, and I'll see what I can do," Harry said.

"All right," Liebowitz said, after Stroud made a formal request, "but we agreed on a time limit of thirty minutes. After that, you forfeit the hand." He laid his watch on the table.

Longstreet listened as Stroud and his friends pooled their assets. The estimated total value of their combined rings, stickpins, gold watches, and pocket money was about three thousand dollars. They looked to Longstreet for assistance. "Where money is concerned," he told them, "I'm the last person to ask." Harry assumed the responsibility. He had friends in Louisville he could call on, but there was no time to have them wire the money. He hurried to the lobby, looking for Richard Canfield. He found him standing on the sidewalk in front of the hotel and approached him deferentially.

"Sir, may I have a word with you?"

Canfield had met Nelson on the Ohio in the early eighties. He was aware of the poker game on the fourth floor. He wished, however, to keep his distance from gambling until his charity project was completed. It irked him to be seen publicly with a known pokerist and short-card dealer. He glanced around to see if any aldermen or civic officials were in sight. He motioned for Nelson to follow him. They went around the corner and turned into the first place they came to, a seafood shop. They stood in the doorway noticing, simultaneously, the odor of fish. The proprietor watched them expectantly, wiping his hands on a messy apron. With side-whiskers and a spindly mustache he vaguely resembled a catfish.

"I'm Harry Nelson of Louisville." Little Harry craned his neck up at Canfield, who was much taller. "We met on the steamer *Fairchild* in 1885."

"So I recall." Canfield continued to watch for anyone who might recognize him. The shopkeeper rearranged bluefish on a bed of ice. He fluffed up his shrimp and brushed away the flies.

"I have a proposition," Harry said. Canfield waited impassively. "Would you be willing to back a full house, jacks over deuces, in a game of straight draw poker?"

"Are you referring to the private game that is going on? On the fourth floor?"

"You know about it?" Harry was pleased. "Well, the situation is, the bet to us is five thousand. We're temporarily tapped out, and there's no time to telegraph Louisville for more funds. We have thirty minutes"—he looked at his watch—"twenty-two minutes before we forfeit the hand."

"What's the pot worth?"

"Twenty thousand plus."

Small-time poker bored Canfield. He glanced up the sidewalk. The shopkeeper held up a lobster for them to see. He toyed provocatively with its claw.

"I realize that twenty thousand is modest by your standards,"

Harry apologized; struck by inspiration he added, "but we would be honored to donate half our winnings to your charity fund."

Canfield blinked and looked at Little Harry with interest. "How many players?"

"Two. Hudson Stroud and Ernie Liebowitz."

"The sequence of the draw?"

"Stroud took three cards, Liebowitz one."

"Liebowitz probably figures Stroud for three of a kind, hey?" Canfield said, thinking out loud for the sake of charity. "Liebowitz himself has a flush or better. Maybe four of a kind."

"This is straight draw poker," Harry reminded the Faro King. "With a full house, we can't just fold and let him have it!"

"Of course the tendency is always to want to see the cards. Too bad. Well, it's always interesting to hear what's going on. I'm afraid I'd better not get involved, this time. Give my regards to your friends."

At a loss for words, Nelson stared morosely at the shopkeeper's lobster. Encouraged, the fishmonger sidled up to them.

"This is a Chesapeake lobster," he said as if in response to their query.

Nelson called Canfield back. "I saw you bet your Rembrandt painting against Davy Johnson's one hundred grand on a single turn at faro. That was something to see."

"Were you there that night?" Canfield was pleased. "That was in my Nautilus Club at Newport. Five years ago, wasn't it?"

The shopkeeper, determined not to miss a sale, went to exchange the lobster for a crab.

"That was one for the history books," Nelson continued.

"Yes, well, I have done some foolish things in my time," Canfield said benignly. "Now I am a businessman."

"You are an artist, sir," Nelson persisted. "You are well known, sir, in Louisville."

"Is that a fact!" Canfield smiled. "Always did like the South. Relaxing place. Decent whiskey and lovely ladies, eh?"

"Speaking of the South," Nelson said carelessly, "General Longstreet is sitting in on our game."

"You don't say!" Canfield thoughtfully regarded the fishmonger, who had reappeared with a large crab.

"Delaware crab, very fresh!" The shopkeeper dangled his

specimen before them. "Just off the boat. Look at the size of this one. Clean and fresh."

"Tell me again about the cards." Canfield was suddenly all business. His change in attitude was like a sea breeze to Harry. "Are the cards marked? Is the deal square?"

"It's a fair game," Harry declared.

Canfield imagined the two old gamblers facing each other across the table, waiting to see if the money would come. He watched the flies circle the bluefish. The proprietor waved them away but they came back immediately. The urge to win at hazard rose up in Canfield.

"If I'm in," he told Harry, "I'd be inclined to push the stakes up a bit—for the sake of charity. I'll back your play for twenty-five thousand dollars. But tell your man not to lose."

"Don't worry," Harry said.

The shopkeeper held up some fillets. "Would you care for cod?"

"No, thanks." Canfield humored the man. "We're after bigger fish."

The fishmonger rushed to the back of his shop, flung down his fillets, and brought out a huge fish in both arms.

"Is this ling big enough? Thirty pounds, dressed. Perfect for a banquet."

Canfield did not look at the fish. "I don't want this to get out," he told Harry. "Nobody knows about this. Nobody knows where you got your backing." He added, "I believe in accountability."

A chill went through Harry. "Mum's the word, Mr. Canfield."

"My man, Ziprenian, will bring the cash to your suite," Canfield said briskly. "Good luck." He walked away without looking back. Nelson and the shopkeeper stared after him.

"Seventeen cents a pound . . . the ling." The fishmonger seemed to be talking to himself. Harry's Southern manners were stirred.

"Do you have pickled sardines?" he asked politely.

"We sold out this morning," the fishmonger exclaimed desperately.

"Too bad."

Nelson left the shop and returned to the Stratford. He allowed

Canfield to precede him at a discreet distance, then followed him into the hotel.

On the fourth floor, while they waited, Longstreet tried to entertain everyone by telling stories. Liebowitz looked at his watch.

"Three minutes," he said.

Stroud drummed his fingers on the table.

"I was stationed in Texas in forty-five." Longstreet resumed his story. "During those long days of waiting for the Mexican War to heat up, we frequently engaged in the game of brag or five-cent ante. We instructed Ulysses Grant in the mysteries of these games, but he made a poor player. The games often lasted an entire day. About the most you could lose was seventy-five cents a day. But Grant lost a bit more than that. Years later, in 1858, I happened to be in St. Louis, and there met Captain E. B. Holloway with some other army chums. We went to the Planters' Hotel to talk over old times and someone proposed to have an old-time game of brag. We were one short of making up a full hand, and Holloway said, 'Wait a few minutes, and I will find someone.' In a few minutes he returned with a man poorly dressed in citizen's clothes and in whom I recognized our old friend Ulysses Grant. We were glad to see him, although we knew that in civil life he had been unfortunate and was in needy circumstances. After the game Grant took me aside and placed in the palm of my hand a five-dollar gold piece. He insisted that I take it in payment of a debt of honor from our Texas days. I had forgotten that he owed me that sum from his disasters at our brag games. I said, 'Old friend, I can't take it. You're out of the service now, and you may need the money.' He said, 'You must take it. I cannot live with anything in my possession that is not mine.' Seeing his determination and desiring to save him mortification, I took the money. We shook hands and said good-bye. The next time we met was at Appomattox."

The gamblers' appreciative murmur was cut short when Little Harry entered the room. "Money's on the way," he said.

Liebowitz frowned. "Who's your backer?"

"That's confidential," Harry said.

The carpeted hall absorbed the sound of Ziprenian's footsteps as he approached the gamblers' suite. In his hand was a paper sack containing five bundles of crisp fifty-dollar bills, one hundred per bundle. During the elevator ride The Zipper had been painfully aware that he was carrying the exact sum he owed Canfield. He also could not put out of his mind the forty-five similar bundles remaining in the hotel vault. He knocked on the door.

"Here you are!" Nelson cried.

"Sign here, please." Ziprenian offered his back as a place for Harry to initial a receipt.

Liebowitz stared at Ziprenian. "Is *that* who's behind you?" he said, meaning Canfield.

"None-a yo' business." Hudson immediately shoved two bundles of hundreds into the pot. "See yo' five and raise you five."

Liebowitz consulted with his partners. "Your five and bump you ten," Ernie told Hudson.

Nelson counted three remaining bundles in the sack and whispered, "If you raise him five more, we can't meet another raise. I'd call."

Stroud looked at his cards: jacks full on deuces. His mind was strong and clear. He looked hard at Liebowitz. They were in a firelit clearing. The cards were on a log. Riley Dunn was alive. Hudson tossed two bundles on the table and laid his cards down.

"Can you beat jacks full?"

"Four nines."

Liebowitz flashed a gold-toothed grin. Stroud did not look at him. Without a word he pushed back his chair. Before he left the room, he motioned for Ziprenian to follow him. Longstreet was the last to leave.

Stroud's room was like a wax museum for gamblers. Surrounded by his companions, Hudson sat in a brown study. After pouring Longstreet a drink, he scarcely paid him any attention. There was no need for them to say what everyone was thinking: when a man is holding the cards, there is nothing you can do about it.

There was a knock at the door. Little Harry let Ziprenian in.

"You gotta tell Mr. Canfield," The Zipper said to Hudson.

"Tell him what?" Hudson snapped. "We still got five thousand in the sack, don't we?"

"Excuse me," Arno said, "but at the rate you're going, it won't last very long."

"Canfield is a professional," Harry argued. "He knows you don't get it all back in one hand. Why wouldn't he stay with us?"

"You want more money?" Ziprenian's voice was shrill, boyish. "*You* ask for it."

Longstreet broke the dispirited silence. "I fear I may be responsible."

"Oh, no, General!" Hudson spoke up immediately and was echoed by his companions. "It's nobody's fault. I would've bet the U.S. Mint on that full house."

"So where do we go from here?" Longstreet asked.

Hudson looked up, encouraged by the *we*. "It may be that the wisest course would be to pack it in." His eyes urged Longstreet to dissuade him.

"You said you received your wound in an attack at the Green River, in Kentucky?" Longstreet said. "Did Liebowitz fight there, too?"

"Yes, sir. In the Twenty-Fifth Michigan Infantry."

"And the sword?"

"He took it off me when he captured me."

Stroud's bony face, with its dogged determination, reminded Longstreet of a veteran of the Army of Virginia who had sought him out at the Richmond reunion, shaking his hand and saying, "They did not beat us. They just outlasted us."

Memory—it is our bane and our glory.

"On April ninth, eighteen and sixty-five, I was at Appomattox," Longstreet reminisced, "in charge of defending against a numerically superior enemy. Lee had sent a courier to Grant to arrange a meeting to surrender our forces. When I realized that news of the truce had not reached General Ord, whose infantry was drawn up in battle formation, I sent Captain Simms to inform the nearest Union commander, George Custer, about the surrender arrangements. Custer returned through the lines with Simms at a fast gallop. I saw he was overexcited. He was wheeling his mount back and forth, calling to me:

" 'I am General Custer. In the name of General Sheridan and myself, I demand unconditional surrender of this army.'

"I said, 'I am not in command of this army. General Lee is, and he has gone back to meet General Grant in regard to a surrender.'

" 'No matter about General Grant,' Custer replied. 'We demand the surrender to be made to us. If you do not do so, we will renew hostilities, and any bloodshed will be upon your head.'

" 'Oh, well,' I said, 'if you do that I will do my best to meet you.' Turning to Colonel Manning of my staff, I said in Custer's hearing, 'Would you please order General Johnson to move his division to the front, to the right of General Gordon. And General Latrobe, please order General Pickett forward to Gordon's left. *At once!*'

"We of course were not capable of such reinforcements. But Custer cooled off immediately. He swallowed it hook, line, and sinker.

"Custer said, 'General, we probably had best wait until we hear from Grant and Lee. I will speak to General Sheridan about it. Don't move your troops yet!'

"As Custer rode off, I remarked to Manning, 'That young man never learned to play the game of brag.' "

The old men stood very still, charmed by the general's story.

"General, sir," Hudson said, his eyes lighting up. "You just give me an idea."

"If there is any way I can help . . ." Longstreet said.

"There *is* one thing," Hudson said. "Would you mind sittin' in on the game tomorrow?"

"It would be my pleasure." Longstreet turned to go.

"I 'preciate it, General." Hudson followed Longstreet to the door and saw him out, then addressed his partners. "They got us backed up. We got to let it all hang out," he said. They nodded their agreement, then glanced warily at Ziprenian, who was pretending not to be listening to their plans. "Thanks for your help," Hudson said, escorting Arno out. "Don't call us. We'll call you." As soon as the door was closed, he said, "We got to cold-deck 'em! Ain't no other way. Harry, you up to it?"

Nelson flexed his fingers, reminding everyone he was the only one in the group without arthritis. "Is a pig full of bacon?" he said.

"Now, the big question," Hudson said. "We'll need at least another twenty thousand, maybe more. Lieberwitz ain't in the credit business. Anybody got any ideas? Would Canfield stay with us one more time?"

"What if," Knot Dickinson said thoughtfully, "we told Canfield we'd guarantee him half the winnings for his charity, *regardless* which side wins?"

"What? You mean, speak for Lieberwitz?" Hudson was amazed and delighted at once. "What makes you think Ernie'd go along?"

"We won't ask, unless he wins." Knot shrugged his big shoulders. "In which case, Hudson, you may have to shoot him."

Hudson cackled. "Still hard as a pine knot, ain't you?" he told Dickinson. "All right, assuming we get Canfield's backing, here's what we do: Knot, you see if you can rummage up a deck of standard playin' cards like the ones we been using. Pitts, you and Harry stack the deck like I tell you. With Longstreet sittin' in, they won't frisk us. Harry's holding the stacked deck. We play fair till the deal goes around once. When the deal comes round to you, Pitts, you call for a fresh deck. McCain will pass a new deck to Harry, who switches decks and gives you our stacked deck. On the deal, Reno gets fives full on jacks. Lieberwitz gets a queen-high straight. Deal me four tens. Harry, you horse the bet up, then drop out. We goin' to clean those suckers out. What do you say?"

"Show me the cards," Pitts said.

Participated in nearly every campaign against Army of Potomac—Lee's mainstay in important tactical movements from Seven Days to Appomattox—Fighting general, superior to Lee or Jackson in battle leadership and appreciation of tactical values— Lee's best general defensively—Instinctively knew moment for counterstroke—Crushing, well-timed assaults at Second Manassas, Chickamauga, and The Wilderness—Sangfroid in battle kept his men steady in desperate circumstances—

"Coach, did you hear me?" King repeated himself.

Stagg looked up from his note-taking with a startled expression. So immersed had he been in Longstreet's book he could almost hear the cannons boom and small arms crackle, while the Rebel yell sounded through the trees.

"What is it?" Stagg said testily.

"We thought we'd get on with the tandem and the turtleback." King glanced impatiently toward the middle of Franklin Field where the team dawdled, waiting for instructions.

"Go ahead." Stagg did not move from the bench on the sidelines, where he sat with a large notebook and *From Manassas to Appomattox* in his lap. The notebook pages were covered with handprinted charts and sketches. King sidled closer, curious.

"Does it matter which formation we work on first?" he asked, trying to read Stagg's notes upside down.

"However you like." Stagg was doodling with a box formation based on Longstreet's troop placement at First Manassas.

"What's that?" King said.

"Oh, one of Longstreet's plays, you might say." Stagg held up his sketch of a formation in which the quarterback and fullback lined up close behind the respective guards, while both halfbacks aligned on them in a box formation.

"You got that out of a military text?" King was incredulous.

"Just reading between the lines."

"We should be going over our game plan, Coach. There's not much time left."

"That's what I'm doing."

"Pardon me, Coach, but I really can't see where Longstreet has anything to do with Heisman and Warner's strategy!"

Stagg looked up, black eyes penetrating. "Heisman said the general was his number-one assistant, remember? I'm doing my homework. Look at this box formation: the center can snap short to the fullback for a quick buck or to either half, to sweep in either direction with blocking in front of him. It's neat, it's tight, it's deceptive."

"And Longstreet thought of it?"

Stagg smiled like a bear with a honey tree. "What we have here," he explained, "is a man ahead of his time. Look at this." He held the notebook where King could see it, flipping through the pages for his assistant's edification.

Battle	Longstreet's Actions	All-Star Strategy
First Manassas	Displays tactical ability, strong leadership, box formation crosses Bull Run.	○○○⊗○○○ ○ ○ ○ ○
Peninsula Campaign	Aptitude for planning and logistics; at Williamsburg, stops retreating and counterattacks in columns of masses; deep penetration checks Union advance.	Tackle-back, with 2 lead blockers through hole, wingbacks cross in downfield blocking.
Second Manassas	Orders artillery enfilade on unprotected Union flank, then follows up with infantry assault.	Right sweep by half, followed by halfback buck cutback left.
Sharpsburg	Orders right flank (Toombs) to hold bridge then execute orderly withdrawal in wide swing to bring men back into position to defend against Federal advance.	Game plan: aggressive defense holds, bends, holds, then counterattacks with sudden wingback reverse.
Fredericksburg	Sound tactical use of terrain: Orders read, "Sustain enemy attacks, repel them until they become exhausted and demoralized."	Use defense and kicking game to establish field position; win in fourth quarter.
Chickamauga	Master tactician at work: overcomes battlefield confusion, organizes makeshift force of various regiments; senses weakened line in front of him and attacks, penetrates, rolls up enemy; successful because of speed with which attack is launched.	After interception or fumble, press attack with quick lateral pass; sweeps followed by bucks in quick succession.
The Wilderness	Arrives in midst of battle with troops marching in double column, thus able to deploy both divisions quickly in counterattack. Sorrel's attack on Union right followed by frontal assault. Textbook example of surprise as cardinal principle of tactics.	Swift exploitation of enemy weakness; Alternate Guard-Crisscross with Running Wedge and End-Around.

King respectfully studied Stagg's notes, then remarked, "You left out Gettysburg!"

Stagg closed his notebook. "Yes, well, Longstreet lost that one. He didn't like Lee's battle plan. He wanted to withdraw and find better ground. I don't blame him."

"So, defense is the key?" King concluded.

"I translate Longstreet's tactics to football thusly." Lonny rared back on the bench, hands behind him. "Hard-nosed, conservative, disciplined, take-what-you-give-me, great line play, blocking and tackling. Then that surprise move that the opposition does not expect. It puts me in mind of Dr. H. L. Williams and the Minnesota Shift."

King whistled. "That's high praise indeed. Well, Coach, let me say that we'd be thrilled to have you join us at practice, whenever you're ready. And . . . Coach?"

"Yes?"

"That last entry of yours . . . you referred to the opposing team as the *enemy.*"

"So I did." Stagg referred to his notes.

"Aren't you getting a little bit carried away, Coach? I mean, football's a long way from *war,* isn't it?"

Stagg looked at his assistant sharply. From the field came the thump of a punt, the cries of young voices echoing from empty stadium seats.

"I never thought I'd hear a Princeton man say that," Stagg said.

"This team is going to hell in a handbasket," Heisman said. He paced back and forth in front of the couch where Kate and Warner sat. They were waiting in the parlor of the Maison Blanche for the players' meeting to end. The coaches had been excluded from the meeting.

"First, Joiner and Carter quit," Heisman fumed. "Then Martin and Wright. I never saw anything to beat it."

"Well, if they can't play on the same team with players whose skin is different from theirs, maybe they belong at home," Warner said.

"It's not just a question of race," Heisman pointed out. "The scrimmage game had a lot to do with it. The bellyaching got serious when we promoted the blacks to varsity status. But like I told Joiner, everybody is going to get to play. This game is supposed to be fun, isn't it?"

"Yeah, well their quitting also had a lot to do with the way the vote for captain turned out," Warner observed. "I must say, Harvey and Nalley took it real well. Did you see them congratulate Riddle and Jones?"

"Now this secret meeting!" Heisman continued to vent his frustrations. "We shouldn't have let this Lopez character within a mile of our squad."

"He had a point about legal rights," Warner reminded him. "Humboldt did invite him. We can't legally kick him off the team."

"Whose team is it?" Heisman exclaimed. "And who is that new Negro? Didn't I see him hanging around practice?"

Kate spoke up. "He's a friend of Brother's. His name is Du Bois. He teaches at the University of Pennsylvania."

"Penn?" Heisman grew thoughtful. "Maybe he could help us borrow some shoes for your players from their athletic department."

"Maybe." Kate looked askance at the Alabama Poly coach. She felt guilty about not sharing what she knew about the planned demonstration.

As if tuned to her wavelength Heisman said, "I don't care if we discard the Rebel flag, do you? What do we need it for? We need shoes and uniforms. What do you say, Glenn?"

"And we need to be left alone," Warner growled. "We don't need any more outside influences."

Kate was thinking about how much her players had changed in the past few days. They were walking on their toes, with a new swagger. They had a faraway look in their eyes. They even dressed differently. Isaiah had a carnation in his lapel, Brother carried a walking stick, B.C. wore white spats, Tree had replaced his belt with a red sash, Weasel had an ascot, Cassius had a tattoo on his arm, a star of David.

Where did he find a Jewish tattoo artist? It seems like only yesterday I caught them smoking rabbit tobacco at recess.

She had never before been excluded from a team meeting. Yet her indignation was tempered by guilt: Was she angry because she was no longer the focus of their attention? She had plotted and finagled to bring her babes out of the woods. Now they were beginning to find their own way.

Shouldn't I be happy for them?

"What's come over those boys?" Heisman asked her.

"I don't know," she said truthfully.

In the players' room down the hall, beds and pallets had been stacked in a corner and chairs brought in, so that the team sat facing a podium and a blackboard. Lopez dragged a wooden box to the front of the room and stood on it so everybody could see him. He was nervous about the strange black man seated on the back row, between Brother and Chase. What worried Lopez was that the man looked right at home. Lopez watched the newcomer whispering to Brother.

"I can't help noticing," Du Bois was saying, "that your team is playing in street clothes. Hasn't anyone provided uniforms and equipment for them?"

"Not yet," Brother said.

"Maybe I can use my university connections to help correct that problem," Will suggested.

"May I have yo' attention!" Lopez said. "Let us talk about our situation in Philly. Let us consider what's *really* goin' on. Let us consider where we stand in this all-star game. Let us consider what we are *worth.*"

Lopez got down off his box and began to strut back and forth. The players on the front row could smell liquor on his breath.

"All the field's a stage, and all the players on it merely actors. Think about it. The spectators pay to see a performance. The field where we play is sump'm like the outdoor the-atres the Greeks used to have. The captains meet in the center of the field for the coin toss. The spectators crowd up as close as they kin git to the sidelines. They start to cheer when the two teams take the field." Lopez paused, bald head shining. "They cain't he'p it, cain't he'p theirselves. All right. The other team kicks off. The audience screams as you score a touchdown. But as the game progresses, you begin to lose ground. The spectators cry and groan. They cheer when you pull yourself up off the ground and face your opponents with grit and pluck. Then you break a long run for a touchdown. It's jubilation time! Folks leap and jump for joy. Men kiss ugly ladies. They love you! They'll do anything for you."

Lopez saw Chase's eyes light up in recognition. Brother, however, looked on skeptically. Lopez moved closer to where Brother and Du Bois sat and directed his comments at them.

"It is drama, that's what it is. The audience boos when the ref makes a call ag'inst you. They give you a nice hand when you get hurt and limp off the field. They moan when you miss a field goal and throw yo'self on the ground in misery. When the game is over, what do they do? They ride the winnin' players off the field, right? Hoisted up on their shoulders, screamin' and runnin' alongside their heroes. It's just as emotional on the side of the losing team. Their loyal supporters are grievin', tears rolling down their cheeks."

Lopez shook his head sagely. "My friends, is it only a game, or is it the best drama in the world? Do the spectators get their money's worth? Standin' on the sidelines gruntin' with ev'ry lick that's passed and worshippin'—yes, *worshippin'*—yo' courage and pluck. Their hearts are with you, win or lose. They're gettin' one hell of a show for their six bits. And that, my friends, is the subject of my program."

The Panthers stared at him without a change in expression. No one had ever paid to see them play. Lopez drew from his pocket some newspaper clippings. "Let's see what your stock is worth these days." He put on rimless spectacles and read aloud from Harry Prescott's columns in the *Inquirer*.

BLACK COLOSSUS TOWERS OVER PHILADELPHIA

The sensational play of the Negro Kentuckians has the South team in an uproar. After the Bardstown natives defeated their white Rebel counterparts, several Southerners from Virginia and Carolina are rumored to have quit the team. Support for the Black Rebels is rampant among the Negro citizens of our city.

"And what about this one?" Lopez continued.

DARK FORCE IN QUAKER LAND

Who are these unheralded Kentuckians, these village lads, these sons of the earth? Fast as horses, strong as bulls, the Black Rebels disdain modern equipment such as leather helmets. "Their heads," says one of their recent victims, "are like concrete posts."

"You are heroes," Lopez said flatly. "Did you know that?" He stared at them over his spectacles. "What are heroes worth these days? Two bucks? Is that fair? Who profits off your sweat, blood, and pain? Businessmen, that's who. Look at this!" He pulled up his pants to show the knobs and scars on his knees. "Some of us have give our lives to football." He took off his glasses and wiped his eyes. "For you, this is only the beginning. For some of us, this is our last hurrah. You have within yo' grasp the opportunity to make hist'ry for the future of football, to give future players sump'm worth bustin' ass for, the chance to make sump'm of theirselves. It's the American Dream. For yo'selves, for the next generation, for the game of football itsownself, let's *STRIKE!*"

For a few seconds no one reacted, then Tree raised his hand. "Say what?"

"As a last resort, of course," Lopez added mildly as he took a piece of paper from his pocket and unfolded it. "I have devised a three-point program to be presented to the organizers of this here all-star game, at a time and place of our own choosin'. They are as follows:

"1. *increased salaries* (we are askin' five hunnerd dollars per man—thass right!—five hunnerd)
2. *performance bonus* (two hunnerd and fifty per player on the winnin' team; one twenty-five to the losers)
3. *guaranteed share of gate* (askin' ten percent, takin' five; with estimated gross receipts of half a mil, thass twenty-five thousand dollars minimum or 'bout five hunnerd per man).

"So you're lookin' at take-home of twelve hunnerd and fifty or thereabouts. It ain't goin' be easy squeezin' that green outa those hombres, but this buckaroo's goin' to work his balls off for you. Count on it!"

Chase stared at Lopez. An unbidden thought came to mind: *I could start my own church with twelve hundred* . . .

Brother could not help thinking of the college tuition twelve hundred dollars would pay, then struggled against Lopez's easy promises. He remembered Du Bois's words: *A man must act on his convictions.*

The rest of the team regarded Lopez in stunned silence. Weasel was the first to speak.

"You mean, they'd pay us all that money to do what we was willin' to do for free?" he said.

"Ain't that wunnerful?" Lopez cried.

Now Brother got up and gravely went to the front of the room. In his hands he held one of the recently delivered jerseys that had been provided for the South team. He held it up for all to see. Over the chest was sewn a replica of the crossed stars and bars of the Confederate battle flag. Lopez started to interrupt, then decided to let the blacks have their say.

"This is the jersey they want us to wear," Brother said.

"Man-oh-man," Cassius said encouragingly.

"Sho' is fancy," B.C. echoed.

"Maybe we have our own reason to strike," Brother said, shaking his head at them.

"Whatta you mean, *we?*" Lopez cried. "Ain't we all in this together?"

"Shall we pray?" Chase said, rising fervently. Nobody paid any attention to him and he sat down.

"What do you mean, strike?" Tree said.

"Look at this emblem." Brother continued, displaying the crossed stars and bars. "What does it mean to you?"

"We from Dixie!" Cassius said.

"By any standard," Brother said patiently, "this is a symbol of white supremacy and racist repression. We must *not* play under the banner of the unreconstructed Old South. Do you understand?"

They looked at him silently. Lopez was wringing his hands.

"We have a responsibility to our people," Brother continued.

"Our mamas?" Lincoln said, trying to understand. Brother's patience snapped.

"Lambs to the slaughter!" he exclaimed in frustration. The word "lambs" brought Chase to his feet.

"For the Lord himself shall descend from heaven with a shout, with the voice of the archangel, and with the trump of God," he quoted, amazed that he had gotten it right. "And the dead in Christ shall rise first: Then we which are alive and remain . . ."

"Amen!" Lopez said, intending to take charge. Brother cut him off.

"Listen up," Brother said, as if in the huddle. The familiar phrase commanded their attention. "There are a lot of people who are counting on us, not just here in Philadelphia or back home in Bardstown but all over—anywhere people read newspapers. We've come this far on our own . . ."

"And with Miz Kate," Tree interjected.

"Yes, Miss Kate, but also on our own ability. Now we must use what we have for a purpose. We must act on our own convictions. Those who control this event may or may not condone a walkout for money, but with all the publicity we've been getting, they can't *not* allow us to make a statement of principle. People are counting on us." Brother glanced at Du Bois for approval. On the back row Will nodded.

"What peoples?" B.C. said.

"Colored peoples, fool!" Tree said. He tightened his red sash. Brother could have hugged him.

"We have an important guest with us," Brother said solemnly. Players sneaked looks at Du Bois, who sat imperturbably on the back row. As small as he appeared among a group of oversized young men, his dignified manner made him formidable. "He would like to say a few words to us tonight, and I think we ought to listen to what he will tell us. I'd like to introduce Doctor W.E.B. Du Bois, of the University of Pennsylvania. Doctor Du Bois?"

Will came forward. Brother moved aside to give him the floor. As Du Bois turned to face his audience, his whole demeanor changed, became elastic, powerful, like a spring tightly wound. He held his arms rigidly at his side, bent slightly at the elbow as if ready for action. His eyes were his dominant feature, dark and shining. The team looked at him respectfully, including the white athletes from Alabama, Georgia, and Tennessee.

"To the white man," Du Bois began, "the Negro is the clown of history, the slave of industry, and the football of anthropology."

Some of the black players chuckled nervously, responding to the word *football.*

"By that I mean Negroes are being kicked around by those anthropologists who say we are an inferior race," Will added. Not wanting to lose them, he asked, in the manner of a teacher, "Do you know what Jim Crow means?"

There was a chorus of *yes* and *uh-huh*. Miss Kate had taught them about Jim Crow legislation. Weasel raised his hand.

"It mean separate laws for colored peoples," he volunteered.

"Jim Crow is here in Philadelphia," Du Bois continued. "That's what I want to talk to you about. I have come tonight on behalf of the Negroes of Philadelphia, especially those who live in the Seventh Ward. I am also here on my own behalf, and yours as well. What we need are fair housing laws and subsidies, protection from slum landlords, and equal treatment by the police and in the courts. Our concerns may be fundamentally human, but bringing attention to them will show that they underlie the broader issues. What is needed is a way to capture the imagination and the purse strings of white Philadelphia. That is where you come in.

"You occupy a position in the spotlight from which to make a profound impression on the conscience of this city. As Mr. Lopez has pointed out, you are big and strong, you are winners on the athletic field, you fight to advance the ball, you fight to cross the goal line. Now I am asking you to fight another kind of battle. Not a physical struggle but a battle of the spirit.

"Protesting the use of Confederate symbols, which are offensive to all black Americans, is an honorable thing to do. I am asking you to go a step further. I am asking you to make a statement on behalf of the Negroes of Philadelphia—yes!—but you too will be beneficiaries of such a noble gesture. In so doing you will shed provincial attitudes and expand your horizons with a greater understanding of the possibilities for advancing your people. I am asking you to play the part of student radicals in advocating radicalism—*real* radicalism, that costs, not mere words and foam. With your help we can *hit* power in high places —white power, backed by unlimited wealth—*hit* it openly and between the eyes, just as you go at your opponent on the football field. *Glory be to god we still own our souls.* Let us not flinch nor falter but fight and fight and fight again."

Du Bois took his seat quietly. Brother looked at his teammates. He saw their struggle to understand. He saw them, then, clearly for the first time, in the diversity of their lives: Tree using his great strength for a community project, such as laying a pipeline for a well; Weasel entertaining an audience at the school play;

Cassius proudly holding his newborn son. Each in his own way now labored to respond to this call which came at them like lightning, in the person of Will Du Bois, Ph.D. Brother's heart suddenly was bursting with pride for them.

Du Bois sat and waited to see what would happen. He had wanted to say more but decided to stop while he was ahead. He had seen the light in their eyes. He himself was quite moved. This was the first call to action he had made since his student days at Fisk. He held his breath and waited.

Lopez seized the moment.

"Down with oh-pression!" he cried. "We got power and we got principle."

"Wait a minute," Brother said. "Our cause may help yours, but how does yours help ours?"

"Are black folks gen'ly po' folks?" Lopez's brain was working so hard he felt that his head was steaming. "You cain't tell me nothin' bout po'. My family come up from old Mexico. I'm talkin' Oh-pression with a capital O. I'm talkin' 'bout ignorance. I'm talkin' 'bout workin' in the white man's fields for twenty cents a day. I'm overloaded with Oh-pression. But I had all I kin take. We can work together. I see an addendum shapin' up to my three-point program:

"1. We ain't playin' in no racist uniforms!
2. No Confederate flags allowed in the stadium!
3. The band cain't play 'Dixie' or none of them Rebel-rousin' tunes!
4. We talk about the Negro problems in Philadelphia!

"I like it! *Do you like it?*"

A spontaneous cheer erupted from the players, black and white. Lopez felt a warm glow of altruism. It had never occurred to him that his minority status might be of some value. In a spiritual state of mind, and also wanting to tie a knot on the deal, he shouted, "All in favor, say Aye!"

"*Aye!*"

Their voices carried to the parlor, where Kate, Heisman and Warner exchanged worried glances.

"All opposed?" Lopez glared. They looked among themselves for a nay-sayer and found none. "Motion carried. Chair appoints a committee *in loco parentis* of me, Brother Jones, and Doctor Du Bois to present our grievances and demands to the Board of Aldermen. And now I'd like to ask Reverend Riddle to put the Lord's blessin's on this endeavor."

Lopez folded his hands and stepped back. Chase came forward to give the benediction. It felt just like being at home. He bowed his head and stretched out his hand.

"May the Lord bless and keep you. May the Lord make his face to shine upon you and give you peace, amen." He almost glanced around to see why the organist had not responded on cue.

"Amen!" Lopez said.

As the players filed out of the room, Lopez spotted Harry Prescott loitering in the hall with a camera in his hands. He motioned Prescott inside. "How 'bout a picture for the paper?" Lopez called to Brother and Du Bois. He herded the group into a pose for Prescott, who was so titillated by the prospect of a team walkout he could hardly keep the camera still.

Du Bois felt the feathery light touch of Lopez's hand on his shoulder. Their eyes met.

"It ain't so bad, is it?" Lopez whispered. "You know, this could be the start of sump'm big for you people. Hell, I can even see a black mayor of Philadelphia someday!"

The click of the camera's shutter caught Will Du Bois staring at Lopez in utter amazement.

Chapter Twenty-one

On Thursday December 19, two days before the all-star game was scheduled, the inhabitants of Maison Blanche arose as usual. The players on the third floor were the first to descend and visit the outhouses, yawning and stretching, shivering in the freezing cold and wasting no time when their turn came to enter a privy. Back inside the building they followed the odor of boiling coffee to the kitchen, coming in one or two at a time until everyone had greeted the cook, Helen, an ample black woman who cheerfully complained about all the flapjacks she was going to have to fry.

Helen put Cassius and Isaiah to work stirring pancake batter, while the rest helped themselves to hot coffee. The white players, including Chase, passed by in the hall on their way back from the privies. They glanced awkwardly at the Post Oak team through the open kitchen door and proceeded into the adjacent dining room. Helen wiped her hands on her apron and went to take their breakfast orders. When she shuffled hurriedly back into the kitchen, Brother had an idea.

"Let me serve them their coffee," he suggested. His dark eyes sparkled.

Seated at the table with Abbott, Burke, Nalley, Price, Glenn and Harvey, Chase looked up sharply when Jones entered the dining room carrying a tray filled with smoking-hot coffee mugs.

"What are you doing?" he asked.

"Serving the coffee," Brother said equably. He set the tray on the table and distributed the mugs.

"Thanks," Harvey told his team's co-captain.

"You're welcome," Brother said and went back into the kitchen. Chase got up and followed him through the door.

"Okay, I see your point," he told Brother, while the rest of the Kentucky players listened alertly. Helen stopped sifting flour and swiveled her head around in consternation. "Half the team oughtn't to have to eat back here. We all belong together. Right?"

"Well, that's mighty white of you," Brother said.

"You hush!" Helen warned.

"I don't like being separated either," Chase said. "And all of us feel that way." He gestured toward the dining room.

"That's hard to believe," Brother said.

"Hush, boy!" Helen said. "Anyway, rules are rules. If Miss Adelaide catch me letting colored people eat in her dining room, I'm out of a job."

"I know how to fix this!" Chase suddenly went to the dining room door and whistled. Seconds later Harvey, Glenn, and the other white players came crowding into the kitchen. The Bardstown team made room for them on the benches around the large kitchen table, grinning at the novelty of it.

Brother grudgingly nodded, but whispered to Chase, "This doesn't really change anything. It's window dressing."

"Got to start someplace," Chase replied.

Blondy Glenn volunteered to turn the pancakes while Cassius poured the batter. The Alabama Poly captain entertained the team by flipping the pancakes in the air, until something made him miss the griddle. A woman stood at the doorway to the hall, clutching her satin dressing gown to her throat. Clearly she had not expected to find the kitchen full of healthy young men. The players' silence made Helen turn to look.

"Didn't you hear me ringing?" the woman said crossly.

"I ain't got time to bring no tray up to the fourth floor," Helen snapped. "You'll have to fetch it yourself, Miss Irene."

All the players' heads turned to see how Irene received her comeuppance. She bristled, glared and pouted. At that moment Kate came through the dining-room door. Seeing the players all together she brightened. Then she spotted Irene and her smile faded. The lady coach and the prostitute exchanged competitive glances.

Irene flounced away. They heard her footsteps on the stairs.

"Who was that?" Tree whispered.

"Who do you think?" Weasel said.

"She was a real pretty lady, wasn't she!" Tree said. Then he realized his teammates were staring at him. "You mean . . ." he said and gazed at the open doorway as if he had seen the magi.

Lopez was just passing the door. He paused and stepped into the kitchen, posing for effect. The players whistled their appreciation. Lopez was dressed conservatively in a dark suit with a black cravat. Instead of his Western hat he wore a bowler. He stuck a hand inside his lapel, Napoleon fashion, and stood with one foot forward.

"Gentlemen," Lopez said, "today is the day we make history."

At 10 A.M. that morning a rented hack stopped in front of the Stratford Hotel. A crowd of curiosity seekers, newspapermen, and demonstrators from the Seventh Ward and the Union League, which conveniently was located next door to the hotel, turned to see who had arrived. Lopez got out of the cab, followed by Will Du Bois, Brother, and Kate. Lopez waved to the people, who responded variously with cheers or angry shouts. Kate noticed a Schuylkill Rowing Not Drifting sign. Women were cheering for her. Another placard read:

UNION LEAGUE FOR BLACK REBELS

Police cordoned off a path to the entrance of the Stratford. Halfway up the steps Lopez paused to address the crowd.

"We seek justice," he cried. When people jeered he shouted them down. "It is a tribute to this great nation that the grandsons of immigrants and slaves enjoy equal rights under the law—and the freedom to negotiate to improve theirselves! I expect to report good news after our meeting today. *Gracias, gracias.*"

Raucous cries followed them inside. The plushly carpeted hotel lobby swallowed up the street noise and replaced it with staid silence. Penrose, Camp, the coaches and the board of aldermen were waiting in a meeting room on the mezzanine. They obviously were surprised to see that Lopez was accompanied by Du Bois, Jones, and Kate.

Ziprenian nervously ushered the player representatives inside. He showed them their places. Everyone was seated. Alonzo Stagg looked around for Heisman and Warner. When he realized that they were not coming he became suspicious.

"Heisman's using the delay to gain practice time!" he complained to Phil King.

Penrose, his face puffy from a late-night debauch, sweat dotting his forehead, rose massively to start the meeting.

"We have gathered," he began, "to hear the demands of the players of the South team. At the outset I would like to ask both sides to conduct themselves in a patient, courteous manner. Let us be aware that no difference exists that does not have a resolution. Will the team representative make a statement now?"

As if Penrose were a narrator standing at the edge of the stage to address the audience, the play began.

LOPEZ ASCENDANT

Act I, Scene i: Business leaders of Philadelphia, in starched collars and gold tiepins, await the entrance of the protagonist. Seated around a table they constitute a chorus, poised to speak in strophe and antistrophe.

LOPEZ *(entering gravely, with a kind of Badlands nobility)* Gentlemen, you may smoke. I am here on behalf of the Negro-Hispanic Coalition of the South All-Star Football Team to present a five-point plan. This plan is the son of democracy, the child of hope and necessity. Hear me out.

The civic leaders light their cigars, grumbling discontentedly.

LOPEZ *(donning spectacles and reading)* First, honorarium: Currently the twenty-five-dollar honorarium is unrealistic in that it fails to meet even the cost of long underwear, wool socks, scarves, and sweaters that we Southerners, unaccustomed as we are to your cold winters, were obliged to purchase. We therefore respectfully request an honorarium increase in the total amount of five hunnerd per player. Dollars.

The chorus gasp, groan, mutter among themselves, puff cigars angrily, vent outrage. Signifying their fury, smoke fills the room.

LOPEZ *(glancing up momentarily over his spectacles, then continuing)* Second, Performance Bonus: In order to create incentive among the players, we request a performance bonus to be computed according to points scored. Thusly: after the first five points, a bonus of twenty-five dollars for each point between six and twenty-three; fifty dollars per point between twenty-four and thirty-nine points; and one hunnerd per point—dollars—for forty points and up. Payment to be allotted uniformly among backs and linemen.

CHORUS *(waving cigars in agony)* No! No! Intolerable. Preposterous. Incomprehensible. Unprecedented.

LOPEZ *(after waiting patiently for cries of protest to subside)* Third, Guaranteed Share of Gate: Whereas football is a violent sport whose players risk life and limb; and whereas said players' acceptance of such risk attracts paying customers; now be it resolved as just and reasonable that players should receive twenty-five percent of gross receipts from ticket sales and concessions.

CHORUS *(some of whom attempt to attack Lopez and have to be restrained by Penrose and Camp)* Bolsheviks! Anarchists! Socialists! Anti-American Subversives! Collectivists! Fourierists!

LOPEZ Fourth, Racist Symbols: Out of consideration for our Negro players we ask that new jerseys bearing only the letter "S" be substituted for present jerseys bearing the emblem of the Confederate battle flag or Stars and Bars; that brass bands or choirs performing at the game or any related functions not be allowed to perform the Confederate anthem "Dixie"; that Rebel memorabilia such as battle flags not be exhibited within the stadium.

The chorus mumbles in confusion, staring dubiously at Jones, Du Bois, and Longstreet, who show no emotion and maintain a united front.

LOPEZ   Fifth, Establishment of Negro Study Commission: We request that a three-man commission be established to study the Negro problem in the city of Philadelphia, said members to include Dr. W.E.B. Du Bois of the University of Pennsylvania, one member of the Board of Aldermen, and one representative of the Union League; said commission to report its findings no later than June the first, Eighteen and Ninety-Seven.

CHORUS   *(buzzing among themselves)* Is there a Negro problem? Does anyone know what it could be? How would it affect football? And vice versa? Who is Du Bois?

KATE   *(voice ringing with bell-like clarity)* Sixth, Women's Rights . . .

Curtain falls.

"That ain't in the script," Lopez whispered to Kate. He motioned for her to confer with him. Du Bois and Brother joined their circle. "Kite won't fly if the tail's too heavy," Lopez continued. "Nobody said nothin' 'bout this."

"I did not think of it until now," Kate explained.

"If Miss Kate wants to do it," Brother whispered, "I know our team will be for it."

"The Union League sponsors women's rights, too," Du Bois said. "Adding it to the list can only lend weight to our other demands."

"Okay, okay," Lopez muttered irritably.

"I feel responsible to the Schuylkill Rowing Not Drifting club," Kate explained.

"Which?" Lopez said.

"It is a local activist group," she said.

"Okay, okay. But let's don't bring up no rowboats or anything. Our agenda is crowded enough as it is."

Curtain rises. Act I, Scene ii.

LOPEZ Sixth—like she said—Women's Rights: we
hereby declare that the All-Star team supports 'em;
and we, uh, request that the City of Philadelphia
recognize their rights and, uh, do something about
'em. Now, in summation, we present these requests
respectfully and in good faith; we expect that, upon
further deliberation, you will find them justified
and will grant them, forthwith. Gentlemen, I thank
you.

*Surrounded by a nimbus of expectations, Lopez seats
himself with the dignity of a prince. He puffs on cigar,
then examines the end and sees that it is not lit. The
chorus gather on the proscenium to talk openly among
themselves.*

WALTER CAMP *(his complexion turning a high pink)* I
never thought I would live to see professionalism
corrupt college football. I will leave the game before I will put up with such as this.

ALONZO STAGG This is all a smoke screen! It is a stall to
give Heisman and Warner more time to drill their
Negroes. They are superior natural athletes. All
they lack is practice time. Well, I won't stand for
such shenanigans. Either we play the game as
scheduled or we go home.

PENROSE *(the voice of reason, chews cigar with equa-
nimity)* Henry Clay Frick once asked my advice
about a strike by workers. I told him, Give them a
little extra gravy to settle them down and raise the
price of goods to pay for it. So let's go back to the
table and find out what compromises they are willing to accept.

*As the chorus, with a grudging murmur of agreement,
return to the bargaining table, Camp and Stagg remain
on proscenium for a telling exchange.*

STAGG All ringers should be shot.

CAMP What ringers?

PENROSE *(back at the table, addressing team representatives)* The Board wishes to point out that your

requests are in violation of the spirit with which this
game is being administered. Our purpose, after all,
is charity.

LOPEZ   Next point.

*The chorus mumbles indignantly at Lopez's callous-
ness.*

PENROSE   *(unruffled)* Your request for a percentage of
the gate is alien to fair business practices. It is the
Board's opinion that such a request is opposed to
progress, contrary to the American Way, and inimi-
cal to amateur athletics. Our position is that we of
the Philadelphia Board of Aldermen are burdened
with responsibility to all our citizens. Capitulating
to your requests would establish precedent that
could have disastrous, wide-ranging consequences.
—And by the way, sir, do you suggest that your
players are, themselves, capable of administering
the All-Star game?

LOPEZ   *(puffing on lit cigar)* Not a bad idea, actually.

CHORUS   *(all together, with doomsday authority)* That
way lies chaos!

*As if to prove their point, the chorus begin to shout and
rage at the protagonist and his company. Angry faces
are seen through a haze of blue smoke. Emotions are at
the breaking point. Penrose is no longer able to maintain order.*

PENROSE   *(shouting to be heard over the bedlam)* Both
parties will meet again at ten o'clock Friday. Meeting adjourned!

                    Exeunt.

In the lobby Penrose made a statement to the press. "What is
clouding the issue," he said, "is the presence of something more
insidious than demands for higher pay. It is, in fact, the embry-
onic presence of a workers' *union* within the ranks of athletes.
The Board finds the idea of dealing with a union both appalling
and disagreeable. Let us remember that our aldermen are donat-
ing their time to this charitable project for the good of the city.
Talks will resume tomorrow at ten o'clock."

Harry Prescott rushed to file his story.

BLACK REBELS DEMAND SHARE OF PROFITS

With the conclusion of the first bargaining session, All-Star player representatives and City Board members remained adamantly opposed. Neither side would say that an agreement could soon be reached. A strike may be imminent. If the Southern players walk off the job, the All-Star game, originally scheduled for Saturday, must be rescheduled. Talks will resume Friday at the Stratford Hotel, but with both sides deeply entrenched on the issues there is little optimism that further negotiations will produce a rapid settlement.

"What is so interesting?" Hudson asked as he settled into his usual place at the poker table. Liebowitz was intently reading an article in the *Inquirer.*

"They're putting off the football game," Ernie said.

"Putting it off? What for?"

"The players have threatened to strike."

"Strike? Like the coal miners in England?"

"What other kind of strike is there?"

"For money?"

"What else?" Liebowitz snapped his newspaper closed and laid it aside. "Let's get started."

Liebowitz was wary of Longstreet returning to the table. He interpreted this to mean that Canfield was continuing to back the Southerners, which meant that Stroud had something going, because Canfield would not back less than a sure thing.

"Hold your horses!" Hudson said. "Let me get this straight. The football players are striking for more money? I didn't know they was getting paid in the first place. What do they pay 'em *for?*"

"To play football," Ernie said wearily.

"To play football?"

"Do you need a laxative, Stroud? What else do football players do? What other possible reason could there be to pay them?"

"I just didn't know they was gettin' paid, that's all," Stroud complained. "Don't get testy. Let's play cards."

Hudson noted with satisfaction that due to Longstreet's presence no one had frisked Harry, who was holding the stacked deck.

Reno O'Shea dealt the first hand. They played cautiously for an hour. When the deal had gone around the table and come to Colonel Pitts, Hudson decided to create a diversion.

"Did you ever sucker a Jew?" he asked Liebowitz. Longstreet looked on, detached, a neutral observer.

"Stroud, I *am* a Jew."

"I know that. It don't stop you from suckering another Jew, does it?"

"You want to tell a Jewish story? Go ahead."

"Well, you know, a Jew wants a sure thing fer his money and mostly stays away from cards. (You must be the only exception, Lieberwitz.) Anyhow, this one time I was travelin' the Ohio, this li'l Jew from Cincinnati come in the salon and said, 'Mr. Stroud, I would like to back yo' play this evening. I heard there is nobody can beat you. I will wager two thousand.' At first I said No, but a little voice said, 'Stick with him and take that two grand.'

"So I told him there would be a game after supper. I found me a horseman to be my 'sucker' and took him to my stateroom. My instructions to him were: 'I'll cold-deck you and give you three kings, a seven, and an eight. Put yo' thumb over one of the spots on the eight so the Jew will think you have a king full on sevens. I will have an ace full and will bet you three hunnerd before the draw. Then you raise me three thousand.' I give him a roll of bills and told him he did not know me but to interduce hisself after supper."

Hudson glanced at Pitts, who motioned to McCain, requesting a fresh deck. McCain obligingly brought out a new, uncut deck. At the same time Nelson reached in his money sack and took out three bundles of hundreds, palming the stacked deck and slipping it up his sleeve. Liebowitz noticed nothing unusual as Little Harry arranged the money in three piles in front of him.

"We got the game started at nine P.M.," Stroud continued. "After a few hands I dealt my phony sucker his kings, seven, and eight. I showed the Jew my aces on treys. Then he edged aroun' and saw the sucker's hand. I bet three hunnerd before the draw. The sucker raised me three thousand. I pretended to be short, and the Jew nearly tore the buttons off his vest getting his money on the table. I called the bet. My Jew partner was dancing in a circle he was so excited 'bout his upcoming winnings. Then my sucker said, 'Gentlemen, I done made a mistake! Cain't I take my money down?' "

McCain passed the fresh deck to Pitts. Harry, keeping his eyes fixed on Stroud as though engrossed in the story, seemed to mishandle the exchange, and in passing the deck from one hand to the other, palmed the new deck and handed Pitts the stacked deck. He managed the swap without ever taking his eyes from Hudson's face. Liebowitz was watchful but did not detect anything suspicious.

"The Jew spoke up: 'We don't rectify no mistakes in poker.' The sucker said, 'What the hell have *you* got to do with it?' The Jew said, 'I thought you was bluffing.' The sucker said, 'I thought I had kings full on sevens but we have not drawed yet.' He throwed down the seven and eight. The Jew said, 'We do not care for yo' mistake.' I dealt him two cards which the Jew did not see. I then bet five hunnerd. The sucker hesitated, then bet five thousand like he wanted to bluff me out. I was again short, so the Jew throwed in his big diamond ring and stickpin and gold watch. He was jumping up and down, he was so excited. I called. We showed down. I had my ace full but the sucker had four kings. The Jew fell on the floor like he was stone dead. We dashed some water in his face. When he came to, he said, 'I go drown myself. I do not want to live.' The guard came and made him put on a life preserver, and he quieted down. Later, the horseman met me in my room and give me the winnings, and I give him three hunnerd bucks and the Jew's watch."

Pitts broke the seal on the stacked deck and shuffled in a way that the cut would not affect his deal.

"I was in Cincinnati three years later and happened to see the Jew. He reckanized me and took me to see his clothing store. He said, 'I mind my business and don't never play that poker.' "

"And I should take his advice?" Liebowitz said sarcastically. "Play cards!"

"Cut?" Pitts waited for O'Shea to cut the carefully shuffled deck. "Cards, gentlemen," the colonel said and dealt.

Stroud looked at his hand. Like magic there were four tens and a king. He did not look at Liebowitz, afraid that he could not keep from smiling to see Ernie stonewalling his joy at getting a straight. He could almost hear Liebowitz thinking: the odds of such a hand were 254 to 1. No doubt O'Shea also was struggling to remain calm about the full house Pitts had dealt him. Hudson pretended to cough, to keep from laughing when O'Shea cautiously opened with a one-hundred-dollar bet and Liebowitz raised a mere two hundred. Hudson raised them five hundred.

Little Harry raised another five hundred dollars, as instructed. Knot Dickinson folded before the draw, as did Diamond Ed and Bones McCain. Pitts dealt the cards. O'Shea stood pat, as did Liebowitz. Stroud discarded his king, for appearance's sake, and asked for one card. He was mildly surprised when Little Harry also asked for one card. Hudson figured that as long as Nelson was going to drop out anyhow, he might as well have called for two cards, to make it look like he was improving treys, not filling a straight or a flush.

Now the betting began in earnest. O'Shea opened with a thousand dollars. Liebowitz raised him two thousand. Stroud raised him five thousand. And Nelson raised everybody five thousand. O'Shea called. Liebowitz called. Stroud, recognizing the possibility that Pitts could have made a mistake or that the Northerners might come back with an unexpectedly high raise from a money source nobody knew about, decided to call.

He was thunderstruck to hear Little Harry calmly raise five thousand. Even with Canfield's extra twenty-five thousand dollars, the money sack was nearly empty. The Northerners pooled their chips and called again. Nelson bet all the money left in the sack. The Northerners had to throw in their rings, stickpins, and gold watches in order to call. Diamond Ed was furious about parting with his famous ten-carat "headlight" tiepin. Longstreet looked on in awe. Hudson was hopping mad, because he had nothing left to call with.

Which hand are we backing? Has Harry gone crazy? He's always bragging how he's the youngest one in the group, but hardening of the arteries can strike all at once.

By borrowing from his associates—a ring here, a stickpin there —Hudson was just able to call. He glared at Little Harry, silently imploring him not to raise again.

Harry looked around the table. He put his cigar stump in his mouth, shrugged his shoulders, and laid down a straight diamond flush.

"Once in a lifetime," he sighed.

As Pitts later explained it, he had stacked the deck for the main hands—Hudson's, Liebowitz's, and O'Shea's—paying no attention to suits. Nelson, who had discarded a pair and held two diamonds on the draw, figured that since he was supposed to fold anyway, he would go for the flush, just for fun. When he saw the cards he was dealt, he could not resist going for the pot. Upon reflection, Hudson saw that Nelson's surprise move had improved his plan. His shock at Harry's final raise had been so genuine that the Northerners did not suspect they had been cold-decked.

Hudson organized a small celebration in the barroom: champagne for everyone and an orchestra to serenade them. Longstreet, who was unaware of the card switch, gave a toast to winning at poker and everything else.

In Liebowitz's room the Northerners sat in stunned silence. They all seemed to have aged ten years.

"Stroud *cheated.*" Liebowitz wanted them to be as angry as he was. If patent medicines came out of pockets, they were finished. "I don't know how he did it, but he cheated."

"He was as surprised as anybody when Little Harry won!" Reno argued.

"I think Pitts accidentally dealt Harry that flush," Liebowitz said. "Too many strong hands on that deal. I think Pitts colddecked us."

"When did they make the switch?" asked Diamond Ed, who was suffering badly from the loss of his stickpin.

"Obviously when Pitts called for a fresh deck." Liebowitz glared. His anger poured into them, restoring their spirit.

We are not whipped yet.

"Any of you heard of Straight Flush Davis?" Liebowitz said thoughtfully. "He worked the river back in the early fifties. Davis had a specialty that he used once in a while, when he had a really fat sucker. He would shuffle kind of awkward, like he screwed up his own deal, and stack the deck. Then he dealt the sucker four of a kind and dealt himself an open-ended, four-card straight flush. The next two cards in the deck would fill either end of Davis's straight flush. The sucker could either stand pat or take one card. —Let's have another crack at Stroud. They beat us with a straight flush. Let's break them with another one!"

"Where we gonna get the kale to bet with?" the Dutchman said.

"Somebody go find Ziprenian," Liebowitz said.

On his way to a quiet place where nobody would bother him, Ziprenian was waylaid by Archie O'Hara and Bird Mahoney, who took him to an even quieter place. The three of them sat at a table. To The Zipper the meeting of the Canfield mob without Canfield had the surreal effect of a six-armed body without a head.

Archie began to clean his fingernails with his knife. Sweat soaked the elastic band of Ziprenian's underwear. He could not get over the fact that these goons were trying to buck the King by setting up their own betting syndicate for the all-star game.

What am I doing here? Is this living?

"The players' strike may work to our advantage," Archie began. "It brought the odds down. These Southern crackers are willing to bet even. They figure the Gray coaches are not dumb enough to let the niggers go on strike if they aren't so good they can do anythin' they want and get away with it. The betting's been wild. We hadda put extra people on the windows to handle the action. Whatta we got on line, Bird, two hundred grand? So natur'ly we are looking for a guarantee. We're counting on you, Zipper. What you got?"

Arno wished Archie would not trim his nails with his knife. Canfield had a rule: conduct your business like gentlemen. Show some class. With a shock Ziprenian realized that, for the first time, he desired Canfield's presence.

"I'm working on it." The Zipper tried to appear enthusiastic. "We could put the girls on 'em."

"So what?" Mahoney argued. "Ain't you heard about black men? Work all day and screw all night. They got no brains. If they stopped to think, they'd drop dead. All you'd do is put the girls outa action for a week."

"You gotta do better'n that." Archie looked up meaningfully, knife poised above fingernails. Arno reached for a fragment of memory.

"When I talked to the blacks the first day, they weren't very clear about where they went to college. What if we put out the word, maybe they aren't college men? Maybe they oughta be disqualified from playing in the game? Maybe some professors oughta be brought in to see if they got a college education?"

Archie's thin lips crinkled at the edges. Ziprenian hoped it was a smile.

On the fourth floor of the Maison Blanche, Irene sprayed cologne on herself and fluffed up her feather-lined satin housecoat. In the vanity mirror she could see Lorraine frowning.

"I don't like it," Lorraine was saying.

"It ain't for you to like or dislike," Irene said, patting some rouge on her cheeks. "It's business."

"I can't face my family again if they find out I done it with a Negro."

"Lorraine, you don't know where your family is at."

"They ain't never left West Virginia! When I went to work for you, you didn't say nothing 'bout no Negroes."

"Look at it from a career standpoint. You've entertained every customer I recommended for six years: lean, fat, old, young, Irish, Italian, Jew, Polish, Arab, Chinaman. You have a good record. Why spoil it?"

"Are you saying if I left your employ over this, you wouldn't put in a good word for me? I give this place the best of my youth! This conversation falls in the category of a threat. I don't cotton to a threat."

They glared at each other in the vanity mirror. Irene was older, wiser, puffier. Lorraine showed signs of puffiness but not much wisdom.

"Get hold of yourself," Irene said. "You are making a peck into a bushel. I tell you, a roll in the hay with a black man is a roll in the hay. Period!"

"Is it true what they say?" Lorraine's face went slack. "That a Negro can work all day and, you know, all night?"

"I never took care of one that had the financial wherewithal for an all-nighter, so I am not qualified to comment."

"Is it true about them being overly developed?"

"They come in all sizes, like the rest of them."

"Well, I speak for the rest of the girls when I say that we did not expect an assignment like this. You might at least have prepared us."

Irene put down her rouge pad. "You talk like I rule the world. I don't. Mr. Dobson is my boss. He makes requests, and I try to satisfy his wishes. This assignment, as you put it, comes directly from Mr. Dobson. And he got it from higher up, like *Mr. Ziprenian.* I naturally try to take care of whatever business comes my way. If you expect to succeed, you'd best take a positive attitude. Now hop to it. Don't let me hear any more grousing."

"We've got to come to grips with the situation," Heisman told Warner. "When you find yourself in possession of a gold mine, you don't worry about the lease. You start carting off the gold. I told Lonny Stagg: this strike is none of our doing. This delay is not our fault. But we'd be fools not to keep practicing."

"Damned fools!" Warner agreed.

The coaches were following the team out to the practice field near the Maison Blanche. They had arranged a scrimmage game between the Gray varsity and a local high school team. When they reached the vacant lot, Heisman and Warner were surprised to see a thousand or more spectators, half black and half white, lining either side of the field. Apparently, the Southern coaches told each other, parents and friends of the high school team had come to support them. Yet Heisman could not figure out why so many Negroes were in the crowd.

Will Du Bois had organized a citizens' party from the Seventh Ward to cheer for the Black Rebels. He had gone from door to door explaining how the players' boycott could draw attention to the need for better housing, jobs, and schools. Accompanied now by some two dozen residents of all ages, Will was leading a Har-

LET THE BAND PLAY DIXIE

vard cheer when he noticed James Longstreet standing among the spectators. By chance the general had come to the same side of the field as Du Bois.

Longstreet, however, did not see Du Bois. His thoughts strayed as he watched the mismatched teams go at each other. The South All-Stars soon led by 20 points. Longstreet asked himself what kept him in Philadelphia. It was past time for him to return to Georgia. His guest lodge in Gainesville needed his supervision. His publisher no longer required him to promote his book. The honorary chairmanship of the all-star game was purely voluntary. Yet something held him, something about these Negro players and the way they had captured the emotions of this Northern city. Longstreet decided to approach the coaches at half time.

"Uh-oh," Heisman told Warner. "Here comes the Confederacy."

"Excuse me," Longstreet said, drawing a piece of paper from his pocket. "I don't mean to intrude, but I've drawn up a bit of strategy. You know, the only sensible way to fight a battle is to take a strong position and hold it. But since football is played on level ground, I reckon you need all the tactics you can get. Here's something I thought up."

He timidly offered Heisman the paper. The coaches dubiously unfolded it and saw:

THE JOHN BELL HOOD END RUN

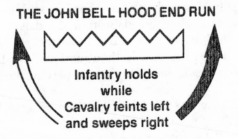

Infantry holds
while
Cavalry feints left
and sweeps right

"Thank you, sir," Heisman said, folding the paper and handing it back to the general. "But where's the *ball?*"

"Pardon?" Longstreet said.

"Thanks very much," Warner put in. "We'll take it under consideration." Longstreet resented the coach's patronizing tone.

"What *about* the ball?" the general doggedly asked.

"Well," Heisman was equally stubborn, "you left it out. Does your diagram mean you are faking a pitch or handoff to the left halfback and pitching to the right? If so, we already have that one in our playbook. In fact, begging your pardon, *everybody* does."

"I see," Longstreet said stiffly, hiding his disappointment. "Well, then, I won't be taking up any more of your time. Carry on."

"Thanks anyway!" Warner called after him.

Longstreet walked quickly away, wanting to put some distance between himself and his mistake. Muttering out loud in irritation, he stopped near the South end zone where the team was resting.

"Who's that?" Tree said.

"Longstreet," Weasel said.

"I've heard that name."

"Yo' Aunt Ethel was a Longstreet, wasn't she?"

Tree gave Weasel a swat to the head, then looked askance at Longstreet. "He fight on the Confederate side, didn't he!" Tree nodded to himself, adding, "I hope we do better'n *he* did."

This conversation providentially took place on Longstreet's deaf side. Unaware that they had been talking about him, he approached them. Tree guiltily moved away. With unerring instinct Longstreet turned to Brother, seeking the team leader.

"I was just talking with your coaches," he said hastily, "about a play I made up." He showed Brother the diagram, mumbling against the back of his hand, "Does that make sense to you?"

Brother studied the sketch, then motioned for Longstreet to hunker down beside him. He drew a play in the dirt with his finger.

"We run a play like that," he said. "It's a reverse. We call it the 'rabbit play.'"

"Excellent!" Longstreet said, getting to his feet. "That's the counterstroke I'm thinking of. I hope you'll use it when the time is right?"

"You can count on us, sir," Brother said gravely.

Longstreet took off his glove and extended his hand. Brother shook it, then stepped back and saluted. Longstreet automatically returned the salute. Moments later it occurred to him that there might have been some impertinence in the gesture, but he was willing to give the young man the benefit of the doubt.

Across the field Du Bois observed this little ceremony take place. He shook his head in wonder.

The gods don't merely have a sense of humor. They are clowns.

By the time the scrimmage was over the South had scored 94 points to 5 for the hapless high school team. Citizens of the Seventh Ward swarmed around their heroes, clamoring for autographs. Wearing a three-piece suit, Lopez stood apart from the commotion and conducted business with concessionaires. Heisman asked Kate to help hustle the players back inside the Maison Blanche and keep them away from politics. The last thing he told the team before dismissing them was, "Think football!"

As they left the vacant lot, looking back Weasel noticed that Burke of Vanderbilt was imitating his style of walking, swaying rhythmically and snapping his head to one side with each step.

"He makin' fun of me," Weasel complained to Brother.

"No, he's not," Brother replied. "After scoring all those touchdowns, you're his hero."

"Aw, naw," Weasel said.

"Yeah."

"Naw."

"Here he comes," Brother said. "Why don't you ask him?"

"Hey, Weasel," Burke said. "How'd you learn how to wiggle your hips and make a tackler jump the wrong way?"

Weasel glanced at Brother before he spoke. "I don't know. It comes natural."

"Do you think you could teach me?" Burke said.

"I reckon I could try," Weasel said dubiously. "Just watch me next practice."

"Thanks," Burke said happily.

Cassius smothered a laugh behind his fist. Weasel chased him all the way to the rooming house. Blondy Glenn took Weasel's place beside Brother.

"Y'all sure can run," Glenn said. "We never saw anything like it, down at Auburn."

Brother gave Blondy a wary look. "What's football like, at Alabama Poly?"

"Our big game is Georgia Tech," Glenn explained. "We played

'em this year in Auburn for the first time. The students held a 'Wreck Tech' pajama parade before the game. They greased the railroad tracks, and when the Tech train pulled in, it slid halfway to Loachapoka, about ten miles away. The Tech players had to walk all the way back to the station. We beat 'em forty-five to nothing."

"Sounds like fun." Brother tried to keep the envy out of his voice.

Glenn grinned at him. "Well, it's supposed to be fun, isn't it?"

"Think appearances!" Lopez told them after they had returned to their rooms. "You are in the public eye. There is more than football at stake here."

There is money.

"It appears likely we will have to go out on strike," he continued, pacing as he talked. "If that happens, you will doubtless come under criticism for holding up the game. The best thing for you to do under the circumstances is to go to ground. Do not—I repeat, *not*—talk to the press. Leave that to me. You let actions do your talking. Brother Jones has come up with a list of good-deeds stuff—local projects, and all—for you to do. I think they want you to lead the Mummers Parade."

"Ain't that on New Year's?" Weasel asked.

"Will we still be here then?" Tree said.

"I thought we'd be back home in Bardstown on New Year's," Cassius said.

"It all depends," Lopez continued, "on how long it takes to get them to accept our six-point program. Now remember, if it comes to a strike we have to stick together. Don't tell anybody sump'm dumb like, 'I'm solid for it now, but I don't know how I'll feel next week.' We got to stick together. They's strength in unity. As Abe Lincoln said, 'A nation undivided cain't stand.'"

"Divided," Brother said.

"Huh?"

"He said, 'divided.'"

"Who?"

"Lincoln."

"Whatever," Lopez muttered. "The point is, we got to stick together or we got nothin'."

After Lopez had left, the Panthers washed up and got dressed and were sitting around with nothing to do when a parlor maid delivered a hand-printed invitation on a silver tray. They crowded around to read it.

The Maison Blanche Ladies
request
Your Presence
at Tea
This Afternoon
or
At Your Convenience
Thursday
19 Dec '96
Fourth Floor

"What do it mean, 'at Tea'?" Tree said.

"It means," Brother said, grinning, "they want to take care of you."

"You mean . . . ?"

"Uh-huh."

The Panthers sat down and considered this startling development. Cassius began to smile. Then Tree told about an earlier conversation he had held with one of the porters regarding the fourth-floor ladies.

"And I ain't got no five dollars," he concluded.

"Me neither," Weasel complained.

"This one is probably on the house," said Brother.

"Why?" they all said.

"I bet Ziprenian had something to do with it," Brother mysteriously replied. He noticed Cassius muttering to himself. "What is it?" Brother said.

"This could mean trouble," Cassius whispered as if the walls had ears.

"You oughta know," B.C. said, "the trouble yo' pecker's got you into." Everybody laughed at Cassius. Then they became serious again.

"What about the white boys next door—Harvey and Price and them?" Lincoln said.

"Invite came to *this* room, didn't it?" Tree argued.

"Maybe if they got a invite, too, we'll see them upstairs," Weasel said shrewdly.

"I ain't never," Ulysses blurted. He looked down at his size sixteen shoes. "With a white woman."

No one said anything.

"What do you think, Brother?" Lincoln asked.

Jones crossed his arms defensively. "Do what you like."

"Will it be all right?" Weasel said.

"Suit yourself."

"Well, are *you* gonna do it?" Weasel persisted.

Brother grinned slyly. "Syphilis makes you go blind."

"Aw, man, don't be spoiling our fun!" Tree cried.

"Then what are you asking me for?" Brother retorted. "Use your own judgment."

Tree looked at B.C., then at Ulysses, Cassius, Weasel, Lincoln, and Isaiah. Without another word, the men of Post Oak rose and went into the hall. No one looked back at Brother. They climbed the carpeted stairs together, their faces rapt and intense.

"Nobody better not tell," Cassius whispered.

"I won't tell," B.C. said.

"Me neither," said Ulysses.

"Me neither," said Lincoln.

On the fourth floor were double doors that opened onto a suite of rooms. They paused and looked at one another. Tree pushed the others aside almost roughly and knocked.

Irene opened the door. It unnerved her to see how big they were up close. "Come in, fellas!" she said gaily. "Glad you could come. Have a seat. —Lorraine, Jeanette, come meet our guests!"

The other women came reluctantly. Irene gave them a steely glance that said, "Hop to it," and introduced everyone. "I am Miss Irene. This is Miss Lorraine and Miss Jeanette." She addressed Tree. "And you are . . . ?"

"Henry Clay Jackson," Tree blurted. The other players chuckled maniacally. Then they spoke their names.

"My goodness," Irene cried, "a Jackson family reunion! Well, here we are. Shall we get acquainted? Miss Lorraine is quite an accomplished musician. Perhaps she would favor us with a number?"

Lorraine went to the piano, plopped down on the seat, and began to play and sing *A Bicycle Built for Two*. The players sat very straight in their chairs.

"There's just three of them for seven of us," Weasel whispered to Tree.

Lorraine sang:

> *Daisy, Daisy, give me your answer, do!*
> *I'm half crazy, all for the love of you.*

"Do this remind you a little of Sunday school?" Weasel asked B.C.

"That's a good one!" Irene exclaimed. "Did you hear what he said, Jeanette? How about some beer, fellas?" When they hesitated, she laughed. "Oh, the invitation said tea, didn't it. Well, what'll it be? Beer or something sweet? We've got cookies and milk, if that's what you want."

Weasel conferred with his friends and took their order. "Six beers, one cookie-'n'-milk," he said.

Jeanette went to get the refreshments. The players listened attentively to Lorraine playing. All of them sat with their hands resting on their knees. They were relieved when Jeanette served them. Cassius was the one who had ordered milk and cookies.

Lorraine sang:

> *It won't be a stylish marriage,*
> *I can't afford a carriage.*
> *But you'll look sweet, upon the seat,*
> *Of a bicycle built for two.*

Everyone applauded politely. An awkward silence fell. Cassius bit into his cookie and saw his friends looking at him. He stopped chewing. Working up his nerve, Tree turned to Irene.

"Did I hear somebody say sump'm about five dollars?" he asked.

"Your credit is good, dear," she replied.

Suddenly everyone was talking at once, laughing and smiling

like old friends. Cassius perched on the piano seat beside Lorraine and picked out a melody with one finger. The players began to sing along, swinging their beer mugs for emphasis.

> *There's a church in the valley by the wildwood,*
> *No lovelier spot in the vale.*
> *No spot is so dear to my childhood,*
> *As the little brown church in the vale.*
> *Oh, come, come, come, come,*
> *Come to the church in the wildwood,*
> *Come to the church in the vale.*
> *No spot is so dear to my childhood,*
> *As the little brown church in the vale.*

Another round of beer was served. Irene tickled Tree with her feathers. After a while, in some mysterious manner none of the players could fathom, the women selected a partner. Irene took Tree, Lorraine took Cassius, and Jeanette took Isaiah. They went to separate rooms. The rest of the players sat down to wait self-consciously.

"They didn't lock the doors," B.C. observed.

"I wonder, do they talk any?" Lincoln said.

"I doubt it," Weasel said.

"What-all do they do?" Lincoln said.

"One thing, they don't allow no kissing," Weasel said. When the others looked at him he added, "I heard."

Inside one of the rooms Tree was astounded when Irene calmly unbuttoned her dress and stepped out of it. He looked down at his shoes. She arranged herself on the bed.

"Aren't you going to undress?" she said.

He stood motionless, great arms dangling at his sides. She patted the bed in invitation. He sat. The mattress sagged, causing Irene to slide toward him.

"My God, how much do you weigh!"

" 'Bout two-eighty."

"I'm going to be flat as a pancake. We're going to have to work out some arrangement. Well, let's wash up. I have a policy about washing up. It saves future embarrassment for everybody."

She got off the bed and directed him to a washbasin. Beside it was a bar of soap and a towel.

"Drop your pants," she said.

Tree slowly did as he was told. When she touched him he staggered and almost fell.

"Have you ever done this before?" she asked conversationally.

"No'm." His voice trembled. "Leastways, we never stopped for no soap."

In another room Cassius sat on the bed next to Lorraine. He glanced nervously around.

"Did anybody tell you I'm a married man?" he said.

"You are? And so young, too."

"I got me two babies. That is, one already borned and one on the way."

"You must be very proud."

"Yes'm."

"You must miss your wife very much."

"I reckon I do. But she mad at me!"

"Oh? Why is that?"

"One of my babies ain't by her."

"Well, you have gotten yourself into a mess. Maybe you should have turned to someone like me a long time ago."

"There ain't nobody like you in Bardstown."

"How nice of you to say. Well, we'd better get on with it. We don't want to keep your friends waiting, do we?"

Chase walked into the black players' quarters on the third floor to see if his teammates were studying their playbooks. He was surprised to find Brother alone, flipping through an old *Harper's*.

"Did you hear singing? Where *is* everybody?"

Brother gave his co-captain a level glance. "On the fourth floor."

"What's hap'nin'?"

"Ziprenian appears to be offering our squad a free ride."

Chase frowned. "We better get up there and break it up!"

"Whoa." Brother put down his magazine.

"What do you mean, *whoa?*"

"I suppose you have a preconceived notion regarding black men and white women," Brother said ironically.

"What? It don't have nothin' to do with *that*. It's just . . . we got a late practice this afternoon."

"The team won't have the old snap, huh?"

"What's the matter with you?"

"I was just thinking—from a negroid point of view, you know—it would be criminal to deprive these *boys* of their first experience with a white woman, except possibly for medical reasons."

"I'm disappointed in you, Brother," Chase exclaimed. "You don't seem to grasp the gravity of the situation."

"Gravity? The law of gravity as pertains to fornication?"

"No."

"Say, what's your position on fornication, Reverend Riddle?" Brother asked flippantly and was surprised to see Chase become congested.

The words "Reverend Riddle" instantly conjured up Big Dad inside Chase, willy-nilly, as real as Jonah in the whale, and he suddenly spouted scripture.

"Abraham begat Isaac; and Isaac begat Jacob; and Jacob begat Judas, and Judas begat Phares and Zara; and Phares begat Esrom; and Esrom . . ."

"Look," Brother interrupted, "Let's just leave them alone. They never expected to do it with a white woman. I mean, in Bardstown the possibility did not exist. We're all finding something new here, something different. Maybe this is what they came to Philadelphia to learn. Leave them alone."

"We got our responsibility."

"To whom?"

"I can't just stand here jawin' with you while they're up there doing God knows what. I'm goin' upstairs."

Chase left Brother shaking his head ironically. He went out into the hall. As he approached the stairs he saw Kate coming up from the second-floor landing, taking the steps two at a time.

"There's mischief afoot!" she cried.

"Better believe it," Riddle agreed.

"Will you go up there and see about it?" she said, less certain.

"I'm on my way."

She held onto his arm and they ascended to the fourth floor together. She noticed that his back was arched, his jaw thrust forward pugnaciously. She tried not to remember him that way.

On the fourth floor, Cassius came out of Lorraine's room. His teammates, sitting on the edges of their chairs, gave him their undivided attention. He looked somehow electric, as if his hair buzzed with current. He spoke with great deliberation. They leaned forward to listen.

"It's good, but not as good as you think it's gonna be."

"Next!" Lorraine cried from inside her room.

"Who's nex'?" Weasel looked at B.C., who looked at Ulysses, who looked at Lincoln, who looked back at Weasel. He squared his shoulders and stood up. "Well, here goes," he said.

Lorraine tiptoed out of her room, robe clutched to her bosom, and knocked on Irene's door. The waiting players heard every word she said.

"They want to do it twice. What's our policy? Same as usual?"

"Mr. Dobson said to take care of them. That's all I know," Irene said from behind the door.

"Where's Doreen? I think we could use some backup."

"Doreen don't work during the day. Hop to it."

As Weasel entered Lorraine's room, Irene's door opened and Tree came out. Isaiah came out of Jeanette's room at the same time. They sat down and stared off into space. Ulysses, Link, and B.C. waited respectfully, then simultaneously asked, *"How was it?"*

"Funny thing," Isaiah told Tree, as if the others weren't even there. "I kept thinkin' 'bout my cousin Henrietta the whole time."

"Yeah," Tree agreed, "the way she bend over to bait her hook."

"Henrietta don't wear perfume," Isaiah observed.

"Henrietta don't need none," Tree said.

On the stairway outside the whores' quarters, Chase and Kate paused to gather courage. *Job thirty-one, three* came quite naturally to Chase's mind: " 'Is not destruction to the wicked? and a strange punishment to the workers of iniquity?' "

"It may not be any of our business," Kate rationalized, ignoring Chase's rantings, "but I promised their folks I'd take care of them."

Chase knocked with authority.

"Who is it?" Irene fixed her eye to the peephole. Chase and

Kate stared back at her, looming indignantly close through the magnifying glass.

"I am Reverend Riddle," he said through the door. "Open up in there."

"This is a private party," Irene called. "Come back later."

"Open up, or we'll break the door down!" Kate yelled.

Irene hesitated, then unlocked the door. Chase barged into the room, while Kate followed hesitantly. Irene clasped her robe around her and gave them a haughty stare.

The seated players cocked their heads apprehensively at Chase. All the years of studying Big Dad suddenly clicked into place, and Chase gave a perfect imitation of Big Dad imitating Christ driving the money lenders from the temple.

"Downstairs!" he yelled. The players in the straight-backed chairs pointed at the private rooms, shifting blame. A door opened and Weasel's head popped through it. Chase planted himself in the middle of the room and quoted for all he was worth.

"*'Know ye not that your bodies are the members of Christ? Shall I then take the members of Christ, and make them the members of an harlot? God forbid.'*"

"Amen!" Weasel came out of Lorraine's room, tucking his shirt in.

"Your mamas and papas would be ashamed," Kate boomed at them.

"We will pray for the Lord's forgiveness," Chase shouted.

Lorraine stuck her head out her door. "What the hell?"

"'I have seen thine adulteries and thy neighings,'" Chase replied, "'the lewdness of thy whoredom on the hills in the fields. Woe unto thee, O Jerusalem!'"

"Goddamn, what is this?" Lorraine said.

"Watch your language, dear," Irene called. She turned to Chase and shot a bare leg through a fold in her robe. "Aren't you a football player too?"

"I am Captain Riddle, and this is Coach Kate."

"I know who she is," Irene sniffed. "Nobody forced these fellas to come up here, you know."

Kate doubled her fist, and Irene took a step backward.

" 'Blessed is the man that endureth temptation: for when he is tried, he shall receive the crown of life,' " Chase said to Kate.

"Whose idea was this?" Kate growled.

"Whose do you think!" said Irene.

"I know my players would not think of it."

"You'd be surprised what your players think of," Irene retorted. Blushing, Kate began to retreat.

Chase hectored his teammates toward the door, saying, " 'Mine anger was kindled against the shepherds, and I punished the goats,' *Zechariah ten, three.*"

The players looked so shamefaced Kate felt sorry for them. Chase paused grandly at the door.

"I will pray for you!" he called to the whores.

"You may be a tad late," Irene said.

At Franklin Field the Blue squad finished practice and headed for their dressing room. The players' cleats crunched gravel. Lagging behind, Stagg lectured his assistants on how to defend against Longstreet:

"We'll have to be prepared to stop a bludgeoning attack up the middle, right at us; but don't get lulled to sleep by it, because he'll hit you with the unexpected flank attack, using the speed of his black dragoons."

"His what?" King said, then diplomatically added, "maybe it's not like you think. Maybe Heisman and Warner aren't listening to Longstreet. Would *you* listen if General Sickles wanted to plot your game plan for you? It's kind of an insult to your coaching ability."

"I know it seems that way to you," Stagg argued. "But there's something about coaching that you haven't discovered yet, my friend. It's coaching on gut feeling, on the unexplainable, the instinctive. There's something about the combination of Negro players, sons and grandsons of slaves, with a Confederate general that sets my nerves on edge. They're a lit powder keg. Something has got to give."

Heffelfinger, who was running extra laps on his own time, stopped beside the coaches, panting happily. "This is fun, Coach," he told Stagg. "I've really missed football, you know. I don't care how long the other team stays out on strike. I like to practice."

"Thank you, Pudge," Stagg said. "Don't let us keep you." He shook his head as Heffelfinger bounded away.

Woodruff, the coach from Penn, had been thinking. "We might be able to defuse that powder," he told Stagg.

"How?"

"There have been rumors," Woodruff went on. "Nobody's ever heard of this Post Oak College. Their coach has supposedly produced records certifying that they are enrolled. But whether they are qualified college men remains to be seen."

"Hasn't anyone checked on the school?" Stagg said, interested in spite of himself.

"A telegram was sent," Woodruff replied, "but it was unanswered. We know it was *delivered*, however, so something is going on, down there in Kentucky. What it is, nobody knows."

Stagg's eyes shone in the gathering dusk. "There ought to be some way to find out if the Negroes are eligible or not."

"Don't worry, Coach," Woodruff said. "We're working on it."

Chapter Twenty-two

FOOTBALL STRIKE IMMINENT
by
Harrison Prescott

Having exchanged charges and countercharges such as "dictatorship" and "just plain greedy," City Board members and player representatives are not likely to reach an agreement concerning the All-Star Football Game. Both sides concede a strike is possible.

At the request of former mayoral candidate Boies Penrose, the two parties have agreed to hold a subsequent meeting at the Stratford Hotel in a last-minute attempt to avoid a players' strike.

Arno Ziprenian, management representative, emphasized that today's session is an "informal meeting" and not a formal resumption of negotiations, which were broken off during yesterday's heated exchange.

Ziprenian was cautiously optimistic, however, in regard to a possible compromise over the playing of Confederate anthems and marching songs. John Philip Sousa, Director of the All-America Band, has offered to compose a medley combining musical themes from "Dixie," "The Battle Hymn of the Republic," "Onward Christian Soldiers," and "The Stars and Stripes Forever."

Police security around the Stratford will be tight. Anti-unionists have threatened a picket line protesting the Southern players' walkout.

Lopez was deliberately late for the second meeting, to obtain maximum exposure. This time he had shed his business suit and wore denim jeans, plaid shirt, rawhide vest, high-heeled boots, and ten-gallon hat. Police escorted him, Kate, Du Bois, and Brother through an angry picket line in front of the Stratford.

Among the aldermen and civic officials awaiting the Southern team representatives were Longstreet and Sickles, seated side by side at the negotiating table.

"I don't see what good we can do," Longstreet complained to Sickles.

"Show of unity," Sickles said. "That shouldn't be hard for you and me to do, Jim."

"Yes, but what, exactly, do they expect of us?"

Sickles shrugged. "We all desire an expeditious settlement of the issues and to proceed on schedule."

"Was it a set-up job?" Longstreet asked shrewdly. "This negotiations business? For the sake of publicity? I don't trust that Ziprenian character."

"You trust *me*, don't you, Jim?"

"Of course."

"I assure you, everything is going to be all right."

As Sickles spoke, Cadwalader and Wanamaker were regarding Ziprenian narrowly, as if they had known from the start that a mixed marriage would not work.

"Can you make Lopez see reason?" John Wanamaker asked Ziprenian under his breath.

"Please, let us remember," The Zipper said unctuously, "This is a joint venture. There is middle ground. All we have to do is find it. I'm sure Lopez will come around. In the meantime, this publicity is good for all. There will be thousands more spectators at the game."

"Yes," Cadwalader interjected, "but do we want the kind of lunatic fringe that this kind of publicity attracts? Our police department is already stretched to the limit to handle the security problem."

"Next, we'll have to call out the Pennsylvania militia!" Wanamaker warned. He glanced suspiciously at his erstwhile rival for the senate, Penrose, who was waiting impassively for the meeting to begin. "If we had known all the facts," Wanamaker muttered, "we might have chucked the whole thing before it started growing on us like a vine."

"A Kentucky pole bean?" Penrose quipped.

Before Wanamaker could bandy wits with his political enemy, Lopez made his entrance. A murmur ran around the table. Lopez gave the businessmen a satisfied look, bit off a plug of chewing tobacco, and said, "Let's do it."

The session began with the questions of honorariums and percentage of the gate. After wrangling back and forth over figures for an hour or more and failing to arrive at a compromise, they came to Point Four of Lopez's plan.

"I can understand your concern about payment," Cadwalader said, "but what's this commotion about something as superficial as flags and songs?"

"Athaletes," Lopez said equably, "have their peculiarities."

"Why get so upset," Wanamaker insisted, "about a bit of flag-waving, for gosh sakes. The war has been over for thirty-one years. Can't both sides afford to indulge in a little nostalgia? Why not let the band play 'Dixie'?" The aldermen murmured their assent. Lopez lit a fresh cigar, cutting his eyes at Brother and Du Bois.

"I have to go along with my boys on this one," Lopez said. "Take it as a given, non-negotiable."

"Aren't you being a bit stubborn, old man?" Cadwalader said mellifluously. "You don't strike me as the sentimental kind."

"Hey, my players feel pretty strong about it. That's all I have to say."

"This is their big chance," Wanamaker said shrewdly, "to see the sights, travel, enjoy themselves. They'll be heroes when they go home to Kentucky. They won't give all that up for a song and a flag."

"It ain't just 'a song and a flag' to them!" Lopez ceremoniously spat under the table. "I know what they're feelin'. Bein' black and pore don't mean they ain't got *pride.*"

The city fathers huddled, then Penrose spoke for them. "The Board would be willing to soften its position in regard to financial arrangements if you and your players would adjust your attitude on the flags and songs."

"Wait a minute!" Lopez exclaimed. "Let me git this straight. You Yankees *want* the band to play 'Dixie'?"

"Businessmen who invest in football games, you might say, have their peculiarities," Penrose said ironically.

"Yeah, but that's *awful* peculiar. Can you explain what 'Dixie' has to do with dollars and cents?"

"I think we all agree," Penrose said expansively, "that a certain amount of flag-waving at such an occasion is not only inevitable but contributes a great deal to the success of the enterprise. From the beginning we have advertised the all-star game as a regional contest. Naturally some regional trappings, outdated as they may be, are in order. We have gone to a good deal of effort and expense to provide colorful promotion for this game. That is our position."

"I believe you gentlemen are tiptoeing around the color of my players' skins," Lopez said. He looked for, and received, a supporting nod from Du Bois.

"This city is well known for its tolerance!" Cadwalader exclaimed.

"Retract that statement," Wanamaker demanded.

"Will not," Lopez said.

"These emblems your players object to," Penrose interrupted, "are traditional expressions of regional pride and surely will be recognized as such by both sides. I don't imagine you would find a dozen Philadelphians who are radically opposed to the informal display of a Confederate flag."

"White people, you mean," Lopez said. Du Bois actually patted him on the shoulder. Lopez beamed.

"This is becoming quite intolerable!" Wanamaker braced himself, as rigid as William Penn's statue.

"The waving of the Rebel flag and the playing of 'Dixie,'" Penrose drew on his diplomatic reserves, "are mere forms of team identification, no more no less, and an innocent means of establishing team spirit."

"Well, we can identify with Yankee fight songs, too. For that matter, I can learn my boys to sing 'When Johnny Comes Marching Home.' And while we're on the subject of songs," Lopez referred to his notes, "besides 'Dixie,' we also reject and exclude 'The Girl I Left Behind Me,' 'The Bonnie Blue Flag,' and 'The Yellow Rose of Texas.' "

"Then the band would be playing all Union and no Confederate songs!" Cadwalader protested. "That's not fair."

"Not fair!" Lopez said. "This Yankee-Rebel stuff is about to start Civil War *Two*. Can you guarantee the safety of my players on game day? Let's forget 'Dixie' and start talkin' Lloyd's of London."

"I'd like to call on General Longstreet at this time," Penrose took a different tack. "We would all be interested, I'm sure, in his views on the question of regional trappings. General?"

Longstreet sat immobile for a few seconds. Beside him Sickles shifted uncomfortably in his chair. At last, Longstreet got to his feet. He spoke solemnly and formally.

"Gentlemen," he said, "you put me at a disadvantage. For it goes without saying that the Stars and Bars has meant a great deal to me—as well as 'Dixie'—more than I can ever say. But since the war, as you must know, my firm policy has been to put aside old feelings and look to the future of my country. My one wish has been to seek an honorable means of saving my people from the extremity of distress. I have followed the course of cooperation with our elected and appointed officials, often in the face of threats against my life. So I must decline to endorse any symbols of a bygone era, one that is best forgotten. For me to do otherwise would be illogical, hypocritical, and dishonorable."

Longstreet sat down. A surprised murmur filled the room. Lopez chewed on his cigar and gave Longstreet an ironical salute, which the general ignored. Du Bois could not believe his ears.

Longstreet and I—on the same side?

For the first time, Penrose found himself at a loss. He turned hopefully to Sickles.

"Perhaps the Honorable Daniel Sickles will comment on the question?"

Glancing at Longstreet, Sickles spoke while remaining seated. "I must beg to disagree with my dear friend Jim in regard to the playing of his beloved 'Dixie,' emblem of a gallant foe. Having opposed General Longstreet on the field of battle, I am bold to say that I have the utmost regard for him, not just as a soldier but as a patriot who defends his homeland. I am sure that all of us appreciate the general's noble gesture of self-denial in respect to anthem and flag. It behooves us to meet him halfway in that same spirit of reconciliation. Let me call on everyone concerned to bury past enmities and prove to the world that 'Dixie' and 'The Bonnie Blue Flag' are mere expressions of history—that is all— but having been purchased in the ultimate currency of human blood are emblems worthy of continued respect. I thank you."

The aldermen applauded vigorously, then looked to Lopez for his response. Lopez did not need to consult his companions before he spoke.

"Begging Senator Sickles's pardon, we'll go with General Longstreet on this. The South stands united against 'Dixie' and the Stars and Bars!"

The board members erupted in cries of angry disapproval. Penrose waved his hands for order.

"Let's sum up, shall we?" he said. "Our side is amenable to a mutually satisfactory settlement on the principal issues of honoraria and profit shares. We agree to the commissions on the Negro problem and women's rights. All that remains is some compromise on your part in regard to the harmless and decorative use of Confederate memorabilia."

"No compromise." Lopez spat for emphasis to the left of the spittoon that had been provided.

"See here," Penrose exclaimed, "we have met you more than halfway. It is up to you, now."

"In that case, we walk." Lopez stood. The aldermen swelled with anger and frustration. Ziprenian hustled Lopez off to one side.

"You have milked them for all they're worth," he whispered urgently. "Brilliant work. Better than we could have anticipated. Now, let's take our gains, cut our losses, play the game as scheduled, put the money in our pockets, and go get drunk. What do you say?"

"That's fine with me personally," Lopez said, "but you realize I ain't speakin' for just myself. I got my boys to take care of."

Ziprenian wished that he could return to the moment when he looked through his telescope and saw a Civil War reenactment in one park and a football game in another. He wished he could beat his telescope to pieces. He wished he had been born female and married to a Lebanese rug merchant.

"Have your Negroes got something on you?" he hissed. "They muscling you? I can take care of you."

"My colored *brethren!*" Lopez was indignant. "You sayin' I ain't got their best int'rests at heart?" Lopez drew himself to his full height. To Ziprenian a monster was emerging before his very eyes.

"We had an understanding," Arno moaned.

"We agreed to disagree," Lopez said firmly.

"For a purpose." Arno rubbed his thumb and fingertips together. The aldermen, watching them across the room, took heart at this universal gesture.

"There is sump'm," Lopez became princely, "more important than money."

"*What?*"

"Self-respect."

Lopez had always thought of himself as a benefactor of mankind. He was glad that others now knew this side of him.

"Are you crazy?" Sweat pricked the skin between Ziprenian's shoulder blades like the point of a spring-knife.

"I'm seriously involved," Lopez said.

"If my aldermen don't back down on the Confederate stuff, your Negroes actually walk?"

"We take a hike."

"I'm gonna level with you." The Zipper tried to keep his voice steady. "If this game don't go on like we planned, I'm a dead man."

"We all got problems."

"I'm asking you. You got such a high regard for humanity, spread a little my way. My people got off the boat without a dime. Just the clothes on their backs."

"That's tough," Lopez said.

Ziprenian forced his mind to follow rational patterns. There was no way to con a confidence man. His last chance lay in convincing the businessmen they would lose profits by not cooperating with Lopez. He went to the aldermen and pleaded with them to see reason. They listened with the sympathy of a brick wall.

"Please ask Mr. Lopez," Penrose said loftily, "to refrain from chewing tobacco next time—if there *is* a next time.

Lopez reached for his hat.

Outside the Stratford, he gave the press a statement: "Our players naturally object to Confederate flag-wavin' which causes them embarrassment and mental anxiety. Which is due cause for legal relief. We ask that the promoters respect our players' rights to their feelin's and substitute unoffensive banners and tunes and such. Our players apologize for any delay caused by these reasonable requests and hope it will be settled as soon as possible."

"Will you strike?" a reporter asked.

"Does shit stink?" Lopez said.

—*Which he answered in the affirmative, one reporter wrote.*

—*Does feces smell badly? wrote an assiduous stringer for the* Pittsburgh *Press, then studiously marked out the -ly.*

—*All-Star dispute reeks of strike, wrote the Wilkes-Barre* Times-Leader *bureau chief.*

—*Fumes of unrest pollute football contest, the Harrisburg* Patriot *correspondent noted.*

—*BLACK REBELS REP SMELLS STRIKE COMING, Prescott hummed to himself.*

A police cordon held back crowds of Confederate and Union veterans who grappled with each other. Black citizens saluted and cheered Lopez. A large man approached him, hat in hand.

"Mr. Lopez, sir, I'm from the Pittsburgh Allegheny Athletic Association," the behemoth said. "We're a professional football team. We just got organized this season. We read about you in the paper. The most any of us gets paid is twenty bucks a game. Maybe you could teach us something about negotiation?"

"A pro team, huh?" Lopez was secretly delighted. "Well, I'll be glad to do what I can for you. I can be reached at the Maison Blanche in North Philly."

Lopez's cab was attacked only twice by demonstrators: at Seventeenth and Walnut, and at Race and Broad.

Brother followed Dobson to the Maison Blanche telephone with a surprised expression. He could not imagine who would be calling him.

"Hello?"

"Robert?" It was Du Bois. "I wanted to alert you to the fact that a group of academics are on the way out there to test the Post Oak players."

"What for?"

"To determine if they are truly college scholars. I just heard about it from a colleague at the university. I'm on my way. I'll do what I can to help, but I've not been asked to contribute officially. Good luck."

"Whose idea was it?"

"I don't know. At any rate, I thought you would want to alert your teammates. I'll see you in a few minutes." Du Bois hung up.

Brother replaced the receiver and went to tell the players. They reacted with stunned silence; then everyone seemed to speak at once.

What'll they ax us?

Where's Miz Kate? Get Miz Kate, quick!

Why us? Why not the white players, too?

We better practice up.

On what?

"What's the capital of New York?" B.C. asked Tree.

"New York."

"No, Albany."

"How'd you know that?" Tree complained.

"What's the capital of Missouri?" B.C. continued relentlessly.

"Ax me the capital of Kentucky," Tree demanded.

"That's too easy." B.C. shook his head.

"Ax me a multiplication question, *somebody!*" Weasel was close to panic.

"What's seventy-two times forty-nine?" Cassius said.

"That ain't in the tables," Weasel objected.

"Wait a minute," Brother told them. "There's no point in trying to cram for a test when you don't know the questions. Doctor Du Bois and Miss Kate will be there to support us."

"You'll be there too, won't you, Brother?" several players said at the same time.

"Yes, I'll be there."

When Heisman heard the news, he swung into action. He called a team practice right away, so that they might put off the "Inquisition," as he termed the unexpected testing. As the team made their way to the practice field, however, they were met by a group of professors and clergymen led by Stagg, Camp, and Ziprenian. Du Bois arrived on the next trolley and hurried to join them.

"What's this about?" Heisman angrily confronted Stagg.

"I apologize for surprising you like this, John," Lonny said, "but there has been a lot of talk about how your Negro players may not be bona fide college men. It was suggested that perhaps they would be willing to submit to a general examination by experts from the Philadelphia educational and religious community. Such a test could serve to clear the air—"

"Who suggested it?" Heisman exclaimed. Stagg looked at Camp, who looked at Ziprenian, who looked into space.

"Since your players are reputed to be seminary students . . ." Stagg continued.

"Reputed!" Warner cried.

". . . we have brought with us lecturers from seminaries in the area."

"This is a waste of time," Heisman said.

"Time seems to be a commodity we have a good deal of, these days," Stagg observed dryly.

"Aha!" Heisman cried. "So *that's* it. Then lead on, Macduff."

Kate pushed Brother forward. The rest of her players held themselves very carefully, as if the air itself might bruise them. Brother's alert expression caught a professor's eye.

"Would you tell us," the professor, a historian, began the questioning, "something about the Magna Charta?"

"It was the first constitutional document in England," Brother replied without hesitation. "It made King John responsible to the law of the land."

"And the year?"

"Twelve-fifteen." Brother added, "The Magna Charta is generally regarded as a democratic document, when in fact it contributed little or nothing to the common man's existence." Jones saw Du Bois nodding his approval.

"Thank you." The historian addressed the rest of the team. "Who can name the U.S. Presidents in order of suc—"

"Washington, Adams, Jefferson, Madison," Brother recited rapidly, "Monroe, John Quincy Adams, Jackson, Van Buren, Harrison . . ."

"Thank you, that's enough."

". . . Tyler, Polk, Taylor, Fillmore, Pierce, Buchanan, Lincoln, Johnson, Grant . . ."

"Thank you so much."

". . . Hayes, Garfield, Arthur, Cleveland." Brother stopped, a bit out of breath. His teammates filled their lungs sympathetically as if to keep him talking.

A science professor came forward. "Would anyone care to comment on Charles Darwin?"

"Author of *The Origin of Species,*" Brother began.

"Oh, please, someone else!" the scientist exclaimed. He looked sharply at the other players. They might have been deaf, dumb, and blind. "Anyone?"

After an awkward pause, the historian spoke up again: "Who can tell me the cause of the Franco-Prussian War?" He wagged a warning finger at Brother to keep him from answering.

A pall fell over the Panthers.

A literature professor spoke up. "How about some Shakespeare, anyone! Your favorite passage?"

Voices joined in a single basso-profundo, as ten student athletes surprised the academics by quoting:

> To be, or not to be—that is the question.
> Whether 'tis nobler in the mind to suffer
> The slings and arrows of outrageous fortune,
> Or to take arms against a sea of troubles,
> And by opposing end them. To die, to sleep—
> No more, and by a sleep to say we end
> The heartache and the thousand natural shocks

> That flesh is heir to, 'tis a consummation
> Devoutly to be wish'd.

Kate could not help applauding. Their voices took her back to the smoky little classroom where she stalked back and forth, staring out a broken window as they stumbled over the foreign words and phrases, ready to whirl and correct them at the first mistake. She was so proud of them she could cry.

She now pressed the advantage. "May I remind the judges," she said, "that these young men are seminarians and therefore should be questioned on religion, not the humanities."

The professors deferred to the clergy, who were Quaker, Catholic, Jewish, and Episcopalian. The Catholic priest, plump and benevolent, addressed a question to any player who would answer:

"When was the Bible written?"

Ten hands shot up. The priest pointed at Isaiah.

"Moses started on it 'bout fifteen hunnerd B.C." The big lineman self-consciously fingered his neck where Jeanette had scratched him.

"Forty writers worked on it," Cassius interposed.

"They finished the Bible up sixteen hunnerd years later," Lincoln put in.

"Who finished it?" asked the priest.

"Why, John!" Weasel cried.

"With the Book of Revelations," B.C. concluded.

"*Amen,*" Chase said, standing at the back of the group. He was so impressed with his young teammates that not only had he begun to believe that Post Oak Seminary existed, he planned to enroll.

"What is the origin of the word 'Bible'?" the rabbi asked.

Cassius consulted with Brother on the word "origin" before he answered, "It come from the Greek *biblion,* which mean book . . ."

"Or little books," Lincoln corrected.

"That's right," said the rabbi.

"The Greeks got it from *Byblos,*" Cassius continued, "name of a Pho-nician town that had papyrus they wrote books on."

"That's right," said the rabbi.

B.C.: *Said 'Do unto others as ye would have them do unto you'*
CHASE: *Amen.*
B.C.: *Said 'Love me and keep my commandments'*
CHASE: *Amen.*
WEASEL: *So God give man the best chance he ever had to save hisself So the Bible teach us man always got a chance if he just repent of his sins and obey God in all things.*
CHASE: *Amen.*

Kate wished that the Revered E. Alphonso Rutledge could have been there to reap what he had sown. She danced a hop and a skip with Du Bois.

The academics and clergymen glanced at each other in open approval. The players waited, bareheaded under the sky.

"Would you mind," the Episcopal priest asked, "naming the books of the Bible?"

Eleven voices (Chase could not help joining in, for fun) boomed:

> *"Genesis Exodus Leviticus Numbers Deuteronomy Joshua Judges Ruth First Samuel Second Samuel First Kings Second Kings First Chronicles Second Chronicles Ezra Nehemiah Esther Job Psalms Proverbs Ecclesiastes Song of Solomon Isaiah Jeremiah Lamentations Ezekiel Daniel Hosea Joel Amos Obadiah Jonah Micah Nahum Habakkuk Zephaniah Haggai Zechariah Malachi Matthew Mark Luke John Acts Romans First Corinthians . . ."*

"That's good," said the priest. "That's very good. Thank you."

Heisman stepped between his players and their inquisitors. He was drenched in sweat. "Have you heard enough?" he said.

The academics conferred. The Quaker minister spoke for them all: "They are college men, so far as we are concerned."

Heisman turned to his team. "All right, we've got a practice to get on with! We'll start with the *Yale modification of the Princeton wedge.*"

Stagg turned away so that Heisman would not see him die a little.

Ziprenian knew what he had to do:
Send Elston all the way to—where was it? Somewhere in Ken-

Kate swelled up like a toad.

The Quaker minister asked, "What does the Bible teach
He pointed at B.C. The big redhead shuffled his feet nervo

"You wants the whole thing?" he said.

"Just hit the high points," the Quaker said. "Anyone who v
to may answer."

"Like Reverend Rutledge's Battle-of-the-Bible quiz," Br
whispered to B.C.

"Oh, that easy," B.C. said, relieved.

B.C.: *The Old Testament: God create the world Adam w
first man God create man in his own image God want man
in Eden but Adam disobey God so God punish Adam by p
him to work*

WEASEL: *But man sin again and again so God punish n
sending the Flood but he give man a chance through No
the Ark with all living things necessary to repop*

BROTHER: *Repopulate*

WEASEL: *Repopulate the earth God made Abraham th
of his chosen peoples the Jews*

CASSIUS: *But the Jews fail God and He send them into l
in Egypt then let Moses lead them out from bondage to
of Canaan give them the Ten Commandments*

TREE: *But they broke them so God deliver them over
enemies again and let them be in bondage to punish th
He took pity on them and sent the prophets Isaiah, Ho
Jeremiah to explain God's will to them*

ULYSSES: *But still they disobeyed so God let the Rom
over Judea so the Jews lost their land and was again u
rule of their enemies*

LINCOLN: *The New Testament: Now God made the
everybody a new promise Instead of just one chosen rac
Jesus as a sacrifice for the sins of the whole world*

ISAIAH: *All man had to do was believe Jesus was the S
and follow his teachings After Jesus was crucified dead
ied He arose from the dead and ascended to Heaven*

B.C.: *His apostles took over They went out preach
gospel everywhere Said 'Believe in me and ye shall ha
ing life'*

CHASE: *Amen.*

tucky. To take stock of this school. What had the black player called it, a few days ago, during the first football practice? Post something. Post time? Evening post? Post Oak.

Ziprenian held on to the name like a drowning man to a piece of wood. The player had said Post Oak Normal. Not Seminary. He had said *Normal.* The Zipper was sure of it.

Ziprenian paused before knocking on Liebowitz's door. He could almost smell a scheme hatching behind the door, ancient and ripe, like a dinosaur's egg. Liebowitz welcomed him into the room, where the old gamblers from the North were waiting. They offered him whiskey and a cigar. Arno, who drank only the wines of the old country, refused.

"We got a sure thing," Liebowitz began. "All we need is some backing."

Ernie explained the famous, no-lose deal of Straight Flush Davis. Ziprenian listened dubiously. Liebowitz was offering half his winnings to his backer. Why would Canfield, Arno thought, decide to back both sides? Then it hit him: there were forty bundles of hundred-dollar bills remaining in the hotel safe. Liebowitz projected a jackpot of $100,000. All Ziprenian had to do was face down the hotel manager and make him believe that Canfield had ordered another withdrawal. Arno stood to make $50,000. Liebowitz saw the Armenian's face light up.

"I think I will try one of your whiskies," The Zipper said.

Liebowitz sent the Dutchman to challenge the Southerners to a showdown. Trott found them in the barroom, surrounded by a throng of well-wishers. He presented Liebowitz's challenge.

"The Fifth Kentuck' don't back away from a scrap!" Hudson entertained his audience. *"We'll be there."* Amid applause he added, "Tell Lieberwitz to bring the sword."

When the excitement subsided, Hudson took his partners aside.

"Remember the trick deal Lieberwitz likes," he told them. Let's go over it again: Ernie deals the sucker four of a kind and hisself an open-ended, four-card straight flush. Don't matter whether the mark stands pat or draws one card. Either of the next two cards fill one end or the other of Lieberwitz's flush. But I got a remedy!"

The gambling men leaned close.

"If any of you gets dealt four of a kind, bet all you got, *before* the draw. Then discard *two* cards. Three of a kind beats a busted flush."

They grinned a hungry grin.

"What if Liebowitz sees you discard two cards," Pitts said thoughtfully, "and deals himself a hole card off the bottom? A regular flush beats three of a kind."

Hudson reached down and pulled his Betsy, the two-shot derringer, from his boot. "I hate to shoot a man over cards," he said.

Some time later the Southerners showed up in the fourth-floor suite. In their ties, collars, vests and lapels they wore the stickpins, watches, and jewels of Liebowitz's men. Pitts wore Diamond Ed's ten-carat "headlight."

Formal as duelists, the two sides exchanged greetings. In this deadly serious mood, no one frisked anyone or examined pockets or hats. They sat down to play. Nobody joked or made idle remarks. Liebowitz casually hung Stroud's sword over his chair by its scabbard loop.

" 'Fore this game is over," Hudson said quietly, "I goin' to git my propitty back."

They began to play, feeling each other out, waiting for cards, watching for cheating. Antes and betting built up a substantial jackpot. Ziprenian watched from across the room. Neither side wanted him seated any closer, lest he give away someone's hand. Before the game he had transferred the money, which he had obtained from the hotel manager with ridiculous ease, to Liebowitz. Ziprenian was fairly certain that Stroud did not know Canfield's money was backing both sides.

Fitzpatrick answered a quiet knock at the door. To Ziprenian's horror, Canfield himself slipped into the room. He gave a backward glance into the hall to assure himself that no one had seen him enter a gambling den. Unaccustomed to propriety, the Faro King had become quite paranoid.

"I'd like to see what happens to my investment with the Southerners," he whispered to Ziprenian. "For charity, of course."

Your investment! The Zipper thought. If you only knew how substantial. *Mother of God.*

He saw high color in Canfield's cheeks, gambling fever. Ziprenian himself was pale as a sheet.

The deal rotated to O'Shea. Liebowitz saw Reno make an awkward overhand shuffle. The time had come. Ernie broke the silence with a subject intended to catch Stroud's interest.

"I've played at cards for cash, gold, jewelry, stocks and bonds, land, houses, ships, cattle, farms, cotton by the bale, and a woman's love," he said, "but did anybody here ever win an *octoroon?*"

Stroud, too, had noticed O'Shea's overhand shuffle and was alert to each card as it was dealt to him. So far he had received a queen and a deuce. "Slaves?" he asked casually.

"I mean, an octoroon *princess.*" Liebowitz ignored the open-ended straight flush building up, card by card, in front of him.

"Naw, them octoroon princess stories is all made up." Stroud now had three queens to go with his deuce.

"I recall that Ruby Roy Stein won a lovely octoroon from a Louisiana planter." Liebowitz scooped up his cards, seemingly more interested in his story than his hand.

"Naw, the goddamned writers made it up." Hudson looked at a fourth queen staring back at him. His heart thudded. He felt congestion in his chest and willed himself to relax.

Here comes Straight Flush Davis.

"White as her master she was and beautiful as a princess." Liebowitz carefully fanned his cards and the makings of a flush appeared before his eyes. "Her owner staked her against Ruby's raise of five thousand. Ruby won her with three jacks and carried her off. She never again saw the plantation where she had been born and raised ; . ."

"Bullshit!" Stroud said. "What use are *writers* anyhow, when they make stuff up? Even when a writer writes down 'zackly what happens he ain't worth much, but who cares 'bout a dressed-up story that bears no 'zemblance to the facts? Now that game you're talkin' 'bout? Ruby Roy did indeed win hisself a slave. It was a big, strong *buck.* Roy turned around and sold 'im at the next port of call. That octoroon princess stuff is for dainty folks that sit around readin' romances. Whose bet is it?"

O'Shea checked. Stroud, under the gun, or next to the dealer, was right where he wanted to be as far as betting was concerned. He pushed all his chips and cash into the middle of the table, amazing everyone, including Canfield.

"Fifty thousand," Stroud said. "Want to count it?"

Liebowitz stared at the pile of cash and chips.

Why isn't Stroud waiting for the draw before betting everything?

"In addition," Stroud was saying, "I'm throwin' in some of yo' jewelry. Stones ain't fake, are they?" He motioned to his associates. Off came rings, watches, gold chains, and stickpins. Liebowitz knew now that the Southerners were expecting something.

Could Stroud have remembered Straight Flush Davis?

Canfield was shocked at Stroud's bet. That's my money he's playing with! thought the King. He'd better be holding the cards.

One by one, the other players folded. The bet came to Liebowitz. He could meet Stroud's $50,000 in cash and chips but was short $25,000, which was the estimated value of the gems, watches, and gold chains. Hudson waited, breathing shallowly, heart palpitating.

"I'll accept the sword agin' the jewels," he said.

You'll what! Canfield thought.

Liebowitz stared at his old enemy. He had not cared a damn about the sword up until now, except that Stroud wanted it so badly. Suddenly it became very precious. He hated to part with it. With no other options, he reached reluctantly for the weapon and shoved it on top of the table. The tarnished brass sheath was greenish brown amid the diamonds and gold.

Canfield was pleased to see that the Northerners had $50,000 in cash but wondered why the Southerners would allow a worthless war relic against $25,000 in jewels and gold. If the Rebels won, the Canfield Children's Hospital would be $50,000 nearer to reality. On the other hand, Little Harry had promised him no less than half the pot, either way. If the Northerners won, he would merely be winning back his own money. He could not lose.

"Cards?" Reno said to Hudson.

"I'll take two," Stroud said.

Liebowitz felt the floor move under his feet. *Two cards.* All was lost unless O'Shea could deal Stroud a discard off the bottom. Hudson had remembered, after all. Liebowitz gave the Kentuckian a bitter glance of respect. Every eye was on the Nevada man as he coolly dealt Stroud two cards. Reno's deal was smooth as glass but Hudson was positive one of his cards came off the bottom. He let the two cards lie face down and made no move to pick them up.

"There's a one-eyed man in the game," Stroud said.

"You calling me a *cheat?*" O'Shea jumped to his feet, fists clenched. In his youth he had killed a man with his bare hands.

"I know sump'm 'bout one of those two cards you just dealt me," Hudson said calmly. He was back in the clearing beside the Green River. "One of 'em will fill one end of a possible straight flush Lieberwitz is holdin'. So will the next card in the deck."

Weapons appeared in hands as if by magic: derringers, snub-nosed pistols, snap-blade knives, even a miniature sawed-off shotgun Fitzpatrick had strapped to his leg. Shedding the years, the old gamblers faced one another, vital and dangerous. Hudson, staring over the evil barrels of a two-shot derringer, was the devil himself.

"You old fool!" Ernie cried. "You hoped it would turn out this way. You think this would be a splendid way to go out, *with dash*. It isn't money you've been playing for. You want to rearrange the past. Well, you can't have it."

"Maybe not," Stroud said, "but puttin' holes in you would be all right, too."

He reached out to turn the cards and prove his case.

"Gentlemen, gentlemen," Canfield interrupted, palms outspread. "There must be a way to settle your differences. I have an idea. Whereas it was *my* football game that brought you here; and whereas part of the proceeds thereof will swell the charitable contributions for the Canfield Foundation Children's Hospital Project; and whereas we must all be desirous of avoiding violence and personal injury, it seems reasonable and appropriate that we allow the outcome of the football match to determine the winner of this jackpot. What do you say?"

Hudson struggled out of the grip of the past. Riley Dunn had been determined for him to remain in the clearing, by the fire. He was drawn back by the crazy logic of Canfield's proposal.

Liebowitz saw immediately that he had no choice. Stroud could prove that O'Shea had rigged the deck.

Ziprenian slumped in his chair. He had aged fifty years during the seconds it had taken Canfield to utter his proposition.

"All right." Stroud laid his derringer on the table.

"All right." Liebowitz lowered his pistol.

Mother of God, Ziprenian thought.

Part III

Chapter Twenty-three

On Christmas Day, Humboldt eagerly led Riddle up the neatly swept brick walk under snow-covered branches. They joined the line of worshippers waiting to be admitted to the morning service at Christ Church. Shuffling along as the line moved forward, Chase entered the vestibule with the curious dread he felt for the Catholic cathedral in Bardstown. He half-expected to hear chanting and to smell incense burning. Instead there was a familiar holiday bustle of people greeting one another, taking off overcoats, hats, and scarves. It was, however, a properly subdued bustle.

"Second-oldest church in America," Humboldt whispered to Chase. "If we're lucky we might get to sit in George Washington's or Ben Franklin's pew or even Betsy Ross's. You know, the Episcopal Church was founded upstairs in a broom closet."

An usher greeted Humboldt politely. The professor smiled and nodded as if they were old friends. Entering the church, Humboldt craned his neck this way and that, looking for a vacant seat. Chase followed self-consciously. Although the sanctuary was nearly filled, Humboldt noticed two empty seats near the back of the church. The professor paused by the pew to genuflect and make the sign of the cross. Chase lingered behind, feeling strangely out of place in a house of God. He stared at the marble slabs of family vaults underfoot, the candlelit chandelier, the stained-glass "Liberty" window which depicted the Founding

Fathers gathered in prayer, and the great pump organ with its powerful song. Then, realizing that Humboldt was seated, he apologized his way down the crowded pew. The professor immediately knelt in prayer.

Chase sat next to a woman wearing a hat with peacock feathers. He stared down at the unfamiliar padded kneeling bench on the floor in front of him and elected to lean forward and bow his head. He closed his eyes and thought of the peacock "eyes" in the woman's hat. He could not think of a single thing to pray about. He felt the smooth, hard finish of the pew underneath him and thought longingly of the roughhewn benches in Big Dad's church. Having finished his prayer, Humboldt seated himself with an air of satisfaction.

As if aware of Chase's hesitation he leaned over and whispered, "Ask Him to let us win the game. It never hurts."

There was a flourish at the rear of the sanctuary as a cross bearer burst in, followed by the bishop in flowing white robe, followed by the choir singing in full voice, "Oh come, all ye faithful, joyful and triumphant . . ." At first Chase thought the church was under attack. The resolute bishop, priest, choir, flag-and cross-bearers were somehow martial, a Protestant machine clanking forward in unrelenting joy. Chase at least recognized the lyrics and was able to sing along. Noticing he was a head taller than anyone else, he slumped just a bit. The bishop ascended to the pulpit shaped like a wineglass.

"Almighty God," said the bishop when the hymn ended, "unto whom all hearts are open, all desires known, and from whom no secrets are hid: Cleanse the thoughts of our hearts by the inspiration of Thy Holy Spirit, that we may perfectly love Thee, and worthily magnify Thy Holy Name; through Christ our Lord. Amen. —The Lord be with thee."

Having recognized the traditional phrasing of the Collect, Riddle had begun to feel better until the congregation's deep response startled him:

"AND ALSO WITH THEE."

"Let us pray," said the bishop.

Everyone knelt, leaving Chase standing. He sank to his knees and wedged in between Humboldt and the lady with the feathered hat.

"Oh God," prayed the bishop, "who makest us glad with the yearly remembrance of the birth of thine only Son Jesus Christ: grant that as we joyfully receive him for our Redeemer so we may with sure confidence behold him when he shall come to be our Judge . . ."

Chase was not familiar with this prayer. Listening carefully, he wondered if Big Dad could have made the wrong lecture notes at divinity school in Mississippi.

A few moments later the congregation was on their feet, singing another hymn not usually sung at the Free Church of the Almighty, although Chase thought it suited to a hilltop chapel.

> Angels we have heard on high,
> Singing sweetly through the night,
> And the mountains in reply
> Echoing their brave delight.
> Glo-oooo-o-oooo-o-ooooo-ria,
> In excelsis Deo . . .

Humboldt thrust a hymn book into Riddle's hands, and he tried without success to find the correct page. The professor had all four verses by heart. Before Riddle found his place the hymn ended and the congregation took their seats.

A lay reader stepped into a second pulpit to read from the Old Testament: Isaiah 1:2–4, 6–7. On familiar ground now, Chase relaxed. He wondered if the bishop's partner also took up collection. The layman read:

> Hear, O heavens, and give ear, O earth: for the Lord hath spoken, I have nourished and brought up children, and they have rebelled against me.
>
> The ox knoweth his owner, and the ass his master's crib: but Israel doth not know, my people doth not consider.
>
> Ah sinful nation, a people laden with iniquity, a seed of evildoers, children that are corrupters: they have forsaken the Lord, they have provoked the Holy One of Israel unto anger, they are gone away backward.

"Amen," Chase said without thinking. People turned to look at him. His ears burned. The reader continued.

> From the sole of the foot even unto the head there is no
> soundness in it; but wounds, and bruises . . .

Chase willed himself not to say Amen again. He had no business attending this unknown Episcopal service. The truth was, he had felt guilty about not going to church on Christmas Day. Humboldt was the only one of their party who planned to attend. The others were off playing Santa Claus in Philadelphia's Seventh Ward.

"You'll love Christ Church," Humboldt had promised. "It's the *grande dame* of them all."

> Your country is desolate, your cities are burned with fire:
> your land, strangers devour it in your presence, and it is
> desolate, as overthrown by strangers.

Glancing around at the fine clothes, the furs and feathered hats, the aura of affluence, Chase experienced a shock of homesickness. He longed for the homely Christmas gathering in the little church on the ridge, farmers solemn in broadcloth, wives and daughters in calico, tithes paid in corn and tobacco, or livestock tethered outside the church. To Chase, Christmas service was a cow mooing outside and Big Dad shouting to be heard and mothers covering their sons' mouths to stifle their laughter. What would the Christ Church congregation make of that?

Chase came to a decision. Obeying irresistible impulse, he whispered in Humboldt's ear, "There's something I've got to do."

Humboldt watched in surprise as Chase made his way down the row toward the aisle, creating a buzzing stir among the worshippers. As he left the sanctuary, however, it died down, and the service continued as though nothing out of the ordinary had occurred.

Chase emerged from Christ Church with a grin of relief and an exhilarating feeling of freedom. For the first time in weeks, he knew exactly where he belonged.

Will and Nina Du Bois woke up smiling on Christmas Day in their one-room apartment above the college settlement. Each had tried to hide the other's Christmas gift somewhere in the room, had discovered the other's hiding place, and by tacit agreement had kept silent. Before Christmas Eve the couple had carefully deliberated on how much they could spend and decided they could afford five dollars apiece, not counting a roasting hen for dinner. Nina had gone to Second Street Market and bought wreaths, a cross, and a fifteen-cent Christmas tree. Now they solemnly exchanged gifts. Will had bought Nina a pair of new shoes; she gave him an umbrella with an ornately carved wooden handle.

The couple passed the morning pleasantly. In a contented mood Will wrote letters to friends and family while Nina prepared the dinner. This connubial bliss was interrupted by a knock at the door. Du Bois wondered who was calling. He opened the door and was surprised to see Brother Jones and James Longstreet, Alonzo Stagg and John Heisman, Heffelfinger and Tree.

"Merry Christmas," Brother said. "We have all these presents and food and things and don't know what to do with them. Can you help us out?"

Du Bois stood dumbfounded. Nina ran to the window. "Look, Will," she called, "it's the football players. They have a wagon full of toys and gifts!"

Brother and Longstreet grinned at the bewildered Du Bois. In their merriment they looked amazingly similar to Will, considering their differences in age, complexion, and philosophy. Du Bois went to the window and looked out. He saw players from North and South standing around an open van filled with boxes of food and toys. Lopez was in the driver's seat, chewing a cigar. Kate and Chase sat beside him. Kate saw the Du Boises and waved. Will turned to Brother for an explanation.

"Lopez went to Wanamaker and got us a deal: toys and goods unsold by closing time on Christmas Eve. We pulled a van up to the back door of Wanamaker's and loaded up. The food was donated by a concession operator who wants the contract for the game. It's mostly hot dogs and pretzels and such, but we can sure enough have us a party. If you round up some children, General Longstreet has volunteered to play Santa."

"I've always thought I was dressed for the part," Longstreet said, tugging at his white whiskers.

Du Bois whooped and grabbed his coat. "Nina," he called, "go light the fire in the cafeteria and warm the place up. I'll spread the word."

Nina was already taking pots and pans off the stove to postpone their dinner. "Let's take our tree," she suggested, "and make the cafeteria festive."

"Good idea!" Du Bois hesitated, elation tempered by habitual caution. "How many children should I bring? We don't want to have too many and not enough toys to go around."

Tree spoke over Longstreet's shoulder. "Bring all you want. If we run out of stuff we'll go back and break into Wanamaker's, won't we, Hiffyfugger!"

While Du Bois and Brother went to spread the word, Nina organized the unloading of toys and setting up the cafeteria. She sent for neighbors to help prepare the food. Soon the lunchroom was filled to overflowing with eager children and their parents. A long line of people stretched out into Lombard Street. Heffelfinger and Tree passed out refreshments while Chase and Lopez handed toys to Longstreet, who, wearing a department store Santa's cap, presented toys to children. Chase could not stop smiling. Cassius and Weasel led the crowd in singing Christmas carols.

Brother discovered the little girl whose parents had been fighting. Her name was Yolanda. He held her in one arm while he escorted the beautiful daughter of the merchant, Mr. Carver, on the other. He saw Du Bois grinning and became self-conscious, as if Will had openly teased him.

"I guess white folks're all right, as long as you take off your hat and say, 'Christmas gift.' "

Du Bois snorted with dry laughter. "Can't you let up when you're ahead? Man, you are a pistol."

When all the presents were gone, the food eaten and carols sung, Du Bois stood on a table and held up his hand. He looked down on the happy faces and had to clear his throat twice before speaking.

"This is one of those moments that renew my faith in mankind. It is, in fact, the best Christmas I can remember. This event came as much of a surprise to me as it did to many of you. I think we owe a hand of applause to General Longstreet and the coaches and players of the All-Star football teams for making it possible."

After the cheering died down he continued, "This gives me hope. Here we are, black and white together, sharing holiday spirit. The greatest gift of all is that it happened. I, for one, will not forget it. The truth is, however, I don't know if I could stand it all the time." Over the laughter he held up both arms and shouted, "Thank you! On behalf of the Seventh Ward—no, by golly, on behalf of Philadelphia—thank you. Thank you all."

SOUTH ALL STARS STRIKE
by
Harrison Prescott

The South All Star football players, represented by I. Lopez, of Fordyce, Arkansas, have gone out on strike. The principal issue concerns the use of Confederate battle flags and emblems.

The Southern players' demands, which apparently would benefit the Northern players as well, also include minimum salaries, profit shares, bonuses, safety regulations, padded helmets and uniforms, hospitalization and disability insurance, retirement plan, the right to negotiate separate endorsement contracts, women's rights, and reforms of city regulations affecting jobs and housing for Negroes, particularly in the Seventh Ward.

"We want everybody to be happy," Lopez said.

Public reaction to the players' strike has exceeded expectations. According to Chief O'Rourke of the Police Department, an estimated 50,000 people jammed the streets downtown. It was three hours before negotiators could leave the Stratford safely. O'Rourke warns that city ordinance forbids citizens to carry arms or deadly weapons and that violators will be arrested.

Citizens of the Seventh Ward have rallied around the Negro-Hispanic Coalition of the South All-Stars. An

anonymous source disclosed that the Cuban Ambassador wired his country's congratulations to the strikers.

In a related development, the South All-Star players
have been invited to serve as marshals for the Mummers' Parade. Police security for the Mummers has been
increased, as attacks on the parade marshals cannot be
ruled out.

Philadelphians turned out to celebrate the New Year. They
lined Broad, Market, and Vine streets to applaud the costumes of
mummers, clowns, "new" women, and diminutive devils sponsored by their favorite organizations. The skies were clear, but
mild temperatures had melted the snow to dirty slush. Various
merchants and businesses awarded prizes at different locations;
thus, individual clubs chose their own parade routes. The major-
ity of the marchers, however, lined up on Broad Street between
Walnut and Locust.

The Black Rebels had been invited to march. Tree Jackson
paraded with the Golden Crown Club, whose mummers dressed
for beauty, not comical effect. He felt splendid and foolish in a
uniform of red plush, with pink and blue satin trimmings, stud-
ded with stones of many colors, and a cape carried by thirty-two
small boys.

Lincoln Jackson was part of the Red Onion entourage. He
seriously intended to win the twenty-five-dollar first prize
awarded by their sponsor. His costume consisted of a red military
uniform with a long cape draped over a flat wagon, on which had
been constructed a miniature football field complete with toy
players and a tiny grandstand. The mechanical players moved
back and forth with each step Lincoln took. Behind him marched
a company of Irish militiamen with red whiskers, red hair, green
uniforms, and green shoes. Instead of hats they wore watering
pots with the spouts pointed down.

B.C. Jackson marched with the Charles D. Dillmore Association of Camden behind a boat on wheels displaying a "Free
Cuba" sign. His broad shoulders supported a white muslin cape
40 feet long and 15 feet wide. On his head perched a miniature
shed from which a toboggan slide extended down his back. A

page walked on either side of him, placing small boats in the shed. B.C. could pull a string dangling inside the cape, raising the shed so that the boats slid down the toboggan slide. He grinned self-consciously and his freckles turned orange.

Lopez was King of Clowns, but fearing retaliation by an unfriendly audience, he was disguised as an ass. He wiggled his ears and made the children laugh.

Kate, embarrassed but determined, rode at the front of the Schuylkill Rowing Not Drifting float. She was dressed as a female Viking warrior in brass breastplate and helmet with horns sticking out of it. She held a wooden shield and broadsword and was seated at the prow of a lifeboat mounted on a trailer and refurbished to resemble a Viking warship. The SRND members, similarly garbed, manned the oars on either side and rowed to the beat of Elizabeth Robins's drum. The trailer was pulled by a team of horses. The driver was seated just beneath Kate's platform. The oars swished the air, forcing pedestrians back up onto the curb. The SRND war drum thudded ominously—*doom, doom, doom*—rising to ram speed occasionally. Ahead of the float Kate could see her players sneaking looks at her. Dressed in Cuban soldier costumes, Weasel and Cassius pedaled tricycles with large front wheels. They circled the Viking boat and waved at Kate.

"Hey, Miz Kate, how you doin'?"

"I don't look any sillier than you two!" she retorted, holding her sword under her arm so she could straighten her helmet.

Directly in front of the SRND float was a group of mummers sponsored by the Union League. Arms linked with Susan Wharton, Du Bois and Brother marched at the head of the Seventh Ward Improvement Committee, whose banner was prominently displayed. Their group included a Negro mummers club called the Hi-Muckety-Mucks and another called The Dutchmen, who wore link sausages around their necks. The entourage was led by a float carrying a Hogan's Alley scene and the Yellow Kid, a masked jester dressed in yellow.

Brother, wearing a suit and hat like that of Du Bois and sporting a cane, unconsciously imitated Du Bois's stalking stride and fearless demeanor, looking straight ahead as if facing the future with optimism and courage.

"I wish they were not so provocative," Du Bois whispered to

Jones, his apprehension belying his stalwart appearance. He nodded toward the Hi-Muckety-Mucks, who cavorted and pranced before the mostly white spectators lining Broad Street. "The crowd doesn't like it. Look how silent they are!"

Brother looked at the mostly white working-class citizenry jamming the sidewalks. Drinking from quart bottles of beer or whiskey, wearing the rough clothes of longshoremen or draymen, the workers of South Philadelphia were hostile and formidable. As Brother regarded the passing faces, Weasel and Cassius blithely pedaled between him and the crowd, which broke silence with a roar of disapproval.

Get those black Cubans!

Cuba-lovers! Go back where you came from!

We don't need your kind.

"Who dressed them in those Cuban uniforms!" Du Bois exclaimed. "Why ask for trouble? Don't we have enough of an identity problem as it is?"

Cass and Weasel wheeled smartly up beside Tree and admired his costume.

"I feel silly," Tree confided.

"You look real good," Weasel said, circling on his tricycle, "but we got sump'm else to worry 'bout. Look up there!" He pointed to an angry group of spectators blocking the street at Broad and Chestnut.

"Don't you worry," called the captain of the Irish militia. "Our regiment's not afraid of rowdies and shoulder hitters."

"On the other hand," Weasel reasoned, "it don't hurt to be a *little* afraid."

Harrison Prescott popped out of the crowd and approached them, pencil and pad at the ready. "Afraid of *what*, did you say? Do you expect something to happen? As a result of your strike?"

"We gotta go." Weasel responded to the parade master's signal to move out.

"Take me with you!" Prescott cried and leaped onto the passenger bar between the tricycle's rear wheels.

The crowd parted at Chestnut Street, but when the parade reached Penn Square people again pressed forward on each side of the street. Weasel and Cassius squeaked the tube horns on their handlebars, and the rowdies sullenly moved out of the way.

"That man got a pistol," Weasel whispered.

"All good Americans hate strikers," Prescott explained over Weasel's shoulder.

"Maybe it's our Cuban uniforms," Weasel said.

"Go home, niggers!"

"Death to the Black Bolsheviks!"

A woman ran alongside Weasel's tricycle, waving a ticket in his face and crying, "Is my ticket to the football game still good? I bought it in good faith. Then *you* went on strike!"

"Don't blame me!" Weasel pedaled as fast as he could. Prescott slowed him down. The woman sprinted alongside.

"I paid two dollars . . . for it . . . when they first . . . put them up . . . for sale," she puffed. "Now the price . . . is seven-fifty. They better honor . . . my ticket!"

"I'll put in a word for you." Weasel pedaled madly away.

In passing City Hall the Seventh Ward Committee received sporadic cheers mixed with boos. Will Du Bois saw trouble ahead and nudged Brother: "Watch out! They're blocking Arch Street just around the corner. It's not safe." Brother saw with a shock that Will was frightened.

"Do you think it's really dangerous?" he said.

"Most assuredly!" Du Bois said. The Committee slowed while the rest of the parade moved on, gaining on them.

Weasel and Cassius passed them and cautiously pedaled ahead. On the north side of City Hall square, looking up Broad, they saw a solid phalanx of hostile men massed in the street. Cassius and Weasel stopped and, as before, politely honked their horns. The toughs moved menacingly toward them. They turned around and pedaled back to the main parade group. They reported what they had seen to the Irish captain, who eagerly suggested a tactic.

"You cyclists ride toward them like you're challenging them, then cut off at Cuthbert Street and divert them. We'll barricade Juniper and hold them back while the parade passes behind us. Just give us two minutes to get into position."

Weasel and Cassius looked at each other for moral support. Prescott had been scribbling notes furiously. He needed the Irish captain's name, for the record, but as soon as the "Cubans" began to pedal he grabbed Weasel's military belt and held on for dear life.

From her perch five feet above the street Kate could see the commotion. A mother's instinct told her that her players were in danger. Gripping her wooden sword and shield, she leaped down from the float. Her helmet fell off. The SRND women wailed in protest and warning. She raced toward the "Cubans" on their tricycles. A spectator lunged at her, for comic effect, and she bashed him with her shield. She kept running. She saw Prescott hanging on behind Weasel and, catching up with Cassius, she jumped on the back of his tricycle. Cassius looked back in surprise. Kate's eyes were as wild as a Viking's.

"Go, Cass, go!" she yelled.

Horns tooting, the tricyclists charged at the mob, which responded immediately with a barrage of bottles, cans, and rotten fruit and vegetables. Kate held her shield over Cassius and whacked at a man running alongside. He cowered from her flailing sword. The cyclists swerved right onto Cuthbert with the mob running behind them. Pedaling for all they were worth, Weasel and Cassius reached Juniper only to find that the Irish militia had not yet arrived. They turned north in panic. The crowd was gaining on them, pausing to hurl sticks and rocks which thumped off Kate's shield.

"Get off, you're holding me back!" Weasel yelled at Prescott.

"I'll be killed!" Harry cried.

"Tell me which way to go."

"Take a right."

They wheeled onto Appletree, where another mob joined the chase. Crossing Twelfth Street, Cassius and Weasel failed to see until too late that Appletree was a dead end. A brick wall supporting an elevated railroad track blocked the street. Without looking back, the athletes jumped off their tricycles and scaled a wooden fence behind a firehouse. Kate covered their retreat, sword at the ready. The howling mob was closing fast. Prescott tried but failed to catch hold of the top of the fence.

"Help me!" he pleaded. He saw Weasel watching him through a crack in the fence. Kate tossed her sword and shield over the fence and hurdled it with acrobatic ease. Cassius led her through the Cherry Street archway beneath the railroad tracks.

"They probably won't hurt you," Weasel called to the reporter. "You could always write sump'm bad 'bout 'em in the paper."

Prescott whirled and faced the mob. "I'm not with them!" he cried.

"It don't matter," a man said.

"I'm with the *Inquirer!*"

"Take his clothes off!" said a man holding a bucket of black paint.

"The *Inquirer!*" Prescott screamed as they ripped his shirt off. A woman tore open a feather pillow and held it poised over Harry.

"Hail to the king of the parade," said the man with the bucket as he poured paint over Prescott's head.

Meanwhile, on Juniper, the Irish militia grappled with angry spectators. Fighting broke out between the Hi-Muckety-Mucks and a gang of toughs. Swinging their waterspouts, the Irish regiment came to their rescue. A man assaulted Tree and tore his beautiful cape. The thirty-two small boys scattered in all directions. Tree picked the man up by the scruff of his neck, opened a sewer cover, and dropped him in.

"This is a mess," he told B.C., whose toboggan slide also had been ruined.

"I ain't goin' to win first prize," Lincoln moaned.

"Doctor Du Bois," Brother yelled, "let's get the hell out of here."

Du Bois had no choice but to lead the Seventh Ward Committee members and the Kentuckians down a side street to safety. When he looked back he could see people still fighting, two blocks away.

Relying on accustomed routine to restore calm, Heisman called a practice after they had returned to the Maison Blanche.

Dressed in new jerseys, moleskin pants, and cleats donated by athletic supply firms vying for advertising endorsements, the players walked to their practice lot. It was not vacant now. Hundreds of fans, well-wishers, and hecklers, black and white, were waiting for them.

"Don't pay them any attention," Heisman told his team.

Will Du Bois arrived just as practice started. He had been afraid that the Mummers' Parade mob might follow the team to the suburbs. As he got off the trolley he saw that his misgivings were well founded. Hecklers had disrupted the practice, and Heisman was talking to police about restoring order. A scuffle had broken out between white and black spectators. As the police moved in, Heisman hustled his team off the field and back to the Maison Blanche.

The crowd quickly dispersed. Du Bois spotted Longstreet lingering behind. He followed the general to a rented hack parked nearby.

"Excuse me," Will said. "May I have a word with you, General?"

"Yes, of course, Dr. Du Bois," Longstreet said. "Would you join me for the ride back to town?"

They got into the hack. Longstreet drove south into the city. The horse's hooves rang musically against the icy pavement. The general was the first to break the silence.

"I don't understand," he said slowly, "what football has to do with politics."

Du Bois shrugged. "What does war have to do with politics?"

Longstreet started. This feisty young Harvard man was full of surprises. "What is on your mind?" he rumbled.

"I, too, am concerned about the team's well-being," Du Bois said. "I confess I did not expect such a violent backlash to what we anticipated could become a popular cause with wide support."

"When you used the South team as cheese to bait a trap, you caught a cat instead of a mouse."

"I joined our cause to theirs." Du Bois was adamant. "I did not intend to *use* anyone!"

"Whatever the reason, the damage has been done."

"I agree completely. I am admitting that I underestimated the emotions involved. I did not realize the pressure that existed on both sides, like a volcano. We released too much, too soon. I am afraid that if this game is played in Philadelphia, my people will be hurt. Our cause will be set back. The game could become a riot."

"I am not insensitive to the problems colored people face," Longstreet said carefully. "But . . . perhaps you should have let time close the breach?"

"Would you have us do nothing to help ourselves?" Will forced himself to remain calm. "But that is not the point. The point is, something must be done to resolve a volatile situation."

"What do you propose to do?"

"I think the game should be moved to another location. For the good of all concerned."

"Where? New York? Baltimore?"

"I thought you might take a hand in the selection, General."

"Why should they listen to me?"

"You command their attention. They made you honorary chairman. But most of all, you do not stand to gain anything—personally, I mean."

"There may be a riot no matter where the game is played."

"No place could be worse than here."

As if to illustrate Du Bois's point, a carter stopped his wagon on the tracks, blocking a trolley carrying blacks from the Seventh Ward, on their way home from the practice session. The conductor repeatedly rang his bell for right of way. Longstreet pulled up.

"Move on!" he called to the driver. The man, who seemed to be enjoying harassing the conductor, stared at the hack. Du Bois could not tell whether the drover recognized Longstreet or responded to the general's authoritative manner, but he grudgingly urged his mule team forward and moved off the tracks.

"Do you have a suggestion as to location?" Longstreet resumed.

Du Bois gave him a penetrating look. "I was hoping you might help in that respect. It would need to be somewhere within commuting distance of Philadelphia, to allow present ticket holders to use their tickets."

"Someplace close by," Longstreet mused and slapped reins against horse's flank.

"Someplace, shall we say, with historical precedent." Du Bois was intentionally intriguing.

"You don't mean . . ." Longstreet looked at him in astonishment.

"Gettysburg."

Longstreet almost failed to stop at a cross street. Just missing them, a horse-powered omnibus clattered past. Du Bois waited patiently for the general's reaction.

"Gettysburg," Longstreet repeated to himself.

"Three hours from Philadelphia by train."

"Can it be done?" Longstreet became excited in spite of himself. "Just like that!"

"Your friend Sickles could do it. Isn't he head of the Gettysburg park commission?"

"But why would the aldermen move the game after they've gone to all this trouble to stage it? Think of the profit they stand to lose."

"This game has already cost the city thousands of dollars for extra police duty, damage to public and private property, disturbing the peace. I think Penrose and the board are desperate for a way out. I think they'd jump at your suggestion. After all, it does have a crazy logic to it."

Longstreet gave him a wild look. *"Who are you?"*

Du Bois grinned. "I'm just an American. Like you."

"How can you, a black man, want us to return to Gettysburg?"

There is no way to answer that question diplomatically, Du Bois thought.

"My side won, General."

Longstreet looked away. Du Bois pressed his argument before the general lost his temper.

"Let's exorcise some ghosts, what do you say? With our Negro athletes, the South has a chance to win. We are in a position to do each other a favor."

"Exorcise the ghosts," Longstreet repeated to himself.

"It's time somebody did," Du Bois said.

Longstreet fought a delaying action. "What are you trying to prove, sir?"

Du Bois spread gloved palms. "We are Americans. We must settle our differences."

"Strange allies, you and I."

Du Bois shook his head. "Not so strange. We are both soldiers."

Longstreet's rugged features were creased by what passed for a smile. "If Penrose and the board agree, the responsibility for what might happen shifts to *me.* Mr. Du Bois, they may shoot the both of us."

Du Bois shrugged elegantly. "I'm willing to let the game decide our fate. Are you?"

"Gettysburg!"

Stagg threw up his hands. King shrugged, messenger of ill tidings.

"How could they change the site without telling us!" Lonny demanded.

"I believe Penrose made the final decision," King explained. "They say it's to avoid a riot. Situation too volatile. Et cetera."

"Why weren't we contacted?"

"Don't ask me, Coach. Seems like we're always the last to know. They say it's best for everybody."

"Except us," Stagg continued. "We've been practicing at Franklin Field for over two weeks now. It's practically our home stadium."

"At least the boycott is settled and the game is on for day after tomorrow."

"How did Penrose manage that?" Lonny asked sardonically.

"They made a deal with Longstreet that if the game was moved to accommodate his people, the South team would agree to end their walkout and play."

"Longstreet." Stagg frowned. "So it was Longstreet."

"He and Sickles went to Penrose with the proposal."

Stagg thought for a moment. "Gettysburg. That's the key."

"What do you mean, Coach?"

"Where's my copy of Longstreet's book? Help me find it."

"Is it in your locker?" King could not suppress a groan of unhappiness.

"That's the one battle I left off my list," Stagg exclaimed.

"Why wouldn't you? He lost, didn't he?"

"That's the point!"

Stagg stared out the window of the dormitory where the team was staying. The University of Pennsylvania campus was deserted for the holidays.

"I don't get it," King said.

"He's returning to the scene."

"Who?"

"Longstreet!" Stagg grew impatient.

"What for?"

"He intends to win *this* one."

"The game or the battle?"

"Both. He's going to fight Gettysburg all over again."

"Aw, Coach . . ."

"And this time, he'll use the strategy he would have used if Lee had let him. Why didn't I think of that before?"

"Coach," King said diplomatically, "I've been meaning to bring something up—that is, Woodruff and I—and the team, too—we've been noticing that you've neglected—I mean, the team feels that you've neglected . . ."

"Help me find that book!" Stagg ignored his assistant's stammering. "What do you remember about Gettysburg? Quick!"

"Huh? Uh, Pickett's Charge. That's all I can think of. I'm not too big on Civil War battles, Coach."

"Pickett's Charge? No, that was suicide. By that time the Confederates had already lost. Even Longstreet would not try to improve on Pickett's Charge."

On Sunday morning a man on horseback urged his mount among the trees of Seminary Ridge. Sunlight glistened on snow-caked branches. The rider reined in near the Virginia Monument and looked across farmland sleeping under a fresh, snowy blanket. The land dipped and rolled up against the Emmitsburg Road like white ocean swells. Except for the clatter of ice falling from branches and a far-off church bell in the town of Gettysburg, the battlefield was still. No birds chirped and called as they had on July 3, 1863, when Longstreet had watched Pettigrew's men form on the left while Pickett's Virginians waited on the right to move into line. He did not know why he remembered the birds.

The general sat motionless in the saddle. The collar of his gray overcoat was turned up. His felt hat was pulled low over his forehead, as if protecting his eyes from the glare of history. Through the steam of his horse's breath he thought he saw waves of gray-clad soldiers streaming across the frozen fields, now pausing to lay down a fence, now disappearing into a shallow ravine or beyond a fencerow; while another wave rose into view, wheeling into position, an officer's sword glinting ahead of them.

Now they are within sniper range.

Longstreet heard a popping of small-arms fire. It was only icicles falling in the trees.

"There's a little swale where you can get your breath, General. The problem is, the whole Union Army is over there in a bunch."

Who said that? Harry Bright of Pickett's staff?

Longstreet glanced about, expecting to see an officer's sweating face. A mile ahead of him Cemetery Ridge squatted on the horizon, the old landmarks unchanged, still beckoning. From left to right Longstreet saw the Bryan house, The Angle where the little cemetery itself stood, the copse of trees and, farther away, Little Round Top and Round Top, which the Confederates had called Rocky Hill.

He spurred forward and entered the arena. He had never actually ridden all the way across the fields where Pickett made his charge. A red barn roof appeared over the first shallow rise, surprising him. It seemed to greet him, saying cheerfully, "Welcome back, soldier." Topping the rise he now could see, off to the left, white houses peeking among the trees of Culp's Hill. He twisted in the saddle and looked back where the Confederate line had first come under artillery fire.

He remembered men falling in clumps beneath bursts of shot and shell and Pickett's troops wheeling in a parade-perfect left oblique to come into line with the North Carolinians, who had started too soon and now were forced to hug the ground and wait while exposed to galling cannonade.

"The oblique is what is killing us off, General! The enfilade is awful."

Longstreet glanced compulsively this way and that. He saw clearly, in the snowy fields, the exact spot where fences were laid down.

"The fences are slowing us down and causing terrible destruction! Yankee skirmishers are behind them and knock us down, one at a time. We're laying them down as fast as we can, but they've brought up cannon and are leveling whole companies with canister."

Longstreet glared at Round Top and Little Round Top, from

which the big guns had fired at will on Confederate soldiers swarming across open fields. He experienced a powerful urge to gallop up to Cemetery Ridge and *take it.* His bearded face was fierce with yearning. He was overwhelmed by the memory of 170,000 men willing to die because other men commanded their loyalties. Regardless of human waste, errors in judgment, the downfall of a nation and preservation of the Union, there remained within Longstreet's heart a secret pride in the unwavering purpose with which his butternut grays had marched, regiment after regiment, toward the guns. The cannonade squeezed Pettigrew's and Pickett's assault forces together until what was left of 12,000 men were advancing shoulder to shoulder within a front of 800 yards. The cannoneers simply could not miss.

Oh, that steady advance.

He strained to hear the shouts of officers directing their troops under fire, the thump of enemy cannon being answered by Confederate batteries.

From among the rooftops of Gettysburg came the peal of a church bell announcing morning service. From Cemetery Hill an echo replied. Longstreet's mount snorted and pawed the icy ground. He saw a horseman ride around the red barn. Longstreet was irritated. He had meant to finish the job before Sickles could join him. He began to search the terrain for a level place to lay out a football field.

He roamed the frozen wheatfields until he found what he was looking for. About a hundred and fifty yards west of the Emmitsburg Road was a stretch of flat ground. Under a uniform coating of snow, dimpled here and there by stray wheat stalks and a flock of feeding blackbirds, the level place had the look of an athletic field. Longstreet shivered inside his greatcoat. He urged his mount forward and rode across a shallow ditch. Brown ice crackled like pistol shots.

"Casualty report, General: We got nine thousand down. They hit us long-range as we came out of the trees, then medium-range the closer we got, then musket and canister and, finally, bayonets. During our retreat they reversed the process. Their long-range artillery is still banging away and nobody left out there but wounded."

The voice belonged to Captain T. J. Goree, Longstreet's aide-de-camp. He wrenched his thoughts away from the past. His eye fell on the lone rider, who crossed the Emmitsburg Road and entered the frozen fields. Even from this distance, Longstreet could see the crutches laid sideways across the saddle. Sickles, too, seemed to be looking for something. He turned his head precisely this way and that. The two riders circled the flat ground counterclockwise to each other. Longstreet reined in where the land began to slope up toward Cemetery Ridge. Sickles's smile flashed beneath a black cavalry hat. The generals' mounts snorted at each other. Longstreet thought that the former Union commander looked more youthful than before, cheeks firm and rosy, mustache barely touched by gray.

"You gave me the slip, Jim," Sickles chided amiably. "Thought we were going to do this after breakfast." He added, "The last time we saw each other here, it was through field glasses."

"Sure it wasn't over a rifle sight?" Longstreet replied with good humor, no longer irritated that Sickles had caught up with him.

Dan smiled brilliantly. "I did not fire a single shot that day."

"Me neither. Maybe we'd be better off if we had."

Sickles gestured at the level field. "This is as good a place as any. Flat as a flounder."

"If you'll direct me, I'll lay it out by myself," Longstreet suggested.

"Did you do it by yourself in July of sixty-three?" Sickles replied. "Let's do it together, Jim."

Longstreet regarded his former enemy from under his bushy white eyebrows. "If you say so, General." He gestured toward Cemetery Ridge, then Seminary Ridge. "It should lie east and west, with your goal here and mine yonder."

"That's a good one!" Dan's eyes sparkled with amusement. "Like old times, eh?"

"Why not?" Longstreet's hands tightened on the reins. "It suits *me.*"

Sickles sobered. "But isn't that configuration a bit obvious? The press would have a high time with that. They do like symbols, you know."

"Well," Longstreet said stiffly, "what's the game being played for, anyway?"

"Still, it's only a *game*," Sickles argued. His mount seemed to sense tension and stamped restively. "Wouldn't you say that this field accommodates a north-south arrangement?"

"You think that would be any more neutral than east-west?" Longstreet said stubbornly.

"Well, if we laid it out north-south, maybe the Gray team could defend the north end and the Federal—I mean the Blue—team defend the south end."

Longstreet thought about Sickles's suggestion, then said aloofly, "Under the circumstances, I reckon the challenger ought to be allowed to select the site."

Sickles glanced up impatiently under his black hat. "All right, then. An east-west configuration it will be! Would your team defend this end?" He pointed toward Cemetery Hill. "And ours that one?" He pointed toward Seminary Ridge.

Longstreet looked across the rolling white fields. Like dancing black dots, birds rose in a flurry and settled farther on.

"I reckon you know," he said, "that each team defends opposite goals each half?" He observed Sickles's quizzical expression. *Dan does not know beans about football.*

Longstreet pressed his advantage. "So it doesn't make a lot of difference which end they defend, does it!"

"Of course it would not matter so much to the players as it would to the spectators," Sickles contended. "Hell's bells, Jim, the entire nation will be following this game. I imagine the wire services will be transmitting the score after every touchdown."

The old generals stared at the frozen battlefield as though each had received a transmission of his own. Cirrhus clouds were spread like gauze across a cobalt blue sky. The clear air was like an ocean of light crashing against the snow-covered battlefield.

"It was hot that day, wasn't it?" Longstreet said.

"Eighty-seven degrees at three in the afternoon." Sickles added, "The humidity killed us. Ninety percent, they say."

"I didn't notice the humidity," Longstreet said ironically.

"How long did it last? Do you know?" Sickles said.

"When Pickett charged? Fifty minutes, I think." Winfield Hancock once told me it seemed like three hours—you just kept coming and coming."

"Yes we did."

Both men simultaneously glanced over a shoulder, as if ghosts were listening in.

"All right," Longstreet returned to business at hand. "We'll lay it out north and south, as you first suggested. Shall I walk it off?"

"You think I can't keep up?" Sickles nimbly swung out of his saddle and, using his crutches as props, eased to the ground on his one leg. "I do it every day," he added.

Longstreet got off his horse and looped the reins over a frozen wheat stalk. He looked around for landmarks to sight on. To the east was a tall tree, between the red barn and a farmhouse; to the west, on Seminary Ridge, a distinctive gap in the tree line aligned perfectly. Fixing these two points in his mind, he reached into his pocket and drew out a wooden stake. He bent over and drove the stake into the hard ground with the heel of his boot.

"Here's the southeast corner of the football field." Longstreet was relieved to have something physical to do.

"Fine." Sickles, who had not thought to bring any markers, was obliged to follow the Rebel general's lead.

Longstreet hesitated. He glanced self-consciously at his companion. "Are we crazy?" he said.

Sickles laughed. "If we are, we're due!"

The generals walked off the east sideline. Longstreet sighted on a church steeple rising above the rooftops of Gettysburg. "Twenty-seven, twenty-eight, twenty-nine . . ." they counted together. From a distance one might have thought they were calling cadence. Boots squeaked in the snow as they paced off 110 yards. Longstreet dug another stake out of his pocket and drove it into the ground.

"That was where we laid the fences down," he said, then stared west for a landmark to align the north goal line. "See that tree?"

"Isn't that where we hid snipers when your troops started to advance?" Sickles said. "I was well out of the battle by then."

"We flushed the snipers out and rested under that tree, on the way up and then back."

They marveled at the oak.

" 'S a wonder that tree is still standing," Sickles said.

" 'S a wonder *we're* still standing," Longstreet said. "A football field is fifty-three yards wide. Let's go."

They stepped off 53 paces. Longstreet put down the northeast corner stake. When they looked south for a landmark they saw the boulder-strewn Round Top squatting powerfully above the snow, jutting against blue sky. Even after thirty-three years the rocky promontory still threatened Longstreet. He half-expected cannon smoke to rise up from it. To Sickles it was the eye of the "fishhook," the finest ground he ever defended.

"Rocky Hill," Longstreet muttered, then corrected himself, "Round Top, you call it."

"Right," said Sickles.

"One hundred ten paces. Let's go."

The old men stepped off the west sideline. Their horses stood nearby, pawing and foraging in the snow. Longstreet pushed in the final stake, then stood back and deferred to his partner. Always sensitive to ceremony, Sickles balanced himself on his crutches and stamped it down. The generals surveyed their handiwork.

"Are the corners square?" Sickles asked, concerned.

"Square as I can make them without a surveyor's transit," Longstreet said.

They looked at the football field they had created in the valley between the ancient ridges. Their tracks in the snow made dotted lines which marked the dimensions of the playing field.

"It's small for a battlefield, isn't it?" Longstreet noted.

"Reminds me of a dueling field," Sickles said ironically.

"It's level, anyhow. There's good sod under the snow." They were silent, their breath smoking in the cold.

"It had to happen the way it did," Longstreet said.

Sickles shifted his weight awkwardly between his crutches. "No way around the killing."

"I reckon not." Longstreet added self-consciously, "I have been forced to defend myself in print."

"There can be no question of your performance," Sickles assured him. "But the battle is over. We must leave it alone."

"Some of us do not have that luxury."

"How long does it have to go on then?"

"I don't know. When they let us be, I reckon."

"You interpret this football game as a means of redress!" Sickles pretended to be astonished, which he was far from being.

"It's a sight easier than going to war again," Longstreet growled.

"The North team is heavily favored."

"We've been there before."

"When?"

"Oh, at Chancellorsville and Manassas and The Wilderness."

"Football is not war!"

"You can't tell me you'd pass up a good scrap." Under his felt hat Longstreet's eyes were smiling in a fierce, bright way both of them understood. Sickles took his time replying.

"No, General," he said. "I won't tell you that."

Chapter Twenty-four

ALL-STAR GAME TODAY
by
Harrison Prescott

The battlefield at Gettysburg is the site for the North-South All-Star Football Game, which will be played today at 1 P.M.—that is, if nothing else intervenes to delay, impede, foil, obstruct, curb, or otherwise inhibit the game from taking place.

Former generals James Longstreet and Daniel E. Sickles were instrumental in coordinating the transfer of location. Originally the game had been scheduled to be played at Franklin Field. According to Longstreet, tickets purchased for admittance to Franklin Field will be honored at Gettysburg. However, spectators not holding advance tickets will find considerably higher prices in Gettysburg: $10 for bleachers seats and from $500 to $1,000 for box seats, depending on yard marker location.

Citizens of Gettysburg vigorously protested the move. A federal court order was necessary to make the battlefield park available to game organizers.

The Pennsylvania Mounted Militia has been called up for active duty to patrol the battlefield. Brigadier

Schwarzeneger requests that spectators do not bring alcohol or firearms to the game.

Temperatures will be in the low thirties. Snow is forecast.

Longstreet spent the night before the game at a boarding-house in Hanover. He was hiding from reporters and their endless questioning about why he had influenced the board's decision to move the game to Gettysburg. He slept fitfully, rose at dawn, and set out, alone in a rented hack, for the battlefield thirteen miles to the west. The day was overcast and cold. The horse's hoofbeats on the frozen roadway were solitary and somber. The closer Longstreet came to Gettysburg, the more he thought of the battle. It seemed to have happened only yesterday.

One of the few times of complete understanding—just before battle. We entrust letters to wives and families to our best friends, take up arms, and face the enemy. We all look ahead.

Arriving in Gettysburg about 7 A.M., he found the streets crowded with parked vehicles. Every hotel, tavern, public and private house was filled to capacity. Woodsmoke hung over the town like fog. Longstreet smelled bacon frying and the unmistakable odor of bourbon. He joined a growing caravan of carpenters, draymen, vendors, and spectators on the Emmitsburg Road. He could hear hammers ringing in the distance. Despite the frenetic human activity, he felt surrounded by ghosts.

"General, the men are ready to move out at your command."

Longstreet reined in, brought back to the present by the sight of a small army of builders and contractors at work on bleachers at the site where he and Sickles had laid out the football field. Longstreet was offended. He had imagined two teams, miniature squadrons, doing battle on an open plain, with spectators removed at a respectful distance. Civilian excess, always a sore spot with Longstreet, was, today, intolerable.

Wagons hauling lumber ripped deep ruts in the muddy ground. Box seats complete with roofs stood atop bleachers on opposite sides of the football field. Marked off by flags and ropes, the field itself stood pristine and untouched in the center of the construction work. The goalposts at either end were wrapped in blue or gray crepe paper, respectively. To Longstreet, the playing field with its white grid lines was like an amphitheater in a bazaar. How could one hope to stage tragedy in such a setting? The general almost agreed with demonstrators from the town of Gettysburg, who stalked self-consciously among the workers hurrying to and fro like ants. Their signs read:

BATTLEFIELD DEFILED!   FREE GETTYSBURG OF
FOOTBALL!
FOOTBALL ROOTERS, ROOT SOMEWHERE ELSE!

Beyond the tiny stadium, smoke from cook fires hung above the woods and fields for miles. Longstreet became aware of a vast tent city that reached from Seminary to Cemetery Ridge. He felt both exhilarated and intimidated at the sight of this civilian army. He parked his hack beside a fence and made his way to the arena, pausing to watch a balloonist lay out his canvas envelope on the ground prior to inflating it. Food and souvenir vendors set up stalls around the stadium as if laying siege to it.

Longstreet noted with disapproval Civil War trinkets for sale: flags, firearms, swords, parts of uniforms, brass insignia, Minié balls, pictures. Seeing a photo of himself, he stopped and examined it. It was not a good likeness. He bought a cup of hot coffee from a vendor whose three cups were to be washed and used again. He drank beside the steaming urn, wondering absently if the cup was clean. As the sun rose behind the clouds, the air seemed to grow thinner and colder. Snowflakes drifted down at the same time spectators began to arrive in earnest, about nine o'clock.

They came from Gettysburg and York, Harrisburg, Baltimore and Philadelphia, Harpers Ferry and Hagerstown, Washington and New York, Richmond and Charlottesville. They arrived in vehicles of all descriptions: Tally-hos, omnibuses, four-in-hands, English breaks, tricycles, bicycles, and shiny new, steam-driven horseless carriages. The rich rode in comfort, under blankets with footwarmers. The boots of their conveyances were well-stocked with picnic provisions: roast chicken, sandwiches, whiskey, champagne. The spectators were dressed in collegiate fashion: greatcoats and ulsters, Newmarket coats, curly-brimmed hats, silk handkerchiefs around necks, canes wrapped in brightly colored ribbons, yellow shoes.

They are ready for war, Longstreet thought.

At noon the football teams appeared. Having traveled by special train from Philadelphia, they arrived in open coaches decorated with gold and gray streamers, or blue and gold. A parade of well-wishers pursued them to the battlefield: hacks, horsemen, bicyclists, roller skaters, and pedestrians. When the coaches turned off the Emmitsburg Road and entered the muddy fields, a great roar went up. Someone discharged a pistol and in the distance weapons were fired all across the valley. The barking of firearms went on for several minutes.

The South All-Stars were stunned by the frenetic activity, the cheering multitudes. Brother, sitting on the front seat of the open coach beside Lincoln and Tree, gave up trying to comprehend the spectacle in its entirety. Blinking against snowflakes, he saw only parts of the whole: a man perched on top of one of the box seats, on the roof, waving his hat high above the grandstand; a woman in a phaeton intent on eating a chicken leg; a hot-air balloon bobbing against its tether; crates of cooing pigeons being hauled into the arena; Arno Ziprenian arguing with a band director; mounted Pennsylvania militia nervously patrolling a wire fence around the stadium; the waving of many Confederate and Union flags, large and small, in spite of all Lopez's sound and fury; a roman candle blazing yellow, green, and red against the cloudy sky to the west, answered by a rocket from Cemetery Hill bursting in a shower of gold sparks.

Brother searched the crowd for Will Du Bois, but the sociologist was nowhere to be seen. He could not help feeling disappointed that, after all they had been through together, the game itself was not worth Du Bois's time.

"Look at them Rebel flags," Lincoln said.

"Don't matter now," Tree replied. "We been plucked and boiled and fried and fricasseed ever' which way till Sunday. Now it's *our* turn."

"Lot of peoples here," Cassius observed, over Lincoln's shoulder.

" 'Bout five thousand," said Weasel, who despite his mastery of multiplication could not conceive of a larger audience.

"Try twenty-five thousand," Brother corrected. "And more out there in the hills."

They looked at the sea of faces. People were packed hundreds deep beyond the wire fencing, occupying every bit of high ground with a view of the football field.

"Double my bet!" a man cried. "Two to one, North."

"The line is *even* in Philly," Weasel shouted helpfully.

The open coaches had separated, delivering each team to its respective end of the field. The South All-Stars got down from their wagon and prepared to make their entrance onto the field. Heisman wore his game face, hard and solemn.

Warner raised his eyes to the heavens. He seemed to be praying. "Barometer's falling," he said.

Kate stood among the players feeling suddenly like a stranger, superfluous, useless. This chaotic mob of spectators was so far from anything she had imagined that she could not believe she had fought to get her players, and herself, where they were. Bardstown had never seemed so far away.

We will never be the same.

Through the end zone they could see a pregame show on the field. Drill teams dressed in Confederate and Union uniforms marched to the music of two brass bands. One played Rebel marching songs while the other battled back with Yankee tunes. The high wheels of bicycles flashed in military precision around the perimeter of the field. Somehow the drill teams became entangled at the 55-yard line, and the drum majors appeared to be dueling with crossed batons. The stadium throbbed with a thunderous roar. Brother and his teammates instinctively looked for Kate. She remembered seeing the same uncertainty on their faces when a tornado passed near Post Oak School.

"Is this what the Roman Colosseum was like?" Brother attempted to joke. "Any of you Christians seen a lion?" Chase, in a state of nervous excitement, took the remark as a cue.

" 'Put on the whole armor of God,' " he quoted resoundingly, " '. . . having your loins girt about with truth, and having on the breastplate of righteousness; and your feet shod with the gospel of peace . . . and take the helmet of salvation, and the sword of the Spirit . . .' "

"I don't need no helmet," Tree interrupted, rapping his head for emphasis. "Bring on Hezzelfigger."

Arno Ziprenian waited near the South entrance gate, presiding over pregame ceremonies with the omnipotence of a khedive. In one hand he held a megaphone, in the other a players' roster. In less than a minute he would run to midfield, command the audience's attention, and introduce the two teams. Life seemed at its fullest. Yet inwardly The Zipper walked a tightrope over the Delaware River while his father sewed a shroud on the shore.

What happened to Elston? It would be just like Elston to take the wrong train and end up in Alabama instead of Kentucky. My last chance to even the odds and save my neck, and who do I send? On the other hand, if my folks had not immigrated to America, the Kurds probably would have got me year before last. Well, as the Kurds say, It's show time!

Ziprenian signaled to an assistant, who led a black stallion forward by its bridle. Mounted on the horse was Hudson Stroud, dressed in a Confederate coat and cavalry hat with a black feather in the band. Stroud's face was calm, almost youthful. He gripped the reins tightly as Ziprenian swung open the gate. He dug heel and peg into the stallion's sides and galloped onto the field. Behind him ran his fellow gamblers, who sucked in liquor-swollen paunches and let out a Rebel yell.

"Yeeeeeehaaaaaahh!"

The great crowd fell silent for a full second before responding with a mighty roar. From the opposite end zone, Ernie Liebowitz, mounted on a white stallion, galloped onto the field waving the talismanic sword over his head, followed by his band of gamblers. The two lead horsemen circled the field, watchful, giving the impression of feeling each other out for the right moment to charge. The audience went berserk. Ladies fainted.

In Canfield's box seats, where aldermen and Philadelphia upper crust had gathered, Lopez gulped down his fourth glass of Dom Perignon and whipped off black cape and top hat to reveal a tight-fitting football uniform with a red "S" on the front. He put out his cigar. "Open another bottle, boys!" he cried. "I'll be back before you miss me. It wouldn't be fair to you Yankees if'n I was to actually *play* in this game." Lopez hurried down the steps and trotted around to the South end-zone area. He joined his teammates just in time for their grand entrance.

"Okay, Rebels," Lopez gasped, *"let's do it!"*

The stadium rocked with a fearsome ovation as both teams ran onto the field and hundreds of white pigeons were released. The birds surged up into a charcoal sky. Stroud and Liebowitz retreated to opposite sides of the field. The teams lined up facing each other across the midfield stripe. Ziprenian raised his megaphone to introduce the players. As their names were called, they stepped forward and shook hands with their opponents.

Official Program
ALL-STAR FOOTBALL GAME
Jan. 4, 1897

South Roster	Position	North Roster
Lincoln Jackson, Post Oak	LE	Garry Cochran, Princeton
Henry Clay Jackson, Post Oak	LT	W. W. Heffelfinger, Yale
Mike Harvey, Alabama Poly		Marshall Newell, Harvard
Ulysses S. Jackson, Post Oak	LG	Charles Rinehart, Lafayette
B. C. Jackson, Post Oak	C	Robert R. Gailey, Princeton
Isaac Juan Lopez, Texas A & I	RG	Truxton Hare, Pennsylvania
Isaiah Jackson, Post Oak		Bill Church, Princeton
Blondy Glenn, Alabama Poly	RT	Doc Hillebrand, Princeton
George Price, Georgia	RE	Norman Cabot, Harvard
Chase Riddle, Centre College	QB	Ernest Liebowitz, Michigan
Robert E. Jones, Post Oak		Clint Wyckoff, Cornell
Eli Abbott, Alabama	LH	Clarence Herschberger, Chicago
Cow Nalley, Georgia		Edgar Allan Poe, Princeton
Levester Jackson, Post Oak	RH	George Barclay, Lafayette
Cassius Jackson, Post Oak	FB	Pat O'Dea, Wisconsin
Orville G. Burke, Vanderbilt		George Brooke, Pennsylvania

Harrison Prescott jotted in his notebook: *Lost Tribe of Israel meets Crusaders/Dark Continent/millennia ago/while demonkind haunts the pale of our souls . . .*

Fireworks lit up the sky like lightning during snowfall. To Longstreet, the bombardment had begun. He left the grandstand and went to the South team bench to review the troops.

Yale and Princeton alumni among the spectators gave college yells. The Aristophanes-Yale yell simulated the croaking of frogs:

> Breka-ke-kex, ko-op, ko-op!
> Breka-ke-kex, ko-op, ko-op!
> O-op, O-op!
> Par-a-bou-lu!
> Yale! Yale! Yale!

Princeton's *"S-s-s boom ahhh!"* was like a skyrocket burst. The Southern partisans across the field roared with one voice.

Prescott noted: *wounded beast with ten thousand screaming heads.*

The teams retired to their respective benches while the captains met at midfield for the toss of the coin. The referee introduced himself and the field judge to Brother and Chase. Then the captains shook hands. Pudge Heffelfinger and Ma Newell were the Blue co-captains. "Sir, would you call the toss?" the referee said to Brother.

Like a field commander seeking his front-line unit, Longstreet was drawn to the sidelines. With a mixture of amusement and curiosity, Sickles watched him climb down from the stands. A stadium attendant went to ask Heisman if Longstreet had permission to climb over the rope separating spectators from playing field.

"He can come," Heisman said irritably, "but ask him please to stay back."

Across the field Stagg saw Longstreet take his place near the South coaches. Nodding to himself, he huddled his team around him.

"All right," he said. "Let's go over it one last time. Let's hear it."

Edgar Allan Poe led his teammates in a dutiful recitation:

"First quarter: Heth, Pender, and Early push Howard's Eleventh Corps off Seminary Ridge and pursue them to Cemetery Ridge. They do not break off pursuit but drive Howard off Cemetery Hill.

"*Equals:* Straight-on offense up their left side, wedge up middle, watch for bucks right then left, then everybody coming—right up the middle.

"*Second quarter:* Hill and Ewell attack Federal right while Hood circles Federal left and rolls up flank.

"*Equals:* Feint left, sweep right—outside speed; watch handoffs that start right and cut back against the flow.

"*Second half:* Lee orders attack in echelon, right to left; division assaults overlap, waves grow in strength; take prisoners.

"*Equals:* Line bucks from right to left by fullback, tackle and end, successively hits holes Eight-Six-Four-Two-One-Three-Five-Seven."

"Good!" Stagg cried. "We're ready for 'em."

"Heads," Brother said. The half-dollar flashed in the air and sank into the snow-crusted turf.

"Heads it is," said the ref.

Brother and Chase trotted back to the sidelines. The air sparkled with snowflakes. Lopez, who was cold without his cape, eased back into the crowd and climbed toward the warm box seats. He had pulled a hamstring while leading the team onto the field. "That's show biz," he told himself. The South team formed a circle of gray and gold. Longstreet looked over their shoulders.

"Watch for the fake kick!" Heisman warned them. "Phil King developed it last year at Princeton."

"Hit low and bring 'em down," Warner growled.

"Play fair," Kate said, "unless they slug you first."

"Hill and Ewell hit the Federal right and keep Hancock pinned down," Longstreet exclaimed, "while Hood and McLaws circle and hit the left flank."

Heisman glanced up in exasperation. The players' heads swiveled back and forth from speaker to speaker. Some of them were chewing gum, the latest fashion. Their jaws worked like gears of a single machine. Du Bois magically appeared in their circle. Brother was delighted to see him.

"There is a tide in the affairs of men," Will quoted, "which, taken at the flood, leads on to fortune . . . on such a full sea are we now afloat." Du Bois had never rallied a football team and wanted to say something useful. Brother nodded his approval.

"What is this?" Heisman said. "A ward meeting?"

Between the thighs of Lincoln and Tree, Hudson Stroud poked his head into the huddle and said, *"Whup the sumbitches."*

Heisman took charge. "Get out there, and, be ready for a fake kick."

The team gave a cheer and ran onto the field. Sensible of Heisman's feelings, Longstreet headed back to his seat in the grandstand. Someone thrust a small Rebel flag into his hand. He looked at it and, isolated by the crowd's roar, thought he heard the cries of company sergeants dressing their lines. He turned and saw Barksdale in front of his Mississippians, white hair ablaze in the slanting sun.

The bands were playing the national anthem.

Longstreet automatically took off his hat and held it over his heart. *"Ohhh, say can you see, by the dawn's early light?"* he sang in a solemn monotone, then noticed that a gentleman in front of him had neither stood to salute the flag nor removed his hat. Without thinking, Longstreet leaned forward and with the end of his Rebel flag tipped the man's hat so that it slid into his lap. Snowflakes gathered on the man's bald head as he sat in stunned surprise. Assuming that someone had jostled him by mistake, he put his hat back on.

"And the rocket's red glare, the bombs bursting in air," Longstreet sang and swatted the hat off. The bald-headed man turned, congested with anger, recognized Longstreet's face, hesitated, unable to believe a famous general capable of such pettiness.

Sickles could not believe it either. "Come now, Jim," he said. "We can't all be patriots!"

Longstreet stared straight ahead and sang, *"Oh, say, does that Star-Spangled Ba-a-an-ner ye-et wa-a-ve?"* The man sat down and started to replace his hat. Something snapped in Longstreet and he broke his Dixie flagstaff over the man's disrespectful head. With an angry cry, the man ran to find a stadium attendant. Longstreet bellowed, *"O'er the la-a-nd of the free and the home of the brave."*

A banshee wail spread from the stadium through the hundreds of carriages, hacks, and wagons parked in the surrounding fields. Fighting spirit inflamed Longstreet. *"Gooooooooo you Rebels!"* he cried.

Prescott jotted: *howling of baboons squeal of rats while ship burns* . . .

The referee raised his arm, signaling to Pat "Toe of the Antipodes" O'Dea, Wisconsin's Aussie kicker, who looked to see if his blue-shirted teammates were set. The timekeeper looked at his stopwatch and fired his pistol. From the far ridges a thousand guns, rockets, and roman candles replied. As Heisman had predicted, O'Dea faked the kickoff, nudging the ball with his toe to put it into play, then scooping it up and lateraling it back to Liebowitz. At that instant, Hudson Stroud yanked the lanyard of a small cannon and fired a blank charge. His friends, not expecting the blast, fell away from him, clapping hands to their ears. Young Liebowitz fumbled O'Dea's pass. Leading the Grays in pursuit, Chase Riddle swarmed upon Ernest and gobbled up the loose ball.

The ref blew his whistle and peeled away the bodies. The North players vigorously protested Stroud's cannon. Stagg danced in fury on the far side of the field. Boos and cheers cascaded down from the grandstands. *"Play ball,"* the ref said, waving his handkerchief to warn Hudson.

In the huddle Chase controlled an impulse to ask God's blessing, nodding instead at Brother, who said, "Rabbit play. Cassius going left, Weasel coming back around. On two." They broke huddle and approached the ball. Heffelfinger's face was as lean and devoid of feeling as a wolf's. He turned his head back and forth as if sniffing the air for the odor of fear.

B.C. centered the ball and Brother passed quickly to Cassius running left. The well-trained Blues reacted swiftly to the feint, burying Cassius but not before he had passed to Weasel, who flew around right end.

"The hole's there!" Heisman screamed. "All right, okay, go wide! Go wide."

"They took the feint," Longstreet bellowed. "Now hit their flank with all you've got!"

Weasel zipped around the line of scrimmage, just avoiding Heffelfinger's frenzied lunge, then swung back brilliantly through a line of would-be tacklers who tried to cut him off, and sailed into the Blue end zone for a touchdown.

Hudson's cannon boomed. Horses whinnied and bucked. A

row of four-in-hands and Tally-hos swayed and creaked as if caught in a snowy typhoon. Seminary Ridge erupted with yellow, orange, and red flashes, while Cemetery Hill remained gloomy and quiet. Stroud shook his fist at Liebowitz who could only stand and watch on the far sideline.

"We hold the high ground!" Longstreet exulted. *"Now roll back the flanks."*

"They're going for Round Top right off the bat!" Stagg yelled to his players. *"Hold the ridge!"*

The Gray players clustered around Weasel, shaking his hand. Cassius embraced him, saying, "I goin' to name my next baby after you!"

In the end-zone bleachers Will Du Bois led citizens of Philadelphia's Seventh Ward in a "Hip-hip, hooray."

Prescott noted: *intrepid rabbit defeats baying hounds, zigzags out of harm's way in harelike haste* . . .

In his opulent box Canfield was so exultant he failed to notice Ziprenian's ashen expression. Lopez lit a Cuban cigar and complimented a millionaire's wife on her cleavage.

The Blues, behind Heffelfinger's raging charge, blocked the Gray extra-point kick. The score read: Gray 4–Blue 0.

The bald-headed man returned to his seat with an usher. "I don't care who he is," he told the attendant. "Throw him out."

Longstreet was concentrating on the game and did not notice them. The usher looked at the broken flagstaff, then realized who was holding it. He blinked against the snow.

"Look here, General, sir," he said, still blinking. "We have a complaint against you."

"Throw him out!" cried the bald-headed man.

Longstreet did not look at them. The usher shifted his weight nervously.

"If maybe you could explain yourself to this fella . . ." the usher suggested. Longstreet was a million light years away.

"Throw him out," said the aggrieved man. "He raised a whelp."

"If you will promise not to bother this fella again, I will overlook it," the usher offered.

"I don't care who he is," the bald-headed man said. "Who does he think he is?"

"Everybody *knows* who he is!" the usher whispered.

"I don't care who he is. He don't have the right to bop a man who's minding his own business."

"I don't think he'll do it again."

"You're gonna let him get away with it?" The bald-headed man looked like an angry seal.

"I think the situation is under control," the usher said distantly.

"How do you know? He didn't promise nothing, did he? He hit me over the noggin. Now you're not gonna do nothing."

"Try to calm down and enjoy the game. No alcoholic spirits allowed in the stands, you know."

"What alcohol? I'm a Baptist, goddammit!"

People glared indignantly at the bald-headed man. Longstreet, however, did not so much as glance at him. The snow came down steadily.

The Blues received the kickoff and marched relentlessly upfield. They had discovered that their skill offset the Southerners' quickness and strength. Tree was frustrated by Heffelfinger's blocking technique.

"Watch the trap, Tree!" Kate screamed from the sideline. "Don't let them trap you!"

"Yessum!" Tree called.

"Lord," Chase could not resist praying in the huddle, "We beseech Thee to let our ends contain their halfback sweep and if it be Thy will, Lord, help our linebackers avoid Heffelfinger and Hillebrand's blocks. We need a big play, Lord. Help those who would sack the quarterback. In the name of the Father, the Son, and the Holy Ghost, amen."

On the next play, instead of rushing headlong as they had been doing, the Grays waited to see where Barclay would go. When the Lafayette halfback committed himself to an end run, they swiftly converged to cut him off. For the first time they caught the Blues for a loss.

"God tells me," Chase told his teammates, his face wild like the prophet Ezekiel's, "to watch for a field goal try. Ends slant in and rush the kicker."

On the next play the Aussie kicker, O'Dea, took a direct snap from center and trotted left, seeking an open space for a 35-yard dropkick. Lincoln was on him before he had time to set his feet.

The ball was knocked loose. It bounced crazily into Weasel's hands.

"*Run, Weasel, run!*" Kate shouted.

"Come to me! Come to me!" Du Bois screamed from the end-zone bleachers.

Weasel ran. The score was Gray 8–Blue 0.

"Roll them up!" Longstreet yelled. The little man in front of him ducked instinctively. Longstreet saw Hood's Texans crashing unopposed through the woods. The Pennsylvania and Massachusetts regiments on Rocky Top were caught off guard.

Hudson's cannon boomed. Fireworks streaked blue and green over the stadium. Ziprenian stared dully through flying snow as the scorekeeper changed the numbers on the board. He felt as if he were watching through a tunnel, or through the final hole his father sewed closed. There were tears in Arno Senior's eyes, but he did not miss a stitch, workmanlike to the end.

With new confidence the Grays exploded on defense and broke up North plays before they could develop. They swarmed Barclay and Liebowitz for successive losses. On third down O'Dea punted. Cassius returned up the middle for 30 yards. As he was about to be tackled he heard Brother call, "*Behind you, Cass!*" and flipped the ball over his shoulder without looking. Brother took it on the fly and reversed his field, leaving the Blue tacklers flat-footed. Du Bois danced to meet him in the end zone, and together they touched the ball down. As the first quarter came to a close, the scoreboard read: Gray 12–Blue 0.

Lopez explained to the millionaire's wife how he had coached punt returns. She fingered her pearls and riveted his attention to her cleavage. He poured them another glass of champagne.

Her husband is in love with his money. Here it is. In two weeks she'll be begging me to accept gifts of stocks and bonds.

The brutal sounds of football players slamming into one another, the rasping roar of thousands of voices provided a comforting background for Lopez's daydreams, for they reminded him that he was not playing.

"Lord says, *Red Dog!*" Chase advised his teammates. On the next play all eleven defenders rushed. The Blues were driven back ten yards. Heffelfinger was so dazed that when he saw Stagg motioning him to come to the sideline for a conference, he forgot to ask for a time-out. His teammates followed him to the sideline, one by one. Stagg was so intent on giving Heffelfinger instructions, he did not see them leaving the ball undefended.

"We've got to hold them," Stagg said, "or we'll soon be out of it. Can't you see? Longstreet went to the Hood Sweep around our left flank—I mean end. Spread out and react to the ball!" Standing with his back to the field, Stagg did not notice the team clustered behind him.

"Hey, ref!" Chase whispered. "Did they call time-out?" The referee shook his head. "My God, it's a free ball!" Chase groaned. "Line up, fellas. Quick!"

"Coach, we're trying," Heffelfinger was saying. "It's just they're so damned quick." When the rest of the team murmured their agreement, Stagg whirled around, horrified that they had abandoned the field.

"Hike!" Chase whispered to B.C., who was confused. *"Hike! Hike!"* Chase cut his eyes to the Blue bench, where Stagg was beating his players back on the field. *"Hike!"* Heffelfinger thundered toward him like a bull elephant. *"God help me!"* Chase cried. B.C. snapped the ball. Riddle ran unopposed for a touchdown. The Blues threw themselves on the snowy turf in agony. Moments later, Chase finally made good an extra point kick and the score was Gray 18–Blue 0.

"They're falling back!" Longstreet shouted, waving his broken Rebel flag joyfully. "We've got them on the run."

Ziprenian looked at the exits and wondered how far he could get before Canfield noticed he was gone, when he saw a familiar figure stumbling along, bumping into an attendant, arguing vociferously. The black coat and stovepipe hat were unmistakable. It was Elston. Ziprenian hurried down to meet him.

"What did you find out?" he cried.

"Hello, Elston, how was your trip? Glad to see you, thank you very much, good to see you, too . . ." Elston whined.

"Cut the crap. What took you so long?"

"I took the wrong train, boss. You wouldn't believe it, but it wasn't my fault. The ticket puncher—"

"The conductor?"

"Yeah, him. In Washington he shoulda told me I hadda change trains. I was sleeping and I heard the puncher say, 'At-a-lanta,

Georgia!' " Elston bared yellow teeth, proud of his imitation of the conductor's singsong voice. Ziprenian danced with impatience. "I wound up in a place called Birmingham. Just a whistle stop. Little mining town. Ever hear of it?"

"Get on with it."

"So I changed trains to Louisville, then to Elizabethtown, then rented a hack. There was this crazy little colored driver, talked his head off—"

"Elston, I'm gonna kill ya."

"All right, all right. So I found this Post Oak School and—"

"And? And?"

"Boss, that Bardstown is so dull you can hear a cow moo from one end t'other."

"Damn you, Elston!"

"Boss, you was right. It ain't no college. It's only a normal school for niggers."

God has spoken. It is a miracle.

"And it took me a little longer but I figure it'd be worth it," Elston continued proudly, drawing folded papers from his pocket. "I got a lawyer to draw up this legal statement that there weren't no college nor seminary nor nothing at Post Oak School and had it signed and notarized."

Ziprenian was kissing Elston violently. He snatched the papers out of his startled assistant's hands.

Stagg forgot military tactics for the time being and unleashed his secret weapon: the turtleback. As the ball was snapped, the Blue team drew in tight and linked arms, bent over so that their backs resembled a shell. Somewhere inside the solid mass of humanity crouched the ballcarrier. The turtle crept forward inexorably against the bewildered Gray defenders.

"What it is?" B.C. screamed.

"He'p me! It goin' to *eat* me!" Cassius disappeared under the crawling mass of bodies.

"Trip them up!" Brother yelled, diving under the moving creature and trying to grasp an ankle or a foot.

"Stand back!" Tree took a flying leap, fell on top of the turtle, and collapsed its shell.

Prescott noted: *bêtes noires rip and tear until portion of tor-*

toise shell is prised loose, allowing them to get at golden egg inside its soft underbelly . . .

The Blues tried the turtleback again, but the Grays collapsed the shell before the play could get started. The Kangaroo Kicker, O'Dea, punted out of bounds at the Gray one-yard line.

Lopez was telling Boies Penrose how he had installed a special defense for the turtleback when he was interrupted by a commotion in the box. Ziprenian was showing Camp some papers. "What is it?" Lopez asked Archie The Knife.

"Something to do with the nigger players," O'Hara said. "They are ringers and won't be allowed to play the second half."

"Holy mother!" Lopez cried.

"Perhaps we will have the pleasure of seeing you play, after all," Canfield said.

The glow of Dom Perignon faded. Lopez's Cuban cigar went sour. He saw Camp hurry off to deal with the emergency. Reluctantly he reached for his cape. The discs in his back made a small, grinding vibration as he bent over. He felt closer to fifty than forty. He wished he had been drinking whiskey instead of champagne. Whiskey had gotten him through three seasons in the Southwest Conference.

The Grays faced third-and-four at their own fifteen. In the huddle Chase asked Weasel, "Do you always shank your punts left, the way you do in practice?"

"If'n I try to kick it straight I do," Weasel admitted.

"Try to kick it straight, then. Cass, you and Brother line up on the left and take off fast to recover the free ball downfield before their safety man does."

The ball was snapped to Weasel. The Blues dropped back to set up a punt return. They watched in astonishment as Weasel's punt spiraled off to the left, bounced once and fell into Cassius's waiting arms. He accelerated and ran 60 yards for another touchdown. The timekeeper's gun sounded to end the half. Amid an uproar of applause and fireworks the teams lined up, with time expired, for the extra point attempt. Tree threw a crushing double block on Heffelfinger and Hillebrand. Chase's kick flew between the uprights.

The scoreboard read: Gray 24–Blue 0.

Alonzo Stagg stood on the sideline looking like a turtle without its shell.

A brightly colored striped tent set up behind the end-zone bleachers served as the Gray team's dressing room. They entered it triumphantly, laughing and slapping one another on the back. A cozy fire burned inside a wood stove, its flue vented through the top of the tent. A large pot of tea simmered on the stove. The players' cleats scraped the hard ground as they arranged themselves on benches, comparing scratches and bruises. Humboldt presided over a table prepared with tape, bandages, salve, linament, tincture of iodine. Amid the sharp smells of medicines, burning wood, and boiling tea, the players relaxed. They could hear bands playing, cannon going off. They touched tender places on heads, arms, and legs, as if seeking proof that they had beaten the North's All-Americas. Kate moved proudly among them, making sure no cuts were neglected. The Post Oak men could not stop smiling. Nobody said a word. Nobody had to. Overhead, the canvas eaves shifted under the weight of sliding snow.

Longstreet slipped inconspicuously into the tent. He went from player to player, shaking hands. He asked Brother, "What do you call it? The rabbit play?"

"Yes, sir."

"It gets the job done."

Their silent celebration was interrupted by the sudden entrance of Walter Camp through the tent flap. He was followed so closely by Penrose, Canfield, Ziprenian, Lopez, and Du Bois that they tripped on one another's heels when Camp stopped. He was holding the notarized statement. Heisman and Warner looked as if they had seen a ghost.

"I am informed," Camp said stiffly, "that you have fielded a team of non-collegians."

"Walter, what in blazes are you talking about?" Heisman said uncomfortably.

"A man was sent to Bardstown, Kentucky, to check on Post Oak 'Seminary,' " Camp continued. "He found that this seminary does not exist. We have a sworn statement. Post Oak is a secondary school. Your Negro players are high school students."

Heisman whirled on Kate. She dropped her eyes.

"This puts us in an intolerable position," Camp fretted. "They'll riot if we call a forfeit." A cannon blast from the stadium seemed to confirm this statement.

"But the oral examination," Du Bois spoke up. "Did the athletes not pass it?"

Camp gave him a long, hard look which said, You've given us enough trouble. Now let us alone. Will glanced at Brother, who could only shrug in disappointment.

"Are you saying my players are ringers?" Heisman went on the offensive. "If so, I would like to lodge an official protest . . ."

"No one is suggesting they are ringers," Camp said hastily. "However, the fact remains that they are indeed ineligible."

Longstreet felt a gentle resignation. It seemed that he had known all along that something like this would happen.

It was so quiet in the tent that tea could be heard bubbling. Kate stepped forward. Somehow she felt vindicated. Established authority had once again shown its bias. She was destined to struggle forever against the way things were.

"I am responsible," she said. "I fixed the records and papers so my players could be here. I would do it a thousand times. I don't care what you do, you can't take the first half away from them. They were magnificent."

Her team made an appreciative little stir. She went and stood protectively beside them. Someone clapped. It was James Longstreet.

"Amen to that, missy," the general said. "They *were* magnificent." Kate beamed at him.

"Are you goin' to let 'em get away with this, Coach?" Lopez cried. Every bone in his body tingled in anticipation of having to play the second half. "Whose word do we go on? This Elston What's-his-face, a known associate of *mobsters,* or Miss Kate, a professional educator? We should postpone the second half till this story can be verified!"

"Postponement means riot," Camp reminded them. "Anyway, we have the proof right here. A written statement signed by the high school principal—let's see, Rutledge is his name—saying that Post Oak Seminary exists in name only. It is still in the planning stage and never received a state charter."

"As player representative, I protest—" Lopez began.

"That player-rep stuff is over and done with!" Heisman cut him short. *"We're* not finished, though. I had planned to make substitutions in the second half anyway. Let's see: who've we got left?"

Heisman counted noses: the Virginians and Carolinians had quit the team, but he still had three Alabamians, two Georgians, Vanderbilt's Burke, plus Riddle and Lopez. That made eight. It was common practice for coaches to play if a team was short, but even with Warner and himself they'd still be one man shy of eleven.

The reserve players, Nalley, Price, Harvey and the rest, were grinning ear to ear at the prospect of playing.

"I assume coaches are eligible?" Heisman archly inquired.

"Of course, college rules," said Camp.

"I'll play!" Humboldt volunteered.

Heisman looked at the skinny academic. Humboldt weighed perhaps 130. "You would be killed," he said.

"I'll play."

Heisman did not look at Kate. He could feel her swell with hope and defiance. His heart sank. From the moment he met her he knew that she would bring him both shame and glory. He looked hopelessly around the dressing quarters. Camp and Warner gave him pitying looks. Professor Humboldt was disgusted.

"You might make a public address announcement," Camp suggested, "to see if there are any college men from below the Mason-Dixon Line who would be willing to lend a hand." Camp glanced at his watch. "There's not much time left in the intermission. I'd hate to delay the game very long."

Kate's offer dangled over them like a noose. Heisman reluctantly sized her up. She weighed perhaps twenty pounds more than Humboldt, was younger and in better condition. He knew she could run. He had seen her romping with her players at practice. The determined look in her eyes convinced him.

"Stay away from Hillebrand," he sighed. "He'll hit anything that moves, man, woman, or child. The rest of them may slack up on you. It could work to our advantage."

"Hurrah!" Kate whooped. "Count on me." Her players congratulated her.

"All right," Heisman summed up, "let's see what our lineup

will be: on defense we'll want Glenn and Harvey at tackle, Burke and Price at guard, Riddle and Nalley at ends, and Lopez at center . . ."

"I ain't played center since high school," Lopez broke in. "Ain't there somebody else you can get for center?"

"You're it," Heisman snarled.

"Ain't that guy from Virginia—what's his face, Martin?—still around? I thought I saw him in the end-zone bleachers. Want me to go look?"

"He went back to Charlottesville," Warner said.

"Coach, lemme tell ya: I got this slipped disc."

"Have you been drinking, Lopez?"

"Yessir!" Lopez was hopeful. "I broke trainin', and under the circumstances, Coach, I realize you'll hafta suspend—"

"You wouldn't happen to have any booze left, would you?" Heisman said. "I wouldn't mind a nip right now." He turned briskly to the other players. "All right, gentlemen . . . and, er," he glanced at Kate, "let's go out there and give it the college try!"

"May I address the troops—er, team?"

Heisman nodded, surprised. It was Longstreet who had spoken. The general faced the players.

"Well," Longstreet said, "you gentlemen from Bardstown did us proud. You won the first half. We are on the defensive, now. I am all for defense. That is the way to win a battle." Everyone stared expectantly at him. "At the battle of Chickamauga," he went on, "General Benning reported to me, 'General Hood killed, my horse killed, my brigade torn to pieces, and I haven't a man left.'" Longstreet paused for effect. "I replied, 'Surely you have one man left, General.'"

The hopeful silence was broken by the referee, who stuck his head through the flap and said, *"Time."*

While the substitute players warmed up, Heisman gave the referee a list of their names.

"Glenn, if we were only ten years younger," Heisman told Warner, draping an arm around the Georgia coach's shoulders.

"It'll be all right," said Warner, who was eager to play. "I'll buy you a beer after the game."

Kate saw her players standing around dejectedly. "Wish me luck!" she said. One by one they shook hands with her.

"Tell Hekkazugger if he hurt you," Tree said, "he goin' to answer to *me*."

Camp went to the Blues' dressing quarters to report that the Post Oak players were ineligible. Lonny Stagg blinked back his joy. He inquired politely if the Grays would be able to assemble a substitute eleven. Camp told him that the coaches—Heisman, Warner, and Kuykendall—were filling in. Stagg blinked even more rapidly.

"Too bad their other players quit," Woodruff said.

"Yeah, that's tough luck," Phil King agreed.

"I was hoping to get another crack at that Tree fella," Heffelfinger muttered, rubbing a deep bruise.

"Under the circumstances," Stagg magnanimously told Camp, "we will waive our right to a forfeit. Let the game be decided on the field."

The Blues were first to return to the stadium and were met by a standing ovation. Ziprenian, upon learning that the blacks had been ejected, went behind the stands and wept in relief. Kate trotted self-consciously onto the field. The stadium grew ominously silent. One by one, men began to boo. Then women began cheering. Kate glanced at the stands and saw SRND members waving and rooting like mad. She gripped her hands together and shook them over her head.

Hudson was incredulous at the sight of the Post Oak players sitting on the bench. "That ain't fair!" he bellowed.

He heard someone yelling at him. Across the field, Liebowitz was waving the sword. "Now we'll see who comes out on top!" Ernie shouted.

Longstreet took his seat in the stands. He dreaded what Sickles might have to say and pretended not to notice him.

"Let us pray," Chase said before the kickoff.

"No time for that," Heisman said. He and Warner continually stretched this way and that, trying to loosen up. "Take your positions," Heisman told them.

Chase kicked off. He did not hear his foot strike the ball amid the din of fifty thousand screaming voices. Babe Rinehart returned the kick to midfield. Somehow they managed to tackle him, although it seemed that the Blues knocked every Gray player to the ground. The North began a drive. There was no finesse in the way they went about it, bucking straight ahead for five and ten yards a crack.

Lopez agonistes.

It was all Lopez could do to dodge the giants of Yale and Princeton, wobble back into position for the next play, and squat down into his stance. His back was killing him. He called upon his reserve energy and found none there. He was still winded from trotting downfield on the kickoff.

Kate was being knocked down on every play. Hillebrand or Heffelfinger or Newell brushed her aside. From a prone position she saw her Post Oak players watching on the sideline. They had begun to run back and forth like chicks mourning the loss of mother hen.

"God is with you," Chase said as he helped her to her feet.

"Can He spare fifty pounds of muscle?" she replied.

In three minutes the Blues scored their first touchdown. O'Dea's extra point kick was perfect. The scoreboard read: Gray 24–Blue 6.

Harrison Prescott noted: *North smells blood/crowd goad their champions/heap derision on foes/Romans turn lions loose . . .*

Lopez limped back to receive the Blues' kick. Everything seemed dislocated: femur, hip joint, lumbar vertebrae, ulna, shoulder joint, cervical vertebrae. A bruised sacroiliac bent him at a 60-degree angle; a detached pelvis caused him to move sideways, like a crab. He felt a cracked rib, a ruptured spleen. There was not enough time to catalog his injuries.

All shot to hell.

He wondered how he had ever played with pain. Looking back across the years he decided that basically he had lied to himself a lot. Lopez watched Rinehart set up the ball, holding for O'Dea's kick.

Do what has to be done: when the wave of tacklers comes, select the smallest, slowest opponent, fake a block, fall to the ground, and remain still until the referee calls down.

"Remember," Heisman instructed the team, "use the clock. Run as much time off as you can. Don't hurry to line up after every play."

"Right, Coach!" Lopez yelled. "Everybody hear that?"

O'Dea kicked deep. Chase returned the ball to the 20-yard line before Hillebrand and Newell brought him down. "Good block, Lopez," Chase said.

Lopez did not reply. He had a collapsed lung. His right side was paralyzed. Even his grin was crooked. He had dodged Heffelfinger but the All-American had changed direction at the same instant and collided with Lopez at full stride. When the Grays broke huddle, Lopez saw Heffelfinger and Hillebrand laughing at him. He staggered up to the line. The old competitive surge began somewhere in his intestines which were more or less intact. He fought it, counseled discretion, but on the ensuing play actually tried to block Truxton Hare, of Penn, who knocked him semiconscious. The Blues held. Chase punted on third down. Again the North began to march. Heffelfinger and Hillebrand continued to laugh at Lopez. In his last act as an athlete, Lopez threw himself at the ballcarrier, Barclay, and sank his teeth into his hand, causing a fumble. Alabama's Abbott fell on the ball in the end zone. The referee signaled a touchback. Will Du Bois led a Seventh Ward cheer in the bleachers. Lopez spit out his next-to-last molar.

On second down Heisman called a quick-kick. Chase's punt caught the Blue secondary by surprise. Both teams chased the free ball downfield. Alabama's Abbott recovered it on the Blue two-yard line.

"Come on, Cow," Warner told his Georgia halfback. "You take it in. Follow me and Price over right tackle."

Newell and Rinehart rose up to stop them, however. Another plunge up the middle was also stopped for no gain. Heisman called the tailback hurdle, in which the fullback and halfback heaved the tailback over the goal line.

"Are you game?" Heisman asked Kate.

"Hmmmmph!" she grunted, insulted.

Lopez snapped the ball directly to Kate. Burke and Nalley escorted her to the line, grabbed her jersey on either side, and hurled her into the air. As she braced for impact, expecting to score her first touchdown, Heffelfinger caught her and threw her back. Her fall was broken by Lopez, who happened to be in the way. Heisman called time. Lopez lay comatose.

"I'm give out," he whispered weakly in Heisman's ear.

Tree and Lincoln brought a stretcher and hauled Lopez off.

The crowd gave him a nice hand, especially the millionaire's wife. Leaving a game always revived Lopez's spirits. He acknowledged the applause with a thumbs-up.

On the sideline Prescott was interviewing the Bardstown players. "Could you have scored that touchdown, if you were in the game?" he asked Cassius.

"That my coach out there!" Cass replied indignantly. "She doin' the best she can."

"How does it feel to be benched for the second half?" Prescott addressed Weasel.

"How would you feel?" Weasel said.

"Can you comment on your ejection from the game?" Prescott asked Brother.

"Inevitable," Brother said.

"Can you expand on that?"

"That says it all."

"Give me some examples? In what ways was the ejection inevitable?"

"I have been reading your columns for the past weeks . . ."

"Thank you very much."

". . . and it seems to me that for the sake of your readers, you might consider economizing."

"That is a racist slur!" Prescott cried.

Humboldt was the only eligible substitute left to replace Lopez. Heisman motioned him on. The professor took off his coat, rolled up his sleeves, and trotted self-consciously onto the field. On his narrow shoulders rode the honor of the University of the South.

From their two-yard line, the Blues drove 108 yards for a touchdown in less than four minutes. The score stood at 24 to 12. Hudson watched Liebowitz taunting him. The next time the Grays were forced to punt, Stroud waited until Liebowitz Junior fielded the ball on the dead run and then yanked his cannon lanyard. The blast caused another fumble. Ernie Senior ran all the way across the field, brandishing the sword and was dragged back by his friends.

"Come on! Come on, bluebelly!" Hudson screamed. He felt a blow to the chest and immediately sat down in the snow. The pain radiated to his left shoulder and arm. He panted for breath. Dickinson and Fitzpatrick knelt beside him.

"I'm all right," Stroud whispered. "Put me in my chair and give me some whiskey."

The Grays ran two minutes off the clock before punting out of bounds. When play resumed, the superior strength of the Blues began to tell. They marched and scored, got the ball back, and scored again. With two minutes left the score was tied, 24 to 24.

Longstreet thought of Sherman's march to the sea.

In the end, they wore us down. But what if Bragg had allowed us to pursue Rosecrans into Chattanooga and consolidate the victory at Chickamauga? What if Stonewall Jackson had not been cut down at Chancellorsville? What if Lee had let us move southeast of Gettysburg and interpose our army between Meade and Washington?

Longstreet concentrated on the game. Something was happening. The tumult was one continuing roar. The South called time out. Less than a minute remained.

"Here we are," Heisman was saying in the huddle. "It's down to one play."

Heisman's face was red and scratched. Tufts of his hair were missing. He had battled younger, stronger players to the point of exhaustion. Kate's face was tortured and wild. Humboldt looked layered, clothes torn and hanging as if Heffelfinger had peeled him like an orange.

"Some kind of . . . pass play." Warner was so winded he could barely speak. "Get the ball outside . . . broken field . . . only chance."

"May I—?" Chase said.

"NO!" they all yelled.

Kate heard someone cheering her. She saw her players shuffling their feet on the sideline. At first she thought they were running in place. Then she made out what they were yelling.

The Abe shuffle do the Abe shuffle do the shuffle the shuffle

Their voices were a summons to the Post Oak playground. She remembered hovering over them, looking over their shoulders as Brother diagrammed one of his fantastical formations in the red dust.

"We've been playing white man's ball!" she cried. "That's not what beat the Blues in the first half."

"You mean . . . ?" Heisman said.

". . . dance with the ones that brought us?" Warner said.

"Look!" Kate drew in the snow. They watched her finger zig-zag back and forth. Her face was as fierce and bright as an angel's.

"It might work," said Heisman.

"I'm for it," said Warner.

"May I—?" Chase offered.

"NO!" they shouted.

They broke huddle and came to the line. Heffelfinger and Hillebrand were grinning, a twin rictus of destruction. Chase smiled benevolently at them. He snuggled close to the center, Blondy Glenn, so the Auburn man could hear him call signals.

Longstreet was on his feet. In the backfield he saw George Pickett at quarterback, Trimble at left half, Pettigrew at fullback, and Armistead at right half.

"By God," he shouted to the ghosts, "we're going to do it, this time!"

Blondy snapped the ball. Chase ran right. Out of the corner of his eye he saw Heffelfinger rip past Harvey to get at him. As powerful arms encircled his legs, Chase tossed the ball to Abbott going in the opposite direction.

"Reverse!" the Blues screamed.

The Alabama halfback gained ten yards around left end before Poe and Barclay trapped him. Abbott pitched back to Kate, who again changed direction behind the blocking of Heisman and Warner. Her path blocked by tacklers, she passed back to Cow Nalley, who cut back and broke into the open.

Suddenly the possibility was there.

Men in blue, spread out raggedly across the field, pursued frantically.

"Gooooo you Rebels!" Longstreet's voice was lost in the pande-monium.

The timekeeper fired his gun. Nobody heard it. Chase took a pass from Nalley and cut into an open lane. He ran past the South bench. Brother and Du Bois were yelling, *Goooooooooo.* Thirty yards from the end zone Chase knew he was going to score. Liebowitz was the only man who had a chance to stop him. Chase did not feel his feet strike the ground. He was borne along on a rising wave of emotion. Liebowitz lunged, Chase offered him a shoulder and cut inside. Ernest Junior twisted as he fell, grabbing helplessly at Chase's legs. With ten yards to go, Chase began to slow down. All motion and sound ceased. He did not hear feet pounding behind him.

Christ was in the end zone. He was dressed all in white, a halo around His head. As Chase approached the goal line, He began to raise His arms. Chase stopped inches short of the goal. He knew that if he scored his life would be over. He simply would ascend with Christ to meet the Lord of Hosts.

Then Heffelfinger was upon him. Instead of tackling him into the end zone, however, the Blue defenders dragged him back. Coming on the run, Heisman and Warner charged into the whole heaving mass and carried it between the goalposts. Through the crush of bodies Chase caught a glimpse of Christ raising His hands to signal a touchdown. Suspended between the quick and the dead, Riddle's one thought was of a white church riding a ridge like a ship on a blue ocean.

Take me, Lord!

Then he saw that the arms reaching to glory belonged not to Christ but the referee. At the bottom of the pile Riddle wept.

The final score went up: Gray 28–Blue 24.

A windy rush of sound swept the stadium like brushfire and spread hungrily across the fields toward Seminary and Cemetery ridges where fireworks set the sky ablaze. Longstreet sat down.

Most of the spectators around him were leaving the grandstands. He saw Daniel Sickles pause and touch hand to hat. Longstreet smiled and returned the salute.

Lincoln and Tree hoisted Kate to their shoulders and rode her triumphantly across the field to receive Stagg's congratulations. Looking down at their ecstatic faces, she had never been happier. Alonzo, who had been complimenting Heisman and Warner, positioned himself between them and Tree Jackson.

"Good game, Coach!" Stagg shouted up at Kate. He then put his hand on Tree's shoulder, saying, "Son, how would you like to play football for me at the University of Chicago?"

Chase and Brother met at midfield. They clasped hands. "Power to you, Brother Jones," Chase said.

"Power to you, Brother Riddle," Jones replied.

Brother found Du Bois among the people milling about on the field. They watched Southern fans tear down the goalposts wrapped in blue.

"What do you think?" Brother said.

"Oh, not bad for a scrimmage," Will said with a straight face.

"A scrimmage!"

"Yes, what do you call it—a warm-up?"

"A warm-up for *what?*"

"What we have to do—you and I. Of course, we've got to get you educated, first. At Harvard we rarely take both cream and lemon in our tea."

Brother grinned the widest grin of his life. "I'll try to remember that."

Hiding in the crowd moving through the exit, Ziprenian walked stooped over to avoid Archie O'Hara. He headed west from the stadium. He had no clear purpose other than to continue the Ziprenian line. Weaving among vehicles parked helter-skelter, he went toward the dark hills of Seminary Ridge. Something made him stop and look back. People of Gettysburg were already tearing down the bleachers. A rocket cut a jagged gash in the sky.

"I created it," The Zipper told himself with a sense of awe. "Now I must live with it."

From his stretcher near the Gray bench, I. Lopez held a press conference and announced a plan to establish an Association of Professional American Athletes.

"I must finish what I have begun," he was saying.

Jubilant fans made way for a man in a wheelchair. Stroud's companions pushed him to midfield to meet Liebowitz. Little Harry, Fitzpatrick, Dickinson, and Pitts were worried about Hudson's pasty complexion and shallow breathing. He did not tell them about the weight which was crushing the air from his chest.

"Find Lieberwitz," he panted.

Stroud held a whiskey bottle in his lap. His tunic was ripped and spattered with mud. He strained to focus on the far sideline. Liebowitz appeared as if from a dream.

Accompanied by Reno, Diamond Ed, the Dutchman, and

Bones McCain, Liebowitz was dressed in a spotless Federal uniform. His brass buttons gleamed. He thrust his crippled hand into a coat pocket, while in his good hand he held Hudson's saber. They met in the middle of the field.

Ernie smiled crookedly and presented the saber to Stroud, hilt first. His smile faded when he saw that Hudson lacked the strength to take the sword.

"Put it in my lap," Hudson whispered.

The weight of the sword seemed to press him into the ground. He sank deeper and deeper. The anxious faces of his friends seemed to recede above him, outlined against a sky bursting with colored lights. Hudson thought he might be in heaven, though he appeared to be going the wrong way. With a tremendous effort he waggled a finger, motioning to Liebowitz to draw near.

"It sure beats sittin' and waitin', don't it," Hudson said and sank back. His eyes remained open as his head lolled to one side. Fitzpatrick felt for Stroud's pulse and listened for a heartbeat. He looked at the others and shook his head.

"Somebody find a doctor!" Harry cried.

"It's too late," Liebowitz said.

"That's a helluva way to go!" Little Harry blinked fiercely.

"He went out a winner!" Pitts declared.

"You old fool," Liebowitz whispered to Stroud. "This is what you wanted all along."

He reached out and closed Hudson's eyes.

From his seat in the stands Longstreet looked down on the circle of grief surrounded by a mob of exuberant fans. Both goalposts had been torn down. Debris littered the stadium. Only an occasional rocket whizzed over the battlefield. Traffic was already backing up on the Emmitsburg Road. Longstreet stood up, stretching his joints gratefully.

"Now we can get on with it," he said to himself.

ACKNOWLEDGMENTS

I owe a debt of gratitude to the following people for their encouragement, support, or advice: my wife, Dean, my editor, Carolyn Blakemore, my copy editor, Chaucy Bennetts, Al Hart, Dr. Chester McLarty, Mrs. Arthur Chitty, Howard Bahr, and P. D. Fyke.

For historical facts and background information I am indebted to these authors and their works: A. Alonzo Stagg, *Touchdown* and *A Treatise on American Football;* W.E.B. Du Bois, *Dusk of Dawn, The Philadelphia Negro,* and *The Autobiography of W.E.B. Du Bois;* Francis L. Broderick, *W.E.B. Du Bois: Negro Leader in a Time of Crisis;* Shelby Foote, *The Civil War: A Narrative;* James Longstreet, *From Manassas to Appomattox;* Donald Sanger and Thomas Hay, *James Longstreet: Soldier, Politician;* H. J. Eckenrode and Bryan Conrad, *James Longstreet: Lee's War Horse;* Edgcumb Pinchon, *Dan Sickles: Hero of Gettysburg and "Yankee King of Spain";* John Lukacs, *Philadelphia: Patricians and Philistines, 1900–1950;* Clyde B. Davis, *Something for Nothing;* Herbert Asbury, *Sucker's Progress.*

I would also like to thank these facilities and institutions: the University of Mississippi Library, the Free Library of Philadelphia, the Bardstown, Kentucky, Museum, and St. Peter's Episcopal Church, Oxford, Mississippi.

L.W.

Oxford, Mississippi
December 1986

About the Author

LAWRENCE WELLS was born in Jacksonville, Florida, in 1941 and was graduated from the University of Alabama. He has been a small-press publisher and college instructor. He is the author of the novel *Rommel and the Rebel* (Doubleday, 1986) and has edited the sports albums *Football Powers of the South, Ole Miss Football,* and *Legend in Crimson.* He and his wife, Dean, live in Oxford, Mississippi.